THE
NORTHERN
CROSS

Also by Hendrik Falkenberg
in the Baltic Sea Crime Series

TIME HEALS NO WOUNDS

THE NORTHERN CROSS

A BALTIC SEA CRIME NOVEL

HENDRIK FALKENBERG

TRANSLATED BY PATRICK F. BROWN

amazoncrossing

Previously published as *Das Kreuz des Nordens* by Amazon Publishing in Germany in 2015. Translated from German by Patrick F. Brown. First published in English by AmazonCrossing in 2016.

Published by AmazonCrossing, Seattle

www.apub.com

Amazon, the Amazon logo, and AmazonCrossing are trademarks of Amazon.com, Inc., or its affiliates.

ISBN-13: 9781503939417
ISBN-10: 1503939413

Cover design by Shasti O'Leary Soudant

Printed in the United States of America

CHAPTER 1

The night was calm and mild. The moon cast a silvery band across the nearly motionless sea. Even though it had been almost a month since the official start of fall, the late summer refused to go quietly. Its strength was waning, but it fought to hold on to each passing October day. The colorful leaves rustled in the slight breeze. A reddish glow on the horizon announced the rising sun. Fresh dew glistened on the grass in the nascent daylight. The first few birds pierced the silence, heralding the end of the night.

The singing came to an abrupt stop when the hammering began. The steady rhythm of metal on metal tolled through the dawn. Soon the silence returned, and the birds renewed their claim on the breaking day. The uppermost edge of the sun was already peering over the horizon when the steady, though this time faster, sound of hammering began again.

Someone out for an early morning stroll on this remote stretch of coast probably would have stopped and stood in astonishment. An eerie figure knelt on a grassy hillside that sloped gently toward the beach, its shadowy arm rising and falling steadily. Then the silhouette paused and shifted before striking the metal again.

The final nail was slightly rusty, but its tip was so sharp that it couldn't withstand the force of the blows. The resistance increased after it had pierced the flesh and hit a hard wooden beam. Labored breathing could be heard. Finally, after one last spirited swing, the defiant nail was firmly planted in the oak.

Silence fell, and the sun climbed a little higher in the cloudless sky. Three massive nails covered in fresh blood, mixed with rust and iron, glimmered in the sun's rays. With a grunt, the figure pushed the lower end of the wooden beam toward a hole in the ground until it protruded slightly over the edge. The grunting grew louder as the figure lifted the beam from the other end and placed it into the hole. Two hands filled the remaining gap with dirt to secure the base of the beam.

The figure took a few steps back and admired its handiwork, which was now illuminated in the soft light. The figure captured the sight with a digital camera before tossing the hammer and shovel over its shoulders and quickly walking away. Not once did it turn around.

The birds remained, eagerly demarcating their territory. A heavy wooden cross remained. Firmly planted in the ground, it looked as much at home on that hill as it would have on the top of a mountain. It was so large that it could be clearly seen from the sea. But only upon closer inspection would it be apparent that there was someone else on this secluded hillside. Arms spread wide apart and face turned toward the sea. Only the nails, which had been driven through the man's wrists and feet, kept him upright. His body hung motionless on that immensely historic symbol, upon which so many others had taken their last breaths thousands of years ago.

A brownish cloth was wrapped around the waist of the young man. However, unlike the itinerant Jewish preacher of two thousand years ago, he wasn't wearing a crown of thorns and showed no traces of having been whipped. He seemed peaceful, almost floating above the ground, and were it not for the blood trickling from where the three iron nails had been hammered into his light skin, the scene might have appeared majestic. But when the first few drops of blood fell to the ground, they served as a reminder that wooden crosses were once a gruesome means of torture and execution.

A gentle breeze toyed with the loincloth, while the immaculate body resembled a sculpture made of marble. He appeared lifeless until suddenly the crucified man trembled and opened his eyes. He struggled to raise his head, and though his vision was blurred, he gazed across the calm sea. Not a sound escaped his lips, and after a few moments his head fell back down. The sun had risen over the horizon by then. It shone warmly on the pale face of the man who, unlike his biblical precursor, would never rise again.

CHAPTER 2

A disgruntled Johannes Niehaus stepped off the bus and shoved his cold hands into his pants pockets. He had decided to leave his jacket at home that morning because it had been unseasonably warm lately. Unfortunately, he had no time to correct his mistake; this was his first day back at work after a special leave of absence, and he didn't want to be late.

Johannes reluctantly headed toward the station. The two weeks he had just spent with the national canoe team at their training camp in Szeged, Hungary, had passed by all too quickly. He had needed some time to process the grueling experiences of his first murder investigation and had wanted to take a breather from dealing with his new boss.

It was expected that Hannes would be assigned a new boss after the involuntary resignation of his old one, Fritz Janssen. That this new boss would be Henning Federsen, however, came as a shock. His colleagues had been divided about Fritz, but not about Federsen. Hannes didn't know anyone who found the chief detective even remotely likable. After Hannes's first day working for him, he understood his colleagues wholeheartedly. At first, he had thought Federsen was having trouble adjusting. But after a week, he had been forced to reconsider.

Hannes knew his colleagues also had differing opinions about him; as a semiprofessional athlete, he was sort of a part-time employee. And at thirty-two, he was one of the youngest detectives to have been taken off desk duty the previous summer. He had overheard others saying that the only reason he enjoyed so many privileges was because the head of the Criminal Investigation Department, Steffen Lauer, was a passionate amateur athlete himself. Hannes thought he might have been assigned to Federsen so all this talk about preferential treatment would finally end.

Hannes pushed open the front door to the station.

"You look like you're already in a bad mood, and you just got back from vacation," said a colleague, whom Hannes had almost hit with the door.

"Sorry, Isabelle," he said, deciding that it wasn't worth pointing out that he was at a training camp. It was definitely not a vacation—especially since his longtime rival, Ralf, had also gone to Szeged and had made a point of pissing him off the entire time.

"I've got a vague idea why you're in such a miserable mood." Isabelle grinned. "Federsen's already in, and he'll definitely be glad to have you back under his thumb."

Hannes muttered under his breath.

"You'll get used to him," she said. Like Hannes, she was one of the younger detectives. "Things didn't go well between you and Fritz at first, but then you started getting along."

"That was completely different. Fritz may have had his issues, but he wasn't a jerk."

"Have you heard anything from him?" Isabelle asked. The sudden end to Fritz's career was still a hot topic at the station.

"No." Hannes was always reticent when it came to questions about Fritz. "I can't be late," he said as he headed for the stairs, "otherwise this day will get off to a really nasty start."

But nothing could change his boss's foul mood. Hannes had only seen him in a good mood once, and that was when Fritz had been kicked off the force.

"So you're back from your government-paid vacation," Federsen said when Hannes poked his head through the door between their adjoining offices.

"Anything happen while I was gone?"

"What do you think? Now that I've got an assistant who's always off training, I'm stuck doing all the work."

Hannes rolled his eyes. Everyone at the station knew Federsen had a knack for disappearing the moment there was a new assignment.

"How can I help?" Hannes asked.

"Until you're caught up to speed, I'd prefer to handle it myself," Federsen said and puffed his small but formidable chest. "Besides, I have a meeting in an hour with the chief. He wants me to present a couple of recommendations I had for improving the force. Ask your colleagues to fill you in."

There was no need telling Hannes twice. Relieved, he shut the door before Federsen had the chance to change his mind. Hannes surveyed his office. The remnants of its original use as a copy room were still apparent.

Hannes wandered down the hall to find someone who could tell him what had gone on in the past two weeks. As it turned out, he hadn't missed much. "At least, nothing your boss would have helped with," said Marcel. Although Marcel was Isabelle's superior, he was still a rank below Federsen. "We had a drug-related homicide—a guy was stabbed to death by another junkie—and a woman died of electrocution, which turned out to be an accident."

Back in his office, Hannes railed at Federsen for being an inveterate blowhard and wondered how he would pass his time. He would have no other choice than to press for a new assignment.

However, his resolve faded when a red-faced Federsen stormed into the room and ordered Hannes into the adjoining office. Short of breath, the overweight detective plopped himself down into a swivel chair and scowled. Since Hannes had a pigment disorder that left him with one blue eye and one green eye, Federsen never knew which to look into. Federsen was a tiny man with a double chin and a face covered in acne and patches of gray stubble. Hannes could even see the red veins in his bloodshot eyes. The chief detective grabbed a cigarette with his nicotine-stained fingers and frantically tried to light it. He often flouted the station's smoking ban in his office. Hannes felt Federsen was the biggest asshole in the city.

"I was just about to present the chief with my suggestions for optimizing the internal structure of our organization when there was a news bulletin on the TV," said Federsen. "A cross was discovered on some beach in the middle of nowhere. It must have been placed there recently." He paused and savored the bit of knowledge he had with an air of self-importance, while Hannes wondered what could be so remarkable about a cross.

"Is that against the law or something?" Hannes asked to break the silence and undermine Federsen's smugness.

"The problem, of course, isn't the cross." Federsen took a few loud puffs of the cigarette. "The problem is that there was a man nailed to the cross." Federsen took a great deal of satisfaction in having impressed his subordinate. But then he quickly frowned again. "We both should take this case. I have already pointed out that we have a lot of catching up to do since you devoted the last two weeks to sports. But the chief thinks that my expertise is needed. Especially since there's already a camera crew hanging around. We'll head to the crime scene immediately. The medical examiner is already on her way, and from what I've heard, it's not a very pleasant sight."

***

After parking the police car along the edge of a small rural road, Federsen and Hannes traipsed through two recently harvested fields. Hannes found it difficult to get used to Federsen's driving style. It took him so long to shift into a higher gear that the engine seemed to be perpetually redlining. They both abruptly stopped when they reached the foot of a small hill.

"What the hell . . ." said Federsen. Hannes couldn't agree more.

Before them was a gently sloping meadow, and a giant wooden cross was towering a quarter mile away. Even from this distance it was possible to see something that looked like a giant doll hanging on the cross. Hannes gulped and followed Federsen.

A fresh wind blew from the Baltic Sea, carrying a salty, musty smell. Hannes felt the cold creep through the fibers of his thin wool sweater. The sky had clouded over, and a fine drizzle began to fall. Police tape fluttered from the metal poles which had been inserted into the ground around the cross. In front of the tape, a number of people jostled to catch what was going on. Hannes was surprised at how quickly the news had spread in this remote area.

"Hyenas from the press," Federsen said.

"How did they get here before we did?" asked Hannes.

"The cross was discovered by fishermen. They headed closer to shore and realized there was a man hanging on it, so they called the local news. They probably wanted their fifteen minutes of fame." Annoyed, he spat on the ground. "Two young guys. After they lured the camera crews, they posted a photo on Facebook. The whole world has probably seen images of this mess by now. What a generation."

Federsen looked at Hannes, as if he were responsible for the behavior of others his age. When they reached the police line, Federsen pushed through the excited press pack. Hannes followed him with his head down, trying to evade the swiveling television cameras.

"Can't you hold them back?" Federsen said to the first officer he saw.

The officer shrugged. "They've already filmed everything anyway. They had enough of a head start. It might be exciting to catch the evening news."

"Well, I better not see your face on there," said Federsen. "Widen the police line. I don't want to see a single one of those bums in five minutes. They've probably trampled over all the evidence."

While the scolded officer struggled to expand the radius of the crime scene, Federsen marched over to the cross. Hannes hastened to follow. He could see the black hair of the medical examiner, Maria Stern, who was staring with great interest at the wooden structure. Hannes nervously followed her gaze.

The crucified man hung above the police officers with his arms outstretched and his head tilted forward. He was about Hannes's age, and his body was remarkably toned. His amber-colored eyes were open and seemed to look directly at Hannes. It was only with great difficulty that Hannes was able to tear himself away from the blank stare. The deceased man's dark medium-length hair clung to his head as a result of the rain that had recently started to fall, and water trickled down his bare, hairless torso. Hannes's eyes moved from the man's arms to his flat stomach to the linen cloth around his hips before finally resting on his feet. The right foot had been pushed over the left, and a single nail tacked both feet tightly to the wood.

Hannes gulped several times but couldn't prevent his body's visceral reaction. He quickly disappeared behind a nearby bush and vomited. Cold sweat mingled with the rain and ran into his eyes. He breathed deeply, then wiped his mouth on his wet sleeve.

As the nausea subsided, anger and shame rose. His stomach had already proven to be a formidable adversary during his first murder case, which still drew some teasing from colleagues. He was so angry with himself for throwing up in front of his new boss and Maria that he reluctantly walked back.

"Congratulations. Who knows what useful clue you just puked all over," Federsen said. "Perhaps you're better off sticking to sports if you can't get used to the harsh realities of police work."

Hannes's ears turned red with his embarrassment. Most of the other police officers stared at the ground, and it was clear the detective hadn't gained any new fans by ridiculing Hannes.

Maria was furious and glared at Federsen with her hazel eyes. In her outrage, her Spanish accent became even more pronounced.

"Not everyone has a stomach of steel, Detective Federsen. And if you're done with your alpha-dog routine, maybe we could talk about the victim?"

Federsen looked at her angrily. His thoughts weren't hard to guess. He couldn't stand her. Actually, he couldn't stand any woman in law enforcement. In his eyes, it was still a man's world. A world for real men, not for wimps like his young partner.

"Oh? Then why don't you begin. Do you have an idea about the cause of death?"

"Not yet. I have to examine the body more closely back at the lab. But"—Maria raised her hand just as Federsen was about to spit out a self-righteous response—"what immediately stands out to me is that the body shows no trace of a struggle or violence. Excluding the nails, of course."

"Are you saying that the guy voluntarily let himself be crucified?" Federsen let out a rare and unpleasant-sounding laugh.

Arms crossed, Hannes observed his boss, who pulled another cigarette from a crumpled pack. It took several attempts until his lighter finally sparked a small flame. Federsen took a deep drag of the cigarette and blew the smoke in Maria's direction.

Annoyed, she stepped to the side and gestured in front of her. "What I also find interesting is the small footrest attached to the cross."

"To make him comfortable?" Federsen asked, causing her to lose her train of thought.

"Comfortable? Only a layman would think that. If this man was still alive after he was nailed to the cross, then the footrest would have prolonged his suffering. Without it, he would have died much quicker. Outstretched arms like that make it difficult to breathe and puts stress on the circulatory system. The footrest was definitely not attached out of consideration."

"How much time would this piece of wood have bought him?"

"I'm not an expert on crucifixions. They're not exactly an everyday affair, and I—"

"Well, since our clearly competent medical examiner can only state the obvious . . ." Federsen turned and waved over a gaunt man in white coveralls. "How's the forensic investigation going?"

The man approached and pushed back his hood, revealing a head of gray hair. Hannes stepped closer so he wouldn't miss out on any information.

"So far we haven't found anything helpful, like tire tracks, for instance," said the forensic investigator. "No objects. There are lots of footprints since the press walked all over the place. But take a look over there." He pointed to the bottom of the cross. "We managed to clear away the loose dirt, and you can see that a shovel was used to dig the square hole. It's slightly larger than the beam, so the gap was filled with loose dirt. It probably came from this pile here, the remains from the hole. We'll take the dirt back to the lab for closer examination."

"There's no way this cross could have been put up by a single person without any tools," said Federsen.

"It's doubtful," said another officer. "But it's not out of the question. With the right technique and necessary strength, it's possible. Then again, the beam alone, which is made of oak, is very heavy. Add to that the victim's body. None of us probably could have lifted it."

Maria opened her mouth as though to protest but seemed to change her mind. Hannes noticed her eyeing him in his soggy sweater.

"We'll take everything down carefully and transport it back to the lab, if that's all right with you," said the forensic investigator.

Federsen continued to survey the scene. Hannes wondered if his boss was really thinking about what he saw or simply wanted to make himself look important.

"Yes," Federsen finally answered, and shivered as a violent gust of wind caused the group to sway. "You'll be able to find out more back at the lab, and I don't want to catch pneumonia out here. Everything points to a ritual murder. Some Satanists or other religious nuts are probably behind this. Hopefully we can learn the name of the victim soon, because I doubt we'll find his wallet in his loincloth."

Federsen laughed as Hannes posed a question to the forensic investigator.

"How long do you think the cross has been standing here?"

"The loose dirt at the foot of the cross is the only evidence we have. We won't be able to know for certain, but the dirt was probably crammed in there pretty recently."

"What do you mean by 'pretty recently'?" snapped Federsen. "Could you be a little more specific? The body still looks fresh, so the guy hasn't been hanging around here for weeks."

"Definitely not weeks. But Maria will be able to tell you more after she's finished with her examination. I think the hole is several days old. If you want me to be more precise, I'd guess two or three days."

"Thanks," Federsen said, then turned around. "I'm not surprised the guy wasn't discovered until now. We're in the middle of nowhere.

Let's head back now, Niehaus. And Dr. Stern, I expect you'll inform me as soon as you've finished examining the victim."

Without looking at Maria, Federsen started to walk away, and Hannes followed with an apologetic shrug. Shortly after, the drizzle turned into a downpour and drenched the detectives. As they ducked under the police tape, they begrudged the curious crowd of onlookers and press and failed to notice that they were being closely monitored by two narrowed eyes.

CHAPTER 3

Hannes shut the door to his one-bedroom apartment and peeled his soaked clothes off. He sneezed several times, and his skin was covered in goose bumps. Federsen hadn't bothered to drop him off at home. He had instead left him at a bus stop and told him to be back at the station in an hour.

Hannes left a trail of water in the hallway as he made his way to the bathroom. He stood in the hot shower for several minutes, then sighed as he turned the water off. He had not expected the day to be so eventful.

He grabbed the thickest sweater he owned and left his place dressed appropriately for the weather. He waited for the bus outside, but it was running late, so he hailed a cab.

"Have you heard?" asked the driver.

"Heard what?"

"About the crucifixion on the coast. Someone was nailed to a cross, just like Jesus. It's all they're talking about on the radio."

"Yeah," said Hannes. "I know. I've seen it."

"What a crazy world, huh?"

No denying that, Hannes thought. The driver continued to philosophize while Hannes got lost in his own thoughts. This could only be the work of a deranged man or a group of lunatics. Who would come up with such an idea?

When the cab pulled up in front of the station, he handed the driver twenty euros, leaving a three-euro tip. The man smiled.

Hannes headed up to the fourth floor. An hour and a half had passed since Federsen had tossed him out of the car. He braced himself for another reprimand. He walked across his office to Federsen's door. After a brief knock, Hannes opened the door, but the office was empty.

All Hannes could think of was Old Fritz, his former supervisor. Fritz had kept the office spartanlike, but after Federsen had moved in, the place was a mess. The desk was covered in piles of paper, and there were plants everywhere.

Hannes closed the door and turned on his computer. As it booted up, his mind wandered again to Fritz. He had mixed feelings. Though it had been difficult at first to get along with him, things quickly got better. Hannes had learned a lot from him, but he couldn't say the same about Federsen. Fritz had been extremely successful, even if he'd had his idiosyncrasies. A few people at the station had predicted that his peculiar methods would be the cause of his downfall. His critics were ultimately right. But even Federsen, his old nemesis, couldn't have imagined that Fritz would end up in jail shortly before his retirement. It had been a very traumatic experience for Hannes, especially because Fritz had been a real mentor to him. And Steffen Lauer had since become extremely cautious and kept his team on a much shorter leash. Federsen couldn't stand the micromanagement and repeatedly blamed the fallen ace detective.

"Always some kind of excuse," Federsen muttered as he passed through Hannes's office to get to his own. When he noticed Hannes sitting there, his face darkened. "There you are. I just had to explain to

Steffen why the press was already blabbering on about the crucifixion before we knew anything about it. Now he's worried about his job, that—" He stopped himself and stood in front of Hannes. "We need to get a leg up on this case, and fast. Steffen expects a daily briefing."

"Where do we start? Until we get the results back from the lab, we've got nothing to go on."

"I'll give you something to go on. Find out who the half-naked man on the cross was. His face has been flashed across every screen in the country by now. Maybe someone who knew him has contacted us. And get in touch with those two idiots who discovered the cross. Tell them to get their asses here immediately so we can question them."

And what are you going to do? Hannes wondered. Federsen walked into his office. The last thing Hannes saw of him was the flicker of his lighter as he lit another cigarette.

Apparently no one had recognized the crucified man, or at least no one had contacted the police about him. A quick computer search brought up nothing. But Maria called with something for Hannes. She probably had little desire to see Federsen a second time that day.

"My first impression was correct," she said in a low voice. "The wounds from the nails were the only ones. There's no evidence that the victim fought back."

"You mean he let himself be crucified?"

"He may have been drugged; we're waiting for the results of the blood test. What do you mean 'let himself be crucified'? Is that your current theory?"

"No idea," said Hannes. "But I have to agree with Federsen. The first thing that comes to mind is some sort of religious ritual. How long was he hanging out there?"

"I can't say for sure. The wounds aren't fresh. Two or three days probably passed before he was found. And he was in his early thirties. I don't have anything else right now. Still want to get a drink after work?" she added, seamlessly changing the topic.

Hannes's ears turned red. He liked Maria a lot. She was around his age and had an excellent figure, a great voice, and a unique effect on him—despite what he saw as her less than ideal job.

"That would be great," he said, then remembered that he already had something planned for that evening. But he was free on Friday.

"Great," Maria said. "I doubt tomorrow will be particularly fun, so a drink would do us some good. I'll call you as soon as I know more about the victim."

Hannes had to gather himself a little before he informed Federsen of Maria's findings. Then he tried to do a little background research on the two fishermen who had discovered the cross. It wasn't difficult. Hannes turned on the TV in the conference room. The crucified man was the top story, though no close-ups were shown. Hannes winced when he saw himself on-screen, ducking under the crime scene tape.

Shortly after, an interview with the two fishermen aired. They excitedly described the discovery without actually sharing anything enlightening. The station didn't report their names, so it took some effort to find them.

They were brothers in their early twenties. The younger one had posted multiple photos of their bizarre find on his Facebook page. The images were slightly blurry, taken from a distance. Nevertheless, they succeeded in getting numerous comments about the photos.

Hannes managed to get ahold of their mother. She told him her sons were back out on their boat and would be home later. Since the family's house was on the way to Hannes's appointment that evening, he said that he would stop by. Federsen disapproved. In his opinion, "Those two idiots would do well to haul their asses down to the station" after having the nerve to speak to the press first. "Tear those two fools a new one for being so irresponsible" was the only order he gave Hannes.

Hannes went home to get his old Ford truck out of the garage. Around seven o'clock, he arrived in the small suburb where the fishermen lived with their mother. He parked in front of the garden gate, and as he approached the front door of the brick house, a dog began to bark. Pressing the doorbell only made the barking grow louder. A middle-aged woman opened the door, and a white terrier darted toward Hannes, jumping at his legs while barking and growling.

"Johnny, no. Bad dog," the stout woman snapped and pointed toward the hallway. To Hannes's surprise, the dog obeyed. "Please excuse his bad manners," she said, astonished at Hannes's different-colored eyes. "Are you the police officer who called? My boys just got back."

She steered him into a somewhat dated kitchen that reeked of rancid grease. The brothers sat at a rough wooden table, wearing navy sweaters. They took a few last bites of steak before they rose to greet Hannes.

"If they hadn't been out there posing for every TV camera, I wouldn't have had to send them on the water again," their mother said.

Hannes took the opportunity to talk some sense into the young men, but his words fell on deaf ears, and the rest of their conversation bore little fruit. The brothers rarely visited that stretch of coast, but were curious about the cross because they had never seen it before. As they sailed closer, they noticed something hanging from the wooden beams and brought out their binoculars.

"When was the last time you visited this stretch of coast?" asked Hannes.

"Two weeks ago," said the older brother. "Have you found anything out about the dead guy?"

"And more importantly, why was he crucified?" added his brother.

"I'm not going to share that information with you so you can post the current status of our investigation on your Facebook page."

Hannes smiled and stood up. He could understand their excitement. Something this thrilling had probably never happened to them, so they wanted to make the most of it.

He headed toward the sea in his rickety Ford. His class in boating safety began at eight, and when the course was over, he would have his recreational boating license. He had long weighed whether or not he should actually follow through with it. His indecision wasn't due to fear, because he had always wanted a boat. The reason was the boat itself, which had come to him as a complete surprise.

Its name was *Lena,* and until a few months ago, it had belonged to Fritz Janssen, who had bought the old shrimp boat several years back and painstakingly and lovingly restored it. Expelled from the force and now serving his prison sentence, Fritz had no more use for the cutter. One day Hannes received an envelope with keys and papers. The handwritten note was brief, in Old Fritz's style.

Unfortunately I can't spend the rest of my days with good old "Lena." Hopefully you feel as much at home on board as I did. I'm sorry how it all happened. Fritz

Hannes hadn't had any contact with his former mentor and pondered whether or not he should accept the gift. He still struggled with conflicting emotions whenever he thought of Fritz. But in the end, the call of the sea had been irresistible.

Ironically, the boat-licensing course was held in an old office building off the small harbor where the first and last case Fritz and Hannes worked on together had fatefully begun. Hannes parked at the edge of the small seawall and sat for a moment, reflecting on all that had happened. Then he shook his head as if to brush off his somber mood and opened the door.

Since he still had fifteen minutes before class, he wandered over to the dock and spotted his cutter. A few tiny fishing boats languished at another dock, the sad remnants of a once-vibrant fishing industry.

Hannes stopped in front of the bow of the fifty-foot wooden vessel. The top was painted brown and the rest white. "Lena" was spelled out in cursive white letters over a dark background. The wheelhouse was also brown and crowned with a white roof. Fritz had removed the boom and tackle so that *Lena* would look like a true old-fashioned recreational boat.

Hannes carefully shooed a seagull from the edge of the deck, climbed aboard, and looked around. Because he had forgotten the key, he could only see the inside of the wheelhouse through the greasy prints on the glass. In the darkness, only the outlines of the pilot wheel and gearshift were visible. The hatches for the ship's hold were also sealed. Down below, Fritz had created a small living area with bunks, a kitchenette, and a folding table.

"What are you doing on that boat?" boomed a man's voice accompanied by rapidly approaching footsteps. Hannes jumped and lost his footing on the wet wood. He fell forward and banged his head on the hatch. When his vision cleared, he saw a pair of sturdy boots. Then two huge hands grabbed him and lifted him up.

"What are you doing here?" asked the old man. He didn't let go of Hannes's shoulders. He was wearing a yellow raincoat and had a gray beard and a large gap between his front teeth. Hannes remembered who he was.

"You're Ole, aren't you? Fritz's friend?" he asked and tried to break free of the man's grip.

"Correct," Ole said, a little surprised. When he took a closer look at Hannes and noticed his eyes, he too remembered. "You're that rookie Fritz worked with."

Hannes nodded, and Ole finally let go.

"Well, that was quite the turn of events," Ole said, and the wrinkles in his face deepened. "Fritz is sitting in jail instead of here enjoying his early retirement. So, why are you snooping around on his boat?"

Hannes explained about the note and the keys. Ole studied him, frowning when he learned that Hannes planned to get a boating license.

"There's already enough people sailing around here who think they're true ocean-going captains after a simple safety course. But if Fritz wants you to have his *Lena*, then it's all right by me. How is he?"

Hannes felt guilty admitting that he had no idea. Fritz hadn't been in the best shape even before his downfall. He had prostate cancer that had metastasized to the spine. Due to severe back pain, he was often hunched when he walked and regularly took painkillers. And prison wasn't exactly conducive to his mental state either. After all, he preferred doing things his own way and took great pleasure in ignoring the rules.

"You still resent Fritz for what happened this past summer," Ole said, which wasn't that far off the mark. "I don't want to give you some big lecture on life, but I've known Fritz since we were little. He was always a great guy. His sense of fairness is what always got him into trouble. But no one would have guessed that he would finish his days in prison. I visited him two weeks ago. No one else had. He blames himself for dragging you into that mess. I'm sure he'd be happy if you went to see him."

Hannes frowned. He had thought about visiting Fritz but couldn't bring himself to do it. It would make him relive those bizarre events, which wasn't an appealing prospect.

"Put yourself in his shoes. How would you behave in his position? It'll make your visit easier if you think about it like that."

The subject was uncomfortable for Hannes. He glanced at his watch and climbed back onto the dock.

"I have to hurry. My class is starting. But maybe I'll visit Fritz as soon as I have some time."

"Yeah, yeah," Ole said as he watched Hannes run off. "There's time for everything, yet no one ever has any."

CHAPTER 4

That was easier than I expected. Not too easy. It was, after all, only my first time. I had often thought about it in the past. What would it be like? Would I be able to do it? But he made it easy for me. I couldn't let him get away with it. I had to make an example of him. I had to show the entire world. They have to understand. But was it the right thing to do? I feel ashamed and . . . maybe afraid? Yes, afraid of myself. Wasn't there another way? I ended his life. I was the one. Me. I killed a man. Even though I really didn't want to. Or did I? At least I accept it. Did he repent in the end? What if he wanted to set things right? I shouldn't second-guess myself. He deserved it. It was the right thing to do. Let him be a warning to others. They all saw it. It takes something extreme to make them notice. I tried to be kinder in the beginning, but that didn't work. Maybe I should have kept trying? Why do bad things have to happen before people finally start to take notice? Hopefully no one saw me. No, I planned it very carefully. I have it all under control and know what I'm doing. It was so easy, ridiculously easy. I couldn't have done it without a reason. And there are plenty of reasons. I can do it again. I have to do it again. I need to be strong. I am strong. One more time, just one more time.

CHAPTER 5

Hannes didn't arrive at the station on Friday until lunchtime. The higher-ups had agreed that he could use weekday mornings for canoe practice. Hannes could still feel the pleasant burn in his muscles after his strength training that day. He inhaled the rest of his sandwich as Federsen opened the door and ordered him into his office.

"Anything new?" asked Hannes.

Federsen handed him a marker. "You got it. Take notes on the whiteboard." He leaned back in his padded swivel chair. Then he paused, clicked his lighter, and lit a cigarette. After three deep drags, he finally got down to business.

"Fact one: the dead man on the cross was Alexander Kramer, early thirties, lived here for five years. He rented a one-bedroom apartment."

"How did we learn his identity?" Hannes asked as he scribbled the information on the whiteboard. "Did his family contact us?"

"No. We haven't contacted his family yet. A woman has come forward. Evidently, they knew each other well enough for her to identify him from the blurry images on the news."

Hannes stared blankly at Federsen, who smiled somewhat lewdly.

"An Inga Bertram identified him. One of his sex partners. Alexander Kramer was a porn star. Well, at least the guy gave one heck of a last performance."

The detective waved his hand dismissively, signaling Hannes to jot down the new information on the board.

"Fact two: Kramer had been hanging on that cross for two or three days. He died, however, only a day before he was discovered." Federsen seemed to take satisfaction from the look of shock on Hannes's face.

"But that means . . ."

"That he was alive for at least a day on that cross. He could have screamed and shouted as much as he wanted out there, but there would have been no one around to hear him. But that's not all. No foreign substances were found in his blood. So we have to assume he was fully conscious while he enjoyed that ocean view, until a heart attack finally did him in."

Hannes gulped. Federsen seemed to relish sharing these gruesome details.

"Fact three: forensics hasn't found anything even remotely helpful, which doesn't surprise me. They still assume that the cross was erected two to three days prior to its discovery. The man was probably nailed to it there."

Hannes stood motionless in front of the whiteboard.

"What are you waiting for?" asked Federsen.

"Uh . . . fact four?"

"Fact four: you'll head now to this . . . what do you call it? Film studio? Porn studio? Interview everyone who works there. Then you'll type everything up in a report and leave it on my desk. Two of your colleagues are already trying to contact Kramer's family and find out more information on him."

"And what are you going to do in the meantime?" Hannes blurted out, feeling uncomfortable about having to go by himself to a porn studio.

"What am I going to do?" Federsen repeated indignantly, his eyes bulging. "You have some nerve. So now you think everything's up for discussion? Get out of here, and don't come back until you have something useful."

He made a point of turning to his desk and picking up the phone. Hannes left the room, the veins in his neck throbbing with anger, and went to check out a car from the motor pool. He had once again been saddled with the more unpleasant task, but he had to admit that he was a little curious about the porn studio. It wasn't like you got to see one of those every day. But he was still annoyed at Federsen. He needed to think of a way to get back at him.

Fall was in full force. Mothers sat enjoying the warm sunshine outside cafés, strollers by their side. Hannes was surprised when the GPS directed him to a ritzy part of town. He would have expected the studio to be in a rundown industrial area. "You have reached your destination," announced the soft female voice as Hannes pulled up in front of a multistory edifice resembling an office building.

There were three businesses listed on the door's buzzer, including Paradise Images & Productions. He was at the right place. Hannes felt the blood rush to his ears. Would he ever learn to control this response?

The buzzer sounded, and Hannes entered a brightly lit stairwell. The directory listed Paradise on the second and third floors. He climbed the stairs and looked at the innocuous landscape paintings lining the walls. He pressed another doorbell when he reached the top, and an older woman opened a steel door. "Finally," she said in a hoarse voice and ushered him through.

Hannes stared at her in confusion, only to be met with an equally puzzled look. Her pupils danced back and forth between his eyes. The woman was modestly dressed and had teased gray hair. She was short and wore a beige cardigan over a tasteful blouse. Reading glasses hung from a gold chain around her neck. Her red leather skirt and white laced boots were a sharp departure from the rest of her outfit.

"Don't worry, hon," she said and patted him on the arm. "They're already waiting for you back there. I'm Gertrude, but everyone calls me Gertie. Come on back."

As she pushed him past a reception desk and a perfectly ordinary sitting area, Hannes felt a wave of panic. Had Federsen even called to say he was coming? There were sketches of nudes on the yellow walls of the hallway that he found more offensive than artistic. The air carried a vague citrus smell, and Hannes felt like he was in a spa.

Gertrude opened a door and pointed to a small room. "You can take your clothes off in here. Everything you need's already on the chair. When you're ready, head down the hall. Studio One, behind the last door."

Hannes was a little taken aback. "Um . . ." he said as Gertrude was just about to walk away.

"What? Come on, quit dawdling. I've only been here for two months, but I know Annette can't stand it when people are late."

"I think there's been a misunderstanding." Hannes looked with embarrassment at the black latex suit draped over the chair. "I'm Detective Johannes Niehaus . . . I've come regarding the murder of Alexander Kramer."

"My goodness." She slapped her hand over her mouth. "I'm so sorry. What must you be thinking? I thought you were—"

"Is he there yet?" came a voice from the hallway. A woman with short brown hair, who looked to be about forty, appeared in the doorway.

Gertrude introduced him as the detective in the Alexander Kramer case. "I'm so embarrassed," she repeated, turning to Hannes. "I thought you were Alexander's replacement. He was supposed to have been here thirty minutes ago. You should take it as a compliment that you could star in one of our films."

"Um, okay." Hannes grinned awkwardly. "I'll keep that in mind if I'm ever in need of some cash."

"You could earn a fair amount here—we pay our actors very well," said the other woman with a slight smile as she held out her hand. "Annette Melcher. I own the studio."

Hannes failed to mask his surprise.

"You were probably expecting someone more in line with the image people have of our industry? Some sleazeball guy and slutty women, right?"

"Uh, yeah, I, uh . . . have to admit I'm a little surprised."

"Why don't we chat in my office. Gertie, when the new guy shows up, send him into the studio."

Hannes followed Ms. Melcher into a brightly lit office filled with Ikea furniture. She pointed to a pair of sofas and invited him to sit down. She sat opposite him, crossing her legs, which were sheathed in a pair of skinny jeans.

"We're very different from other producers. We specialize in making films that appeal to women."

"Oh, like soft porn?" asked Hannes, too aware of his colorful ears.

"What a modern image you've got of women. It's not that women don't like explicit films. We just give them the necessary touch. We make them less misogynistic. But that doesn't mean we don't make different types of films. And we must be onto something because the demand is huge."

"And Alexander Kramer was one of your actors?"

"That's correct. We have a pool of fifteen women and ten men. We choose the appropriate actors depending on the genre. There's a lot of interest in being one of our actors. We pay well and provide excellent working conditions. Alexander had been with us for about six months and played the leading role in two of our recent films. Our customers immediately took to him—the sales figures were phenomenal. He was very talented and nice. He also looked amazing."

Ms. Melcher sighed and knotted her fingers together. Unfortunately, she didn't know too much more about her favorite star but immediately agreed to provide Hannes with contact information for all the other actors. She called Gertrude to print out a list.

"We don't do your typical job interview like other companies. All I need to know is that an actor can do the work. I couldn't care less about personal matters or background checks."

"Are any of Mr. Kramer's former colleagues here? Would they know him better?"

"At the moment, only Inga and three crew members are here. They were supposed to be filming a few scenes with Alexander's substitute. But since he hasn't shown up yet, we can head into the studio. Inga was the one who recognized Alexander from the paper."

Hannes followed her down the hallway. The studio had been transformed into a sumptuous room in a palace, and a spotlight cast its warm glow on the set. A woman and three men were sitting on the ground in front of a fake fireplace. They were chatting quietly and smoking. Inga Bertram had on a skimpy red cocktail dress. Her long dirty-blonde hair was undone, and she strutted past Hannes in her high heels to a couple of chairs off set.

"Alex was a sweetheart," Inga said in a pleasant voice. "We made two films together, and he was a professional, even though he'd never worked in our industry before."

"How'd he get the job? According to Ms. Melcher, it's extremely difficult to get hired here."

"Well, that depends." Ms. Bertram eyed him up and down. "There are always casting calls to discover new talent. Screen tests. Alex showed up one day and blew us away. His predecessor hadn't been all that great to work with, so Alex was hired to replace him. Now his predecessor's back, unfortunately." She flicked the ash from her cigarette and sighed.

"What did Mr. Kramer do before he started working here?"

"Various odd jobs. He was a nice guy, but he also had his share of problems. He liked to wear expensive clothes, party, gambled, and . . ."

"And?"

"Well, it's not like it matters anymore. He did a lot of coke. Alex led a lavish lifestyle and needed money. One time we went to a party after a shoot, and he told me he owed his dealer."

"Did he ever tell you the name of his dealer?"

"No. We weren't really friends and only went out together that one time. I prefer to keep my work and private lives separate."

"It shows. You don't seem like you're in shock."

"Of course I am. But I would also be shocked if one of these stage lights fell on your head. I liked him, and I liked to work with him. When I saw the picture in the paper, I was suspicious. It wasn't a clear photo, but the longer I looked, the more certain I was that it was Alex. Of course I'm sad. But I've worked for quite some time in this industry. I've learned that it's better to keep your distance."

"Do you know anything about his friends or family?"

"His parents died in an accident. I don't know much about his background. He came from Bayreuth. Don't know if he had friends here or not."

Hannes remembered his and Federsen's initial impressions at the crime scene. "You know how Mr. Kramer was killed. This could point to some kind of ritual act. Do you know if he ran with such groups?"

"I'd be surprised. He once said he had no use for religion. I think there's another explanation for the cross. In our last film, Alex played a devout priest, and I bound him naked to a cross. Maybe that's why I recognized him in the photo. The scene popped into my head immediately."

Hannes eagerly leaned forward. It couldn't be a coincidence.

"You can watch the movie for yourself," she added.

***

"The crew didn't have anything more to add about Kramer?" Federsen had read Hannes's report, and the two of them now sat at his desk.

"Men talk about different things with each other than they would with a woman."

"Kramer was probably someone who kept his professional and personal lives separate. As soon as they were done shooting a scene, he'd shower and leave."

"Hmm, a junkie porn star who's dominated by women on camera, owes money to his dealer, and says little about his personal life. Seems like a real saint."

"It's a bit much to call him a junkie. He looked healthy and was in perfect shape. Here." Grinning, Hannes handed Federsen two DVDs. "You can see him in action for yourself. He's dominated only in the second movie."

"You've already watched them?" Federsen pushed the DVDs away. "What's this world coming to? It's a good thing I've got you. Since you apparently have no moral qualms, track down the rest of the studio's cast."

Hannes had been relieved to get out of the studio. Gertrude had handed him the two DVDs along with the list of actors and staff. Alexander Kramer's predecessor—and successor—had arrived, and Hannes had found him instantly unappealing.

Gertrude had walked Hannes to the door and patted his chest. "Come see us again if you ever feel like trying something else. We haven't had someone with different-colored eyes before. You'd certainly be a hit."

"I'm sure I would," Hannes said. "Not just because of my eyes either."

She had looked at him in surprise, and her laughter had accompanied him on his way down the stairs.

Ben laughed even longer. Hannes stared at his friend in consternation. Maria had had to cancel their after-work drink because a woman's body had been found on a dock that evening.

"Marcel's a nice guy, unlike your boss," she had told Hannes over the phone. "That's why I want to have the results on his desk first thing tomorrow morning."

Fortunately, Ben was never averse to getting a beer, and as a student he rarely had any important commitments. So Hannes still spent a relaxing evening at the bar. After Ben's assistance with his first case, Hannes had absolute confidence in his lanky sidekick. Since he couldn't talk normally with Federsen, he was happy to share his experiences with Ben.

"You at a porn studio?" Ben pushed one of his blond dreadlocks out of his face. "You turn red the moment you're alone with a woman."

"You think I'm some total prude," Hannes said. "Besides, it wasn't how you imagine it in that dirty mind of yours."

"Sorry, man." Ben patted him on the shoulder. "But you've got to admit that's some story. Did you ever think you'd see the inside of a porn studio? By the way, I saw you the other day on TV eyeing Jesus up and down." He pulled a rolled-up newspaper from his pocket and placed it on the table. "New Leads in Jesus Murder" was emblazoned in large letters atop a panoramic shot of the crime scene. Hannes scanned the article and photos of the two-page spread.

"New leads? What's so new? It says absolutely nothing new." Hannes had feared there was a leak in the police force.

"Well, if the headline read 'No New Leads in Jesus Murder,' no one would buy the paper."

"Let's talk about something else. I'll be busy with Jesus tomorrow anyway. Yesterday was my first boating safety class."

"So you finally want to take your old boss's boat out on the water? Awesome. Hurry up so we can make your maiden voyage before it turns cold. I'm sure the class is real easy for a canoeist."

"Doubtful. My head was spinning last night. We started with navigation and learned the different types of lights. Do you know how many types of lights there are? Flashing, blinking, I could go on."

"Green, go; red, stop; yellow, drive like hell?" Ben smirked.

"Very funny. I'll have to cram for the test. I wonder if Fritz ever bothered to get his license."

"Have you visited him?"

"No." Hannes had promised himself a more exciting evening with Ben. The topic of Fritz and the scratch in his throat didn't bode well. "Don't you start too. I know I should see him. I need to look up the visiting hours and see if they fit into my schedule."

Since Ben knew all about Hannes's conflicting feelings, he decided to change the subject.

"What's Anna up to? Shouldn't she be back by now?" Ben asked. Hannes had had his eye on the key witness from his first murder investigation.

"She comes back in two weeks," Hannes said. "She e-mailed me yesterday from Indonesia to say that she'd be hanging around there for a few more days."

"Well, at least she wrote you."

Before Anna and Hannes could really get to know each other, she had quit her job as an executive assistant at a pharmaceutical company and had flown to Southeast Asia for several months.

"I need to clear my head first and then think things over. I hope you understand," she had said to Hannes after they'd kissed good-bye at the airport. Their first real kiss.

Hannes had understood only too well after the events of the past summer. Yet he had also been reluctant to let her go. The right words had been on the tip of his tongue, but he never said them. After staring at him for a moment, Anna had hugged him one last time before joining the security line, never once turning around.

"You know what?" Hannes said, his eyes fixed on his beer. "You're right. I'm completely inept when it comes to women. When I said good-bye to Anna, I wanted to tell her something, but I couldn't. Sometimes there's only one right moment, and if you miss that moment, it's probably too late."

CHAPTER 6

The mood at the station plummeted over the next few days. It was fifty degrees outside. The summer was gone, and the gray, rainy weather cast a pall over the city. Steffen Lauer made for an even tenser mood, demanding routine updates even when there was nothing new to report.

Alexander Kramer's apartment had been thoroughly searched. There were plenty of sex toys found in the process, and Hannes's ears had burned as he'd reported the discoveries to Federsen. The items did little to improve Federsen's opinion of Kramer, and the apartment had provided no clues. It was the typical apartment of a man in his early thirties, with workout clothes and exercise equipment.

Federsen seemed almost giddy when he opened the door to Hannes's office on Thursday.

"Those reporters aren't as bad as everyone here says," he said.

His wool sweater hiked up his paunch as he walked over to Hannes's desk. Upon noticing Hannes's red nose and watery eyes, he stepped back. Their field trip to the wet and windy crime scene had given the ill-dressed Hannes a severe cold.

"Just yesterday you were cursing those bast—" Hannes blew his nose into a tissue.

"True, but that was before I dealt with this woman from *The Daily Courier*," Federsen said as he took a few more steps away. "Unlike those pompous asses from the national media, she has a very good understanding of our situation. We spoke last night, and I wish all members of the press would follow her example."

Despite his headache, a bit of life sprung back into Hannes. He pulled a copy of the current *Daily Courier* from his bag and unfolded it on his desk.

"I wondered," Hannes said and sniffed, "how the reporter knew so much. Her article fills the entire front page, and your name pops up."

Federsen stepped a little closer. The look of satisfaction suddenly vanished once he saw the headline, which was clearly intended to drum up sales.

"'Police Overwhelmed in Jesus Murder'?" Federsen read, breathing hard. His face turned dangerously red as he skimmed the article. He came off as utterly incompetent.

"That damn bitch. What's she trying to suggest? 'Detective Federsen seems far from capable and doesn't give the impression of being up to the task. As an excuse, he cites the department's lack of staff.' Excuse? If that bimbo wants to dig up dirt, maybe she should start by looking on her own desk. Of course we don't have the man power." He glared at Hannes. "If they'd given me a couple of competent detectives, we'd be much further along. Instead, I get stuck with some semipro athlete who produces little more than snot." He pointed a nicotine-stained finger at Hannes. "That bitch has underestimated me. I'm going to give her editor a piece of my mind."

Federsen slapped the desk with the now rolled-up newspaper and stormed into his office. He slammed the door behind him and got on the phone.

Ten minutes later, Hannes was in Federsen's office when Steffen Lauer walked in with a copy of the *Daily Courier*.

"Detective Niehaus, would you give Detective Federsen and me a moment alone?" he asked in a forced voice, his mustache twitching. Hannes was happy to comply. Lauer closed the door, but Hannes listened in for a moment.

"Henning, you've gone too far this time. Not only did you give the newspaper an unauthorized interview, but now you've gone and insulted the editor-in-chief and his 'dimwitted intern' over the phone. Not to mention threatened to . . ."

Isabelle was sitting at a rickety table. She was also in her early thirties, but Hannes hadn't talked with her much before. Although she wasn't very attractive, she was the indisputable Pollyanna of their floor. Isabelle stared out the rain-washed window, and Hannes startled her with a loud sneeze.

"Well, misery always loves company," she said.

"So you haven't gotten anywhere with your case either?"

"No, not at all. Fortunately your crucifixion has overshadowed everything else, and nobody's interested in the dead woman found at the dock."

"You're welcome," Hannes joked, settling into a chair across from her. "Plus you have a nice boss. Mine's a rabid dog."

"Nice." Isabelle smiled, and the shine returned to her blue eyes. "What's he done now?"

"Nothing. His fangs are being filed down as we speak." Hannes pulled out a tissue in the nick of time. When he told Isabelle about Federsen's battle with the press, the mood brightened a little in the small break room.

"This is the first good thing I've heard all day," Isabelle said.

"Well, I'm sure the worst is yet to come." Hannes knew his moment of triumph would not last long. "If we don't come up with a lead soon, Lauer's going to nail us to the cafeteria door."

"Where do you stand at the moment?"

"I've interviewed all the people Alexander Kramer worked with at the porn studio. Nobody really knew him. At least they could all recognize him in the photos. One of the cameramen knew he had a sister, but we haven't been able to reach her."

"Why not?"

"She seems to be out of town. She lives in the city and is some sort of artist. Their parents died a long time ago."

"Have you checked all the alibis of the people at the studio?"

"Yup. Unfortunately, it's impossible to say when exactly the crime took place. So not all of his colleagues have solid alibis. However, the gaps in their whereabouts aren't big enough to warrant suspicion. Right now, we're trying to find out more about his family and friends."

Hannes and Federsen hadn't yet successfully identified the dealer Alexander Kramer owed money to. Questioning the victim's neighbors hadn't unearthed much.

"Maybe you should reveal his identity in the press and ask for the public's help?" suggested Isabelle. "Your boss has a good contact, I hear . . ."

"We'll probably have to." Hannes had already wondered why the public didn't know the victim's name, given the enormous amount of media attention the case had garnered. But the police had questioned a number of potential witnesses, so it was only a matter of time before the first newspaper touted, "Jesus Was a Porn Star."

"How's it going with you?" Hannes asked.

"Not much better. The dead woman had a horse farm about twelve miles outside the city. She ran the operation with her husband and lived an unobtrusive life."

"How'd she die?"

"Painfully. Found curled up against a wall in a secluded area of the port. Some sort of poison was injected into her abdomen, but there were no signs of a struggle. She was discovered relatively soon after she died by two young lovebirds. Maria thinks she died a few hours before."

"So you're taking a break from doing nothing," Federsen said from the doorway, and a frightened Hannes looked over. "Finish your chitchat. We've found Kramer's sister."

***

Half an hour later, the detectives stood in the small courtyard in front of Antje Kramer's workshop. It was surrounded by a thick row of hedges and situated at the end of a narrow dead-end alley. Gravestones and a variety of other finished and semifinished bird baths, sculptures, and fountains littered the ground. Antje Kramer was a stonemason and sculptor.

Hannes hated meeting with victims' relatives because he didn't know how he should behave around them. The woman's tears slowly ran dry, and Hannes handed her a tissue. They blew their noses at the same time.

"I can't believe it," she kept saying.

"We also find it hard to believe that this is the first time you've heard about your brother's death," Federsen said. "The story's all over the news, and you should have been able to recognize the blurry images."

"I only heard about it on the radio," Ms. Kramer said, glaring at him. "I was at a training course in the mountains at Bergisches Land and had other things to do than watch the news. Had I known that—" A sob cut her short.

While Ms. Kramer fought to regain her composure and Hannes struggled to control his legs, the detectives scanned the courtyard. Federsen didn't believe women belonged in professional trades either. He frowned when he saw a particularly kitschy gravestone with two angels leading a man over a bridge.

Ms. Kramer followed his gaze and said, "What I want doesn't matter when I do commissioned work. The customer gets what the customer wants. I prefer to do sculpture." She pointed at some of her works in the corner of the yard. "Unfortunately, sculpture doesn't pay the bills, hence the gravestones. They're recession-proof." She grimaced.

"What kind of gravestone will you make for your brother?" Federsen asked.

Hannes suffered a violent fit of coughing, and his face turned red.

"Uh, Ms. Kramer. What my colleague meant to say was: What kind of person was your brother, and why might he have been killed in this bizarre way?"

"You mean because he starred in pornos?" Ms. Kramer asked while glaring at Federsen again. "Do you think he was a bad person? Because he wasn't. He was honest and sincere. And definitely more sensitive than this jerk."

"My dear Ms. Kramer," Federsen said, "I want to find your brother's murderer as quickly as possible, and pussyfooting around won't help. Who knew your brother, and who could have wanted him dead?"

Ms. Kramer sat down. Then she shrugged and turned to Hannes. "I have no idea. He never said he was in trouble. We had a close relationship, so he would have told me. I just know . . . Well, my brother did do cocaine every now and then and wasn't particularly good with his finances. He owed some money to his dealer, who began to pressure him to pay him back."

"Do you have a name?" Federsen asked.

Ms. Kramer thought hard and, ignoring Federsen again, directed her response to Hannes. "I can't remember. Dennis or something."

"Last name?" demanded Federsen.

Ms. Kramer shook her head and looked down at her chapped, dust-covered hands. "Please find the person," she said softly. "Find whoever did this to my brother."

It was clear she could offer no more help at the moment. Federsen nodded, and Hannes handed her his business card. As they were leaving, Hannes saw a knee-high figure peering from a window in the workshop. A lifelike man wearing a loincloth and crown of thorns hung on a cross atop a small hill. The figure stared in torment at Hannes, his eyes following him as he shuffled behind his boss.

They returned to the station, where Federsen bitterly watched from his office chair as Hannes blew into a tissue. He wreathed himself in cigarette smoke as if it were an impenetrable wall against the germs.

"If you infect me, you can kiss this job good-bye. What do you think about this sculptress?"

"I called the school in the Bergisches Land. She was there at the time in question, so the alibi checks out. She was also understandably beside herself. We should question her again once she's had some time."

"She can't be that sensitive. She's not exactly the dainty type. I find it hard to believe she didn't know much about the murder. A hermit would have heard all about the story by now. Anyway, she's the only person who can help us right now. Call her later when she's calmed down. Damn it, pull yourself together." He pounded on the desk and stared at Hannes as he let loose another sneeze. "Steffen scheduled a briefing in five minutes. Stay here, and update the facts on the whiteboard. Use your brain. There has to be a clue somewhere in that scribbling."

Hannes watched Federsen leave, then searched with disgust through the used tissues in his pocket to find his nasal decongestant and choked the pill down. Then he wiped the whiteboard clean and wrote down everything they knew about Alexander Kramer again. With every sneeze, he made sure to cover Federsen's office a little bit more in his germs. When he had all the facts before him, he shook his head. If there was a crucial piece of information hidden in there, he didn't see it. No suspects, no motive.

As soon as he had left Federsen's contaminated office, his desk phone rang.

"Johannes Niehaus," he answered.

"It's Antje Kramer. You were just here."

"I was about to contact you. How are you doing?"

"I need to make arrangements for my brother's funeral."

"His body is with the medical examiner. Unfortunately, I don't know when it will be released. But if you'd like to see him, I can schedule an appointment."

"No. I don't think I want to see him like that. Incidentally, I've made a list of all the people Alex knew. Should I read it?"

"No, I'll come by and see you again." Hannes coughed and hung up.

***

Hannes looked at the stone cross on the windowsill in the small workshop. The eyes of the sculpted Jesus were fixed on him, as if they wanted to tell him something.

"That was my journeyman's piece," said Ms. Kramer, following his gaze. "It was a challenge. I didn't know where to begin. My brother really liked it, even though he was usually critical of Christian symbols. Tragic, huh?"

"How did you get into stonework? Isn't it a rather male-dominated profession?"

"It is. During my apprenticeship year, there was only one other woman. I had an office job, but I wasn't happy. I always liked being creative, and I fell in love with stonework after taking a video course. It's fascinating what you can make out of a rough block of stone."

Hannes looked around the dusty workshop and nodded. Ms. Kramer knew her craft. He picked up a small hammer; it was surprisingly light.

"That's a lump hammer. I use it with a chisel to engrave headstones. I prefer traditional hand tools. They're more enjoyable. The work takes longer, but it's more exact. I get a better feel for the stone."

She led Hannes to a wooden bench with various almost medieval-looking devices. Had Hannes not known any better, he would have guessed they were the tools of a torturer. His head began to spin when Ms. Kramer explained the functions of the strange items: crandalls, round mallets, bush hammers. Only the splitting hammer looked familiar.

"How long does it take to learn to use these tools?"

"You apprentice for three years. But I haven't passed the exam to become a master craftsman yet. Did you know that it's one of the oldest craft professions in the world? Chiseled rocks discovered in the Dordogne are about four thousand years old."

It was obvious Ms. Kramer had found her passion. Hannes listened as she continued to proudly explain the history of her craft. For a moment, it seemed she had forgotten her grief. Her unruly blonde hair framed a face that must have usually looked young and full of life.

"Was your brother also creative?" he asked. By this point, he desperately wanted to crawl into bed and sleep.

"Not really. He once jokingly tried to carve a horse out of a stone block. He loved horses. But the result looked more like a mythical creature." She smiled and leaned down to dig out a small object. Her hair fell to the side, revealing a small tattoo on her upper neck. It looked like a Nordic rune, but it could have also represented a cross being split in two by lightning. Hannes had noticed the same symbol on several works in the yard.

"Here." Ms. Kramer handed him a lump of stone. "This was the result." She smiled when she saw the look of doubt on his face, because it took a great deal of imagination to recognize the shape of a horse.

"What's the meaning of that rune you carve into the stones?" Hannes asked.

"That's my mason's mark. It's how a mason designates his or her work. It's kind of like a signature. There's not really any deeper meaning to it. I used to be more religious and am still very interested in sacred buildings, because they often have masterpieces by earlier sculptors.

Sometimes I'm asked to restore monuments or statues on historic buildings. But I don't want to bore you any longer about my stonework. You're here for the list." She wiped her dusty hands on her black jeans and pulled a folded piece of paper from her pocket. "I hope I didn't forget anyone."

Hannes scanned the list, but none of the names jumped out. "I'll need you to help me a little," he said and pulled out a pen.

They hunched over the list together. Hannes already knew the first three names: Kramer's film partner, Inga; Melcher, the head of the studio; and quirky Gertrude.

"Unfortunately, I only know four people at the studio. Alex didn't talk much about it. He knew I was a little uneasy with my little brother starring in pornos."

"Hold on. Which four? I spoke to everyone at Paradise Images & Productions, but I only recognize three people on this list."

She pointed to the fourth name from the top. "Manuel. I don't know his last name. He'd been promised the lead role in Alexander's first film. But then Alex replaced him, and he wasn't cast again."

Hannes remembered the young man he'd seen as he left the studio. "Do you know why Alexander was given his role?"

"Manuel didn't get along with his female costars." Ms. Kramer shrugged. "He wasn't thrilled at being upstaged by my brother. After Alex's first day of filming, he ambushed him outside the studio. He didn't show up after that, and Alex never mentioned him again."

Hannes jotted this information down next to the name. He had focused solely on Kramer's current coworkers—a stupid mistake on his part. Federsen would be delighted.

Ms. Kramer said there were no other close family members. Her parents had no siblings, and her grandparents had died many years ago. The next names on the list were five childhood friends, all still living in Bayreuth. As far as Ms. Kramer knew, her brother had been in sporadic contact with them. Hannes would have to ask for assistance from his Bavarian colleagues to find them, because he had no desire to take a trip to the city of the Richard Wagner Festival. That would have been something for Old Fritz, who preferred to work on his most difficult cases while listening to classical music.

"Did your brother have any friends here?"

"Not really. Alex worked out a lot because he had to be in great shape. And before he started his career in porn, he modeled off and on. He also spent a lot of time with his horse, so he didn't have much free time. His costly hobby wasn't exactly good for his financial situation. He had two friends here in town. They're on the list. He met Mirko at the gym, and Jonas at the stable."

Hannes was sure he'd be able to track them down.

The last few names on the list were grouped together by a large bracket with "New Way" written beside it.

"Who are these people?" Hannes's head and body ached, and he was burning up.

"They're all from New Way. It's a sort of nondenominational community. A place for people who want nothing to do with traditional church."

"So a cult?" What better place to find a killer?

"We're not a cult," Ms. Kramer said. "New Way is a group for people who support core Christian values, but do not agree with the Church as an institution. Heavy-handed moralizing, male-only priests and their misogynistic views, medieval rituals—we reject all that. We're the exact opposite of a cult because we condemn, patronize, or exclude no one."

"I can imagine, if a porn actor's allowed to join. Still, I'm surprised. This is the first time I've heard that your brother had religious tendencies."

"He didn't. I was trying to explain it to you. We're a community that focuses on moral truths rather than traditional religion. We may discuss the Ten Commandments, but for us, they're simply fundamental moral values. Religion doesn't really play a role. Alexander didn't believe in God or Jesus."

Instead of making a beeline for his bed, Hannes made a detour to the police station to share the new information with his boss. He opened the door to the office and stepped into the middle of a conversation between Federsen and Steffen Lauer.

"You don't look too good," said Lauer.

"Where have you been?" Federsen asked.

Hannes handed him the list of names and explained how he had gotten it.

"How dare you visit the murder victim's sister again without talking to me first. There, you see, Steffen? The guy can't be controlled. He's just like Fritz."

"That's enough, Henning." Lauer turned to Hannes. "In the future, please check with your supervisor before you go out on your own. Are there names we didn't know before?"

Lauer relaxed when Hannes explained everyone's backgrounds. "This is good news," Lauer said and patted Hannes on the shoulder. "We've finally shed some more light on Alexander Kramer. But you should head home and get to bed. I'll lend Henning a couple of your colleagues to help him go over the list."

Before heading home, Hannes called the prison to inquire about visiting hours. He was so fed up with Federsen that he was finally ready to visit his former boss. He was a little taken aback to learn that visits were possible on Fridays—tomorrow. He hadn't planned on visiting Fritz so soon. On the other hand, he would have skipped his workout anyway since he was sick, so he might as well visit.

On his way out Hannes stopped by Isabelle's office. Cat photos hung everywhere—she was legendary at the station for her love of felines. He thought about Antje Kramer's list of names. Her inclusion of Sylvia Böhm on the partial list of New Way members stood out.

"Alex got along best with Sylvia," she had explained. "She owns the horse farm where he rented a stall for his gelding. They spent a lot of time together. And now I have to figure out arrangements for the horse. Hopefully Sylvia's interested in keeping him."

"You look exhausted," Isabelle said, snapping Hannes back to the present.

"Hey, what was the name of the dead woman found on the dock?"

"Sylvia Böhm. Why?" Isabelle asked.

Hannes stared at her, his feverish eyes now wide.

CHAPTER 7

Hannes had slept for twelve hours, thanks to a healthy dose of cough syrup. His reflection in the bathroom mirror, however, showed that his health had only marginally improved. The whites of his eyes had turned reddish. His nose was rubbed raw after his all-day tissue marathon, and his lips were chapped. At least his fever seemed to have broken.

Fritz Janssen didn't look much better as he limped toward Hannes an hour later. Hannes had been led to a bright room with several tables. Partitions between the tables at least gave the sense of some privacy. A prison guard sat behind a desk at the front of the room, carefully observing the interactions between prisoners and visitors.

The only other visitor was an elderly woman who sat at the far end of the room opposite a dangerous-looking man. Hannes chose the farthest table from them. He looked self-consciously at Fritz. A mix of feelings came over him: anger, insecurity, sympathy, pity.

Fritz's face had two new scars. Evidently, the wounds from his fall had not yet healed. His slightly wrinkled face looked pale, and his hair had lost its last remaining patches of brown. Even his bushy eyebrows had changed color, making him look like an old, slightly injured owl.

However, the most serious consequence of Fritz's fall was his stiff right knee. It took great effort and difficulty to hobble over.

A broken Fritz groaned as he fell into the chair and stretched his right leg to the side. His light-blue eyes had lost their luster. Hannes sat there with his arms crossed defensively.

"I'm very happy you came," Fritz said. His chronically hoarse voice sounded even more like a rusty saw. "But you don't look too good."

"Thanks. I caught some stubborn cold. You've looked better yourself. How are you doing here?"

"I was more comfortable in the infirmary than I am in my cell. I was there for the first month. In any case, I managed to score a coffeemaker for my little apartment." Old Fritz briefly returned in a flash of his foxlike grin, but he was still only a shadow of his former self. He'd considered coffee a basic necessity ever since his sixteenth birthday. "I can listen to music too, and they gave me a small TV. Congratulations, by the way."

"What for?"

"I watched the Canoe World Championships. You know, I'm not really a fan of sports, but . . . well, you don't really have anything better to do here," he said, trying to hide his interest in Hannes's life. "I'm no expert, but ninth place at the world championships is pretty good, right?"

"I'm happy with it. I may have come in last in the final heat, but it was enough to qualify for the Olympics." Hannes uncrossed his arms. He was glad to talk about something more innocuous.

"So I can catch you on TV next summer in the Olympics?"

"Only if I make it to the finals. I doubt they'll broadcast all the heats. I only qualified for the thousand meters. Unfortunately, I didn't make the two hundred—I lost in the prelims. I was too slow out of the gate, and there's not enough time to catch up in that race. But whatever. I'm just proud I made it to the Olympics."

"I hope my successor's giving you enough time to train. Who is it?"

When Hannes told him the bad news, Fritz frowned. "That bum? How are you two getting along?"

He wasn't surprised when Hannes told him they were constantly at each other's throats.

"The best thing to do is avoid him as much as possible. You need to make sure his bad reputation doesn't rub off on you. Try to do your own thing and go to Marcel for good advice. He's one hell of a cop and can't stand that dope either. Henning should be happy having you. He can't handle anything by himself, and you've already proven you're a talented investigator."

The memory of the past summer caused them to grow silent.

"One request, Hannes. Let's not talk about what happened. I'm sorry for what you had to go through, but beyond that, I'd do it again. I'm guilty of justice and paying the price for it. But I don't want to dredge it all up. Nor, incidentally, would I like to talk about my cancer. Let's not waste the short time we have discussing medical reports. Tell me something positive. How's my *Lena*? Have you already been out on her?"

Hannes didn't want to let Fritz off the hook so easily. They still needed to talk about the dramatic events of last summer. He could understand why Fritz wanted to avoid the issue, but sooner or later they would have to broach it. However, after looking at the former detective's scarred face, he decided to let it go for now.

Hannes reluctantly explained that he intended to get his boating license in the coming weeks. His newfound enthusiasm for boating got the better of him, and they engaged in an animated discussion about buoys, nautical charts, and meteorology.

Fritz looked at the large clock on the wall. "We've only got ten more minutes. I'm allowed an hour visit each week. Besides you, Ole's the only other person who's visited, and he came once. So I'm far from being booked up. If you have nothing better to do next week, you could visit your old boss. I'd be very happy."

He stared in embarrassment at the edge of the table, and Hannes felt sorry for him. He realized that despite everything he had actually grown fond of the old man. The last few minutes had flown by. When Hannes promised to return next week, Fritz beamed.

"Tell me, what are you working on at the moment? I don't mean to interrogate you, but maybe I could give you a few tips here and there . . ."

"Geez, Fritz." Hannes had to smile. "I was wondering how long you'd be able to hold out."

"My body might be a wreck, but I'd at least like to keep my mind sharp. I've started doing crossword puzzles. I never would've thought to do them before, not even at my most bored. I have a lot of time to think. If you give me something to gnaw on, I might be able to come up with a few theories."

"Absolutely not. Federsen would have my head. Then Lauer would feed the rest of me to the lions in the zoo. I'm sorry, but that's not an option."

"I understand." Instead of pressing Hannes, Fritz gave him some more tips on how to handle *Lena*. "And don't forget," he said as he shook Hannes's hand good-bye. "You're never happy on land until the ship is sinking."

***

Perhaps Steffen Lauer doubted Federsen's competence as much as Old Fritz, because after lunch he rounded up the detectives investigating the two murder cases and personally chaired the meeting. He shared what Hannes had learned and commended him for discovering that the two victims had known each other. After all, it was a well-known fact that Federsen liked to bask in the glory of others. Lauer looked around and stroked his bald head with one hand, while the fingers of the other fiddled with his mustache. It was a nervous tic of his. He nodded at Hannes.

"Let's start with Alexander Kramer. Please give us a brief overview."

Surprised that he'd been chosen and not Federsen, Hannes quickly collected his thoughts. He first went over the victim's personal details before turning to the current status of the investigation. "In the meantime, Bavaria's gotten back to us about Kramer's childhood friends. At the time in question, all five of them can prove they were in Bayreuth. No one could have driven up here, crucified Kramer, and driven back. His cell phone gave us no new names, at least none of any help. He had the numbers to modeling agencies, his landlord, gym, and so on. We've also read all his text messages and found nothing unusual."

"When was he last seen alive?" asked Isabelle.

"At a New Way function. A member teaches a fitness class from time to time, and Kramer participated in the class on the Monday night before his death. He walked alone to the bus stop, and there's no trace of him after that."

"I paid a visit to that other porn star, Kramer's predecessor, yesterday," Federsen chimed in, seeking attention. "His name's Manuel Birkholz, and he's thirty-two. He made it clear that he didn't like Kramer but denied threatening him. There are enough holes in his alibi for him to be the perp."

"What about the dealer?" Hannes asked.

"Dennis or whatever his name is? The two colleagues who stepped in for you yesterday afternoon asked around. The name didn't ring a bell for anyone in narcotics. Unfortunately, Ms. Kramer didn't give us much to go on. We also questioned Kramer's sex partner from the studio again. She didn't recognize the name either."

"Well, let's hope we find him anyway," Lauer said. "There were two other friends on the list. What'd they have to say?"

"I questioned them myself." Federsen seemed to have had an unusually productive day yesterday. "The guy from the gym, Mirko, was on a business trip. His alibi checks out, and he couldn't give us anything to go on. The other guy's name is Jonas Talmann. He works at the stable owned by the late Sylvia Böhm. He grooms the horses and handles minor repairs."

"He's still fairly new there," added Isabelle, since this was the point where the two murders overlapped. "Mrs. Böhm's husband told us that he has been there only a year. Apparently, they haven't been particularly pleased with him, because Mr. Böhm's considering firing him. Mr. Talmann can prove he was at the stable when Mrs. Böhm was murdered, so he's been ruled out."

"Does he know he's on the chopping block?" Hannes asked.

"Mr. Böhm hasn't mentioned anything to him about it. Whether his wife made any sort of hints to that effect, we don't know."

"So far, Mr. Böhm and Jonas Talmann are the only two with connections to both victims," a pensive Lauer said. "We have only a rough estimate when the crucifixion took place, but in the case of Mrs. Böhm, they both have alibis. Let's take a closer look at this religious community the victims belonged to. It can hardly be a coincidence, and a crucifixion strongly suggests that the crime was religiously motivated. Marcel, please fill in Henning and Detective Niehaus about Mrs. Böhm's murder, so you're all on the same page."

Like Lauer, Marcel was totally bald, even though at forty-one, he was nearly fifteen years younger and an outspoken ladies' man. He had strikingly attractive features and a carefully trimmed beard. He was a passionate runner and father of two. He was very popular, but he wasn't particularly great at managing stress. Although he rarely lost his cool, in times of great tension, he would get nosebleeds. He pulled a large color photo of an attractive blonde woman from a file and placed it on the table.

"Sylvia Böhm was thirty-nine, and strangely enough, we share the same birthday, April 1."

Federsen mumbled a bad April Fool's joke, but Marcel continued, "She bought the horse farm with her husband three years ago and grew the business significantly in a very short amount of time. She used to be a competitive rider and even made it to the German national championships. She had grown up with horses and knew how to run a horse farm."

"Unlike her husband," Isabelle added. "Matthias Böhm is forty-two and was originally an insurance broker. He doesn't ride and has stated that he isn't much of a horse lover. He manages the farm."

"Rumor has it that the two had been going through some sort of rough patch," Marcel said. "Mrs. Böhm wanted to start growing organic produce and open up a bed-and-breakfast. Her husband thought it was a bad idea."

"He also didn't think much of her involvement in New Way," Isabelle explained. "He's a practicing Catholic, and in his opinion, the group is nothing short of blasphemy."

"What can you tell us about Mrs. Böhm's death?" Hannes asked and attempted to stifle a cough. He sneezed twice instead, and Isabelle moved away from him.

"She was found last Friday night, so a week ago today, by a young couple—Japanese tourists who continued on their European tour. Neither is under suspicion. She was last seen alive by her husband that morning. She left the farm in her car, but he didn't know where she was headed. We found the car near the crime scene. So it's possible she had planned to meet with the perp. Her cell phone's missing. It wasn't on her, and her husband can't find it in the house. Nothing else is missing, though. Her purse was beside her at the scene. Her wallet and jewelry were untouched."

"There were no signs of a struggle," Marcel said, "and no other DNA. No clues at the scene either. Maria did find something, though. A strong poison had been injected into her abdomen, causing an extremely painful death. That's probably the reason why she was found curled up." He placed another photo on the table, and Hannes's stomach turned at the sight of her distorted face. He quickly looked at Isabelle.

"Was Maria able to determine the time of death?"

"Mrs. Böhm died last Friday at approximately three o'clock. She was found five hours later."

"So she died two days after Kramer," Hannes said. "But Kramer was crucified before he died, maybe right after the fitness class, so sometime Monday night or early Tuesday morning. Mrs. Böhm was killed three or four days after that."

"What interests me the most is the connection between the two victims," Federsen said. "We have to assume it was the same perp or at least the same person who ordered the murders."

Lauer shook his head. "We should be careful not to jump to conclusions."

"What do you mean?" Federsen said, annoyed. "Mrs. Böhm was attractive, Mr. Kramer had a knack for women, and things weren't great between the married couple. We already know that Mr. Kramer and Mrs. Böhm got along. What's more, both were involved in this strange sect that Mr. Böhm is so dismissive of. The motive is obvious."

"But why go to that expense?" Marcel asked. "If Kramer really was his wife's lover, why would Mr. Böhm bother to nail him to a cross? On the other hand, we do have some evidence that would support your theory and provide an explanation for the strange circumstances surrounding Mrs. Böhm's death."

He nodded to Isabelle. They clearly respected each other.

Isabelle took the floor. "Maria discovered that Mrs. Böhm had had an abortion shortly before her death. This was confirmed by the clinic. It was her husband's child, not a lover's. At least that's what she told the doctor."

Before the meeting ended, Lauer instructed the two teams to continue working separately but consult with one another often. The number of suspects was manageable: Mr. Böhm, the one who potentially ordered someone to commit the murders; Dennis, the drug dealer; and Manuel Birkholz, the porn star. Federsen and Hannes were given the task of investigating the religious community—the appearance in the case of a crucifixion and an abortion were reason enough. The two colleagues Clarissa and Per, who had been searching without much luck for the dealer, were relieved of their other duties, so both teams could rely on them for support.

Hannes was pleased. They could use the help, and now he would no longer be the only one Federsen could vent his frustrations on. He also remembered Fritz's advice to stick with Marcel. He'd be able to do that without Federsen's knowledge now that the teams were collaborating.

At the moment, however, he was stuck with his boss.

***

Federsen shifted up instead of down, and the engine howled as the Passat turned down the driveway of Böhm Horse Farm. Two young girls struggled to control their Haflingers as they shied away from the police car.

The farm was well kept. It was situated on the outskirts of a small village, only a few hundred feet away from the sea. It was bright and warm, and Hannes was relieved he could breathe more freely. Federsen, however, sneezed so loudly that the two Haflingers snorted in fear. Hannes handed him a tissue. Evidently, his germ warfare was showing its first signs of success.

"I warned you. If this turns into a cold, you'll pay," Federsen said, then blew his nose. He marched toward an elongated barn and lit a cigarette. It was clear that it was fall break, because the farm was inundated with children of all ages, mostly girls. An ill-tempered Federsen made his way through the children and horses, using his belly like a snowplow.

"We're looking for Mr. Böhm," he said to the first adult he saw.

"I'm here to pick up my daughter. I have no idea where Mr. Böhm is," the irritated parent said.

"Over in the main house," a younger man said. His work clothes suggested he was a farmhand, and he pointed to a large residential building.

Hannes thanked him while Federsen took off. The farm appeared to have been expanded in recent years, because unlike the stables, the main building seemed much older. But it was evident that its owners placed a great deal of emphasis on upkeep. The window frames and doors of the large brick house were painted glossy white, and its red-tile roof seemed recently redone.

The front door opened, and a tall man eyed the two detectives through thick glasses. He wore brightly colored pants and a dark-gray turtleneck sweater, hardly appropriate for farm work.

"Can I help you?" It was clear he had little desire to do so.

"Detective Federsen. We'd like to have a word with you."

"Have you taken over the investigation? I've already told your colleague everything I know. Come on, we can sit on the terrace."

Next to the large front door was a spacious wooden deck with comfortable patio furniture from which it was possible to watch all the activity on the farm. Although it was protected from the wind and warmed by the sun, Hannes was grateful for his thick winter jacket. This time, Federsen was the one who was poorly dressed.

"How many horses do you have on the farm?" Hannes asked.

"Currently eighty-six," said Mr. Böhm with some irritation. He turned to Federsen. "Forty of them belong to us, the remaining are boarded here. I'd be glad to give you a tour later. We have three stables, two riding arenas, a riding lawn, and over there is the riding hall. There's also a round pen and numerous pastures. Six staff take care of everything."

"You can spare us the tour—I'm allergic to horses. My colleague and I are not here about your wife, the officers you've already met are taking care of that investigation."

"So why are you here then?"

"I'm sure you've heard about the so-called Jesus Murder, right?" Hannes asked.

"Of course. What a crazy story. It happened near here. But I don't see how I could help."

"You knew the victim," said Federsen. "Your wife too. Alexander Kramer. His horse is boarded on your farm."

Mr. Böhm's eyes widened. "The man . . . the crucified man was Alexander Kramer?"

"How well did you know him?" Federsen asked.

"Not well. His gelding has been with us for about six months. I only take care of the paperwork and had little to do with him. He was late twice on payments, so I was ready to give him notice. Sylvia spoke with him, and we had no trouble after that."

"Well, that's about to change," Federsen said. His gaze wandered. "Your wife knew him better?"

"Sylvia was in charge of the day-to-day work, so she was in close contact with our customers. She interacted with him more than I did." It was obvious that Mr. Böhm felt uncomfortable discussing the topic.

"Weren't your wife and Mr. Kramer also active in a kind of . . . religious community?"

"That's correct. She knew him from there. The group has little to do with religion. They supposedly live by Christian values, but they tolerate the most perverse lifestyles."

"Like acting in pornos or homosexuality?" Hannes asked.

"Exactly." Mr. Böhm was becoming increasingly agitated. "I'm a tolerant person. But some things are just sick and depraved. Pretending like everything's compatible with Christian values is just pushing tolerance too far. Although Alexander Kramer was the only person from this group I knew personally, Sylvia told me enough about the other members for me to make my own judgments."

"Yes, what's this world coming to?" Federsen asked. "But your wife thought differently?"

"My wife was just naive. A typical do-gooder. Everyone has the right to do what they want so long as it doesn't hurt anyone. But where does it end? Alexander Kramer, for example, with these sleazy films . . ." He shook his head in disgust.

"Then I assume you weren't very pleased that your wife got along so well with Mr. Kramer?" Federsen asked sympathetically.

"Of course I wasn't. I also didn't want her participating in that pseudoreligious group. But if you'd met my wife, you'd have known how pigheaded she was."

"Your wife and Mr. Kramer were apparently very close. Is it true that the relationship between you and your wife had been strained?" asked Hannes.

"I don't think that's any of your business," Mr. Böhm said. "But I do realize what you're trying to get at. You're insinuating that my wife was having an affair with this porn star and that I took them out? That's absurd. At the time of my wife's murder, I was with our accountant. You know that. I've been at my wit's end since Sylvia died, and now you show up and suggest—"

"We're not suggesting anything," Federsen said, and shot Hannes a warning look. "My young colleague misspoke. But you certainly understand that we need to pursue every lead, even those we can quickly rule out."

"You have an alibi for your wife's murder, but not one for the crucifixion," Hannes continued, unfazed. "Besides, you don't necessarily have to be the perpetrator. There's always someone willing to do the dirty work. We'd like to know what you were doing late Monday night and early Tuesday morning of last week."

For the first time in several minutes, Mr. Böhm looked directly at Hannes. "I can tell you exactly what I was doing. As I've been doing for the past few weeks, I spent the night going over our finances and looking for a way out of our current difficulties. I went to bed around midnight."

"Do you have any witnesses?"

"Yes. My wife. Ask her." He laughed bitterly.

Hannes fell silent, then said, "According to the autopsy report, your wife recently had an abortion. It's our understanding that you didn't agree with her decision. However, because your wife was still in her first trimester, she was free to choose and had an abortion against your will."

"Of course I was against it. You can't do that to a child. But I wouldn't kill my wife for that." Mr. Böhm took a deep breath. "Look, like I just mentioned, we've been having financial problems. The renovation and expansion were more expensive than planned, and our occupancy rate still isn't as high as it should be. My wife thought it wasn't the right time to have a child."

"Your wife was already thirty-nine," Federsen said. "She wouldn't have had a lot of time left to get pregnant."

"That's what I told her. We risked not having children at all. Not to mention, it's a mortal sin to kill an unborn child. But these free spirits at New Way supported her decision, told her it was perfectly fine—Kramer more than anyone else, even though he was always fond of the kids here."

"I don't know," Federsen told Hannes on their way back to the city. "Sure, Mr. Böhm didn't have very much of anything nice to say about his wife, and even less about Kramer, but he would've tried to hide that from us if he were actually behind the murders. He also doesn't give me the impression that he'd be able to kill a man, and certainly not in such a sadistic manner. To nail someone to a cross or to pay someone to inject your own wife with poison, you need to have a pretty cruel streak in you. And there can't be any financial motive—his wife didn't have any life insurance."

Hannes hadn't left with a positive impression. He may have listened to one too many of his sister's esoteric explanations, but he believed the eyes were a window into a person's thoughts. And Mr. Böhm's eyes seemed cold and calculating. The horse farm's six employees confirmed this. Everyone had spoken very well about Sylvia Böhm, who regularly pitched in with the work and was a very warm person. Her husband, on the other hand, could rarely be found around horse manure and limited himself to a few words of encouragement.

"Mr. Böhm doesn't seem to know the difference between encouragement and excessive criticism. It's clear he doesn't know the first thing about horses and isn't interested in learning," Jonas Talmann had said.

His opinion, however, was presumably lacking in impartiality, since he had received written notice of his termination. But he'd been indignant at the suggestion that Mrs. Böhm was unsatisfied with his work.

"We were always on the same wavelength," he had said. "Unlike her husband, she understood that you can't run a farm based solely on finances. Of course, you have to make ends meet, but you have to respect certain basic principles in breeding and keeping horses. Ignore them and your bottom line might be good in the short term, but in the long term, it'll all go down the drain. If things get really bad, animal control can make your life very difficult—and rightly so."

Hannes was unsure what to make of Jonas Talmann's and Matthias Böhm's arguments. But it was clear that the employee had repeatedly opposed what he saw as his boss's delusional cost-cutting measures in favor of the alleged welfare of the horses. Talmann was floored by the gruesome deaths and couldn't imagine who was behind them. He also knew that his friend owed money to a dealer but wasn't familiar with the details. While the professional horse groomer seemed rather likable to Hannes, Federsen had a very different view.

"We should keep our eye on Talmann," he said as he hit the horn to shoo a group of young cyclists off the road. "He strikes me as suspicious. It is obvious he was attracted to Mrs. Böhm, and unrequited love can elicit strong reactions. Especially if his buddy Alexander got with her."

That seemed far-fetched to Hannes. Federsen was aware that Talmann claimed to be with his girlfriend on the alleged night of the crucifixion. And he couldn't have been responsible for the murder of Sylvia Böhm—the other staff had all confirmed that he had been at the farm all day. Federsen didn't seem to be bothered by this fact. He thought the employees weren't "very bright," as he'd put it.

"His girlfriend could've lied for him, and the staff seems pretty clueless. His alibi's questionable. At least we don't have to search for the murderer among the rest of the staff."

Mr. Talmann was the only professional groomer at the farm. The other employees were placed by an organization that helped individuals with developmental disabilities find jobs. Mrs. Böhm had set up the agreement. According to Mr. Talmann, her husband had been against it, until he realized that the mentally challenged were a cheap labor force that made few demands. None of them alone would have been physically able to nail a large man like Alexander Kramer to a heavy wooden cross and raise it. This was in stark contrast to Jonas Talmann, who had the arms of a lumberjack.

"Mr. Böhm isn't exactly lacking in the upper-body department either," said Hannes. "On the other hand, it wouldn't have required much physical force to murder his wife."

"No, only chemical or medical knowledge. Knowledge which these five numskulls hardly have. It's an entirely different story with Talmann. I've seen it all before."

"Yeah?" Hannes rolled down his window as Federsen lit a cigarette and puffed frantically.

"The chemical that caused Mrs. Böhm's death is a drug commonly used for deworming horses," Federsen said. "It's also used on the Böhm farm. However, Mr. Böhm, unlike Jonas Talmann, knows absolutely nothing about horses or any other animal. It's a neurotoxin, and in extremely high doses like the one found in Mrs. Böhm's system, the drug inevitably leads to death—a rather painful one."

Federsen eyed Hannes. "It's obvious you're in no shape to train," he said. Hannes's cold had taken a brief hiatus at the stables but was now back in full force. Instead of sending him home, though, Federsen had a different idea. "We'll pay a visit tomorrow morning to this religious—or antireligious—group. Find out some more background info on them and set up a meeting with the group's leader, if there is one."

Tomorrow meant Saturday, and Hannes was surprised that his boss was willing to work a weekend shift. He had never worked one before—Lauer obviously must have upped the pressure.

Back at the station, Hannes huddled over his computer. He found the group's website and opened a Word document to type notes.

New Way had celebrated its tenth anniversary that year, the festivities captured in a photo gallery. Its meeting location was in a residential neighborhood, and those interested in finding out more were invited to join them every Friday night. Evidently, the group had a skilled IT person, because the website was modern with a clean interface.

They clearly valued transparency, because under "Our Finances" was a spreadsheet of the group's revenue and expenditures. The previous year, the club had earned about 8,000 euros, mainly through donations and events. Membership dues accounted for only a small portion. Almost all proceeds went toward group activities, administration, and event-related rentals. The remainder was allocated to its capital fund, which had grown to 200,000 euros. The group intended to use the savings to purchase its own building.

New Way was a registered charitable organization. Its purpose was a bit vague, described as the "promotion of civic engagement for charitable purposes." In the next section, the aims of the group were more specific. Hannes scanned the bullet points: support of persecuted people, equality, religious tolerance, integration of the disabled, support for children, and the creation of a vibrant community within the group.

The members had some lofty goals, and Hannes wondered how they were implemented. He was surprised to find not a single reference to religion, until he clicked on "Our Tenets." New Way referred to the Ten Commandments of the Bible as the basis for moral behavior, but only a few of the Commandments were mentioned. The association provided a justification for their selectiveness: "When considered abstractly, the Ten Commandments include all the essential elements of moral behavior. The key messages are love and tolerance. Everyone should be allowed to live as he or she wishes, so long as his or her actions do not infringe on the freedom of anyone else. For this reason, we firmly reject religious rites and dogmas, institutionalized forms of religion, and fundamentalist interpretations. Far too often have they triggered war and persecution. We wish to create a community of fellowship for all those who place moral principles above blind religious obedience."

Pretty grandiose, Hannes thought. He wondered how serious the group really was. But at least he wasn't surfing the website of some fundamentalist religious organization. If their words reflected reality, then the perp wouldn't be one of them. Hannes suspected, however, that this professed aversion to organized religion didn't attract only like-minded individuals. He briefly surfed the "Our Activities" page, where there were write-ups of afternoons spent playing with refugee children, theater performances, and Christmas bazaars.

He also looked elsewhere for information on the group, but apart from a few newspaper articles on activities he already knew about, he found nothing useful. Nor did any comments about the group, positive or negative, pop up; apparently, public awareness of the group was very limited. The club didn't have a Facebook page or any other social media presence, so Hannes jotted down the contact information listed on its website.

His nose was dripping like a leaky faucet, and he had used up all his tissues. He ran down to the station cafeteria, where Mrs. Öztürk reigned supreme. In addition to the daily meals she served to officers, she also ran a sort of minikiosk; she was always prepared.

"Ah, our canoeing policeman. What's wrong, Hannes? Was your boss being a jerk again? The next time he comes in here, I'll spit in his food."

"No, Mrs. Öztürk," Hannes said. "Or yes. But I don't look this miserable because of my boss. I have a cold. Do you have a pack of tissues by chance?"

"Of course." Mrs. Öztürk rushed into the small storage room. She came back with a pack of tissues that would tide him over for the next few days.

"These clearly won't be enough," she said. "I have a special recipe from Turkey: Ottoman Sultan tea. Why don't you sit down, and I'll make you a cup."

It was clear that this wasn't an invitation, but an order. Hannes took a seat at one of the cafeteria tables. Although he was skeptical, Mrs. Öztürk had once given him a tea for an upset stomach, which had worked wonderfully. He cautiously sniffed the tea, then gulped it down as it brought tears to his eyes.

"What's in it?" he cried before noticing that his voice was almost completely clear along with his sinuses.

"You see," Mrs. Öztürk said, "it helps the moment you smell it. The recipe's a secret, but here's a small bag of it. Mix two teaspoons in some hot water, and it's ready. Make it three more times today, and tomorrow you'll be much better."

CHAPTER 8

Federsen called in sick Saturday morning, while Hannes felt much better. He had downed three cups of the Ottoman potion the night before and slept through the night. He had to hand it to Mrs. Öztürk—her concoction had miraculous powers—and he thanked her accordingly.

The last day of October was overcast. The pale light offered a dreary foreshadowing of the coming winter. The city was filled with tourists enjoying the last weekend of fall break. Hannes drummed on the steering wheel as he waited for a line of cars to move. He crossed over the railroad tracks near the main train station and parked in a largely residential area. He was ten minutes late to his meeting at New Way and hurried along the street toward what looked like a residential building if not for the large metal cross.

Hannes tentatively pulled open the door. He entered a small vestibule, where an elderly gentleman was in the middle of filling a brochure rack.

"Hello. Are you Mr. Lück? I was supposed to meet you at ten. Sorry, I'm late."

The gray-haired man turned around and cringed. He wore a crisply ironed shirt and a striped tie. Hannes detected a slightly bitter odor.

"What's this about? I'm the pastor here. There's no Mr. Lück."

Hannes was surprised. A pastor didn't jibe with what he had read about New Way.

"I'm looking for Mr. Lück from New Way," he said, and the man grimaced.

"You're at the wrong place. We have nothing to do with those people—and we don't want to. They're on the other side of the street. However, you should think twice if you're searching for salvation there. The one true faith—"

"I'm not seeking salvation. I'm here on business. Sorry for the mix-up."

Hannes left the building and glanced across the street. It was hardly surprising he had entered the wrong place, because New Way apparently met in a former café. In front of the two-story building was a small gravel terrace with three weathered tables and several folding chairs. There was no sign or other indication of a religious-type group. The large glass window of the former storefront was decorated simply.

As Hannes climbed the front steps, he saw a waist-high stone sculpture in the form of a welcoming outstretched hand. He remembered having seen this hand on the website—it was the group's symbol. "New Way" had been meticulously carved in large letters, and he recognized Antje Kramer's mason's mark.

"Pretty, don't you think?" asked a high-pitched voice.

Hannes looked up. Standing in front of him, dressed in a dark suit, was a man of about forty with a blond ponytail. He smiled and greeted Hannes with a clammy handshake.

"We spoke on the phone yesterday. Benjamin Lück. You must be Detective Niehaus?"

"Correct. Please excuse me for the delay, but there was a lot of traffic. Also, I walked into the wrong building." He pointed to the church.

"The cross outside should have been a clue. That's a fundamentalist church. The so-called Church of the Creator takes the Bible very literally. They weren't very excited when we moved in."

"Was it mutual? I took a look at your website. A fundamentalist church stands for everything you reject."

"You're right, but we don't really care." Mr. Lück shrugged. "Live and let live. We have our opinions, and they have theirs. Actually, we haven't had any serious problems with each other. Although that may be because our meetings no longer overlap with their services. We used to hold our general meetings on Sundays, but we've since moved them to Friday nights. Since then, we've hardly crossed paths."

He led Hannes inside and gave him a tour. The group had rented it several years ago after an old bakery had gone out of business. The members had renovated and remodeled the place to give them sixteen hundred square feet. The furnishings were mostly the worse for wear—the organization seemed to place little value on appearances.

The largest room on the ground floor served as a meeting space with comfortable couches and a long table. Chairs were stacked along the walls, and in the back there was an open kitchen.

"We have different committees and groups, like choir and theater. We also host a number of activities, and anyone is welcome to get involved."

He led Hannes up a rickety spiral staircase to a converted attic.

"We meet twice a week in the evening, and every member's welcome. There's no fixed program on Mondays, and for about a year now, we've held an alternative service on Fridays. Some members missed the spiritual context they knew from church. And one of our goals is to strengthen the sense of community."

"So a kind of atheist service?" Hannes remembered an article stating that such events in England already had large followings.

"I wouldn't call us atheists, just moderate believers. Some of us feel more connected to religion and reject only the Church as an institution. Others are searching for moral values. So our meetings are a mixture of religion, philosophy, and anything that moves us. We're religious and nonreligious. It may sound incompatible, but it isn't."

"But your group's basic tenets cite the Ten Commandments. That sounds very religious to me."

"Every community has to agree on commonly shared values. We see the Ten Commandments as representative of fundamental moral values. The same rules could be derived from a humanistic standpoint. Since the founders of New Way were all once members of churches, they chose something familiar which anyone could respect."

Hannes glanced around. He had to stoop over due to the low sloping ceiling and exposed rafters. Open shelving and low filing cabinets lined the walls, and a wide desk with a phone and computer sat in front of a recessed circular window.

"How many members do you have?"

"Forty-three."

Questioning all the members would take a long time. It was good that Isabelle, Marcel, Clarissa, and Per had also been assigned to the investigation.

"I've put together a list of their addresses like you asked," Mr. Lück continued. "Of course, some members are more active than others. Maybe twenty are heavily involved."

"How long have you been with the group?" Hannes asked when they reached the foot of the stairs.

"I was a founding member ten years ago and have sat on the five-member board ever since. I've been responsible for public outreach for several years, though we don't actively recruit new members. Religion's a touchy subject, and it's easy to step on somebody's toes. Besides, space is already at a premium."

"How involved were Sylvia Böhm and Alexander Kramer?"

"Sylvia was very active, and Alexander showed up sporadically. What happened to them came as a big shock. They were well liked, open, and friendly. But as they say, only the good die young. We talked for a while about it at our meeting yesterday."

Hannes could imagine that there was some need for discussion, and he was annoyed that he hadn't visited the group the night before with his colleagues. They probably could have interviewed half the members and gotten a better impression of New Way.

"How were they active?"

"Sylvia taught German to asylum seekers once a week and helped them with paperwork and administrative procedures. She and Alexander loved kids. They organized play times for refugee and mentally challenged children. It was always very lively in here on those days."

Mrs. Böhm had sacrificed so much of her time to give foreign children a few happy hours but had opted to terminate her own pregnancy. According to the doctor, the fetus was healthy, so her decision hadn't been in response to an anticipated disability. He considered raising the issue, but decided against it. Mr. Lück had had a good and trusting relationship with both victims and had no idea who could have been behind the heinous acts. Neither victim had felt threatened.

"How was Mr. Kramer received by your group?"

"Everyone knew about the pornos, and no one has to hide or justify his or her actions in our group. I'm gay and make no secret of it. God doesn't care. And if I can't be open here, where can I be?"

Self-professed understanding didn't necessarily mean actual tolerance. On the other hand, the key message of New Way was that everyone was welcome.

"When did Mrs. Böhm and Mr. Kramer join?"

"One moment." Mr. Lück went over the membership list he had given to Hannes. "Sylvia joined two years ago, Alexander just last May."

So Kramer had joined around the time of his first porno. His second film took place in a church and likely offended religious sensibilities. Maybe he felt a need to belong to a community that didn't judge him, that gave him some sense of absolution?

"I'm supposed to meet with Mr. Beck in fifteen minutes," Hannes said. "I called him last night after you recommended him."

"He and his wife also sit on our board. If you were to compare us to a church, he's something like our chaplain. Thomas used to be a priest before he left the Church. Since then he's worked as a freelance therapist, and many of our members rely on him. He should be able to tell you more about Sylvia and Alexander."

Although Hannes was convinced that Mr. Lück was innocent, he inquired about his whereabouts during the murders. He had ironclad alibis. He worked as an actor, and on the night Alexander Kramer had disappeared, he had been onstage. After the performance, the cast had hung out together until after midnight. At the time of Mrs. Böhm's death, he had also been at the theater, this time rehearsing a new piece. The details were easy to verify and a perfect task for Clarissa and Per.

A few minutes later, as Hannes approached Thomas Beck's home, he saw the man kneeling in front of a waist-high picket fence, carefully painting the wood white. In the garden, a woman was hanging laundry on a line stretched between two apple trees.

The property was situated on a quiet street in a well-to-do neighborhood. It was a typical brick house with a generous bay window overlooking the garden and a spacious terrace. Thomas Beck had a bushy brown beard, and as he rose, the forty-some-year-old almost matched Hannes in height. His brown eyes and brown midlength hair with its crooked part gave the impression of a kindly man. He had the build of an avid outdoorsman and a firm handshake.

"Oh, I'm sorry." Mr. Beck had accidentally covered Hannes's hands in white. "We bought the house recently and still have a ways to go."

Mr. Beck led Hannes through a crooked gate, where he noticed a bronze plaque stating psychological counseling was available by appointment. Once they crossed the garden, Mr. Beck introduced his wife.

Few people struck Hannes as so immediately likable. Mrs. Beck was a bit younger than her husband. She was a little plump, and her curly strawberry-blonde hair was tied into a ponytail. Although Hannes guessed by the look in her eyes that she had experienced much tragedy, she radiated warmth and friendliness. He credited them for not reacting to the unusual coloring of his eyes, which was rare.

"What a shame you have to spend such a beautiful Saturday investigating murders," said Mrs. Beck.

The sun had fought its way through the clouds and bathed the wild garden in an idyllic light.

"I can't stop thinking about Sylvia and Alex." The tiny woman wiped her eyes. "Sylvia was always ready to lend a hand, and Alex . . . well, Alex was very special."

She bit her lower lip, and Mr. Beck patted her on the arm.

"Let me show our guest to the bathroom." He pointed to Hannes's hands. "I got paint all over him."

"Leave the bucket, and I'll paint while you talk," Mrs. Beck said. "I need something to get my mind off things."

After Hannes and Mr. Beck had washed their hands, they headed into the living room.

"Would you like something to drink?" Mr. Beck asked after Hannes sat in a soft leather chair. He declined and gave a brief summary of his conversation with Benjamin Lück.

Mr. Beck smiled. "Benny built up our initial membership and would increase it tenfold if he could. He works as an actor and devotes his free time to our group."

"You work as a psychotherapist, correct?"

"Not as a psychotherapist, since I don't have the appropriate training. I was originally a Catholic priest at a parish in North Rhine-Westphalia. I left the priesthood five years ago because I no longer agreed with some of the Church's teachings. Otherwise I wouldn't have been able to marry my wife."

He smiled again, and for a moment, there was a coltish look in his eye. He had the habit of accompanying each of his sentences with emphatic waves of his arms, probably a holdover from his time as a priest.

"But the sign by your gate says you offer psychotherapy sessions."

"It says I offer psychological counseling. There's a crucial difference. You see, I always liked working with people when I was a priest, and I think I was good at it. But I didn't want to have to go back to school for several more years. So I took a couple of courses to become certified as a counselor and life coach."

"Did Mrs. Böhm and Mr. Kramer avail themselves of your coaching?"

"Not as patients. But we often chatted at group activities. I've slipped into the role of substitute chaplain there. At least that's what some members call me."

Mr. Beck had moved to the city almost five years ago, but only learned about the group a little over a year ago when he came across their table at a festival. His involvement grew, and he now led the Friday meeting. It was obvious he enjoyed the role and was in his element.

"You know, many people find it hard to shake off traditions. Here, for example." Chuckling, he pulled a silver cross from under his sweater. "Some habits die hard. But it gives me strength and comfort, so I wear it around my neck. Sometimes I even catch myself making the sign of the cross when I visit a church."

He put the chain back under his sweater before continuing.

"People yearn for a sense of belonging, and many feel a spiritual need. We want to make that possible outside the Church. Part of the group has been campaigning for a sort of nonreligious confession, even though the others think that's going too far." He smiled. "But none of us can be forced to participate in anything, and people can pick and choose."

"Did the murder victims confess anything to you that might help us?"

Mr. Beck scratched his beard.

"Please treat all details as confidential, even though our members already know some things. Like, everyone knew Alexander worked as a porn star. But I'll gladly help you as best I can to shed light on these terrible crimes."

Mr. Beck didn't know much more than the police, but he was well informed about Sylvia Böhm's abortion.

"We discussed it often. Sylvia loved children and would have liked to have had her own. She had been trying for some time. It wasn't easy for her to admit that she didn't want to have the child. Life was sacred for her. It was a real dilemma."

"What advice did you give her?"

"That it's a decision individuals have to make for themselves. And whatever the decision, it accompanies that person for the rest of his or her life. I listened, and we explored alternatives. As far as I know, she talked with Alexander a lot about it. They got along well."

"Why did she decide to have the abortion? Her husband was completely against it, right?"

"Yes and no. He was ultimately the deciding factor. Things had been getting increasingly ugly between them. Sylvia wanted to file for separation and had turned to a divorce lawyer. Recently, it had devolved into an all-out war. In the end, Sylvia realized she didn't want to have a child with her husband under any circumstances."

Mr. Beck could say very little about Alexander Kramer. He had joined six months ago, but never came on a regular basis. Mr. Beck had known about his drug use, but it seemed only recreational. It was his first time hearing that Kramer had had any problems with a dealer. On the other hand, he had noticed that the relationship between Kramer and his sister had seemed a little tense recently, but he didn't know why.

He was more familiar with Sylvia Böhm because she had been one of the group's most active members and had grown very dear to his heart. He wiped his eyes more than once. Her death left a gaping hole in the group, especially since she led two of the group's activities.

"But that's the least of our problems at the moment." Mr. Beck sighed and promised Hannes that he would help however possible.

Mrs. Beck likewise offered her help when she entered the living room a little later. She seemed extremely upset and unable to process what had happened. During the conversation, she kept shaking her head and blowing her nose. She had been close to both victims. No one sprung to mind as a potential suspect.

Hannes asked them to account for their whereabouts during the crimes. Mrs. Beck recalled having a severe migraine around the time of the crucifixion. She was unable to get out of bed for two days, which her doctor could confirm. Her husband said he was interested in adventure expeditions, and that night there had been a television special on research expeditions.

On the day Mrs. Böhm had suffered her agonizing death on the dock, Mrs. Beck had been visiting her mother in Cologne, while Mr. Beck had received patients in the morning. On Friday afternoons he was usually free, and on that day, he had taken a trip to the sea on account of the nice weather. He grabbed his wallet and pulled out a ticket for Sea Life. The date on the ticket matched.

After all Hannes had learned about New Way and its members, it was difficult to imagine that the murderer could be one of them. Nevertheless, all members would be interviewed and their alibis checked. That meant a lot of work without any prospect of success. The detectives would lose valuable time.

***

Ben had invited everyone in their circle of friends to a pasta dinner for that Saturday evening, but only Elke and Hannes could make it. Ines and Kalle had left for a two-week stay at a spa resort in the Seychelles after several stressful weeks at work, and Anna had not yet returned from Asia. Ben rented a small garden cottage from a doctor, who lived with his family in the large main house. As Hannes opened the garden gate, a bundle of black-and-white fur darted toward him.

Socks, Ben's dog, jumped onto Hannes. His white paws glowed in the dark, and Hannes laughed as he stroked the dog's soft fur. He, too, was always happy to see Socks and gave him treats. This time, it was smelly jerky.

Hannes heard laughter from the rear of the garden, and as he approached the cottage, Elke and Ben waved from the patio.

Ben tossed Hannes a beer. "Socks picked up your scent five minutes ago."

"I think it was the snacks in my bag," Hannes joked as he hugged Elke. Her long blonde hair got tangled in his stubble. "Why are you sitting out here in the cold?"

"Don't look at me," said Elke, who had pulled her hands into the sleeves of her black wool sweater. She pointed to a half-filled ashtray.

Ben was fond of the "grass of the gods," as he called marijuana. Hannes looked at Ben, whose pale blue eyes had a somewhat glazed veil. Evidently, he had chosen a lighter strain tonight.

There were pots of three different pasta sauces in the kitchen. Ben always experimented, so Hannes never recognized any of his creations.

"What are you torturing us with this time?" Hannes joked.

Ben placed the pots on the small dining table and presented the menu for the evening. "The first course: cannelloni with an exotic sauce of tomatoes, onions, garlic, chili pepper, and mangoes. Next, we have farfalline with a leek and lime sauce. And for the grand finale, festonati in a spinach-peanut sauce."

"Good thing my cold's almost gone and my taste buds are working," Hannes said and tried a forkful of the first course. His tongue caught fire, and he quickly reached for his water glass. "Now I know why you smoked a joint before eating." He wiped the tears from his eyes.

"I tried a new chili variety," Ben said and swallowed a mouthful.

"At least the sauce is likely to kill all the germs." Elke had tears in her eyes after the first bite too. "This is exactly what I need. I woke up this morning with a scratchy throat."

"If you get sick, you can get your revenge and give it to the kids this time, not the other way around," Ben replied.

Elke rolled her eyes and tossed her hair back. "I'm so glad our preschool was closed for break. Almost every kid was sick. I didn't even think about germs when becoming a teacher."

The second course wasn't nearly as painful, and Elke and Hannes licked every last drop of the third dish—much to the chagrin of Socks, who cocked his head and watched. It was only a matter of time until the conversation turned to Hannes's investigation; the crucifixion was the hottest topic in town.

"Do you know who nailed the porn star to the cross?" Ben asked, wiping remains of spinach sauce from his beard.

Elke was surprised. "You're investigating the crucifixion?"

Hannes was uncomfortable discussing his work. Although he trusted everyone, he couldn't discuss the details. He limited himself to a vague description of the circumstances which the media had already covered.

"It reminds me of a news report I saw on the Philippines," said Elke. "On Good Friday, men nail themselves to crosses in a bloody ritual to recreate the pain and death of Jesus."

"You're not serious." Ben was fascinated. "How sick is that?"

"Well," Elke said, pointing to Ben's eyebrow piercing. "Some men like having metal driven through their flesh."

"Hey, you wear earrings," Ben said. "But you wouldn't whack nails through your hands. It just goes to show what religion's capable of."

"You just lump everything together." Elke's bracelets jingled as she gestured at him. "Just because you don't get religion doesn't mean you paint everyone else as delusional idiots."

"Did I hit a nerve?" Ben said and grinned. "I didn't know."

"I used to go to church," Elke said, much to Hannes's surprise. "I actually used to enjoy it, but I stopped going."

"Why?" asked Hannes, who had last attended church fifteen or so years ago.

"As a lesbian, you don't feel very welcome. It's a shame because sometimes I miss it. Mass is so solemn and dignified that it makes you want to reflect. But what I was actually going to say was that maybe this man let himself be nailed to the cross. And then the ritual somehow got out of hand."

"I don't think so," said Hannes, and he explained with some hesitation that Alexander Kramer was a member of some kind of nondenominational church.

"I don't want to hurt Elke's feelings again," Ben stated, "but sometimes these fundamentalist churches are much more extreme than established churches."

"It's not a fundamentalist church," Hannes said and explained New Way's goals.

"That sounds all right," said Elke. "Throws my theory out the window. Maybe the group has enemies?"

"Unlikely. There aren't that many members, and they don't publicize themselves. Maybe someone just wants to give the impression that it's religiously motivated."

Hannes couldn't shake the feeling that there was something more to the killings. Something that had yet to be uncovered. And that was precisely the problem.

CHAPTER 9

She knew it was coming. She looked up at me and knew it. It was already too late for her to repent. Why do people only realize it when they're confronted with death? It didn't have to be this way. She didn't have to do it. But I did. Her deed couldn't go unpunished. But was this really the only way? Absolutely. It was too late to make amends. How could she? It was easy this time as well. Even easier than before. The perfect plan. But I also had a good adviser. I have it all under control. It was the right thing to do. I just hope I don't have to do it again. I didn't enjoy doing it. But if need be, I could. Now I know how it all works. I know the game and the rules. I could do it again if I had to. Please don't make me. Is it possible they might suspect something? I doubt it. But what if they do? It's certainly possible. Should I take the risk? Leave everything else to others? I can't do that. I've done it twice already and can do it a third time. She can destroy everything. I have to do it. She's making me do it.

CHAPTER 10

Four more days had passed. It was now two weeks since the crucifixion, and the pressure was mounting. There was, however, a bright side: Federsen had called in sick at the beginning of the week and would be out sick until further notice. Steffen Lauer had merged the investigation teams and temporarily placed Marcel in charge. The marathon of witness interviews had to be split among fewer colleagues, but Hannes was convinced that they had been able to work much more effectively without Federsen's interference.

This was a welcome change, and it wasn't long before the team had bonded under Marcel's levelheaded command. Even Isabelle and Clarissa, who hadn't gotten along before, had interviewed several witnesses together without incident. But the lucky streak didn't last long, because soon Per was out with a severe cold.

The crowd in the cafeteria at lunchtime had also thinned, and Mrs. Öztürk could barely keep up with the incoming prescriptions. Federsen had apparently denounced Hannes as the one responsible for the contagion, which explained the dirty looks.

That Thursday afternoon, just four detectives sat before Marcel, who was often rummaging for a tissue. He summarized the results of the previous days. As usual, he was wearing faded jeans and a perfectly ironed, form-fitting shirt.

"Thanks to Per, we were finally able to track down Alexander Kramer's dealer. His sister had given us the wrong name. His name's Daniel Novak, not Dennis. He's a small-time crook."

"How'd you identify him?" Lauer asked.

"Per has built a reliable network of informants, but no one knew a Dennis. One individual remembered Daniel Novak boasting about some porn-star customer he'd regularly put the squeeze on. So we put the squeeze on Novak."

Clarissa, who in her late twenties was the youngest member of the team, had conducted the interrogation. Her advantage was in being regularly underestimated. Hannes could picture her backing the dealer into a corner with her barking voice and no-nonsense demeanor. She toyed now with her long fingernails.

"Daniel Novak said Kramer owed him 2,000 euros," Clarissa said. "He denied any involvement in the murder. His alibi's shaky, but why would he have killed him? He wouldn't get his money, and Kramer was just about to come in to some serious cash. There's no connection to Sylvia Böhm. According to her husband, she never did drugs."

"What about the guy Kramer stole the porn gigs from?" Lauer asked.

Isabelle took the stage. "Manuel Birkholz is thirty-two years old and has been working in the porn industry for years. He got his first role at twenty-five."

"There's another difference," added Hannes, who had visited him with Isabelle. "While Kramer was everyone's favorite, no one liked Mr. Birkholz. He might think himself irresistible, but some of his costars refused to continue working with him. His return to Paradise Images & Productions didn't last long. The boss kicked him out the door for good."

Manuel Birkholz had claimed that he had been taking on various odd jobs to stay afloat. But word had it that he also worked as a call boy specializing in married women. That could explain why he was unable or unwilling to provide alibis.

Twirling his mustache, Lauer paused to sneeze. He rose from his chair and shuffled over to the water cooler. He downed a vitamin and came back.

"We need to find out if Birkholz had any connection to Mrs. Böhm. Can we put some pressure on him? Take him into custody?"

Marcel shook his head. "On what grounds? No one heard him threaten Kramer. All we have is Ms. Kramer's vague statement that her brother felt harassed by him. We need a lot more."

"Then see to it you get more," Lauer said. "Pay him another visit and put him through the wringer. I have another meeting in ten minutes. So let's move on. Who else is still on the list?"

"Matthias Böhm," Isabelle said. "He couldn't stand Alexander Kramer, was against the abortion, and his wife wanted to leave him; however, at the time of her death, he was with his accountant."

"Though he could have hired someone to commit the murder," Hannes said. "Maybe he suspected an affair between Kramer and his wife. And from what various New Way members have told us, it might have been true. So he had a motive."

"What else came out of all these interviews with the members?" Lauer asked.

Marcel summed up the interviews. The murder victims had been very popular at New Way. The group was a hodgepodge of characters, but the one thing they had in common was their lack of strict religious attitudes. In many cases, religion played no part in their lives. The members were artisans, housewives, businessmen, and even a local politician.

"The politician insisted his membership be kept confidential," Clarissa said. "Apparently he doesn't want to alienate religious voters."

"In any case," Marcel said, "several people have indicated that the victims were very close. They met a few months ago. No one has any idea who might have had an interest in killing them. So far, none of the members have any significant gaps in their alibis. We haven't checked out all the alibis, but so far there's been nothing unusual. We still have a couple more interviews left. There are forty-three of them and only four of us."

"I know." Lauer sneezed. "And if I get any worse, next time you'll be updating me in my bedroom."

Hannes wasn't sure, but he sensed a certain reproach in Lauer's voice. He'd been looking at Hannes when he spoke. Evidently, his star was waning.

***

For the remaining interviews, Hannes had paired up with Clarissa, while Marcel had left with Isabelle. Clarissa tossed on her leather jacket and walked toward a drab-looking row house. It wasn't random that she and Hannes were starting here. Since the Schweigers were teachers, they would be home in the afternoon.

The investigators squeezed past an old Passat on their way to the front door. A few minutes later, they were sitting in a messy living room and being eyed suspiciously by a pair of identical six-year-old boys. Mrs. Schweiger had likewise stared at Hannes and asked about his different-colored eyes. Hannes preferred that over hushed comments and furtive glances, so he explained the pigment disorder called heterochromia iridis.

The twins had left their toys all over the room, and they began to fight.

"Marius, if you don't stop, I'll remove a star from the chart," Mrs. Schweiger threatened, and the two police officers stared at each other.

Mrs. Schweiger looked young for a mother, while her husband appeared to be ten years older. The couple were New Way mainstays. It became clear over the course of the conversation that Mr. Schweiger liked to lecture. It was easy to picture the high school science teacher making his students break into a sweat during class. He had also served as president of New Way for the past four years.

His wife was an elementary teacher, and her love of children was so obvious that Hannes found it almost grating. Her eyes kept constantly wandering over to the boys, who were playing quietly. It took a while for her to explain all the extracurricular activities and school projects she led. She also sat on the New Way board and coordinated all the children's activities.

"Children are the most precious thing in this world. Unfortunately, too many are growing up in dysfunctional families or under difficult circumstances."

Mrs. Schweiger explained that she had left the Church in the wake of the abuse scandals and sought a stable community based on fundamental values.

"I enjoyed working with Sylvia. She loved kids and had lots of great ideas. Which made it all the more incomprehensible why she"—she glanced at her husband—"why she had no children of her own."

"Why didn't she have children?" Hannes asked.

"Well . . ." Mr. Schweiger started, but his wife couldn't control herself.

"She could have had a child, but decided not to. Imagine that. She was so set on having children, and then . . . then she kills the one growing inside her."

"Sabine," Mr. Schweiger said. "That was her decision and none of our business."

"Of course it's our business. We're a community, and she was making the wrong decision. Not to mention the whole Alexander thing."

"What do you mean?" Clarissa asked.

"He didn't really fit in from the beginning," Mr. Schweiger said. "I mean, his whole way of life was so—"

"Undignified!" Mrs. Schweiger burst out. "Can you imagine? A porn star playing with children? Sylvia encouraged him because he was good with the kids. But it's inappropriate." She lowered her voice, probably so her sons didn't pick up any "bad" words.

"What went on between them?" Hannes asked.

The teachers looked at each other in embarrassment. Mr. Schweiger stood up and ushered the children out of the room. The TV came on in the next room. Shortly thereafter, the overprotective father returned.

"We're not intolerant," he began, but his wife interrupted him.

"This has nothing to do with intolerance. It was an open secret that they had a relationship."

"Are you sure?" Hannes asked. "We've heard they got along but that it was purely platonic."

"Platonic?" Mrs. Schweiger said. Her cheeks turned red. "During one of our afternoon play times, they disappeared. I went to get some supplies out of our storage room, and I caught them . . . well, you know. What if a child accidentally wandered into the room?"

Obviously, not everyone in the group was as tolerant as they claimed to be. These two certainly would have liked to kick Sylvia Böhm and Alexander Kramer out of the group.

"What did the others have to say about it?" Hannes asked.

"Some saw it how we did. But others stretched the definition of tolerance."

"You can say that again," Mr. Schweiger said. "I had a long conversation with Mr. Beck. He is, after all, sort of like a chaplain. But even he didn't want to take action against them. And his opinion carries weight. I'm sure the press will find out sooner or later that they were members of our group. It won't reflect well on us. A porn star in New Way. We wanted to increase our outreach efforts to attract new members."

"Don't get us wrong," added Mrs. Schweiger. "It's terrible what happened to Sylvia and Alex. But it's also terrible what they did."

"What a nice couple," Clarissa said as she started the engine and drove away. "Only confirms my image of teachers. Miserable, stuffy know-it-alls who pass judgment on everything."

"You don't have good memories of your school days, do you?" Hannes said.

"Whatever," Clarissa said. "Who's next?"

"Rebecca Köhler." Hannes entered the address into the GPS.

The neighborhood was in a rough area. Clarissa raised an eyebrow and shook her head, her green earrings swinging.

"At least that last visit gave us a different perspective," Hannes said. "The Schweigers were the first ones not to gush about the victims."

"That got me thinking. Either the others were better able to hide what they really thought, or this couple is alone in their thinking. Perhaps the group's split into two factions?"

"An internecine religious war? That seems hard to believe. Could you picture the Schweigers being involved in a murder?"

"No, but a group dynamic is always difficult to assess," Clarissa countered, and Hannes wondered what in her less than thirty years of existence she hadn't experienced.

The teachers also provided verifiable accounts for their whereabouts at the times in question. Around the time of the crucifixion, they had hosted friends from Munich. On the following Friday afternoon, they had both been at teacher meetings.

Rebecca Köhler lived on the ninth floor of a drab high-rise. Clarissa searched for the buzzer while a group of bored teens looked on. The elevator was being serviced, so the officers headed for the stairs.

Ms. Köhler was on welfare, and her sparsely furnished apartment was tastefully decorated. She was in her twenties, seemed educated, and had a misty-eyed look about her. She had a completely different take on the victims. Ms. Köhler didn't have a close relationship with Sylvia Böhm and had nothing bad to say about her. It sounded as though she had felt self-conscious and awkward around her. On the other hand, she gushed about Alexander Kramer. Her eyes turned even mistier. The last time she had seen him was at the fitness class before he disappeared. She didn't notice anything unusual about his behavior that evening. Afterward, she had met up with a friend. On the day Mrs. Böhm died, she had attended a job training course at the unemployment office, which was easy to verify.

"Alex was a super nice guy. He didn't look down on anyone and was always friendly. I liked him a lot." She burst into tears and took several minutes to continue.

"Did he get along well with everyone in the group?" Hannes was pursuing the idea that there were two warring factions.

"As far as I know. How could anyone not get along with him?"

She refused the bait when questioned about an intimate relationship between Mrs. Böhm and Alexander Kramer, claiming she knew nothing. Hannes assumed she only saw what she wanted to see. She painted an incredibly glowing portrait of Kramer.

"Alex was always helpful. I broke up with this guy who wasn't right for me. In the beginning, he was very kind and loving, but then he started trying to brainwash me. He was very religious and demanded I change my life. I finally broke up with him a few months ago when he started hitting me. But he kept calling and even attacked me in front of New Way. That was three or four weeks ago. Alex grabbed him and told him to leave me alone. He hasn't bothered me since."

"What's the name of your ex-boyfriend?" asked Hannes.

"David Bach."

"You said he's very religious. Could he be a member of a cult?"

"No. He goes to the Church of the Creator, so we kept running into each other."

Clarissa and Hannes informed their colleagues about David Bach over the phone. They made their way to his apartment, but he wasn't there. The station told them he worked as a forklift driver at a filter-systems factory. His rap sheet was fairly long.

They left the factory empty-handed. David Bach had been sent by a temp agency and worked Monday through Wednesday. A call to the temp agency didn't help either because he hadn't been sent to any other jobs. Apparently, a three-day work week was enough for him to survive.

"Eh, it's probably a false lead anyway." A testy Clarissa drummed her long fingernails on her cell phone. "Just because he hit his ex-girlfriend and was put in his place by Kramer doesn't mean he would have killed him."

"He didn't just beat her up," Hannes said as he turned onto the main road. "To get a rap sheet like his, you really have to try. Theft, repeated assault, property damage, trespassing. I mean, the guy's your age."

"Just goes to show how boring my life is," she joked. "My biggest crime was running topless through the red-light district in Hamburg because I lost a bet."

"Really? How old were you?"

"It wasn't all that long ago," she said and smiled. "What's your biggest offense?"

Clarissa's phone rang, saving Hannes. She spoke for a few minutes, and Hannes guessed it was Isabelle based on the bits he overheard. She had gone with Marcel to the Church of the Creator to find out more about David Bach.

"That was Isabelle," Clarissa confirmed as she placed the phone on her slender thigh. "They met the pastor, who said he hadn't seen Bach for weeks."

"So much for his piety," Hannes said.

"The pastor claimed Bach hadn't done anything wrong for a year. Said he deeply regretted his earlier actions and was leading a decent life."

"Very decent, beating and stalking his girlfriend."

He remembered Elke asking him whether New Way had enemies. The information about David Bach would certainly suggest
it. After all, the murders pointed to a religious motive. There were
no apparent fanatical tendencies within New Way. The moral objec-
tions of the Schweigers had so far been the most serious and seemed
the only point of contention. Otherwise, the group appeared to be
extremely liberal and averse to dogma. That could attract enemies
from across the street perhaps. Clarissa also felt this was a reasonable assumption.

"Where are we going, by the way?" She hadn't been paying attention while Hannes explained his theory.

"Alexander Kramer's sister lives here," Hannes said as he turned
down the familiar dead-end alley. "Maybe she was there when her
brother had his chat with this pious whipping boy."

Antje Kramer remembered the incident. She was working on a
gravestone, and as the detectives approached, they realized she had been
carving her brother's name. The stone was simple and dignified, and she
must have invested a lot of effort in its design.

Exhausted, Ms. Kramer wiped her sweaty hair from her forehead
and stood up. "It must have been a month ago," she said. "Rebecca had
told us before that her ex-boyfriend abused her. It happened on a Friday
night after our meeting. Rebecca had already left to catch her bus. As
we were leaving the building, we noticed she was arguing with a guy
who grabbed her by the arm. When he started jerking her around, Alex
stepped in."

"Were there any problems with him before?" Clarissa asked.

"I saw him from time to time. We've had verbal altercations with
people from the Church of the Creator before. When Alex stepped in
to protect Rebecca, the guy jumped him and started punching him. I
ran over with Sylvia, and the three of us were able to subdue him." She

shook her head. "I can't believe I forgot about that. It's a good thing you talked to Rebecca."

Unfortunately, not much else relevant to the investigation stuck out in her mind.

"Have you found a new owner for your brother's horse?" Hannes asked as Ms. Kramer walked them to the door.

"Sadly, no. I went to see Mr. Böhm yesterday, but he isn't interested. Apparently, he wants to sell the farm."

"Understandable. After all, it was more his wife's project and probably a daily reminder for him that . . ." Hannes caught himself, realizing how tactless that sounded.

"I didn't get the sense he was too burdened by it. The marriage hadn't been working for months. I felt like he was trying to shoo me off the farm yesterday. I'll leave the horse there for now. I've paid for boarding through the end of the year."

"That's a beautiful bowl," Clarissa said as she picked up a stone vessel.

"It's not for sale," Ms. Kramer said and gently took the bowl from her. "It's supposed to represent a Celtic sacrificial bowl."

"Who commissioned it? Are some of your customers druids?" Hannes joked.

"No, I use the bowl." Ms. Kramer sheepishly turned the vessel in her hands. "Actually, the Celts carved sacrificial bowls into the rock. So this isn't a very realistic interpretation."

"So what do you use this Celtic bowl for?" asked Clarissa.

Ms. Kramer blushed. "You'll probably think I'm some wacky New Age person. I've always been fascinated by Celtic myths and gods. Every now and then, I go out into the wilderness and hold a small ceremony. Of course I don't sacrifice animals in this bowl, just plants."

Clarissa shook her head. "Doesn't pagan magic conflict with your membership in New Way? After all, there are references to Christianity."

"Well, we only refer to moral values. Those don't have to be the Ten Commandments. Alex often said I always pick the god who best suits me." Ms. Kramer smiled. "But why opt for a single religion? There's something fascinating and distasteful in every faith. For some reason, I feel magically drawn to Celtic mythology. That's probably why I feel so at home in our group—we accept more than one truth. Unlike, for example, the Church of the Creator."

***

Hannes hadn't forgotten the key to *Lena* that evening. He stuck it into the lock of the small wheelhouse. After missing the second class in his boat-safety course the previous week, he wanted to return motivated. Unfortunately, the class he had missed was on navigation, which he found the most difficult.

The door groaned, and Hannes entered the dark room dimly lit by the small harbor. He heard the ocean smack against the hull and harbor walls and felt *Lena* tug against her ropes as she bobbed. The ship creaked as he placed his hands almost reverently on the worn wood of the old steering wheel. He could already see himself crashing heroically through the stormy waves. Then he explored the belly, which had been expanded and comfortably furnished by Fritz. Hannes plopped down on the bed. Between passing the boating-license test and his maiden voyage, he would have to do some dusting and get rid of the moldy odor.

On his way to the small harbor building, he once again ran into Ole, who held hands with a familiar-looking boy with platinum-blond hair.

"How's the boating license going? This is my grandson Fiete."

Hannes confessed he had missed an important class and that he was still confused by navigation.

"At least manual navigation is still being taught," Ole said. "Most people just rely on technology, but a real captain must be able to deal with a chart and compass. Even on a little boat like yours."

Hannes told Ole about his visit with Fritz, and Ole scratched his beard.

"Decent of you to see him. I honestly didn't expect you would. Hmm, speaking of navigation, if you show up an hour before your class, I'll teach you everything you need to know."

CHAPTER 11

Hannes and Fritz sat opposite each other at the same table as the week before. The guard on duty looked as though she had never left the room. A nod hello, however, proved that she was made of flesh and blood. There were no other visitors that day, so the former colleagues had the space to themselves. Fritz looked much better. As always, he wore a wrinkle-free polo shirt over a pair of black jeans, and his face seemed less gaunt. Hannes had felt a little uneasy at their first meeting and had remained more or less reticent, so he looked forward to a more relaxed reunion this time. But he suspected that it would take some time before he could feel completely at ease.

"How come you're allowed to wear your own clothes?"

"In principle, we're supposed to wear a prison uniform, but you can request to wear your own clothes. You're responsible for washing them, though. As you can see, I know how to use the washing machine."

He smiled, and Hannes wondered how this restless man could endure his days in captivity. Because Fritz couldn't stand or walk for very long, he worked in the prison kitchen, where he could sit while preparing meals. Given his former—and what Hannes had thought an almost suicidal—diet, this opened him to a whole new world of experiences. Since he had to serve out the rest of his days in a seventy-five-square-foot room, he figured he might as well make the best of it.

"Ole's going to help me because I missed the class on navigation. Can't fail the exam now, he'd take it as an insult. He wants to visit you next week, so I won't be able to."

"I doubt that." Fritz grinned. "I could probably arrange for extended visiting hours. You'll have to come up with a better excuse."

Hannes wasn't about to let his visits become a regular habit. He presented a stack of papers, which after a lively discussion at the security gate, he had been allowed to bring in. "Don't want you rotting away. Lots of crosswords and a few sudoku puzzles. Now you can enjoy your new hobby even more."

Although the former Fritz would have never considered such a pastime, his face lit up. "That's very kind of you; the ones at the commissary are too easy. But let me return the favor. Since you don't want me to turn into some useless lump, let me share some of my gray matter with you. I understand you won't discuss any details of the investigation, but I've had a lot of time to read the paper, and I couldn't help but notice that you and Henning are investigating the so-called Jesus Murder. By the way, you looked good in the pictures, unlike him." He grinned. "We can limit ourselves to what's already public information. Maybe my outsider's perspective can provide some insight? Sometimes in an investigation, you can't see the forest for the trees. I certainly know that."

Dumbfounded, Hannes stared at Fritz. The sparkle in his eyes spoke volumes. Hannes had seen this look before—Old Fritz was caught up in the thrill of the investigation.

"There's no giving up with you, is there? Well, what the hell. Why not? That said, I'll only discuss the facts that the press already knows."

"Great." Fritz leaned forward and patted Hannes on the shoulder. The prison guard eyed them suspiciously. "I've prepared a few notes." He pulled out two folded pieces of paper.

Hannes leaned back in his chair. "Am I that easy to read? Did you think you could just win me over?"

"I hoped I could," said Fritz with a laugh. "But I know you. We're not so different. All you can think about is catching the killer and whether or not you're overlooking some crucial detail. That's how it was with me. The only way I could get my mind off the case was to solve it."

"Well then, tell me what you've figured out so far."

Fritz massaged his big ears. Hannes could picture him hunched over the desk in his cell, listening to classical music while he put his thoughts on paper.

"The most obvious and strangest thing about this murder is the cross," Fritz began. "It can have only one of two meanings: either the crime is religiously motivated, or the perp wanted to make it seem that way. It was stated in the paper that the victim was a porn star. This might suggest a religious connection. The perp considers the porn industry immoral and wants to take action against it. Maybe the victim even starred in a film that used religious symbols."

He looked at Hannes, who had the uncomfortable feeling that Fritz was reading his mind.

"So far, so good." Hannes kept a straight face. "If this theory is true, then we might as well quit while we're ahead, because this world's full of religious fanatics."

"Not so fast. There must be a reason why this man in particular was crucified. It's rare to see a victim chosen at random. You need to find out if the dead man came into contact with a religious group."

They discussed the pros and cons of this theory until Fritz glanced at the clock.

"If it's just to create a diversion, then it becomes more difficult. Why crucifixion? After all, it's quite a hassle. It takes more than a few minutes to nail someone to a cross and hoist it up. It'd be easy to spot you. In this regard, my second theory overlaps with the first. If the diversion is going to work, then it has to appear realistic. The crime would need a religious connection, even if it's only incidental. The perp would need to know the victim well."

"Do you think it's an individual or group?"

"If religious fanaticism motivated the crime, then my gut feeling would say group. Maybe just two or three people. If the act was committed for personal reasons, then it's more likely a single perp. Crucifixion might be a physically demanding task, but hatred can awaken unseen strength."

"So either a group of fanatical religious warriors or a strong, hate-filled individual."

"At least, that's my first guess. Either way, you're looking for someone who knew the victim personally, that much I'm sure of."

Hannes nodded, but he was reluctant to share. He could never have a conversation like this with Federsen, and he would have preferred investigating the crime with Old Fritz by his side. But it was Old Fritz's fault he had to bother with Federsen in the first place, and Hannes resented him for it.

I have a long way to go before I'm a pro like him, Hannes thought as he left the prison. What annoyed him the most was that he had accidentally disclosed information regarding the murder of Sylvia Böhm and its presumed connection with Kramer's death. On the other hand, Hannes was also curious as to what theories Fritz would come up with. It didn't occur to Hannes that he was already planning for the following week.

***

"We're slaving away over two murder cases, while you just paddle across the water," Federsen said.

Hannes had actually skipped his morning workout to see Fritz and was not happy to see his boss back at the office. He asked if Rebecca Köhler's abusive ex-boyfriend had surfaced.

"Still no trace," Clarissa said. "We posted an undercover cop outside his apartment building, but no luck. Either he's out of town, or he's up to something."

"Hopefully, he isn't up to something," Marcel said. "I have a bad feeling. The minister at the Church of the Creator probably tipped him off."

"Spare us your doom and gloom," Federsen said. "It's still unclear whether he had anything to do with the murders. The pastor wasn't wrong. David Bach hasn't misbehaved for a while."

"But only because Rebecca Köhler didn't press charges." Clarissa said. "You know that with guys like him we only see the tip of the iceberg."

"We've been looking for him since yesterday. He has to come out of hiding by Monday," Hannes said. "That's when his three-day work week starts. Is Per still sick?"

"Not just him," said Federsen. "You've done a great job spreading your germs. Half the force is bedridden. Steffen too."

Clarissa and Marcel headed out to pay another visit to Daniel Novak, the drug dealer, while Isabelle and Hannes went to see Manuel Birkholz one more time. The members of New Way had all been interviewed, and the group hadn't shown any radical religious tendencies and had offered mostly solid alibis.

For his part, Federsen claimed to still be sick and not yet ready to hit the streets. There was no protest from his colleagues.

"I feel sorry for you," Isabelle said a little later in the car. "I couldn't stand dealing with that guy every day. Can you drive a little slower? I need to change my contacts."

She flipped down the visor and took the contacts from her bloodshot eyes. Then she opened a new pack and put in the new contacts.

Hannes merged onto the highway. "Still can't find the right lenses?" he asked, aware of her sensitive eyes.

"No, I'm testing a different brand. I can't stand these things. I should probably get laser surgery."

"Or a pair of glasses."

"Easy for you to say. It's annoying wearing glasses all day. Besides, I don't have a face for them. Do you have any problems with your eyes?"

"Not with vision. But people always look at me funny. They're used to glasses, not different-colored eyes."

"You could always try color contacts. You could turn your green eye blue or your blue eye green."

"Why? Are you bothered with how they look?"

"Not at all." She giggled. "Whenever I see you, I think of my father's husky."

Isabelle's cheerfulness was a refreshing change from the drab rides with Federsen. Her outfit wasn't very flattering, and her short black-dyed hair didn't do her any favors either. But he felt comfortable around her and wondered if that might be enough to ask her out. That was when he realized he still owed Maria a drink. And he had almost forgotten that Anna would be returning from Asia soon. At least he wasn't hurting for options.

Manuel Birkholz lived in the southern part of the next town over. Hannes drove along the main road and parked at the curb.

A visibly annoyed Manuel Birkholz was waiting for them on the fourth floor of a well-maintained apartment building. He led them into a messy apartment and plopped down on a shabby couch.

Hannes sat down in a rocking chair while Isabelle stood, her arms crossed. The living room was as chaotic as it had been during her previous visit; clothes and fitness magazines were strewn across the room. Mr. Birkholz ran his hands through his hipster-style hair and flaunted the impressive array of tattoos on his arms.

"Why are you here again?" he asked, looking Isabelle up and down.

"Certainly not because of your decorating skills," she said, looking at the pinup calendars on the walls.

"They're harmless. You should see my bedroom."

"I don't give a damn about your bedroom. I'm interested in why you killed Alexander Kramer."

Both Manuel Birkholz and Hannes were surprised.

"You don't . . . What makes you say that? I barely even knew him."

Hannes quickly picked up on Isabelle's strategy. "You didn't think too highly of him, though."

"He was a wimp. Ladies' man. No idea what he was doing in our industry. I know women. I know what they want. They want to be fucked properly. And those who don't are—"

"We've heard otherwise," said Isabelle. "Some of your costars have refused to work with you, because you're rough, insensitive, and aggressive."

"Then you spoke to the wrong women. I should have never gotten involved with Paradise and lady pornos. If you asked any of my customers . . ." He realized he had said too much.

"Your customers?" Hannes said. "So you are a call boy. In our last conversation, you said you worked odd jobs in addition to your porn career."

"Who said I worked as a call boy?" Birkholz's eyes narrowed. "Well, so what? Since when is it against the law to help out women whose husbands can't take care of them properly?"

"Of course it's not against the law," Isabelle said. "But what you did to Sylvia Böhm is."

"Who?"

"One of your customers," suggested Hannes.

"Bullshit. I've never heard that name."

"Mrs. Böhm was close friends with Alexander Kramer," Isabelle said.

"Well, then she could have really used my help. Unfortunately, I've never heard of her. But do put in a good word for me."

"That won't be possible. Sylvia Böhm was also murdered."

"Oh, and let me guess, I'm responsible for that too? I told you I don't know her."

"Then let's get back to Alexander Kramer. You resented him for stealing your job. And you threatened him and assaulted him."

"Bullshit. I never threatened him."

"Strange," Hannes said. "Mr. Kramer told his sister you ambushed him outside the studio."

"His sister's lying. I ran into him one evening, and we chatted briefly. Sure, we had a little disagreement. But I didn't give a damn about him. If I was really out to get him, he wouldn't have gotten off so light."

Isabelle and Hannes got stuck in rush hour traffic on their way back.

"You really let him have it," Hannes said and grinned.

"We wiped that smug look off his face. But I don't think he's lying about not knowing Sylvia Böhm."

"I got the same impression. Unless he's a good liar. If the same perp is behind both murders, we can rule him out. But if there are several perps, we can't eliminate him as a suspect in Alexander Kramer's murder."

Hannes's phone rang, and he answered on speaker. Clarissa's gruff voice boomed through the car. She was with Marcel on their way back from questioning Daniel Novak again.

"So we didn't get much more out of the dealer," Clarissa began. "He denies any involvement in the crucifixion and says he had nothing to do with Mrs. Böhm, which is probably true, but he knows Antje Kramer. She only came up because Novak asked about Kramer's sister. After dodging questions, he admitted she's also a client of his."

"What?" exclaimed Hannes. "She told us she didn't know anything about him. She even gave us a fake name."

"What kind of drugs does she buy?" asked Isabelle.

"Not cocaine like her brother, but hallucinogenic mushrooms. Magic mushrooms. They're very popular in stoner circles. So, why did she hide this from us? There are worse drug offenses than that."

"Especially since it's her brother's murder investigation," Hannes said. "Maybe she was afraid of being arrested and thinks the dealer's innocent?"

"But how could she be so sure? Unless . . ."

"She knows more than she's been telling us," Marcel said. "Hannes, you've got a good rapport with her. Attend New Way's meeting tonight. Just say you want to get a better understanding of the victim's life. You can chat with Ms. Kramer while you're there."

Hannes thought an unannounced visit wasn't a bad idea. He gave a brief summary of their time with Manuel Birkholz before saying good-bye for the weekend. The phone rang again, and Hannes rolled his eyes.

"Are you on your way back?" Federsen asked. "Report directly to me. I haven't heard anything from Marcel."

Hannes summed up the two interviews.

"Okay, why don't you go to the meeting tonight," Federsen said. "If you find out anything interesting, call me. Otherwise, I'll see you Monday."

***

It was dark when Hannes arrived at New Way's meeting place. The meeting was already in full swing. He climbed the front steps and noticed that the stone sculpture of the outstretched hand was gone.

There were over thirty people inside, and they generated a considerable amount of noise. He spotted the towering figure of the group's leader, Thomas Beck, standing in a corner next to his wife, engaged in a lively discussion with a few members. He looked up, recognized Hannes, and waved him over.

Hannes weaved his way through the members. Some of them he had questioned; others had been interrogated by his colleagues. He noted a slightly higher number of women, but almost all age groups were represented.

"I'm glad you came," Mr. Beck said. Then he introduced the board members around him, whom Hannes already knew: the Schweigers, the Becks, and Mr. Lück.

"Full house tonight," said Hannes. "Your members are very devoted."

"Well," replied Mr. Lück, who looked dapper in his suit, "our Friday meetings are only attended this well around Christmastime. And people have heard of the deaths. They're probably the main reason."

"You came at the right time. We've just been attacked," Mrs. Schweiger said.

"Attacked? What do you mean?"

"That might be a bit of an exaggeration," Mr. Beck said. "Next to our front door used to be a statue of our symbol. When I got here at six thirty, the statue had been smashed."

"And that's not all," his wife added. "Someone had spray-painted 'No Blasphemy' on the wall. Someone's trying to intimidate us."

"It was someone from the Church of the Creator," Mrs. Schweiger said. "We've had problems with them before."

Hannes hadn't noticed the graffiti outside. Was there any connection between the vandalism and the murders? It could also just be a stupid prank, of course. He went outside to look. Next to the entrance, he found small bits of stone, the larger pieces having been already taken away. As he looked at the wall, the red lettering caught his eye. The message had been sprayed in spidery letters that weren't particularly big. The work didn't appear to be done by someone skilled at using a spray can—or an especially gifted speller, because there was an extra *m* in "blasphemy."

"Where's the statue now?" he asked the group when he had returned.

Hannes was led to the storeroom. The statue was no longer recognizable. Hannes knelt down and ran his fingers over the chunks of stone, which had to have been hit with a giant hammer.

"Have you reported the incident?"

"We're still debating what to do. We don't want to make a big deal about it and encourage copycats. We can easily take care of the graffiti, but the statue's a total loss," replied Mr. Beck.

"Poor Antje," Mrs. Schweiger said. "She worked on the piece for so long. She'll be so upset."

"Where's Ms. Kramer?" Hannes asked.

"She's unfortunately one of the few who didn't come today," Mr. Beck said. "It's probably better that she doesn't see her destroyed artwork."

"Really a shame," Hannes said. "I strongly advise you to report the damage. You can also ask that the incident be kept quiet. Did you find any cans of spray paint or a hammer or something?"

"No," Mr. Schweiger said. "We looked around. We also asked the neighbors. Nobody noticed anything."

"If something like this happens again, please leave everything as you found it," Hannes said. "You'll make our jobs easier and prevent any tampering."

Soon the members took their seats among four rows of chairs, and Mr. Beck stepped in front of a festively decorated table. A white floor-length tablecloth had been placed over the small table. In the middle was a colorful bouquet and next to it, a smaller version of the destroyed outstretched hand, probably also made by Antje Kramer. To the left and right were two lit candles, the flames of which were reflected in the two small framed photos of the murder victims.

As solemn music played, the members rose, took each other's hands, and closed their eyes. Hannes spotted the petite figure of

Rebecca Köhler, who stood holding the hand of an elderly woman in the front row.

When the music ended, the members let go of one another's hands, opened their eyes, and hugged the person to the left and right of them. Hannes suddenly found himself in the arms of a stout little man. Bewildered, he took his seat and waited anxiously for the meeting to continue.

The last time he was in a church—his cousin's wedding—was many years ago. But he realized New Way's ceremony was similar to a church service. A Bible was nowhere to be seen, but an image of the Ten Commandments painted on the wall did suggest a connection with Christianity, and Mr. Beck had worked as a priest for many years. Although he made no mention of the Bible, his voice was solemn like a homilist, and he knew how to captivate the audience.

"Hard days are behind us, and sad days still lie ahead. Two people were torn from our midst, Sylvia and Alexander, whom we all knew and loved like a sister and a brother. But as we care for each other in life, so too do we do so in death. It is our duty to ensure that they will never be forgotten. We will hang these photos on the wall, so that Sylvia and Alexander continue to be with us. Please rise for a moment of silence."

There was silence for two minutes. People had tears in their eyes. Mr. Beck placed two black ribbons on the frames and hung them on the wall next to the Ten Commandments. A woman stepped forward and read a poem in honor of the victims. After that, several members played two instrumental pieces, evidently favorites of the deceased.

"The police have released Sylvia and Alexander for burial," Mr. Beck continued. "We'll say good-bye to Alex tomorrow at ten o'clock at the cemetery. Antje has shared with me how she'd like the burial, so I'll organize everything on her behalf. Anyone who wishes to contribute something may do so. A traditional funeral Mass will be said for Sylvia at eleven o'clock. Her husband insisted on this and will take care of everything." He cleared his throat; his baritone voice had lost some of its strength. He slowly looked over the members. Hannes felt his intense gaze rest on him for a moment.

"I wanted to talk today about courage. About the courage which we constantly seek and so easily lose. Instead, I think it would be better if we discussed steadfastness. It too demands courage. Today our group's home was vandalized and our symbol smashed. We must remind ourselves why we gather here. We must focus on our values and our convictions. We must not let ourselves be intimidated. We must remain true to our symbol of the outstretched hand and offer it to anyone in need. Let us not forget that."

Many of the members nodded, and as music began playing, everyone rose and held hands. As the last notes died away, Hannes was once again embraced by the man next to him, and he patted him on the shoulder. Before people left, Mrs. Schweiger stood up and announced the group's activities for the coming week.

It was already past eight. Hannes listened to her talk about play rehearsals and a music night, then slipped away. Outside, he took a deep breath and strolled to his car. He was impressed by the togetherness of the group. The sensational nature of the murders had contributed to the rise in attendance. The group satisfied a need to come together and help one another. And everyone had clearly benefited from Mr. Beck's collected manner.

Hannes glanced back at the building. Through the windows, he could see Mrs. Schweiger had not finished her announcements. As he was about to open his car door, he noticed a shadow lurking by the Church of the Creator. He watched as a man hurried across the street to New Way.

The man crouched in front of one of the windows. He was wearing a dark-green jacket, black knit hat, and gloves. As he peered through the window, light fell on his face. Hannes held his breath. Rebecca Köhler had shown him a photo of her abusive ex-boyfriend, David Bach. The man looked very similar, and he was holding a crowbar.

Hannes moved away from his car. Bach had already ambushed his ex-girlfriend here, and Hannes didn't want to take any half measures. He cursed himself for leaving his gun locked in his desk drawer. He discreetly crossed the street. Suddenly, the door opened, and the Becks stepped outside.

When Hannes saw that the man was now holding the crowbar with both hands and approaching the entrance, he shouted and raced over. The attacker jumped up and stared in Hannes's direction.

"Police! Drop your weapon!" Hannes roared.

The man lunged at Hannes, swinging the crowbar. It grazed his cheek and left a deep gash. Then the man ran off.

"Get back inside!" Hannes shouted to the group that had gathered at the door. Mr. Beck directed everyone back inside as Hannes pursued the attacker. He had no doubt: David Bach had resurfaced.

Bach leaped over a fence, got caught on a picket, and tumbled to the ground. As Hannes jumped after him, Bach was back on his feet and darting toward a small residential building. He climbed up a pile of wood onto the roof of a garage and jumped into another backyard.

Hannes was close behind him. He was just about to jump on top of Bach and wrestle him to the ground when a cat bolted out of a bush and caused him to stumble. He scrambled to get up and saw Bach race toward the street. Hannes raced after him and stormed out of the front gate. He saw the silhouette of the man about a hundred yards away and chased him.

As Hannes turned the next corner, he saw Bach fumbling with the lock of a blue Opel. He opened the door, jumped in, and started the engine. Hannes pushed himself to the limit, but his fingertips only managed to brush the car as David Bach sped off.

***

Antje Kramer closed her eyes and breathed in the smell of damp earth and moss. The night was cold and quiet. This was one of her favorite places. She had discovered the clearing by accident one day when she had gotten lost picking mushrooms. She was carrying mushrooms this time as well, in a small basket from home. She also had her small Celtic sacrificial bowl, a camping stove, and two thick candles.

She had decided to seek out nature that night rather than attend New Way's meeting. Although she appreciated all the group had done for her, she had little desire to go through another evening of condolences. She wanted to be alone, especially since it promised to be a full moon. An ancient oak stood in the middle of the clearing, with a small stream flowing nearby. Whenever she visited this spot, Antje Kramer felt she could grasp the mysteries of Celtic culture as the magic of nature invaded every fiber of her being.

This was partly due to the spell the place cast on her and partly to the small mushrooms she brought. When the moon was high enough to illuminate the tree and the glistening stream, she got out the camping stove. She took a large cup of water from the creek, threw in a couple of vegetable bouillon cubes, and placed the mixture over the flame. Then she added the dried mushrooms. While the concoction simmered, she walked over to the mighty oak and placed her hands on the cracked bark.

She had often addressed the Celtic mother goddess Danu in this clearing. Danu was her favorite figure in Celtic mythology, in whose honor midsummer bonfires were still lit. Her thoughts turned to her brother and tears welled in her eyes as images of their childhood flashed before her. That night she wouldn't call upon the ancient goddess of the Celts, but instead implore Donn. According to tradition, he was the Celtic god who guided the souls of the dead to the so-called Otherworld. It was the last thing she could do for her brother.

She returned to the small gas burner and lifted the tin pot. She sniffed the rising steam and sat down with her back against the oak's trunk. She grimaced as she swallowed her first sip of the mushroom soup. Apparently, she hadn't added enough bouillon, because the bitter taste of the mushrooms was stronger than ever. Bit by bit, she emptied the pot and turned her head to the side to rest her cheek on the trunk. She sat there for a while, listening to the gentle gurgle of the stream and waiting for the mushrooms to take effect.

After twenty minutes, a feeling of warmth came over her, and her perception sharpened. She rose to fetch the small sacrificial bowl and candles. She stumbled slightly and shook her head. Had she eaten too much? The onset seemed faster and the effect stronger than usual. Breathing heavily, she steadied herself against the trunk and fought back the dizziness and nausea. After a few minutes, the symptoms subsided, and she was overcome by a relaxed, warm feeling. She breathed in relief and prepared her offering. Soon after, she thought she saw Donn standing before her, but she hadn't anticipated that he would reach out to touch her. The process inside of her had already begun.

CHAPTER 12

With the start of the new week came a ferocious storm of wind and pelting rain. First responders were clearing roads, pumping flooded basements, and caring for the injured. There was a great deal of frantic activity at the police station.

Hannes watched the raging storm through the conference-room window. He had a vague feeling that the darkness of the overcast day had dulled his senses.

David Bach had still not been found. After the foiled attack, there was increased concern that more people were in danger. Federsen sat at the head of the conference table.

"What's the point of letting you train every morning if you can't even keep up with a forklift driver?"

"If it weren't for that stupid cat, he wouldn't have had a chance."

"At least now we know Bach has it out for New Way," Marcel said. "It's a good thing you went to the meeting. Even if you ended up getting that nasty cut on your cheek."

"We already knew from his ex that he had it out for New Way," Federsen said.

"But now it's clear he's targeting the entire group," Isabelle said.

"Do we know that for sure?" Clarissa asked. "Maybe he was only going to attack Ms. Köhler. And we also don't know if he's the one behind the graffiti and destroyed sculpture."

"He was hanging around there, so he's clearly suspicious," Federsen said.

"We ran the getaway car's tags," Marcel said. "The car's in his name, and we've put out an APB. Teams are posted in front of his apartment building as well as the factory where he works. He was supposed to be back working the forklift today, but he hasn't shown up."

"Well, no wonder in this weather. The radio was advising people to stay at home."

"But he hasn't," Per said. Like Isabelle and Hannes, he was in his early thirties, though he had a pronounced receding hairline. "I'm sure his fellow believers have told him we're looking for him. We've paid them quite a few visits already. He's in hiding. He doesn't care about the weather."

"Nor do I," said Federsen. "And you shouldn't care about it either, because you and Niehaus are driving over to see Antje Kramer now."

"True, we still need to ask her why she lied to us about the dealer."

"That too. But the real reason is to check on her. Mr. Beck from New Way called. He's worried because he hasn't seen or heard from her in days."

"She probably just wants to be alone and skipped the Friday meeting," said Per.

"The meeting, perhaps, but not her brother's funeral," Hannes said with some worry. "The funeral was on Saturday morning. It's odd she didn't show up."

"Especially since she was involved in the preparations," Federsen said. "Mr. Beck last saw her in her workshop on Tuesday. They discussed how and when the funeral should take place. Since then, she hasn't been at home or answered her phone."

There were many obstacles on the road. Several underpasses were blocked off due to flooding, forcing Hannes and Per to take numerous detours. Hannes strained to see through the windshield, since the wipers barely made a difference.

"Maybe we should have called Ms. Kramer rather than put ourselves in danger," Per said.

"I tried. She's not answering."

"Why are we heading to her workshop? There's no way she'd drive to work in this weather."

"She works on the ground floor and lives in the loft above. Anyway, we're already here."

He turned off the engine and looked at Per, who was not a handsome man. In the dim light, his acne scars seemed more pronounced.

"Ready?" asked Hannes. Per nodded.

They jumped out into the raging weather and ran through the rain. Every time their feet hit the ground, water splashed to their waists. The high winds nearly knocked them over, and within seconds they were soaked.

"Let's hope we don't catch the flu again," Per said when they finally made it under the awning.

"Don't tempt fate." Hannes pounded the glass, but there was no movement inside. "She's not down here. Let's go around. The entrance to her apartment's over here."

Unlike the door to the workshop, the door to Antje Kramer's apartment had a bell, which Hannes repeatedly pushed. Still no response.

"She couldn't have gone on vacation, not before her brother's buried," said Hannes, his concern growing.

"Maybe that's why she left. Maybe she thought she was too unstable to attend. She could be staying with a friend for a while."

Hannes shook his head. "Of course she's mourning the loss of her brother. But she wasn't one to wallow. She seemed to be holding up pretty well." He took a few steps back and looked up at a small gable window. The rain dripped into his eyes, and a shiver ran down his spine. "Look up there. There's a light."

"It's probably just a nightlight."

"That's enough for me." Hannes walked back toward the workshop. He picked up a stone and weighed it in his hand.

"What are you doing?" Per asked. Then Hannes smashed the glass in the door.

"There's no way we can break down the door to her apartment. It's massive." Hannes slipped his arm through the window, careful to avoid the shards of broken glass, and unlocked the door from the inside. "Maybe we can access the apartment from in here."

"We could have called a locksmith," Per said.

Hannes flicked on the light. The place looked significantly more cluttered than on his last visit. In the back, half-hidden by a large shelving rack, was a wooden door that opened easily.

"What smells so funny in here?" Per sniffed. "Reminds me of . . . of . . ."

"A public restroom," Hannes said and hurried down a short hallway. He opened another door, but it led to a small kitchen. "She's not down here. Let's look upstairs."

With each step up the creaky staircase, the smell grew more and more intense—a mixture of excrement and vomit. By the time they had reached the second floor, they were only breathing through their mouths. Two doors led from the landing, and when they opened the first, the stench overwhelmed them. It was the bathroom, and it looked as foul as it smelled.

"That's what I call a gastrointestinal bug," Per said.

"I've had bugs too, but my bathroom never looked this bad." Hannes opened the second door. It led into a living room where the repulsive smell was almost as strong.

"Something's not right here," Hannes said and pinched his nose. There were pools of bodily fluid on the parquet floor. "It must lead to the bedroom."

They bounded across the living room, dodging the residue on the floor. Hannes shouted for Ms. Kramer and banged on the last remaining door. When no answer came, he pushed the door open and gasped as he looked inside.

Ms. Kramer was by no means a sight for sore eyes.

***

Meanwhile, Isabelle, Clarissa, and Marcel were dealing with Federsen. He waited until the rest of the team had taken their seats and said, "There's been an interesting development: Matthias Böhm was arrested an hour ago."

"Why?" asked Isabelle.

"Tax evasion. He's awaiting arraignment."

"That's pretty serious," said Marcel.

"What's serious is that we had no idea he was under investigation. That's some shitty communication on our part," said Federsen. "All the text messages on Matthias Böhm's cell phone have been deleted, but they found his wife's phone when they executed the search warrant for his house—the phone he claimed not to have found. There were a number of texts from him on that phone. Mostly insults and threats. He also railed against Alexander Kramer."

"Well, this is quite the turn," said Clarissa. "Do we have printouts of the messages?"

"Of course," Federsen said and waved two sheets of paper. He tossed them into the middle of the table, and everyone huddled to read them.

Clarissa frowned. "The messages aren't nice, but they're not death threats either. The closest to one is this: *If you go through with this abortion, you'll pay for it in this life and the next.* But he could also just mean that in religious terms."

"At the very least, it does seem he knew about her relationship with Kramer," Marcel said. *"Go ahead. Sleep with him for all I care. Can't fool me anymore."*

"Mrs. Böhm responded to almost none of these," Isabelle said. "It's as if she were already through with her husband."

"How was he evading taxes?" asked Marcel.

"I don't know the specifics," Federsen said. "It seems our colleagues don't like to share."

"At least we have cause for suspicion," Marcel said. "He can only provide an alibi for the time of his wife's murder. He was at home around the time of the crucifixion, and the only other person who could vouch for him was his wife. So it might be worthwhile if we coordinated with our colleagues."

Federsen said, "We'll get more info soon. Either way, he seems to have been having a hard time financially."

"Now would be a convenient time to sell the horse farm," said Isabelle. "But Mrs. Böhm would have been against that. And his financial problems would have only gotten worse if they had gotten divorced."

"And from his point of view, his wife wasn't the only one to blame for the impending divorce. How soon can we interrogate Mr. Böhm?" Marcel asked, excited.

"He's all yours in an hour," Federsen said and leaned back in his chair.

***

Hannes looked in alarm at Per, who stared at the chaos in the small bedroom. Next to the bed was a nightstand and a rocking chair. A floor lamp lay on the ground, weakly shining. The bright wool carpet was covered in stains. Several garments were scattered on the floor. The bedspread was smeared with dirt. Antje Kramer was huddled, naked, on the formerly white bedsheets, her face turned to the wall.

"Ms. Kramer." Hannes approached the bed. "It's Detective Johannes Niehaus. Are you okay?"

No reply. He walked over to the edge of the bed and bent over the motionless woman. He tried to turn her on her back, but her body was too tense. Her expression seemed pained, her eyes closed. She felt ice cold.

"Call an ambulance." Per was already one step ahead, dictating the address to the dispatcher. "I think she's dead," Hannes whispered as he searched for a pulse. Was that a faint beat? He placed a hand over her mouth; he could feel breathing. "She's still alive. But her pulse is barely detectable."

Per hung up. It was unclear what might have put Ms. Kramer in this state. Given the severity of the symptoms, a stomach bug seemed unlikely.

Per checked her mouth for vomit. "Her mouth's clear," he said. "Let's try to roll her on her back."

"Do you think that's a good idea? We don't know why she's lying here all curled up. She seems to be in a lot of pain."

"She doesn't feel the pain; she's unconscious. But I guess it's possible we might make things worse if we move her."

Hannes heard the rapidly approaching sirens. Relieved, he took a step back. It was only then that he realized how sick he felt.

"Can you go down and get the paramedics?" he asked in a weak voice before vomiting on the carpet.

The paramedics suspected poisoning and rushed Ms. Kramer to the emergency room. The diagnosis was acute renal failure. Judging by the look on the doctor's face, Ms. Kramer's chances of survival were extremely poor, and it was still unclear what had triggered the renal failure. The doctor listed a number of possible causes, but none of them stood out. On the other hand, when the physician's assistant suggested that such symptoms could have been caused by poisoned mushrooms, Hannes perked up. He remembered Daniel Novak stating that Antje Kramer had often purchased hallucinogenic mushrooms from him.

He and Per raced once more through the storm to Ms. Kramer's loft, which they then tore upside down. When they searched downstairs in the workshop, they found remnants of what looked to be mushrooms. They also discovered a small tabletop convection oven in which Ms. Kramer had apparently dried her psychedelic mushrooms. Hannes placed the remnants in a plastic bag and brought them to the hospital for testing. The results were pending.

Meanwhile, Clarissa and Marcel hauled Daniel Novak in for questioning. He was adamant that the goods he sold were pure. Since he was unwilling to name his supplier, Marcel had him locked up in an attempt to make him talk. Searching the dealer's apartment was a disappointment. Only minor amounts of marijuana were seized; evidently, the man stored the majority of his goods elsewhere. The interrogation of Matthias Böhm was likewise unsuccessful, since he refused to talk. After a few minutes, the detectives reluctantly led him back to his holding cell.

***

"What are you thinking about?" Anna asked and furrowed her brow as she smiled at Hannes. She had returned the previous weekend from her months-long trip to Southeast Asia. It was their first time seeing each other since their awkward good-bye at the airport. The kiss hello she had given him on the cheek had been relatively innocent in comparison to the kiss they had shared when she left. This only reinforced Hannes's belief that Anna had left the country at the worst possible time. Everything was back to square one.

"Um, I had a bad day at work. Sorry if I'm not totally with it right now. Why don't you tell me more stories from the other side of the world? It'll be a good distraction. So, what about this Hindu monastery in Gung Kavi?"

"It's Gunung Kawi," Anna said and laughed. "It's an amazing temple cut into rock. You can only reach it from this small wood-carvers' village, which alone is worth the trip."

As she described how peaceful and quiet it was, Hannes gazed at her face. Though her tanned skin made them difficult to see, the Asian sun had multiplied the freckles on her cheeks. Her light-green eyes glowed. Hannes was a little jealous—the trip sounded really fun.

His eyes lingered for a moment on the little dimple in her chin, and her engaging smile enchanted him just as it had the first time they had met. Nevertheless, he sensed some distance. He hoped he was only imagining it. His life in comparison to her stories seemed boring. After all, he had never ventured too far from Germany. Anna, on the other hand, had spent a whole year backpacking around the world before she worked at the pharmaceutical company and had seen all the continents except Antarctica. She had hundreds of amazing stories, while he didn't have much to show for his life.

Anna had suggested that they meet at Chameleon, the bar where they had met up for the first time a few months back. At the time, the purpose of their meeting had been completely different. Anna had worked as the assistant for a pharmaceutical-company executive whose murder Hannes had been investigating. It quickly became apparent that there was some sort of spark between them.

"So tell me how you've been over the last three months," Anna said. "You make it seem like it's a secret. And what happened to your cheek?" She gently ran her finger along the cut. Her touch felt electric.

"Um, I had an unfortunate run-in with a crowbar last Friday," he said as he struggled not to blush after her touch. "I was chasing a suspect."

"And you claim nothing happened while I was gone." Anna's eyes widened. "I hope you repaid the favor?"

"Unfortunately, no. A cat got in the way." He gave a brief summary of the failed chase and the so-called Jesus Murder. She was totally fascinated.

"That's incredible. The moment I leave, a murder straight out of Hollywood happens. Well, at least you can't pin it on me."

"No, you have the perfect alibi," Hannes said and grinned.

"That reminds me of a movie I saw a long time ago," Anna said. "A serial killer went around torturing people to death because they had allegedly committed one of the seven deadly sins. Each murder was made to look like one of the sins."

"Was anyone nailed to a cross?"

"I don't think so. But you said the dead man was a porn star. Maybe some maniac wanted to punish him. Isn't lust one of the seven deadly sins?"

"No idea, I'm not particularly versed in the Bible." Hannes looked at Anna and thought about the "attack," as Mrs. Schweiger had called the incident on Friday night, and David Bach with his iron rod. Was this guy some kind of copycat? It was worth considering.

"If you ever wanted to change careers, you'd make a good detective," he said. "Have you thought about what you want to do now?"

Anna shook her head. Her brown hair fell into her face. Hannes liked the way it looked—it was considerably longer than it had been in the summer. He also liked that she wore little makeup, which set her apart from the other women in the bar. She shrugged and rubbed her nose.

"I'm sure you've heard that the company's new managers brought their own assistants. I was going to quit anyway, but at least now I got ten months' salary, so I'm not in a rush. I'll probably get another job as an assistant somewhere. I'd hoped that I'd think of something else while I was traveling. Unfortunately, I'd barely be able to afford rent with the ideas I came up with. I'll start looking at job postings soon. Are you still half cop, half canoeist?"

"Yes, but I plan on retiring from sports after next summer. I'll have to think about what to do after that, because there's no way I'm working full-time under my current boss." He told her about Federsen.

"So you were sent to a porn studio alone?" She giggled. "What was it like?"

"Different than you might expect," Hannes said and recounted his visit to Paradise Images & Productions. When he told her how the receptionist had mistaken him for the new porn star, Anna burst out laughing.

"What's so funny? Do you think I couldn't be one?" he asked with slight indignation and glanced at the large mirror behind the bar.

"No, I didn't mean it like that." She continued to laugh and touched his forearm. "I'm just picturing the look on your face."

Then she became serious and blushed. Hannes squirmed in his chair. He finally relaxed, and Anna smiled.

"If I don't have a new boss by next summer, I'll have to think about a new job too."

"That reminds me," Anna said and nudged his shoulder. "You didn't tell me about the world championships. You needed it to qualify for the Olympics, right?" She seemed embarrassed. "Or did you not make it?"

"I did. I screwed up the two hundred meter, but I'll be at the starting line for the thousand."

"That's awesome." Anna came around the table and hugged him. "And you're only telling me now?" She jokingly tried to choke him, then signaled the waiter. "This calls for another drink."

Of course, it didn't stop at one drink. Hannes felt as though the ice had finally been broken. For the next two hours, they talked about everything and nothing. In her presence, Hannes found it easy to forget about police work and enjoy the time.

It was already after midnight when they stood outside the bar. The storm had died down. Hannes felt the effect of the numerous cocktails and doubted if he'd be able to practice in a few hours.

"You'll probably get seasick," Anna joked.

"Speaking of that, I'm getting my boating license. Fritz gave me his old shrimp boat. He renovated it completely. We should go out on the water once I get my license."

"Good idea." Anna linked arms with him, and they headed to the taxi stand. "But maybe wait until spring? Or at least until I get used to the cold weather again."

Two cabs were waiting. "Lucky us," said Anna, pointing to the beige cab. "We don't have to fight over who takes the first taxi. I had fun tonight, Hannes. Do you want to go out again sometime?"

Although he wanted to see her again the next day, Hannes reluctantly suggested that they see each other on Saturday. He didn't want to come across as moving too fast. Anna seemed somewhat disappointed by his suggestion, but Hannes could have also imagined it.

"I'll dream of Asia tonight," he said and hugged her. She placed her arms around him and held him for a moment longer than seemed necessary.

"I will too. It'll probably take some time before I've processed all the images and experiences. Everything was just so different. It was exactly what I needed. Meeting people who see things differently and live life differently is the most enriching experience," she said.

Hannes thought it was a very perceptive and uplifting note on which to end the evening.

CHAPTER 13

Hannes's Tuesday morning training session didn't go all that well. He felt as though the alcohol had taken up residence in his muscles. It took nearly twenty minutes for the stiffness to wear off. But it did just in time—the coach wanted to simulate racing situations with the team sprinting against each other in pairs. Hannes was partnered with his archrival Ralf, because old coach Fuchs knew that he could tease the most out of both athletes by making them compete. It was best of five. The temperature was around forty degrees. Fleecy tufts of cloud drifted across the sky, pushed by the chilly headwind.

The other canoeists watched excitedly as both athletes threw their paddles into the water upon hearing the starting pistol. Their rivalry was legendary and had already resulted in a fierce wrestling match. Their coach had thought that wrestling would be a perfect way to teach them coordination and give them a better feel for their bodies. In theory, he wasn't all that wrong. But after ten minutes of intense grappling, the outcome had been far from desired. They may have gotten a better feel for their bodies, but Ralf had walked away from the mat with a missing tooth and Hannes with a laceration above his right eyebrow. The coach had immediately scratched wrestling from his training schedule.

Hannes had already won two sprints that morning. Now he wanted to set the record straight and capture the series with a third and final win. As the familiar burn warmed the muscles in his arms, he gritted his teeth and doggedly pushed himself through the dark water. From the corner of his eye, he noticed that Ralf was just behind him. He could hear the recognizable sound of the athlete's panting. As Ralf glided past him, Hannes was ready to write the sprint off and save his strength for the next round. Federsen was his saving grace. Normally Hannes's head was empty during a race, but at that moment, the image of his boss's face flashed before his eyes. He could almost hear the man jeering, "You just don't got what it takes, Niehaus."

Hannes snorted in anger and summoned his last reserves of energy. He slowly closed in on Ralf's red canoe. Water splashed as his boat cut through the waves raised by the wind. As he worked the paddle in the water, he imagined hacking his boss to pieces. Just before the finish line, he pushed his boat ahead of the red canoe with one last power stroke. Completely exhausted, he gasped for breath and slumped down. Ralf steered his canoe beside him.

"That was a tie," huffed the competitor, his face bright red.

"My ass it was," panted Hannes. With lightning speed, he shoved his paddle under Ralf's canoe and flipped it over with a quick flick of the wrist, sending Ralf crashing into the ice-cold water. Then he calmly paddled back to the start, while a floundering Ralf began ranting and raving.

"Who won?" the coach asked when Hannes reached the dock.

"I did. By a nose. Ralf disagrees."

"Okay, hit the shower. No need for another race. I'll send Ralf to the finish line. He can be the line judge if there are any more close calls."

Hannes pulled his canoe from the water and carried it to the boathouse. If the two rivals ran into each other again that day, fists would definitely fly. With this in mind, he took a look at his face in the locker-room mirror and ran his finger along the wound David Bach had given him with the crowbar. He didn't realize that he was imitating Anna's gentle caress from the night before. He stared at his reflection and hoped there wouldn't be a scar—for Bach's sake.

An hour later, Hannes stood opposite the red-haired doctor. He had gone straight from practice to the hospital in order to find out about Ms. Kramer's condition.

"Nothing's changed," the doctor said. "We'll continue to keep her on dialysis, but I'm not hopeful."

"Is she conscious?"

"No. We've been able to analyze the mushroom sample. Most of it is so-called magic mushrooms, which contain the active ingredient psilocybin."

"What's that?"

"Psilocybin is converted in the body into psilocin, a substance that acts as a psychedelic hallucinogen."

"What are the effects?"

"Similar to LSD—intense feelings, relaxation, heightened perception, and so on."

"Can you overdose on magic mushrooms?"

"In theory, yes, but that wouldn't explain such an adverse reaction like kidney failure. The active ingredient content is quite high, but an overdose usually results in a bad trip, so loss of control, massive panic attacks, or paranoia. We determined that the sample primarily contains *Panaeolus cyanescens* and *Psilocybe semilanceata*."

Hannes scratched his wound. Why couldn't the doctor just speak plainly? "So most of what we found belongs to these varieties?"

"We also identified *Cortinarius orellanus*, otherwise known as fool's webcap."

"What are its effects?"

"It is not hallucinogenic; it's highly poisonous." She arched her brow to emphasize the last point.

"And that's the reason for Ms. Kramer's condition?"

"The symptoms suggest it. Nausea and vomiting set in one or two days after consumption, followed by severe lumbar pain, then kidney failure."

"Well, she definitely suffered severe nausea. The evidence was all over her apartment. When would she have eaten these mushrooms?"

"Due to the severity of her kidney damage, she must have ingested them a few days before her arrival here. I can't give you an exact date, unfortunately. We spoke to her primary-care doctor, but he says she never contacted him. Presumably, the patient believed she just had a severe virus."

Hannes thanked her and walked down the hallway. He passed a woman pushing an infusion cart and hastened to leave the building. A contaminated batch of mushrooms. That little bastard dealer was in big trouble now.

***

Ms. Kramer died late Tuesday night without ever regaining consciousness. Hannes thought of the many uncut stones at her workshop that would now never bear her mason's mark. It was as if New Way's destroyed sculpture had foreshadowed its creator's death. Another picture with a black ribbon would have to be added to the wall.

"The woman's now dead," a red-faced Federsen barked at Daniel Novak, "and you're the one responsible for supplying her with the mushrooms that killed her. We're no longer talking about assault, but murder—or at least manslaughter."

Novak looked up at the two policemen who towered over him in the interview room.

"Tell us already. Where did you get the poisonous mushrooms?" Hannes asked. "If you didn't give them to her, then they could only have come from your supplier."

"Antje must have gotten the poisonous ones from someone else," Novak whined. "She also foraged for her own mushrooms. She once asked me about the best way to dry them."

"So you're telling me she picked the poisonous mushrooms herself?" Federsen yelled, spraying spit across the room.

"That's ridiculous," Hannes agreed. "Why would she ever buy mushrooms from you when she could pick them herself?"

"Because they're not very common, and you have to find them first. They don't grow year round and aren't the same as the ones she bought from me. Those are specially bred. Maybe she mistook the poisonous ones for harmless ones?"

"We've consulted an expert. Fool's webcap isn't easily confused with other mushrooms. If she went foraging, then she'd have known better than to commit such a fatal error. Tell us where you got the goods. This is your one chance to save yourself, provided you tell the truth."

Novak kneaded his cramped fingers. "All right, all right," he blurted out and reluctantly named a dealer in the Netherlands.

"Well, it's about time," Federsen said as he stormed toward the door. Hannes followed, and Federsen slammed it shut after them, leaving behind only the smell of stale sweat. "Niehaus, contact our Dutch colleagues so we can shut down the supply operation. But I get the feeling it's not going to do much good. This asshole's bullshitting us."

"Who knows," Hannes said. "For some reason, I don't think he's behind it. He lacks a motive."

"Motive? Maybe the guy's just crazy. Maybe he takes pleasure in making other people suffer. Think of the crucifixion and the poison injected in Mrs. Böhm's abdomen. It all fits."

"True. But what did Daniel Novak have to do with Mrs. Böhm? If the killings are related, we can't rule out the possibility that someone else tampered with the mushrooms."

That evening a report came from The Hague. Novak's supplier operated a large mushroom farm just outside Amsterdam. Although the sale of dried hallucinogenic mushrooms was banned in the Netherlands, the sale of fresh ones at so-called smart shops was permissible. Daniel Novak insisted that he had purchased fresh ones.

According to the Dutch police, the supplier was considered reliable, although the fact that he had built up an illegal side business distributing the goods abroad, of course, spoke against this. But the German investigators had to concede that it seemed virtually impossible that poisonous mushrooms would be accidentally grown on a farm, much less intentionally sold—there was no better way to destroy a business. So it was assumed that Antje Kramer was now the third person from New Way to be murdered. The urgency of solving the case grew, along with the fear that there could be more victims.

The crucial question was whether Daniel Novak had committed the lethal tampering or whether someone else was behind it. Everyone found it practically inconceivable that Ms. Kramer would have accidentally picked and consumed the fatal fungi. Although fool's webcap grew in the fall in deciduous forests, its occurrence was relatively rare.

A thorough search of her apartment and workshop offered no new suspicious findings; a look at her phone records led nowhere; and interviews with her neighbors and friends weren't helpful. Her death fit the perp's MO perfectly. Like with Alexander Kramer and Sylvia Böhm, there was a delay between the crime and an agonizing death.

The teams assembled later that evening. For Federsen, the matter was clear: "If it's not some crazed serial killer, then I'm quitting."

On the one hand, Hannes was inclined to agree with him, but on the other hand, this hasty declaration made him hope for another resolution. In any case, he couldn't see Novak committing the murders. Apart from a sound motive, he didn't come across as cold-blooded.

Clarissa raised yet another possibility. "Maybe Ms. Kramer ate the mushrooms on purpose?"

"I didn't get the sense that she was suicidal," Hannes said. "And she certainly wouldn't have chosen such an unpleasant way to go."

"Cut the crap," said Federsen, and the red blotches on his face darkened. "We're not going to get anywhere speculating like that, and let's not indulge any of your fantasies."

"Pull yourself together, Henning," Marcel said.

He was tired and had wanted to head home to his family three hours ago, fearing his wife's reproaches. Police work and family life were difficult to reconcile. Now his youngest had come down with the measles, and he felt guilty. He also felt another nosebleed coming.

"We have Matthias Böhm, David Bach, and Manuel Birkholz," Hannes said. "All members of New Way have been questioned, as well as family and friends. None of them gave any cause for suspicion."

"Let's start with Böhm," Marcel said.

"He does have the perfect motive for murdering his wife, but he also has an alibi," Isabelle said, then glanced at her watch. It was pitch-black outside, which was hardly surprising given that it was already nine thirty.

"But what would he have against Ms. Kramer?" Hannes asked. "Unless she supported her brother in his relationship with Mrs. Böhm."

"Too weak." Federsen shook his head. "You wouldn't kill someone for that unless you're completely insane."

"Well, what isn't insane about all this?" Hannes said. "Mr. Böhm not only knew about his wife's affair, but he's also very critical of New Way. Ms. Kramer was active in the group and even designed its symbol. Maybe he blamed his failed marriage on New Way, then punished Antje Kramer as its representative."

"That sounds like speculation," Federsen said. "I'm not convinced."

Per raced into the room. "Bach's car was found in a parking garage downtown. The tank was almost empty. And guess what was found in the trunk."

"Just spit it out," Federsen said.

"A hammer and a can of spray paint. The color matches the graffiti on New Way's building. That proves he destroyed the sculpture and sprayed the message on the wall."

"So he hasn't been targeting just his ex-girlfriend!" Clarissa cried. "He either thinks the group's corrupting her or has actually become a religious fanatic. He might not stop at property damage and could be a danger to the other members. He did attack Hannes with a crowbar."

There was a moment of awkward silence, then everyone spoke at once.

"Quiet." Federsen banged his fist on the table twice. "We can't offer all the members personal protection. The best protection is to catch the perp. We finally have enough against Bach to secure a search warrant. Marcel, take care of that. He's now our prime suspect."

"Let's not forget about Manuel Birkholz. He's also on the list," Hannes said. "But I can't think of a specific motive. Unless he wanted to punish Antje Kramer for her brother's actions. I mean . . . No, that can't be it."

"What?" Marcel prompted.

Hannes ran his fingers through his hair. "I went with Isabelle to see him. I mentioned that Ms. Kramer had claimed he had ambushed her brother and threatened him. Perhaps he wanted to punish her for tipping us off. Or maybe he was afraid that she knew more."

"Are you crazy?" said Federsen. "You never tell a suspect the name of a witness or what the witness said. Unbelievable. That was such a dumb mistake." It was one of those rare moments when the detective was at a loss for the right insult.

Hannes stared at the table in shame. His stomach tightened at the thought that his carelessness might be responsible for Ms. Kramer's death. Federsen was probably right. He was an amateur.

"Well, so far that's only a theory," Marcel said, trying to defuse the tension. "Besides, right now everything seems to point to Bach. And there's still the possibility that the murderer isn't even on our radar yet. That would be even worse."

"But since these four suspects are all we've got, we ought to focus on them," said Federsen. "Novak's already in custody, so he's no danger, unless he's planted a time bomb somewhere. But we're going to have to release him tomorrow because the evidence against him is too flimsy. Mr. Böhm landed himself in jail for tax fraud. David Bach is still on the lam, which is our biggest problem. Birkholz is also a free man, and God have mercy on us all if he strikes again. But for you, Niehaus, there will be no mercy."

***

Federsen's words still rung in Hannes's head as he looked into Maria's beautiful face later that evening. She wouldn't let him forget about that drink he owed her. She had dragged him to what in her opinion was the best Spanish spot in town, and since she was half Spanish, she knew what she was talking about. Hannes studied the various tapas dishes on the table. He wasn't a fan of these mini portions, even though he could try lots of different flavors in one evening. Before them was a large pitcher of sangria which had twice been refilled. How someone could drink buckets of this was a total mystery to Hannes. His head felt heavy. He had just told Maria about the reprimand he had received from his boss earlier as well as their difficult relationship.

She shook her head. "I don't get how you can work with this guy. He's ugly, has no manners, stinks, and is the laziest police officer I know."

Hannes shrugged. The waiter appeared, and Maria studied the menu to choose a dessert. She was a real beauty, her year-round tan accentuated by her ivory teeth. Her hair was long and black, and her figure earned the stolen glances of all the neighboring tables. Hannes smirked. He was probably the most envied man in the room. His gaze wandered down from her face, and he gulped. Maria wore a tight top, which showed off her shapely bust.

He was completely receptive to her erotic charm. His ears glowed. They had gone out a couple of times, and Hannes had always enjoyed her company. He even got the sense that Maria found him somewhat interesting. But although they were both single, there was a problem. Every time he saw her manicured nails, he couldn't help thinking of her job. Those hands handled dead bodies all day, and there was nothing he found more repulsive. He couldn't even look at a corpse from far away. As a homicide detective, he ought to feel more neutral about dead bodies, but he always told himself that every job had its drawbacks.

"What are you having?" Maria's low voice pulled him from his thoughts.

"I have no idea. What about you?"

"*Crema catalana.* It's similar to crème brûlée—only better, of course." She winked, and Hannes seconded her choice.

"By the way, I wanted to try this new rock-climbing gym out." Maria leaned toward him. "Any chance you'd like to join me? If you're there, I wouldn't be afraid of falling."

Hannes felt slightly dizzy, which he attributed to his fourth glass of sangria. But maybe it was also the intensity of Maria's gaze, which always made him sweat a little.

"Uh . . . I've never been climbing before."

"Then it's time you tried." She placed her hand on his, and the image of an autopsy table immediately flashed in his head. He discreetly withdrew his hand as he reached for his glass.

"Yeah, maybe I should. After I pass the test for my boating license, I'll be looking for a new project anyway."

"Then it's settled." Maria smiled, pleased.

Hannes was also pleased. At least he had managed to win himself a grace period. Who knew what would happen in a few weeks? He liked Maria a lot, and there were definitely worse pastimes than watching her climb up a wall. Maybe he could even learn to control his fear of dead bodies. But then he thought about Anna. There were no phobias to fight with her. He just didn't know where he stood or how to assess the situation. At the thought of her, his stomach turned to knots. He reached one more time for the center of the table, where a new pitcher of ice-cold sangria had just been placed, and chugged another glass.

Hannes had never slept so badly in his life. In fact, he barely slept. Even when he was able to doze off a little, his dreams were haunted by images of Manuel Birkholz creeping into Ms. Kramer's workshop to plant the poisonous mushrooms. When he awoke in a cold sweat, his nightmares were replaced by the memory of how he had found the naked and motionless sculptor in her dirty apartment.

He finally gave up at five o'clock and got out of bed. Racked with guilt, he struggled to choke down a slice of toast with jam. He felt he was in no shape to attend practice that morning, nor did he think he could bear to see Ralf. He sent his coach a text message saying that he was needed at the station, which wasn't a complete lie.

Hannes should have guessed that he would be Federsen's punching bag for the day. He spent half the morning enduring his boss's snide remarks until Marcel stepped in.

"That's enough. Hannes gets it. And it's not like you've never made a mistake."

"At least not one with deadly consequences," Federsen said.

But from then on, he kept his comments to himself, and Hannes breathed a little easier. He vowed to upstage the self-righteous creep and was determined to redeem himself by making a positive contribution to the investigation.

The first opportunity arose at ten o'clock, when he and Marcel interrogated Matthias Böhm. The evidence of serious tax fraud seemed solid. Mr. Böhm must have realized that the tax authorities were slowly tightening the noose they'd placed around his neck, because he had clearly lost his confidence and was ready to talk.

"I have nothing to hide. I can't tell you anything more than I already have," he said.

"We have some more questions for you," Marcel began, his tape recorder on the table. "Alexander Kramer's sister, Antje Kramer, is dead. Did you know her?"

"I met her for the first time a few days ago. She came to the farm wanting to know if I'd buy her brother's gelding. I said no."

"Why? Is the horse sick?"

"Not as far as I know. But I want to sell the farm. There's little point in filling up the barn."

"I'm sure you could really use the proceeds of the sale," Marcel said. "You could at least pay some of the taxes you owe."

"I'm not discussing that with you. If you don't desist, I'll call my lawyer."

"Fine. The accusation of fraud is only relevant to us as an indication of your financial trouble. A divorce would have given you even less leeway . . ."

"Has anyone come to mind who might be responsible for your wife's death?" asked Hannes.

"I have no idea, and that's not going to change no matter how many times you ask."

"Then let's forget about your wife for a moment," Marcel said. "So you only met Ms. Kramer once. What kind of impression did you have of her?"

"I didn't care for her. Shows up unannounced and wants to pawn the nag off on me. She was so obtrusive that I had to ask her to leave."

"Ms. Kramer mentioned you were rather unfriendly. Your employees have confirmed that there was a heated discussion."

"Who said that? Jonas? Now that he's being let go, of course he's going to bad-mouth me."

"Presumably, Antje Kramer wanted to discuss more than just the horse with you," speculated Hannes. "If she also brought up the two murder victims, that would explain the heatedness of the discussion. Especially if she suspected you and had something against you."

"What did she say about our meeting?" Mr. Böhm asked.

Hannes shrugged. "What do you remember about the conversation?"

"Like I said, it was about her brother's horse. I didn't have much time that day, and I was annoyed that she wouldn't let it go. That was all. How did she die, by the way?"

"Poisonous mushrooms," Marcel said.

"So what's the issue?"

"Well, she's dead." Hannes spoke carefully. "What's more, she wouldn't have taken poisonous mushrooms intentionally."

"So you assume I placed a poisonous mushroom in front of her and made her eat it? Listen . . . We were outside the entire time. My employees can testify to that. And I've been stuck here since Monday."

"That doesn't matter, because Ms. Kramer ate the mushrooms last week. You were still free then. She endured horrific pain and died only two nights ago, in case you're interested."

"No, I'm not interested. You know why? Because I had absolutely nothing to do with that woman. It was bad enough that her damn brother hung around our place. I'm done with these absurd questions, or I demand to see my lawyer."

"That won't be necessary," Marcel said and turned off the recorder.

The search warrant for David Bach's apartment had been issued, and Federsen looked for colleagues to accompany him. Marcel felt that Hannes and Federsen should work together as little as possible and thought it would be appropriate to visit New Way again after Antje Kramer's death. Hannes learned from Benjamin Lück that play rehearsals were being held later that afternoon.

Practice was in full swing when Marcel and Hannes entered the main room of the group's meeting place. As they opened the door, they heard a familiar line recited in a fervent voice: "Enough words have been exchanged; now at last let me see some deeds."

Mr. Schweiger continued with his lines, undeterred by the appearance of the two investigators. New Way's theater group was evidently trying to put on a production of Goethe's *Faust*. *How fitting*, Hannes thought.

Benjamin Lück and another person entered from the hallway. They were both perfectly dressed for their parts. It was only after the other man took off his white mask that Hannes recognized Mr. Beck's bearded face. Dressed in black and donning a red cape, the group's chaplain had been transformed into Mephisto.

Mr. Lück rushed over to greet the detectives and excitedly shook their hands. "I'm sorry everyone's in costume, but we want to perform the piece at Christmastime and still have a ton of work to do. Even though Antje's death has given us a lot to worry about, we've decided not to cancel the performance."

"Unfortunately, we also had no choice," added Mr. Beck. "Our performances are always well attended, and admission goes a long way to covering expenses. Last year, we made over 10,000 euros. Antje certainly wouldn't have wanted us to cancel some of our activities."

"You've certainly bit off a lot with *Faust*," Marcel said.

"We're putting on an abridged version," Mr. Beck explained. "Fortunately, we have a professional in our midst. Benjamin pushes us to give our all."

Hannes recalled that the group's public outreach coordinator was also a stage actor. But here, Mr. Lück modestly explained, he served as director, prompter, and makeup artist.

"Unfortunately, everyone has to play multiple parts, since we're short members without stage fright," he said. "With Alexander, we lost our Mephisto, but Thomas is talented and proving an excellent understudy."

"A chaplain as Mephisto is a rather unusual combination," Hannes said.

"But it makes a lot of sense." Mr. Beck smiled. "As chaplain you gain profound insight into the dark side of human behavior. But I'll be playing another role in addition to Mephisto. That's why"—he patted the white mask—"we're doing without makeup. It lets me switch between the characters quickly. Besides, I don't really want to shave or dye my beard." His eyes twinkled.

Marcel cut to the chase. "Antje Kramer died from eating poisonous mushrooms. Can you explain how she got them?"

Both men looked at each other in embarrassment. "Well," Mr. Lück began, "we knew Antje had a weakness for Celtic mythology and performed ceremonies. She even gave a few lectures here on the subject."

"It was a real passion of hers," Mr. Beck added. "Her enthusiasm was contagious. She used mind-altering drugs in these ceremonies to heighten their intensity. We knew she experimented with mushrooms for that reason, but never thought they would be dangerous."

"They're not," Hannes said. "But she ate more than just hallucinogenic mushrooms. She also ingested a poisonous variety. We are wondering where it came from."

The two men stared at him, their eyes wide. "That's horrible," Mr. Beck said. "But I have no idea where she got her mushrooms."

"She sometimes foraged for them, but she also purchased them from a dealer," said Mr. Lück. "Her brother told me about it once when we talked about his cocaine use. He bought his drugs from the same dealer."

"We know," Marcel said. "He was briefly in custody."

"Do you think he purposely . . ." Mr. Beck paused. "That would be so terrible. Was she murdered?"

"That's a possibility," Marcel said. "One of many."

"We've got to warn our members," Mr. Beck said. "It's like someone's targeting us."

"There's no need to panic," Marcel said. "There's no harm in a little caution, but please don't frighten your members."

"You're right," Mr. Beck said. "We should be careful when we bring it up tomorrow at our meeting. Do you have any suggestions how to best proceed?"

"If you've been promoting yourselves recently," Hannes said, "it would be a good idea to keep a low profile and not draw too much attention."

"Well, we've already started advertising our theater performances, and in recent weeks we've been preparing to launch a new membership drive," Mr. Lück said. "Maybe we shouldn't be so active over the next few weeks. Otherwise, I can't think of anything else. We've been hosting our children play groups and offering refugees support for some time now without any real incidents."

"I agree," Mr. Beck said. "As a precaution, we should lie low and not open ourselves up to further attack. If necessary, we'll cancel the play."

"What were your disputes with the Church of the Creator about?" asked Marcel.

The men looked at each other hesitantly. Mr. Lück looked uncomfortable.

"We don't want to slander anyone or cast suspicion," Mr. Beck said. "They've insulted us. Other times, they've distributed pamphlets. And there was a pretty ugly scene during our summer festival. Yet I can't imagine that someone would go so far as to—"

"Did any individuals in particular stand out?" asked Hannes.

"Two or three were always there."

"This man, for example?" Marcel showed David Bach's mug shot.

Mr. Lück's face turned pale. "He led the attacks. Does that mean that he . . . ?"

"There could be an entirely different explanation," Hannes said. "But this is the man who damaged your property. Your members should definitely beware of him. However, we're investigating several leads at the moment. It's possible that membership in New Way was not the real reason for the deaths."

His attempts at calming the two achieved little, and Hannes hoped the group wouldn't break out in a panic. After the investigators had said good-bye, they stood in the back and watched the rehearsal for a bit. It took a while before Lück and Beck regained their composure. The other actors looked surprised when Mephisto began to stumble over his lines. Since no one had overheard the conversation, they didn't understand the director's pale face or their chaplain's distracted performance.

A few minutes later, however, the two men returned to their former roles and were engrossed in Mephisto's devious deal with Doctor Faust. Benjamin Lück mouthed each line silently with the actors and wandered excitedly around the stage. Rebecca Köhler played Gretchen, while Mr. Schweiger assumed the role of Faust and the director in the opening sequence of the play. His wife starred in three different female roles, and the man who had hugged Hannes at the meeting the previous Friday appeared as the Earth Spirit.

"That's Wolfgang Hartmann," whispered Marcel. "I remember him because he's pretty sociable. Clarissa and I interviewed him about the first two murder victims. He owns a department store downtown. Must be in his early fifties."

Benjamin Lück did a good job directing the amateur actors. Mr. Beck's acting and facial expressions were so convincing that Marcel and Hannes had trouble tearing themselves away.

"Maybe I should buy tickets," Marcel said. "It would probably make my wife happy. She complains that we never do anything cultural." He stopped on his way to the car and pointed to the opposite building. "Wasn't that the Church of the Creator's pastor who just walked in?"

"No idea. I wasn't looking."

"Come on," Marcel said. "While we're here, we might as well grill the neighbors."

The front door wasn't locked, and Hannes followed Marcel inside. The vestibule was empty except for a coatrack and two brochure racks. Opposite the two restrooms on the left was a locked office. Marcel leaned into the double wooden doors of the large, plain-looking main room. The space could easily seat three hundred. The floors were dark oak, while the rest of the room, with the exception of the curved wooden beams on the ceiling, was completely white. At the far end, three steps led to a raised platform with a plain wooden altar on the right and some musical instruments on the left. Behind the altar was a gigantic wooden cross; otherwise, there were no pictures, no gilding, and no pulpit.

A single person was in the room, bent over and adjusting a few chairs. Marcel cleared his throat. The man turned around. Indeed, it was the minister. He wore a striped tie and a dark shirt, and his pale, ascetic face showed little warmth. He approached the two detectives.

"Good afternoon, Mr. Ahrendt," Marcel said. "This is my colleague, Johannes Niehaus."

"We've met briefly," Hannes said and shook the minister's hand.

"Yes, you were the young man who assumed this was New Way. I remember your eyes. Did you find what you were looking for?"

"I did. But as I said before, I'm not interested in their religious aspects."

"Religious? *Pfsh.* If those people are religious, then I'm the Devil. They're no Christians, no matter what they say."

"Is that so?" Marcel asked.

"Yes. They invoke the Ten Commandments to lure people in. Why can't they just admit they're atheists? That would be honest. Those people are a disgrace to Christian values."

"So you wouldn't have a problem if they identified as atheists?"

"No, I would, but at least they'd be admitting that they don't share our values. Of course I consider atheism dangerous. After all, it's the ultimate denial of God. The Devil created this movement so real Christians would falter. The true faith and the true Word of God can only be found with us."

The minister's eyes were fixed on the detectives. Hannes looked at him in fascination. It was the first time that he had met such a fervent believer, and he wondered if this man actually believed what he was saying. The fanatical glint in his eyes certainly suggested so. Amused, he wondered what Mr. Ahrendt would say if he could see New Way's chaplain onstage wearing a Mephisto mask. Mr. Ahrendt noticed the smirk on Hannes's face.

"There's no need to make fun," he said in anger and pointed to the exit. "I can see that you're more inclined to accept their nonsense over the true faith."

"We don't wish to discuss any theological questions with you," Marcel said, trying to calm him down. "Actually, we just wanted to ask if you've heard from David Bach. We're still looking for him."

"What do you want from him? He's a faithful member of our church. He's mended his ways. Forget about his past and let him enjoy his new future."

"It's not his past but his present we're interested in," Hannes said. "Have you seen him or not?"

"No. And if he comes, I'll tell him to confess his sins. It's only by confessing that he acknowledges the one true authority."

"Are you implying that your religious rules take precedence over the law?" Marcel asked.

"God's laws supersede any worldly court," said the minister.

"How many members does your church have?" asked Hannes.

"Around two hundred. Why?"

"Do all of them share your theological beliefs?"

"Of course. What kind of question is that? If they didn't, they wouldn't be members. We don't preach some feel-good gospel here. We don't bend God's rules to suit our own. Here you will find deep faith and eternal laws. It may be tough, but it's the only way to salvation."

"Mr. Ahrendt," Marcel said, "three people who belonged to New Way have recently died. At least two of them were murdered. Last Friday, someone smashed a stone sculpture by their entrance and graffitied the building. What do you think about that?"

"Anyone who invites sin should expect punishment."

"But New Way is no den of iniquity," Hannes said.

The pastor glared at him. "It's not surprising you see it that way, but I've heard otherwise. I don't wish to go into details. The worst sin is their claim that their behavior is compatible with the Ten Commandments. That's outright blasphemy."

"So you think blasphemy is a sin worse than murder?" Marcel asked. "Do you preach such views here?"

"I didn't say that." Mr. Ahrendt was apparently aware that he had just walked onto thin ice. "Of course, murder is a sin. After all, it's written in the Bible: 'You shall not kill.'"

"That didn't deter the Crusaders from their bloody campaigns," Hannes said. "But you probably have a justification for why killing in some cases is not a sin. I find your views to be very troubling. I also find them to be very dangerous when considered in light of the murders. We have since learned that David Bach smashed the stone sculpture and spray-painted the message against blasphemy on the wall. Moreover, there have been repeated confrontations between your people and the members of New Way. And Bach is not the only person implicated."

"Are you implying that we had something to do with the murders?" The indignant pastor began to walk away. "We wouldn't dirty our hands with those people. What an outrageous accusation. I'll be filing a complaint against you. Please leave the church immediately."

"All right," Marcel said. "But you can be sure we'll be investigating your church and its members."

He pulled on Hannes's sleeve and motioned toward the exit. Mr. Ahrendt followed their every move until the heavy double doors swung closed.

"Sorry," Hannes said once they were outside. "I couldn't listen to his nonsense anymore. I won't listen to someone preach hate. I wonder what he says during his services."

"You'll never know." Marcel grinned. "If you ever showed up on a Sunday, he'd definitely kick you out. He probably considers your eyes a mark of the Devil."

"I wonder if the roles aren't somehow reversed," Hannes said as he glanced over at New Way and then back at the Church of the Creator. "You're more likely to find Christian charity on the street than in his church."

"You utter nothing but blasphemy, you shameless heretic," Marcel joked. "But seriously, if someone really is targeting New Way, there are probably several pews full of suspects in that church. If everyone there shares Mr. Ahrendt's views, it's possible someone could have been goaded into action."

"Especially Bach," Hannes said.

"Indeed. But there are still around two hundred other potential crusaders. We need to find out who was involved in the clashes with New Way."

"Should we interrupt the rehearsal again?" Hannes asked.

"No, let's call it a day." Marcel had little desire to exacerbate the situation with his wife. "Beck and Lück could only name David Bach. I'll put Clarissa and Isabelle on it first thing tomorrow. They can also visit the church on Sunday to get a better idea of its members. Besides, I'm curious what Ahrendt has to say in his sermons."

"I just hope he doesn't convert them," Hannes joked.

***

Hannes looked around Ole's apartment. The fisherman lived in a small house on the harbor and hadn't forgotten his promise to help Hannes prepare for the test. Ole had lived alone since his divorce, and it was clear he didn't have a very good grip on housekeeping. But the clutter must not bother him too much since he spent most of the day on the water.

Ole sat next to Hannes at the wooden table. The instruments in question included a navigational triangle, parallel rulers, dividers, and a chart—plus a pencil, which Ole had mostly chewed to a nub. He was a patient and motivating teacher, which could perhaps be attributed to the regular contact he had with his grandson Fiete.

Ole watched closely as Hannes worked on the last exercise of the evening: charting a course from Lübeck to Copenhagen. So that it wouldn't be too easy, Hannes had to include stops at Kiel, Flensburg, and Svendborg, which meant navigating between small islands. After drawing the pencil lines and double-checking the distance, he presented his work to Ole.

"One hundred percent correct," Ole said. "You didn't run onto a sandbank and reached Copenhagen without incident. And believe me, the girls in Denmark are worth it." He grinned impishly.

"Actually, it wasn't so hard," Hannes said with satisfaction. "What I'm more concerned about is all the other material for the test, because I don't have very much free time right now to study."

"How many more classes are there?" Ole asked and tapped the ash out of his pipe.

"Today's basic maritime law, and that's it. This weekend, we'll go out on the water and practice everything we need to know for the test."

"And when's the test?"

"At the end of November. If everything goes smoothly, I can celebrate Christmas on the Baltic Sea."

"With the right first mate, that sounds like a great idea." Ole laughed, while Hannes wondered if Anna would feel comfortable on a boat. But before he could even answer that question, he needed to know if Anna actually felt comfortable with him.

"Well, who knows," Hannes said. "I'll probably have to sail to Copenhagen to find the right first mate to spend Christmas with."

CHAPTER 14

I do not doubt you. Never again. But why were they not found in time? They could have been. They did not have to die; there was enough time. I know why. Because it was not your will. Yes, it was not your will. They should have died. I know the enemies. I watch them. I know where they are. Who they are. I no longer doubt you. Not with you by my side. I could do nothing else. And you take pride in me. Do you? Of course you do. For too long I have turned a blind eye. I will not give up hope halfway. I knew the way before, but I was too weak. Today, I know the way, and I am strong. Your way. I thank you for that. I will not be stopped—by anyone. I follow my destiny. I do what you ask of me.

CHAPTER 15

Hannes had been really looking forward to visiting Fritz that Friday. Although an argument was still inevitable, present circumstances now far outweighed memories of the past summer. He was curious to learn what theories the experienced detective had come up with. He was also so racked with guilt over the supposed mistake he had made when questioning Manuel Birkholz that he would have gladly accepted any help imaginable—and that included Old Fritz's. To increase his chances of solving the case, he was even prepared to divulge more details than he had been a week ago. Who would tell?

Certainly not the guard. Although four tables were occupied that day, she leafed through a magazine in boredom and rarely looked up. Fritz seemed like a wind-up toy in comparison to her. His mood had continued its upward trend. His voice was chipper as he greeted Hannes.

"Ole was here for half an hour today. He's confident you'll pass your test on the first try."

"I hope he's right," Hannes said.

"Why the long face? Is the stupid test getting to you?"

Hannes was silent for a moment before he pulled himself together and anxiously recounted the mistake he made while questioning Manuel

Birkholz and the subsequent death of Ms. Kramer. "Do you think I put her life in danger? If so, then I should quit the force."

"Listen," Fritz said, peering through the rectangular lenses of his glasses with an almost paternal look on his face. "Honestly, I don't see the problem. Henning's making a mountain out of a molehill. Of course you shouldn't have mentioned her name, but everyone's messed up during an interview. The question is whether this Birkholz is the actual perp. I have my doubts."

"Why?" Hannes already felt a little calmer.

"Intuition," Fritz said, pointing to his forehead. "I mean, obviously I haven't met him, but his possible motives seem weak, even in the case of Alexander Kramer. Ditto for Mrs. Böhm."

"True. Mr. Birkholz denies knowing her. And there's no evidence to suggest he's lying."

"Tell me about Mrs. Böhm, so I can get a better picture."

Hannes hesitated and looked around the room as if Federsen might turn the corner at any moment. All the other people were engrossed in their conversations, and the prison guard was flipping to the next page. Hannes lowered his voice and gave Fritz a rundown on what they had learned about Mrs. Böhm so far.

"That doesn't sound like a woman who would hire a call boy. Even if she had needs which weren't being met, she already had Alexander Kramer to satisfy them. Not to mention that he was better in the sack— at least according to the women at the film studio. They're professionals, so they know what they're talking about." He had a lecherous grin on his face.

"Right." Hannes's continued to grow more and more relieved and grateful to Fritz. "So you think Birkholz is innocent?"

"I didn't say that. I just strongly doubt he's guilty, at least in the case of Sylvia Böhm. If it turns out we're wrong and it was multiple perps, then he of course could be behind the crucifixion. In that case, it would be possible that he feared Alexander's sister might pose a danger."

"But only theoretically."

"Purely theoretically," said Fritz. "To make a more realistic judgment, I'd need more information about the other suspects. That's up to you. If you want, you can tell me more, and I promise that it stays between us. I do, after all, have a few wrongs I need to right by you. But if you don't want to tell me anything, I understand."

Fritz looked earnestly at Hannes. Presumably, he already knew the outcome, because he took out several folded pieces of paper and a pen from his pocket. When Hannes finally decided to tell him, Fritz listened attentively and jotted down a few notes or corrected what he had previously written. Hannes's face was flushed by the time he finished with his description of the pastor at the Church of the Creator. They only had a few more minutes.

"That's quite a mess of information," Fritz said, almost out of pity. His face beamed with excitement. It was clear that his crosswords would have to wait. "I need to organize this information. Hannes, I have a bad feeling about this and wouldn't rule out the possibility that more people are in danger. I'll try to see if I can get more visiting hours on another day so we can swap ideas more often."

"But nothing jumps out at you so far?" Hannes was disappointed. He had hoped for more, especially since he had violated regulations and put his career on the line. But he realized Fritz was not a magician.

"Up until now, you've only questioned the New Way members about the deaths and whether they noticed anything unusual. I recommend asking them about their own lives. Maybe something unusual happened to them in recent weeks. Maybe something presaged the murders."

"Do you suspect a religious motive?"

"The evidence certainly suggests it, otherwise there would be a few too many coincidences. You should take a closer look at this Church of the Creator and see what kind of people belong to it. And you should definitely track down David Bach."

"What do you think we've been doing?" Hannes angrily replied. "Easy enough for you to say. Why don't you snap your fingers? Maybe he'll turn up then." He lowered his eyes and returned to using his normal voice. "Clarissa and Isabelle are going to the Sunday service at the Church of the Creator, and we have an APB out on Bach. He's the one we've got the biggest case against."

"Of course it could also be fanatics who don't belong to this church," Fritz said, ignoring Hannes's outburst. "Just because the Church of the Creator set up shop across the street and there have been several confrontations doesn't mean the church's followers have resorted to such drastic measures. Religious sentiments can flare up easily. If that's the case, then you're standing knee-deep in a pile of shit, looking for that famous needle."

Fritz looked like he was ready to plunge headfirst into that pile to search for the missing needle. He finally had a challenge and was clearly happy. Old Fritz was back in business.

***

"Where's my esteemed partner?" Hannes asked when he arrived at the station.

"He's been with the boss for two hours," Marcel said with a smirk. Although Steffen Lauer had succumbed to the office epidemic, the new developments in the case had driven him out of bed. Hannes could already picture Federsen tattling on him, denouncing the mistake he had made while questioning Manuel Birkholz. However, according to Marcel, there was another reason.

"Their search of David Bach's apartment proved very helpful. Although nothing there points to the murders, we have much better info on him. There were pictures of Rebecca Köhler all over his place. He's still obsessed with her, so we got a restraining order on him and put her under police protection."

"How's she handling all this?"

"She's scared but glad she's protected. We also searched Bach's computer. There's a ton of religious material stored on it, and he's collected all sorts of things on New Way. It seems like he's been monitoring the group. He has notes on who does what, and he paid close attention to those who were in contact with Rebecca, particularly the Kramers."

"Damn it," said Hannes. "And I almost caught him a week ago. Is there any evidence he's been working with someone else?"

"No, but it seems likely. This guy's impulsive and aggressive. He's not the type to plan something and carefully cover his tracks. Take the crowbar episode, for example. It's a completely different MO than the murderer's. If he's the one, then he's got help."

"Probably from the Church of the Creator."

"Per's already researching it. Isabelle and Clarissa have begun calling New Way members to ask about other incidents with people from the church. We need to know which churchgoers we should take a closer look at. After all, nearly two hundred people belong to that church."

"I just had another thought," Hannes said. "When we talk to the people from New Way again, we should ask if anything unusual has happened to them lately. Maybe it would give us a clue about the murders."

"That makes perfect sense," said Marcel. "But we need to be discreet. We don't want to trigger a panic in the group. Ah, here comes the rest of the team. We can discuss it now."

Federsen trudged into the room and ignored Hannes. He threw himself into the only seat to assert his place in the pecking order. Marcel balanced himself on an exercise ball behind his desk to manage his back pain. The young detectives were forced to remain standing for the duration of the meeting.

Per spoke first. He had done some research on the Church of the Creator and had learned some interesting facts. In his assessment, it was a conservative fundamentalist group which had sparked controversy before due to its literal interpretation of the Bible and its promotion of antiliberal values. The church attracted new members with promises of salvation, which evidently worked quite well.

"In the last three years, its membership has increased nearly 30 percent. The church now has around five thousand members in Germany, with two hundred in our city. Founded in Stuttgart, it now has multiple locations. It's completely independent and doesn't belong to an umbrella organization like the German Evangelical Alliance, which includes a wide range of independent churches and Evangelical Lutheran churches. However, these aren't cults or religious fanatics. In total, the Alliance counts some 1.3 million active members, and some of the constituent churches are a little quirky. One religious community—"

"Get to the point and stick with the Church of the Creator. The rest is irrelevant," said Federsen.

"Uh, right. So, the Church of the Creator was founded in 1988 and has gradually expanded from southern Germany all over the country. It maintains a particularly dogmatic interpretation of the Bible. However, it doesn't belong to the so-called Charismatic Movement, where firebrand preachers whip people up into a frenzy."

"That Mr. Ahrendt was by no means charismatic," Hannes said.

"How's the church financed?" asked Marcel.

"Like other independent churches: exclusively through donations. It doesn't receive any government funding. Donations are supposedly voluntary, but a certain amount of pressure is probably placed on members. It's been noted that members of independent churches show much greater commitment than attendees of established churches. For example, as a rule, they attend religious services more regularly. What's more, there's a surprising number of high earners in the church's ranks. The Church of the Creator is unlikely to go broke anytime soon."

"Five thousand members. Well, have fun questioning everyone," Clarissa said. "And if we add all the other independent churches as a precaution, we'll be at it for years."

"Per pointed out that these churches represent a broad spectrum," Marcel reminded her. "So we shouldn't lump them all together. The majority of members practice their faith peacefully. You'll be in a better position to determine whether this also applies to the local branch of the Church of the Creator after attending their service on Sunday."

"I'm sure you'll get a warm welcome," joked Per, who was obviously glad to have avoided the assignment. But Federsen burst that bubble.

"You'll go with her. After all, you're the one with the most background information. You can find out if what you learned is correct and hang out with some truly radical Christians. Where are we with the New Way interviews? Any evidence of incidents with certain people from the Church of the Creator?"

"We've only been able to reach a few so far," Isabelle said. "We'll probably have more luck this afternoon when people start their weekends. So far all we've heard is that they've gotten dirty looks and comments. But the situation calmed down after New Way started meeting on Fridays."

"There's only been a few isolated confrontations since the beginning of the year," said Clarissa. "A woman was told at a children's party to stop spoiling the kids. And at this year's summer festival, a few people from the Church of the Creator distributed pamphlets. An argument ensued, and in the end, two cops had to intervene."

"Well, at least that's a start," Hannes said. "Maybe they took down names and addresses."

"We checked. It's not like we were born yesterday," Clarissa said. "There were five names, including two from New Way: Mr. Lück and Mr. Beck."

"Did it get physical? I'd have a hard time picturing those two getting into a fight. They must have been provoked."

"A fight might be a little exaggerated. Let's just say there was some shoving," Isabelle said. "Who pushed who first, we'll never know.

However, two members of the Church of the Creator did get into a scuffle with our colleagues."

"One of them we already know by name—and Hannes at least from behind," Clarissa joked.

"We need to catch that guy!" Federsen shouted as if David Bach had just waltzed through the door. "Who were the other two?"

"A Ludwig Obermann and a Frank Meister. Neither has a criminal record. Obermann is forty; Meister, thirty-four. He was the other guy who couldn't keep his hands to himself. Obermann, however, behaved."

"Let's teach those two a lesson." Federsen banged on the table. "Niehaus can stay here and continue calling New Way members. No more slipups."

Isabelle and Clarissa had been able to reach the first seven members on the list, so there were thirty-four left for Hannes. Although many numbers were for cell phones, his success didn't start improving until after five. As was to be expected, many from New Way remembered the incident at the summer festival as well as David Bach. One member mentioned finding a pile of dog poop on the group's doorstep, but he couldn't be certain if the Church of the Creator was to blame.

Hannes asked if anything unusual had happened to them personally. What constituted unusual was, of course, subjective. A few of the statements made Hannes laugh. He did, however, learn of incidents which couldn't just be attributed to anxiety, exaggeration, or bad luck.

Wolfgang Hartmann, the department store owner, stated that he had been the recipient of repeated calls on Sundays in July until he finally had his number changed. He was one of the few names that Hannes could put a face to. He remembered Hartmann as the plump man who had hugged him at the meeting last Friday and as the Earth Spirit at the rehearsal. Hartmann hadn't reported the alleged telephone calls, but he insisted that his phone had rung hourly every Sunday for a month.

"It started at six in the morning, and it didn't stop until eleven at night. Whenever I picked up, nobody answered. The first Sunday, I kept thinking it was just kids playing a prank."

"Who did you think it was the following three Sundays?" Hannes asked.

"I assumed it was just some crazy person who randomly dialed numbers. So I just put my phone on silent and then got a new number."

Alarm bells went off in Hannes's head. Of course, it could also have been completely harmless. After all, the incident was several months ago, and Mr. Hartmann hadn't experienced anything out of the ordinary since. A Beatrice Reichert, who sounded elderly, told Hannes about a burglary of her ground floor apartment.

"I made it easy for the burglar," she said, somewhat embarrassed. "I always forget to close my patio door in the summer. He didn't even have to break in."

"But let me guess, you didn't use the insurance money to replace anything," Hannes said.

"That's the thing. Nothing of value was stolen."

"How do you know you were robbed when nothing was stolen?" Hannes asked.

"They took only items of great personal value, not material. Mementos that meant a lot to me. I used to be a successful ballet dancer. Then I got sick and couldn't dance anymore. My world collapsed. But I still had souvenirs that I could look at, and they would take me back to those wonderful days."

"What sorts of things were taken?" Hannes asked.

"Photos from my performances, my old ballet slippers, awards, newspaper articles."

"Strange," Hannes said. He had never heard of burglars who specialized in ballet memorabilia. "Where did you keep the stuff?"

"In a box, which my friends jokingly called my treasure chest. I kept it in the living room under a large picture that had been taken during my last performance. That photo's also gone."

"Otherwise nothing else was stolen?"

Mrs. Reichert was insistent. Hannes made a mental note to ask his colleagues about their impressions of her from when they had questioned her. Perhaps she was just some scatterbrained old lady who had misplaced the souvenirs while cleaning the house.

His next two interviewees couldn't think of any mysterious or odd incidents and were suspicious about the reason for the question. Hannes had hoped that "investigating all leads" would be a satisfactory explanation, but neither sounded convinced.

After speaking to twelve more people, Hannes hadn't learned anything new. A glance at the clock showed that he still had time for one last phone call before heading downtown to meet Ben and Elke at the movies.

Vanessa Brinkmann picked up immediately and didn't seem very surprised by his question.

"Oh, you know," she said, "these last few weeks have been a complete mess. In late summer, I endured the loss of my children, then the murders, and now the death of Antje. Work's been nonstop. I've barely had time to visit my parents in the nursing home."

"I'm so sorry," Hannes said. "I didn't know."

"Didn't know what?"

"That you lost your children this summer."

"I said that the wrong way. They're not dead. It's more that I'm dead to them."

"Oh, okay."

"My daughter and son are in their midtwenties. When my daughter was two, I separated from my husband and raised my children on my own. I didn't want to have any more contact with their father. It wasn't easy because I worked full-time, which was still unusual then, and there wasn't childcare like there is today." She sighed, and Hannes hoped she would get to the point. His bus was coming in a few minutes. He quickly sent Ben a text message telling him to buy the tickets and only half listened.

"They probably lacked a father figure. It often wasn't easy. We had a somewhat complicated relationship in recent years. I . . . well, I didn't agree with everything they did. Anyway. I always maintained that their father had died in an accident. I had even thrown out all my photos of him. We moved back then, so there was no danger that they'd run into one another. But in September, my children received a letter telling them that their father was still alive and that I'd lied to them all these years. They were so upset that they broke off all contact with me."

"Hmm," Hannes said. "Certainly took some gall on your former husband's part to send the letter. But I'm sure your son and daughter will start talking to you again." He glanced at his watch.

"But the letter couldn't have come from my ex-husband," Mrs. Brinkmann said. "He died before it was sent. He was run over by a truck in June after running out into the street drunk. My kids never got a chance to meet him."

Despite an all-out sprint, Hannes just missed the bus. Fortunately, the driver stopped again to let the wildly waving cop on.

"Thank you very much," Hannes said as he tried to catch his breath. The bus driver nodded. Hannes squeezed past a group of young people who had evidently been pregaming and were now on their way to a party. There was an empty seat in the rear.

"Well, what a surprise," someone said.

Hannes looked over. "Oh, hello, Mr. Beck," he said and shook the man's outstretched hand. "Was your meeting canceled tonight?"

"No, no. I'm just running a little late because I was visiting Mrs. Schlichter. She's also a member but unfortunately can't make it because she's bedridden. Her mind's still sharp, though. I visit her every Friday.

It took a little longer today because the recent incidents have really upset her. I hope you're getting somewhere with your investigation. Our members are very concerned."

Hannes tried to give the impression that they had everything under control. He also seized the opportunity to ask Mr. Beck about any unusual events.

"You could say that I was unfortunately somewhat of a guinea pig. When I was working as a priest in North Rhine-Westphalia, we had problems with a small group of anarchists. They'd disrupt Mass, hold demonstrations, and once even urinated in the baptismal font. Now I'm the chaplain of a secular group, and it seems I've still pissed someone off."

"How so?"

"Mr. Ahrendt from the Church of the Creator keeps accosting me for, in his words, 'going astray.' But since I know that I live out Christian values today just as much as I did before, I can take it. This summer, however, my tires were slashed outside our meeting place. Since then, I started taking the bus. Then, someone put a picture of the Devil in my mailbox a few weeks ago, and there was an anonymous complaint against me that I was supposedly working as a psychiatrist without proper qualifications. As you know, that's complete nonsense. I've never called myself a psychiatrist, and the sign on my gate doesn't say that either."

"Did you report any of this to the police?" Hannes asked.

"No. I'm used to a lot by now and have learned that there's not much the police can do. I'm sorry—I don't mean you personally. My wife's a bit worried, especially after the murders. We had hoped we'd be able to lead a quiet life here. We went through a lot when the parish found out we were a couple. Celibacy is still a prerequisite for being a Roman Catholic priest. It was not an easy time."

Hannes now realized why he'd gotten the impression when he'd first met Mrs. Beck that she'd endured a tragic life.

"I have to change buses here," said Mr. Beck. "Have a nice weekend."

Hannes's mind raced for the remainder of his ride. Fritz had once again demonstrated a sixth sense. Some of the New Way members actually had incidents to report, and the list of interviewees was still quite long. The question was whether or not these incidents were connected in some way to the murders.

Hannes's phone rang. Clarissa's voice soon thundered in his ear.

"Federsen, Per, and I had the pleasure of visiting Frank Meister at his home. We shouldn't have contacted him first, though. He's definitely friends with David Bach. And if Bach was hiding out there, then we gave him enough time to escape. Meister claimed he hadn't seen him in a while."

"Why'd you call first?"

"It was Federsen's idea. He didn't want to have to travel all the way there just to stand in front of an empty apartment," Clarissa said.

"Ah, but he never makes mistakes," Hannes said cynically. They were even now. He wouldn't forget this slipup the next time Federsen accused him of botching the Birkholz interview. He listened intently to the rest of Clarissa's report.

Frank Meister had been a member of various independent churches since he was a child. His deeply religious family had joined the Church of the Creator several years ago. He worked as an optician in a small shop and had, in Clarissa's opinion, been "thoroughly brainwashed."

"Although he didn't come across intellectually stunted, the stilted language he used to explain his beliefs did seem odd. And he kept going on and on the entire time," Clarissa said. "He'd make the perfect missionary. I wonder if he gives a free Bible with every pair of glasses. He had an answer for every question or comment. He'll make your head spin."

"It's odd that he's friends with a daredevil like Bach."

"We only found that out because in addition to the umpteen crosses and other religious junk, there were a ton of photos hanging on his walls. Most were of church events, and it was obvious that they got along quite well. There were pictures of a pilgrimage they went on together. But it's true, he seems more the brains while David Bach's probably the muscle. And it shows."

Unlike Bach with his imposing stature, Frank Meister hid his spindly, anemic-looking body under some pretty stodgy clothes. He had a razor-sharp side part and wore round John Lennon glasses. Clarissa was convinced that his eyes had a fanatical glint, but Hannes did not want to read too much into this interpretation. As expected, Meister did not have a very high opinion of New Way, but he chose his words carefully and refused to be finessed. Outraged, he denied the involvement of any members of the Church of the Creator in instigating conflict. The dispute over the summer was provoked by New Way, and the scuffle with the police was purely a misunderstanding.

"Have you heard anything from Isabelle and Marcel?" Hannes asked as he stepped off the bus one stop early to continue the conversation without being disturbed.

"Yes. They met up with Ludwig Obermann, who runs a small carpentry business and does wood carving. He apparently has a very impressive collection of Madonnas and saints. You could say he's the religious counterpart to Antje Kramer, only he works with wood."

"Making a wooden cross like the one Alexander Kramer was nailed to wouldn't be too difficult for him then," Hannes said. "And I assume he's also strong enough to set it up."

"But Isabelle described him as somewhat oafish and not very thoughtful or noticeably aggressive. He claimed he was just trying to defuse the situation during the confrontation with New Way."

"He contradicts Frank Meister, who said it was all just a misunderstanding."

"Like I said, he doesn't seem to be the brightest. He's unwittingly stabbed his coreligionists in the back. Unlike Meister, it should be easier to get him to talk. He's just as deeply religious, though."

"He might have been used," said Hannes. "He innocently threw together a cross, and the others finished the job."

"Maybe. He couldn't deny ever having made a giant wooden cross. Well, at least we have a promising new lead, though we shouldn't forget Matthias Böhm."

"At least he's in custody."

"Didn't you hear? Böhm was released today—he posted bail. But he supposedly doesn't pose a risk of absconding. No idea how he got the money."

"Damn it," Hannes said. "We couldn't hold him for longer?"

"Marcel tried, but there wasn't enough evidence against him. How far did you get with the phone list?"

Hannes picked up his pace as he approached the movie theater. Elke and Ben would surely be waiting impatiently. He quickly filled Clarissa in about the phone calls and running into Mr. Beck, then they agreed to divide up the remaining calls on Saturday morning. Clarissa and Isabelle would meet at the station, while Hannes would make his calls on his way to his boat-safety course.

"Catch all the murderers?" Ben teased when Hannes finally arrived. He was forty minutes late, and the movie was half over. Elke had chosen a French-German comedy.

"I'm really sorry." Hannes looked around. "I hope Elke's inside watching the movie, otherwise she'll kill me."

"Don't worry, she canceled, which is why I've taken the liberty of making a last-minute change to our viewing program. And fortunately for us, the movie doesn't start for another five minutes. If we hurry, we can catch the previews."

"Is Elke sick?" Hannes asked as he followed Ben into the small lobby.

"No, she found something better to do. Apparently, you inspired her at our pasta dinner. She really is full of surprises." They got in line to buy drinks and popcorn. "Elke took a look at the group's website and wants to join. She's going to tonight's meeting to see if it's for her."

Hannes stared at him in shock. "New Way? You're joking, right?"

"No. She told me earlier. She's been looking for something like this for a long time, and maybe she'll fit in there."

"I think it's a very bad idea," Hannes said.

"Oh, stop." Ben laughed. "If anyone can take care of themselves, it's Elke."

"Well, I don't know," Hannes said and looked at the ticket Ben handed him. The movie couldn't be more different than Elke's choice: an adventure drama, in which a former drug-addicted woman spends three months crossing the Rocky Mountains on a trip of self-discovery. Hannes immediately thought of Anna and her journey through Southeast Asia. While they looked for their seats, armed with popcorn and two bottles of beer, he told Ben about their reunion.

"Too bad you ended the evening at the taxi stand," Ben said, his mouth full of popcorn. "But at least it was a good start. When are you seeing her again?"

"Tomorrow night at her place," Hannes said. "After my boat course. So no taxi stand this time."

"Just make sure you take a shower before you show up," Ben said and laughed as the theater plunged into darkness. The movie was starting.

CHAPTER 16

November smiled on the budding sea captain that Saturday. Though the strong wind promised to create a few whitecaps, the sun was shining brightly in the cloudless sky. Hannes had intended to head straight home after the movie, but his resistance to Ben's entreaties had been halfhearted at best. So Friday night had lasted a little longer than expected. At such times Hannes envied his friend's carefree life. Ben had little ambition to finish his degree in history and instead dedicated himself to anti-Nazi causes—which had gotten him beat up more than once by the opposing side.

Hannes studied the list of New Way members at the breakfast table and called Isabelle. As expected, she was easier on him in divvying up the remaining calls than Clarissa presumably would have been. His opinion of her grew.

"We can handle most of them since we're at the station anyway," Isabelle said. "How many calls are there?"

There were twenty left. Isabelle and Clarissa each took eight. Hannes dialed the first of his four numbers after exiting the underground parking garage in his decrepit Ford. It quickly became apparent that the call would lead nowhere. He spoke to the bedridden Mrs.

Schlichter; Mr. Beck had visited her the previous day. Not surprisingly, given the limited excitement in her life, she seemed quite happy to get an unexpected call. Hannes was halfway to the port when he was finally able to hang up. The next interviewee had nothing unusual to report.

The last two names on the list belonged to a married couple, Bernd and Bettina Graf. After more than several rings, an unfriendly male answered.

"Were there incidents? Why don't you take a look at that police computer of yours? But you probably won't find much. So far the investigations have turned up nothing."

"What happened?" Hannes asked.

"A few weeks ago on October 2, our house was set on fire. Luckily, we were visiting my in-laws, so neither of us was hurt. It happened early in the morning. We probably would have burned to death."

Hannes pulled over. This interview deserved his undivided attention. After all, it was the first incident in which lives had actually been at stake.

"Are you sure it was arson?"

"Yes. Your colleagues initially assumed it was an accident. Listen, we own several apartment buildings and know a thing or two about fire prevention. We followed all safety precautions. Then, they discovered traces of an accelerant. They made it sound like they were accusing us of insurance fraud, like we set our own house on fire."

"We have to investigate every angle," Hannes said. "It happens sometimes."

"What investigation? So far, there's been no lead on who might have burned down our house. We've been living at a hotel for weeks and won't be able to move back in until Christmastime."

It was clear this incident needed to be pursued in greater detail. Hannes relayed the information to Isabelle and asked her to find out more about the arson case. It didn't take her long—she called him back just as he arrived at the small port.

"Neighbors called the fire department at four o'clock in the morning. They always sleep with the window open and were woken up by the smell. The fire department estimates that the blaze was started about half an hour before that. It intensified very quickly. The building sustained significant damage and is uninhabitable."

"Was it definitely arson?"

"No doubt about it. Several Molotov cocktails were lobbed through the windows. The fire marshal found the remains."

"Is there a suspect?"

"No one definite. The investigation's ongoing. Apparently, the couple hasn't made very many friends recently. They own several old buildings and have been carrying out luxury renovations so they can jack up the rent. Several tenants have complained that the Grafs either pressured them or forced them to leave. Some have hired a lawyer."

"Do the Grafs make a lot from their properties?"

"Mrs. Graf has a full-time assistant to help her manage the properties. Mr. Graf runs a software company that created New Way's website as probably some kind of donation."

"I'm surprised the couple even belongs," Hannes said, stunned. "Their behavior doesn't seem to be all that in tune with New Way's principles."

"They're only moderately active. But according to Mr. Lück, they've been giving larger and larger donations. Without their support, they wouldn't be able to host many of their activities. Either the Grafs have two sides to them or they see the donations like bribes."

"Did you learn of any other incidents? I'm through with my list, and except for the house fire, I've got nothing."

"Nothing here, but we still have eleven more people. I'll talk to you later."

Hannes parked beside a battered sedan and glanced at the dock. His classmates had already gathered and were nervously eyeing the waves beyond the jetty. The wind was even stronger on the coast than it had been in the city; it promised to be a very eventful session.

***

"Man overboard portside!" yelled the instructor.

Hannes tried to remember the correct sequence of maneuvers. Of course, no one had really fallen into the icy waters of the Baltic Sea, just an orange buoy.

The future seafarers had been split up into two inflatable boats. After the last person had managed to cast off while shouting out all the commands in correct order, it'd been time to try docking in tight spaces. The harbor offered the perfect practice setting; the boat collided repeatedly against the dock or a fishing boat during the repeated attempts.

So far, Hannes had done well—at least, the *Lena* wouldn't suffer any scratches on account of his steering skills. He now had to prove whether or not he could safely pull a person from the water. Since he wanted to take Anna out on the water as soon as possible, this exercise was very important.

After the fake panicked cries of the instructor, Hannes slammed the lever of the outboard motor and took his hand off the accelerator. He steered the stern away from the buoy, so the motor's propeller blades wouldn't butcher the individual. Hannes checked the wind direction before assigning tasks to his crew.

"Ute, deploy flotation devices. Karl, keep your finger pointed at the victim. Anke, note our coordinates."

The instructor had no comments, which was a good sign. Hannes carefully gave the motor some gas and steered leeward before turning and heading for the buoy. He decided that the rescue should take place on the starboard side and shouted the appropriate commands. But in the process, he forgot to approach an overboard passenger slowly and to ease off the gas. Although the inflatable boat nudged the imaginary victim only slightly, a human head wouldn't have fared well. When Hannes repeated the maneuver, he imagined Anna's face on the bobbing sphere. This time, the maneuver went flawlessly.

During the lunch break, the instructor entertained his students with his knotting skills and gave everyone a small piece of rope on which to practice. As usual, Hannes tangled his when rolling a hitch knot and hoped he wouldn't be asked to make one when he took his test. After eating his sandwich, Hannes called Isabelle and Clarissa. They had nothing new to report.

"A woman thought it was odd that her dog had died," Isabelle said. "It was sixteen years old. That's Methuselah in dog years." She laughed. "By the way, Clarissa knows the woman you talked to yesterday. Hold on, I'll pass her to you."

"When I was still walking the beat, we were constantly having to haul Mrs. Reichert down to the station," Clarissa said. "Petty thefts every time. She'd get caught by store security guards."

"Oh? I took her for a harmless old lady."

"I wouldn't say old—she's in her early sixties. You'd never suspect her if you ever ran into her. She's tall, slim, and has an almost aristocratic face. Her husband's a banker, and they're extremely wealthy. She wasn't stealing for lack of money."

"Do you know when she last went on a stealing spree?"

"Well, she wasn't caught every time. I last had to deal with her about a year ago, just before I got off patrol. She started going to see a therapist. It's possible she's done stealing."

"I don't think there's much more to her story," said Hannes. "But as for Mr. Hartmann and Mrs. Brinkmann, I'm not so sure."

"Mr. Hartmann kept getting those calls on Sundays, right?" Isabelle was back on the line. "It could have been a form of intimidation, but it could also have been a prank. The letter to Mrs. Brinkmann's children regarding their unknown father points to a more personal connection.

Perhaps a relative's behind it. Very few people would have known about the story."

"I think so too," Hannes said. "She was very eager to keep it a secret. The incidents the Becks and Grafs experienced are the only cause for concern. We need to ask Marcel and Federsen how to proceed."

Isabelle was skeptical. "I don't think it's enough to warrant personal protection. I'm curious to see what happens tomorrow at the Church of the Creator."

"Just be careful you don't join and give them all your money."

"Well, it's not like they'll get much out of me. How's class? Fallen into the water yet?"

"Nope, but it could still happen. We leave the harbor after lunch and head a little farther offshore. It's windy here. The boat will definitely be rocking."

"Better take a Dramamine."

***

Ute cowered in the rear of the motorboat, her face completely green. The group was practicing navigating by compass. It hadn't been a good idea to have Ute at the wheel. It was virtually impossible for her to keep a steady course. Cold water doused the occupants every time Ute hit a wave head on.

The instructor sat grumbling in the bow. "New course one hundred eighty degrees!" he shouted before he was hit by a wall of water. "What's she want a boating license for?" Hannes heard him mutter. He tried to maintain his composure and directed Ute back to the dock. As the boat bounced across the waves, he gave his students some tips for the exam.

"If you get Mr. Naumann, keep a low profile. He can't stand wise-cracks. Always keep calm and think before you perform the required maneuver. He will try to confuse you and trip you up."

These tips were somewhat wasted on Ute. When the boat finally reached the dock, she stumbled out and collapsed onto the wet wood. It took some cajoling to get her up.

Two hours later, Hannes had not quite yet made the transition back to dry land either as he walked across the dock. "Completely normal," a classmate reassured him, but it only took Hannes a few more moments before he was once again accustomed to walking on solid ground. He was in a euphoric mood. The afternoon had been fun, and he hadn't thought once about the murder investigation. He looked forward to starting up *Lena's* motor for the first time and sprinted to his car to change out of his wet clothes.

Federsen had called three times. Hannes's good mood vanished. Hopefully there weren't any new developments which might ruin the rest of his weekend.

Federsen was just returning from Antje Kramer's funeral, where he had mingled with people from New Way. Hannes was strangely curious who had made her gravestone. Definitely not her. But he was wrong.

"These artists are weird," Federsen said. "Ms. Kramer designed her gravestone years ago. Perhaps she was afraid of dying in an accident and wanted to be prepared."

"What's it look like?"

"Pretty bizarre. Celtic and Christian symbols. Even in death, she's torn between two worlds."

Like all the members of New Way. According to Federsen, the fear among the funeral attendees was almost palpable. But there was also a noticeably defiant attitude.

"Fortunately, Mr. Beck's a trained chaplain. He called upon the other members to observe the fundamental principles of the group, so they don't make themselves vulnerable to further attack. There's a great need for discussion, and he seems very capable of reassuring them."

"Some will probably need special encouragement." Hannes summarized the results of his recent phone calls.

"We ought to keep an eye out on this group," he said. "We should pay another visit to David Bach's friends. Everyone claims not to have seen or heard from him in days."

Hannes grew annoyed. If not for that damn cat, he would have caught Bach. Since he had a little more time before his date with Anna, he called Elke on his way home to see if they could get together for a bit. He wanted to hear her impressions from the meeting and to know why she was interested in New Way. They planned to meet up at seven that evening, which would leave him enough time to pick up Anna. There would even be time for a long shower—he couldn't ignore Ben's advice.

After showering and brushing his teeth, Hannes stood in front of his closet and considered his options. He pulled out his favorite pair of jeans, then put them back. They already looked well worn. He decided instead on a pair of dark-blue chinos that he'd only had on once. He owned only white and blue shirts, but even he realized a blue shirt would not go with a pair of blue pants.

"Where are you off to?" Elke asked as Hannes plopped down on her couch.

"I've got a date with Anna tonight." He tried to sound casual, but Elke raised an eyebrow.

"That explains a lot. Where are you taking her?"

"Um . . . nowhere. We're going to spend a quiet evening at her place."

"Uh-huh. Hence the really comfortable clothes, I see," Elke teased with a laugh. She was lounging on the couch in sweatpants and a T-shirt, while he wore a white shirt and chinos. But it was clear that she was happy for him.

Hannes quickly changed the topic to the New Way meeting and asked her why she attended.

"I'm not a deeply religious person, but I'd like to belong to a community that seeks to shed light on life's deeper meaning. Everyone's constantly talking about money, status, and what awesome things they're doing. But I don't want some close-minded religious group with outdated morals. I don't want to have to justify my homosexuality all the time. After you told me about New Way, I looked at their website and it appealed to me."

"Did the group meet your expectations?"

"I can't say yet. But they were very welcoming, and I liked their service. Solemn, but not too uptight. A woman read an essay about her husband who has cancer. It was very moving."

"Did the deceased members come up at all?"

"Of course. Antje's funeral was today, so they discussed the program and assigned tasks."

"My boss was at the funeral and said some people seemed scared. Did you get that impression?"

Elke concurred. Members had been given the opportunity to voice their feelings and fears. Some had already been toying with the idea of quitting New Way. Everyone had been in agreement that they should keep a low profile for the next few weeks and postpone the group's public activities. Whether this would also include the theater performances had yet to be decided.

"I don't think it's a good idea for you to be hanging around there right now," Hannes said. "There's some indication that the killings were related to the victims' involvement in New Way. We've also learned that some members have experienced a few serious incidents."

"I know," said Elke. "They talked about that. You called all the members. But don't worry, I only wanted to see what it was all about. A choir group meets on Tuesdays. I might try that out once or twice."

"Did you mention at all that you know me?"

She shook her head. "Should I have?"

Hannes thought for a moment. "No, it's better if you don't. No one should feel as though everything they say could come back to me. But if you hear that someone feels threatened or if you notice anything strange, please tell me immediately."

"So you want me to infiltrate the group?" Elke joked, and her blue eyes sparkled.

"I'd prefer it if you didn't go there at all, but I can't talk you out of it. If you're already attending, then you might as well keep your eyes and ears open. I want to protect these people."

Elke's joke about being an undercover agent left Hannes wondering if he had approached the issue the wrong way. It hadn't occurred to him that she might be attracted to New Way and the latent danger because she thought her life had recently been a bit boring.

"I'll be careful." Elke hugged Hannes good-bye. "Focus on your date and enjoy the evening."

***

Anna's small one-bedroom apartment was located in a new three-story building. The open hall led straight into a simple but tastefully decorated living room. Nothing seemed to have changed since Hannes's brief visit several months ago, except the atmosphere. In addition to a single floor lamp, a veritable armada of candles lit the room. And from the front door, Hannes could see two glasses of red wine waiting on the table.

Embarrassed and nervous, Hannes stood in front of Anna. He had to steady himself against the doorframe when he caught sight of her radiant green eyes and tanned face. Her short brown corduroy skirt and light-blue blouse highlighted her figure. Anna seemed to look at him admiringly. Her smile widened as Hannes, his ears beet red, awkwardly handed her a colorful bouquet.

"Welcome home again," he said in husky voice and leaned down to kiss her on the cheek. He caught a subtle whiff of perfume. "And of course thank you very much for inviting me," he added and hoped his socks weren't sweaty as he took off his shoes.

"Thank you," she said. "Glad you could make it. I hope I don't bore you with my photos from Asia. I kept telling myself it was a bad idea. But to compensate, I cooked something delicious."

Hannes of course would have accepted her invitation even if there weren't photos or food. He toddled behind her to the little table. Anna was a little flushed, but that could be because she had just been standing in front of the stove.

The meal began with a curry-lemongrass soup, followed by a Thai curry that was somewhat too spicy for Hannes. His battered tongue was soon soothed by her mango pudding. The conversation was slow at first since both of them tended to be shy.

After Hannes had checked his teeth in the bathroom mirror, they moved to the sofa, where Anna showed him pictures on her laptop of her five-country Asian tour.

"These are just a few of them," she said. "I took more than a thousand, but I saved the best ones in a separate folder."

There were two hundred and fifty photos to look through. Hannes could have listened to her vivid descriptions for hours—and gazed at her for hours too. His eyes kept slipping from the screen to her as she leaned forward to click on the next image. Her long brown hair was draped over her left shoulder, and her neck glistened in the candlelight. As they simultaneously reached for their glasses of wine, Anna's fingers brushed his wrist and his whole body tingled.

Hannes kept wondering if she really had invited him over just to look at pictures. He'd had a few girlfriends before, but flirting had never been his strong suit. He was always unsure whether or not he was missing signs or crossing signals. But there wasn't much danger at that moment, because all he had to do was listen, ask a few well-timed questions, and gasp.

The slideshow came to an end, and Anna smiled as she closed her laptop. She turned to look at Hannes. Her knee touched his leg.

"I hope it wasn't too boring for you," she said. "I love to travel so much that I get caught up in the memories. Of course that's not very interesting or fair to everyone else who wasn't there."

"That wasn't boring at all. I'd love to go on a trip like that."

"Maybe I'll take you sometime." Anna smiled mischievously, and 99 percent of men would have correctly interpreted the look in her eye. Hannes watched with fascination as she played with a strand of hair.

"Yeah, that would be awesome."

"I'd protect you from snakes," Anna teased. She knew about his snake phobia. Then she eyed him coyly and moved a little closer. Her arm slipped, spilling wine onto Hannes's white shirt.

"Oh damn," she said and jumped up. "I'm so sorry!"

"It's no big deal," Hannes said and dabbed himself with a napkin. "I almost never wear shirts like these. I won't notice if it goes missing."

"Still, it's a shame. You look great in that shirt. I hope I didn't get any on your pants." Anna walked to the small kitchenette. "The best thing to do is to sprinkle salt on the stain. Take your shirt off."

Hannes's hands shook as he unbuttoned his shirt and walked over to the sink. Anna turned around, and her gaze fell on his muscular torso illuminated by the warm glow of the candles. Then her eyes wandered back up to his unique eyes. Like magnets, Hannes and Anna moved closer to each other until Hannes could feel her breath on his skin. Her fingertips grazed his stomach and ran slowly up his chest. Hannes gently touched her cheek, and she leaned her head into his palm and looked up at him. Their lips drew closer, and when at last they touched, their bodies were overcome by a warm sensation. Button by button, Hannes undid her blouse and caressed her body. Their tongues playfully explored each other, and Anna pulled Hannes down onto a small, somewhat rickety kitchen stool.

For a few minutes, the world around them disappeared, and only the creaking of the stool—followed by its collapse—brought them back to reality. Laughing and breathing heavily, they lay on the ground surrounded by pieces of wood.

"Maybe we should go into the other room," whispered Anna. He followed without protest. The shirt with the red-wine stains lay forgotten on the kitchen counter.

CHAPTER 17

Fritz had managed to get a second weekly visit approved for Tuesdays. Unfortunately, it wasn't in the afternoon, which meant that Hannes had to rush his training. He found it frustrating that he couldn't go full throttle in the final stages of his sporting career. After all, there was nothing more exciting for an athlete than competing in the Olympics. On the other hand, he was determined to solve the case as quickly as possible, and the mornings spent at the gym gave him the perfect cover—he wouldn't be able to slip away from the station so easily in the afternoons. Nevertheless, it was still risky. If word got out that he was discussing the investigation with his former boss instead of working out at the gym, he'd find himself in a tight spot.

At the moment, however, Hannes wasn't wasting his time thinking about it. He was floating on cloud nine. He had skipped boat practice to spend Sunday with Anna. He grinned as he relived the events of their day together.

"What are you smiling about?" Fritz asked.

"Oh sorry. What were you saying?" Hannes struggled to pull himself together.

"Just that I find what's happened to some New Way members disturbing," Fritz repeated, shaking his head.

Hannes had given him a rundown of his phone calls, and Fritz had frowned as he took notes.

"Some of them really laid it on thick, though," Hannes said. "I doubt Mr. Hartmann's phone calls or Mrs. Reichert's stolen mementos are really cause for concern."

"This Wolfgang Hartmann," Fritz said in a feverish voice, tapping his pen on the table while he pondered what to say next. "Isn't he the owner of a department store?"

"Yes. He's also said to be a socially conscious individual and very popular with his employees. He's been described as your typical Hanseatic merchant who runs a tight ship, but doesn't forget the needs of his employees. Sounds nice, right?"

"Perhaps. He's a member of the chamber of commerce. I forget what his position is, but I've interviewed him a couple of times before. The group's been lobbying for years to do away with restrictions on business hours, specifically on Sundays. The tourism board supports the push. They want visitors to be able to shop all weekend."

"Maybe that's why he received those harassing phone calls? An employee who doesn't want to work on weekends?"

"It's possible. Sunday's also supposed to be a day of rest for Christians. Don't want to prevent the flock from going to church, right? I'm sure the Church of the Creator isn't a huge fan of Hartmann's campaign. Have you looked into that?"

Fritz's expression darkened when Hannes reeled off what the investigators knew. He also shared Isabelle's and Clarissa's impressions from Sunday's service. Over one hundred members were in attendance, including Bach's friend, Frank Meister, and the carpenter, Ludwig Obermann.

"It was the most absurd thing I've ever been to," Clarissa had said. "I didn't think church was all fire and brimstone anymore. You could practically feel the flames of hell. Sin, punishment, the need for repentance—that's all he spoke about. But the people hung on the minister's every word and kept shouting out, 'Amen!'"

"New Way also came up," Isabelle had added. "As an example of how the Devil tries to lead vulnerable people into temptation. I doubt they were happy when this alleged Antichrist moved in across the street."

"Have you questioned any more people from the church?" Fritz asked.

"Of course. But it seems like they've coordinated their responses. They tolerate New Way, even if it's not a Christian organization. No one claims to have been in contact with David Bach recently. Their alibis seem coordinated too."

"And still no trace of Bach?"

"Unfortunately, no. We searched his apartment again yesterday. We didn't find Mrs. Reichert's stolen items. He did have a printer, though, and our tech specialists think it could have been used to print the picture of the Devil that Mr. Beck found stuffed in his mailbox. Fortunately, Mr. Beck saved it."

"The way I see it, you should definitely focus on the religious angle and forget about the previous suspects," Fritz said, "especially if they don't show any fundamentalist leanings. It's true that Mr. Böhm has a convincing motive and is a strict Catholic, but the Church of the Creator is in a completely different league."

"Besides, he has an alibi for his wife's murder. Federsen won't let us rule out the others, including Alexander Kramer's rival, Manuel Birkholz."

"Well, I don't know," Fritz said. "I wouldn't bother with the dealer or Birkholz. You should focus on the Church of the Creator and maybe Mr. Böhm too. Forget about the others. Don't waste your time chasing false leads."

That was easier said than done, since Federsen still had the final say. He decided which detectives explored what leads, and Hannes was currently sidelined. Evidently, his boss feared that the young detective could put another witness in danger with his reckless comments.

"Speaking of which, Anna got me thinking about the killer's possible religious motives," Hannes said. "There's a movie called *Seven* about a serial killer who is obsessed with the seven deadly sins and slaughters his victims for their respective transgressions. Maybe someone's copying the movie?"

"The seven deadly sins," Fritz said. "What are they again?"

"I wrote them down." Hannes pulled out a piece of paper. "Pride, avarice, envy, wrath, lust, gluttony, and sloth."

"Hmm. Lust might apply to Sylvia Böhm and Alexander Kramer. But what about Kramer's sister? The way you've described her to me, none of the seven deadly sins apply to her. Still, it's an interesting idea . . . So, there's still something between you and Anna?"

Fritz watched in amusement as Hannes's ears changed color. He winked when Hannes told him they were dating.

"Took you long enough. So when's the wedding?"

***

The distance between cloud nine and reality could be pretty short, as Hannes learned that afternoon.

Groaning, he wiped his mouth and looked at the remains of his lunch on the ground. The reason for this acute episode of nausea lay, his face blue, only a few feet away behind a bush. The shrubs grew on the edge of a parking lot which belonged to a paint manufacturer located in an industrial area near the highway.

This industrial park was ideally suited for the discreet disposal of a body. Hardly anyone wandered around this area after hours. Maria had no doubt that the body of Benjamin Lück had been lying there for several hours before it was found. And this time, the forensics team was lucky enough to discover several shoe prints in the soft ground which didn't match those of the corpse. It was, after all, very unlikely that New Way's public outreach coordinator had lain down behind that bush.

His tongue had been cut out with a blunt instrument while he was still alive and then shoved down his throat like a plug. There had been no chance for survival. He had on a suit. His eyes were closed, while the mouth still seemed to gasp desperately for air.

"Feeling better?" Federsen shot him a dirty look.

Hannes didn't bother answering. Although he had yet to get used to the violent reaction of his stomach at the sight of a fresh corpse, he was now able to recover quickly.

"The cause of death is clearly suffocation." Maria pulled her gloves off as she walked over to the group. "It must have occurred last night. Like the other victims, there's no evidence of a struggle. Presumably, he was sedated. I took a blood sample—maybe we'll find something."

"We still don't know whether or not it's the same killer," Federsen said and exhaled a cloud of smoke. "Lück was gay. Maybe he was cruising for sex?"

The rest of the group shook their heads. Apparently Federsen still thought gay men all met in secluded locations to have depraved sex.

"This isn't a known cruising spot," Marcel said. He had stuck bits of tissues in his nose to stanch bleeding brought on by this new development. Everyone had his or her own way of dealing with the sight of a dead body.

"Besides, he didn't hide the fact he was gay," said Hannes. "There are lots of other places where he could have found a partner."

"You seem to know what you're talking about," Federsen said. "I guess you're the right guy to investigate Mr. Lück's personal life. Find out if he had a boyfriend or arranged a hookup. But leave the members of New Way out of this one. We don't want to start a panic."

"How am I going to find out about his personal life? Besides the theater, New Way's the only clue we have. The group will find out soon enough once we talk to his stage colleagues."

"Well, talk only to a few key people, like maybe Mr. Beck and the manager of the theater where he worked. I want to wait until we get the autopsy report before we make people go crazy."

"Do you really think that's a good idea?" Marcel asked. "We might lose time that could be spent gathering valuable information."

"There was no one around last night who would have seen anything. And if they had, they'd have contacted us already. The man who found him stumbled upon him only because he wanted to take a leak behind the bush," said Federsen.

Hannes looked at Clarissa. "I just realized I've been here recently."

"Yeah," she confirmed. "Two Thursdays ago. We wanted to pay a visit to David Bach at his job and didn't know he only worked Monday through Wednesday."

"The company he works for is only two blocks away," said Hannes. "Coincidence?"

"Coincidence or not, we should investigate," Federsen said. "Dr. Stern, get this queer . . . um, this guy back to the lab as soon as possible."

Clarissa and Marcel went to visit Bach's work, while Isabelle and Hannes headed over to Mr. Beck's house and the theater, and Federsen and Per left to question Ludwig Obermann and Frank Meister from Church of the Creator.

Mr. Beck was just about to head to the group's weekly choir practice when Isabelle and Hannes showed up on his doorstep. To say that he was shocked to hear the news would be an understatement. His powerful shoulders slumped. He reluctantly agreed to keep the murder a secret but insisted that his community had the right to know.

"It's clear we're the target. Our members should be careful," he said. As far as he knew, Mr. Lück didn't have a boyfriend. He also hadn't been in contact with his family for years. They saw his homosexuality as a disgrace.

"Your theory isn't panning out," Isabelle said to Hannes as they headed from the Becks' house. Isabelle had interviewed the victim a few days before and asked whether he had received any threats or experienced any unusual incidents. He had said no. "The murders aren't obvious in advance. If they were, we'd be investigating the deaths of Mr. Beck or the Grafs today."

"Maybe it's not their turn yet," Hannes said. "Although Lück didn't mention anything, there may have been an incident. Maybe something scandalous he was ashamed of?"

"It's possible. Anyway, I think Federsen's decision not to inform the members of New Way is extremely dangerous. Four of them are dead. If someone drowns in a baptismal font tomorrow, he's to blame."

The theater was located close to the movie theater where Hannes had met Ben last Friday. He'd never been inside the impressive Art Nouveau building before. The manager's office, however, was a little more utilitarian. As expected, he reacted with shock at the news of Mr. Lück's death.

"Mr. Lück was supposed to star in Lars von Trier's *Antichrist*. Opening night's in two weeks," he said. "It's a tough piece, and he was given the lead. There's no way we'll find a replacement."

"Did you notice anything different about him lately?" Isabelle asked. "Was he anxious or upset?"

"You'll have to ask his colleagues; I don't work too much with the actors. I didn't notice anything. Just last week he mentioned that he was playing the role of Faust at New Way. He apparently led an amateur theater group there. He seemed very enthusiastic about it. He was also really looking forward to the premiere of *Antichrist*."

Isabelle and Hannes knew there was little sense in talking with someone who barely knew Mr. Lück, though it was worth noting that he was to star in a play called *Antichrist*. From the Church of the Creator's perspective, he certainly was the ideal candidate.

"Are his colleagues from the play here?" Isabelle asked. "They must have known him pretty well, having worked with him on a daily basis."

The manager looked at the clock. "Rehearsals should have started fifteen minutes ago. They're probably still waiting for him. Let me take you down. There are only two characters in the play—a married couple who have reached an emotional low point following the death of their son—so there's only one other actor. And of course the director."

Ilka Markwart's whole world seemed to implode when she learned of the news. Whether this was primarily due to her costar's death or the issues that it posed for the play's premiere remained unclear. Isabelle and Hannes spent the next few minutes trying to find out, but it took a while for both the actress and the director to regain their composure.

Both knew about Mr. Lück's involvement with New Way and described him as the same man the detectives had gotten to know: committed, cheerful, and thoughtful. But he seemed to lead a rather lonely existence outside of New Way, Ilka Markwart informed them. He hadn't been in a relationship since a nasty breakup with his boyfriend earlier that spring. He would often go to a gay club in the city.

"Do you remember the name of his ex-boyfriend?" Isabelle asked.

"Karl or Carlo, I think. But Benjamin usually just referred to him as 'my darling.'"

Lück had a small circle of friends, and the few names that Ms. Markwart and the director gave were all names of New Way members.

"I think the people in the group took advantage of him," Ms. Markwart said. "He worked his ass off for them—he handled the administration almost entirely on his own, but found few real friends. I got the feeling that his involvement was a kind of escape. It gave him a sense of purpose. It made the loneliness and emptiness a little easier."

Hannes wondered if Ms. Markwart spoke for herself and not Benjamin Lück. He had seemed anything but unhappy or lonely.

The investigators made all three of them promise to keep quiet about Lück's death. The manager pointed out, however, that he had to find a replacement as soon as possible and postpone the premiere.

At seven that evening, Steffen Lauer once again gathered all the detectives. His bald head dripped with sweat. He knew it was only a matter of time before the press would sound their next attack. Lauer decided on a further course of action after Isabelle and Hannes presented their meager findings.

"Detectives Niehaus and Hoffmann, visit this gay club tonight and ask around about Benjamin Lück, but be discreet. It might be a weeknight, but I'm sure at least some patrons will be there. And I'm putting an end to the secrecy. We can't have another death on our hands."

With these words, he glared at Federsen, while Hannes and Per anxiously stared at each other. Hannes saw his evening with Anna slowly fade; Per shot Marcel an imploring look. Federsen reported on his conversations with Ludwig Obermann and Frank Meister.

"Obermann has an ironclad alibi. He's laid up in bed with a broken leg and couldn't have cut out someone's tongue last night."

"Did a cross fall on his leg?" Isabelle joked to lighten the mood.

"Meister, on the other hand," Federsen continued, "can't prove where he was after eight, when he closed up the optician's shop where he works. He claims he went home, watched TV, and went to bed early."

"Dr. Stern, does that make him a suspect?" Steffen Lauer turned to Maria.

"Absolutely. The time of death was around ten last night. We found traces of Rohypnol in Lück's blood, which would explain why there's no evidence of a struggle. The drug was probably also used on Sylvia Böhm and Alexander Kramer. There was no sign that they had defended themselves or that the killer had to use force."

"Then why didn't you find any traces of the drug in those two?" asked Federsen.

"Rohypnol metabolizes quickly. Kramer hung alive on the cross for hours. And in the case of Mrs. Böhm, the killer probably waited for the effects to wear off before he injected her with the poison. He wanted her to be conscious so she would suffer just like Alexander Kramer."

"Clues?" Lauer asked.

"There were no traces of anything else in Benjamin Lück's body. The perpetrator's still being very cautious. Except for the footprints, forensics didn't find anything else."

"And that's where we come in," Clarissa said. "We paid a visit to the factory where David Bach works. It's a giant complex—you need to swipe an ID card to get in and out."

"What's that got to do with anything?" Federsen asked.

"I'll tell you if you let me finish," Clarissa snapped.

It had evidently been a trying day for her as well, and what little restraint she had seemed to crumble. The other investigators grinned, and even Steffen Lauer smirked.

"So, when we asked if anyone had seen Bach, they said no. When we asked if anything unusual had happened, they took us to a secluded area of the warehouse where they keep extra parts. Bach apparently knew about it, because he'd been hiding there for a couple of days."

Everyone began talking over one another in excitement.

"Unfortunately, he'd already hightailed it out of there," Clarissa continued, earning a disappointed sigh. "There was only a camping pad, sleeping bag, and some leftovers."

"How can you be so sure it was his hideout?" a red-faced Federsen asked. "It could have been some bum who hopped the fence."

"That's what the people at the factory had assumed," Marcel said. "But it would be pretty hard to jump the fence. So Clarissa came up with the idea of checking who'd swiped their card."

"Since I'm such a good listener," Clarissa said and glared at Federsen, "I remembered that they explained the ID system to us. And lo and behold, Bach was recorded entering the premises last Friday evening, the day we visited Frank Meister. It's highly likely Bach had hidden out at Meister's place until Friday. Since some idiot contacted Meister before visiting him, Bach had enough time to escape. Bach left the premises early yesterday morning and returned in the evening after the factory had closed. Seems he didn't want to risk being caught during the day. He entered the premises at exactly ten twenty, which possibly makes him the killer. He left the premises at five this morning and hasn't returned since."

"Because he doesn't want to be near the scene of the crime!" shouted Per.

"Just in case, we've posted a couple of guys in uniform there," Marcel said. "But there's one more thing: the workers must wear protective clothing when on the job, including special boots. We had them break open Mr. Bach's locker. The profile of his shoes doesn't match the print found at the crime scene, but the size does. He wears a ten and a half."

***

At first glance, La Bella Vita looked no different from other social hot spots. The gay club was located in a former warehouse and looked unassuming from the outside. At the entrance stood the obligatory bouncer; however, he wasn't the typical muscleman, but instead a polite and well-dressed middle-aged man. Hannes and Per introduced themselves as detectives investigating the murder of Benjamin Lück, which came as a shock to him. The doorman immediately assured them that the actor had never given him or the patrons any problems. He had last seen him two weeks ago. Lück had been a regular at La Bella Vita for many years, and the two men had talked from time to time. The bouncer was even familiar with Lück's religious views.

"He believed in God. He just never felt welcome in a church, which upset him. But he had that group, and it didn't seem to bother anyone. Only the neighbors weren't too friendly. Some fanatical church. He was even attacked last February—had his ponytail cut off."

"Come again?" Hannes blurted out. "He never told us that. He still had long hair."

"He got hair extensions. No one could tell."

"Did he say who it was?"

"He guessed it was people from that church. Benjamin didn't want to make a big deal out of the attack. He didn't want to fan the flames."

The bouncer confirmed that Lück was single. He had never seen a Karl or Carlo at the club, but then again, he didn't know all the patrons by name. He vaguely remembered Lück's mentioning something about a difficult relationship in the spring. The guy's name could have been Karl. The bouncer recommended that the detectives conduct their questioning undercover.

Hannes and Per passed through a heavy velvet curtain and entered the lobby. The cover charge was eight euros, and next to the cashier was the coat check. After they had taken off their thick winter jackets, Per looked at the metal staircase which led down to the club.

"So what's that? The dark room or something? I feel out of place here."

"Quit it," Hannes said and began to walk down the stairs.

Hannes paused after a few steps to take in the main area of the club. A long bar was situated behind the stairs, and the restrooms were down a hall next to the bar. Small square tables surrounded by leather armchairs lined the walls, and the dance floor was in the center of the room. The club was mostly empty, and the DJ had not started spinning; his booth was lit but deserted, and the strobe lights and lasers were off.

"Let's get a beer, then we'll talk to the boys. It's best if we split up."

"Are you crazy?" Per said. "If we stay together, maybe people will think we're a couple and leave us alone."

"Per, we're not here to be left alone. Start with the bartender. No one's going to hit on you."

"Fine." Per sighed. "I'll go get us some beer."

There was no hiding the stiffness in his legs as he awkwardly made his way to the bar. At least he wouldn't have to wait long. Hannes watched him in amusement and considered whom to question first. After a brief look around, he noted that there were maybe twenty people in a space meant to hold at least ten times that number. The majority stood in pairs, waiting for the night to get started. Hannes headed in the direction of a man leaning against a pillar. On his way over, he grabbed his beer from the bar.

"Pretty empty, huh?" Hannes said as he walked up to the forty-something man.

"It's still early," he said. "And things don't get too crazy here until Thursday."

"Do you come often?"

"Not really. Five or six times a month."

That didn't seem too infrequent to Hannes. He went out to a club maybe once a month.

"Then you must know half the people by name," he commented.

"Nah, I don't really care about names. But I recognize faces."

"Maybe you've met two of my friends before, Benjamin and Karl?"

"Doesn't ring a bell. But that doesn't mean I've never seen them."

Hannes wondered whether or not he should describe Benjamin Lück's appearance. The decision, however, was made for him when another man joined them and eyed the detective with suspicion. He placed a muscular arm around the man.

"What do you want?" His loud voice made the other bystanders turn their heads and look.

Hannes didn't want to cause a scene and put up his hands. "I'm just looking for a few friends of mine. My boyfriend and I are supposed to meet up with them tonight." He nodded at Per, who stood at the bar with a forced smile. He turned his shaved head, revealing his receding hairline and acne scars.

"Huh? That ugly weirdo's your boyfriend?" the man said and seemed even more suspicious.

Hannes shrugged and casually walked away. To drive his point home, he put his arm around Per's bony shoulders. Per cringed in fear, then sighed with relief when he recognized Hannes.

"The guy over there thought I was hitting on his boyfriend," Hannes whispered in Per's ear. "I had to say you were my boyfriend."

"Oh," Per said. "Well, then you've blown my cover. I let the bartender think I was single."

With a sigh, Hannes plopped down onto the bar stool next to his supposed boyfriend.

"I don't know if this was such a good idea. We can't go around chatting up random men and asking if they know Lück. Maybe he didn't even use his real name here."

"He did," Per said.

"How do you know?"

"Nico told me." He pointed at the bartender.

"See? You're not so lost here, are you?" Hannes said and grinned. "So Nico knew Lück?"

"Yeah, but he was better known as Benny. Nico works here every night and saw him at least once a week. But the name Karl doesn't ring a bell."

"Anything else?"

"Lück was always very reserved. He wasn't some wild dancer or Don Juan. He'd have a few drinks and mainly watch the scene on the dance floor. He'd come here from time to time with other guys, but he didn't seem to have a steady boyfriend."

Hannes thought for a moment as he took another swig. He turned to Nico and signaled for two more beers, which he quickly brought over.

"So Lück didn't come here to find one-night stands," Hannes said. "Does this Nico guy know anybody Lück hung out with here?"

"Like I said, he mostly kept to himself and was only here to blow off steam."

"What did you tell Nico when he asked why you were interested in Lück?"

"What do you think? Said I liked him and wanted to know if he was available."

The explanation seemed natural to Per. Hannes looked at him in surprise and approval, then swung around on his stool. Newcomers traipsed down the steel stairs in dribs and drabs, and the club gradually filled. Apparently, the club didn't have a specific target audience, because the crowd was very mixed in terms of age and attire. Hannes gathered up some courage. Talking to strangers wasn't one of his strengths, but that didn't matter. If he wanted to spend time with Anna that evening, they would have to start now. He reluctantly got up.

"Let's go, Per. Talk to as many guys as possible, and then we can get the hell out of here."

Without waiting, Hannes strolled off. He looked around, trying to assess the men. The scene didn't seem all that different from most straight clubs. A few were obviously looking for a quickie, some for the love of their life, and others just wanted to have fun. Meanwhile, the DJ had taken his place and upped the volume. Hannes walked over.

DJ Micky was wearing a loose yellow T-shirt and a gray cycling cap. He took his giant headphones off as Hannes leaned toward him.

"Say, Micky, do you take requests?" he asked.

"Yeah, sure. What do you want to hear?"

"'Bitter End' by Placebo?"

"No problem, I'll put it on next." He tried to put his headphones back on, but Hannes wasn't finished.

"Can I request something later? I'm waiting for a friend and want to surprise him with his favorite song. Maybe you know him. Benny. He comes here often."

"I don't know him. I get a lot of requests, can't make any promises." He ended the conversation by rummaging through his records.

Hannes was partially consoled by his music request which played shortly after. He looked around for Per, who was engaged in an animated conversation with a couple.

"You've got good taste!" a voice shouted into Hannes's ear.

He turned to see a smiling face.

"I saw you make that request to Micky. Bands like Placebo aren't played enough here."

"Thanks," Hannes said. The man was casually dressed and sported stubble on his chin.

"Don't come here often, do you?"

"Nope. My first time."

"I thought so."

"Why?"

"Because club rats notice everything. Newcomers always stick out."

"What do you mean?"

"Don't tell me you haven't noticed." He grinned and stuck out his hand. "Tommy. I'm here with my boyfriend and friends. They're standing over there. We've been having fun watching everyone look at you. They told me to come over and tell you to cut it out before you give all these horny guys blue balls."

Hannes laughed halfheartedly and looked over at Tommy's friends, who were all smirking. He guessed they were students, which Tommy confirmed. He was studying German and physical education. Hannes immersed himself in a lively discussion about training methods. Unfortunately, Tommy knew little about Lück. He did remember a man at the club who always looked a little lost or forlorn, but that was about it.

The music faded and a slight murmur arose. A sleek figure with long brown hair and green eyes marched across the dance floor toward Tommy and Hannes. Hannes's jaw dropped.

"I just wanted to see if I needed to save you from the clutches of these jealous men," Anna whispered mischievously in his ear.

"How'd you get here?"

"On the bus," she said and laughed. "I wouldn't miss this for the world."

"And they just let you in?"

"Why wouldn't they?"

"Because . . ."

Per walked over, and Hannes quickly introduced him. Per didn't seem surprised by Anna's presence and got straight to the point.

"Hannes, I've had enough. Let's get out of here. I really can't take it anymore."

"We still have a lot of people to talk to."

"I don't give a shit. If they know Benny, they all say the same thing: nice guy, a bit reserved, and that's it. Nobody's ever heard of a Karl or Carlo. We've done our duty."

"What's wrong? With a face like yours, no one's going to pounce on you anyway," joked Hannes.

"Shows what you know. Someone cornered me on my way out of the bathroom!" Per cried.

"Well, at least it wasn't *in* the bathroom," Hannes said.

Anna had a more convincing argument. She placed her hands around Hannes's head and directed his eyes to the cleavage visible under her pink top.

"Put your colleague out of his misery. Besides, I've got something else planned for us tonight. I'll show you something no one here can offer you . . ."

CHAPTER 18

Hannes scowled as he scanned the news the next morning. It had been a month since the cross was discovered. The police had decided to go public with the search for David Bach. The media had run photos of him for two days, but it had yet to prove useful. And a few editors with good contacts in the force were able to deduce a few facts about the murders. If coverage of the so-called Jesus Murder had died down over the past month, there was now renewed interest in the story.

"Religious Rampage?" read the headline on Hannes's tablet, and his appetite quickly disappeared. The article established a clear link among all four murders, and it was noted that the victims had been members of New Way. The group was cast in such a positive light that Hannes suspected the writer was an avowed atheist. And with that, their attempts to keep the group out of the limelight crumbled. There was even speculation about the use of Rohypnol—someone had obviously been unable to keep his or her mouth shut. Fearing a copycat, Steffen Lauer now had a patrol car regularly drive past New Way.

Potential witnesses kept calling the hotline, claiming to have seen David Bach. The detectives had been busy investigating every tip, but they all led nowhere. There hadn't been any time to chase down other leads. Efforts at pinpointing Bach's cell phone had also failed.

Benjamin Lück had last been seen alive by his colleagues at the theater. Rehearsals had taken place on Monday afternoon, only a few hours before the actor was murdered. Those who had known Lück described him as a nice man who'd been particularly close to a couple of people there. But Lück had evidently been pretty tight-lipped—only two men at the theater knew about the attack on him, and only one friend knew about his former boyfriend. Although the name Karl or Carlo didn't ring a bell, the friend did recall that Mr. Lück had once mentioned having a steady boyfriend at the time in question. They had dated for over a year but had never been seen together. Even the members of New Way were unaware if Mr. Lück had had a boyfriend or not, despite the fact that he was openly gay and often told others that "God loves me just the way I am."

In Clarissa's opinion, it wasn't a big surprise that Lück had not kept in contact with his family. She and Marcel had informed the parents of his death. Although Benjamin Lück had been an only child, his coming out had resulted in the family's estrangement. According to his mother, he had told them about "his disease," as she put it, on his thirtieth birthday and had adamantly refused to seek treatment. Her husband had sat next to her the entire time, never once opening his mouth; evidently, his son had been dead to him for almost fifteen years.

Hannes went with Per, Isabelle, and Federsen to search Lück's place. It was a one-bedroom apartment located in a somewhat dilapidated building. The furniture proved there wasn't money in acting. The walls were covered in theater posters illustrating the man's career. He didn't seem to place much value in collecting things other than high-end fashion, which became immediately obvious when they opened his closet.

Per rifled through a drawer of DVDs, pulled two out, and walked over to his colleagues with a grin.

"Either Mr. Lück was also interested in straight sex or he was fond of the group's new member."

"Those are the pornos Alexander Kramer starred in. Maybe he didn't just demonstrate his skills to Sylvia Böhm."

"I doubt that," Isabelle said and eyed the DVD covers. "He's gorgeous. A lot of people are into these metrosexual types. Lück was probably just looking for a little inspiration."

"Niehaus, have there been any rumors that Kramer was interested in men?" Federsen asked.

"I haven't heard any. But if he was, people at the studio certainly would have known. Is there any more straight porn in the drawer, Per?"

"No. Mostly just regular movies and gay porn."

A call to Paradise Images & Productions revealed that no one knew anything about any bisexual tendencies. Kramer's friends, Mirko and Jonas, were similarly skeptical when Per asked their opinions. Isabelle was probably right. Although Lück's phone showed that he had occasionally called Alexander Kramer, he had also contacted other members of New Way.

Frank Meister received yet another visit from the cops. This time, the investigators shoved a search warrant in his face and inspected every inch of his apartment. He watched in surprise as they thoroughly examined his shoes. He wore size eight and a half, meaning that the police couldn't place him at the scene of the last crime. Meister remained surprisingly calm for the duration of the search and only lost his cool when the police seized his laptop. The investigators didn't exactly know what they hoped to find on it, but sometimes a shot in the dark brought the desired result to light.

***

Hannes quickly put down his tablet when he heard the patter of Anna's bare feet across the floor of his bathroom. They had spent the last few nights alternating between apartments, but Hannes had been getting off work so late that he had usually found Anna fast asleep. At least that morning they could have breakfast together. Hannes was scheduled to see Fritz until ten that morning. Anna wrapped her arms around him from behind. Her hair smelled like his shampoo.

"Late night again?"

"Yeah. I thought about waking you up, but you looked so peaceful."

"Oh, I would have sprung back to life," she said and laughed, and her eyes fell on his tablet. "Are you obsessing over the case again?"

She made a point of placing the tablet facedown on a chair, and Hannes managed not to think about the killings for most of breakfast.

He was late arriving at the prison, but the precious few minutes he had gained with Anna were well worth it. Fritz had already spread his notes on the table and looked at him impatiently.

"They almost took me back to my cell. Where were you? We only have an hour now."

One look at Hannes's face revealed his reason. Fritz couldn't begrudge him for wanting to spend a few extra moments with Anna. He didn't press the subject. Instead, he let his investigative passions run free. He had also read about Lück's murder in the papers, and thanks to the heads-up, he was able to put two and two together before the reporters could. Still, he insisted that Hannes clarify the details, then shared his impressions.

"I've been thinking about your interviews with the members of New Way. Some of what they said is a little far-fetched, but there have been some unusual incidents. It all fits."

"What fits?"

"Listen, your new girlfriend's comment about that movie on the seven deadly sins got me thinking. You said that New Way uses the Ten Commandments as their guiding principles, right?"

"Yeah, they even have them displayed on the wall."

"So what are they?"

"Um . . . You shall not kill, you shall not steal, you shall not . . ." Hannes struggled.

"I'll help you." Fritz slammed a piece of paper onto the table. "I've listed the incidents in chronological order. Let's start with the Third Commandment: 'Remember to keep holy the Sabbath.' Think. Who in the group hasn't obeyed the Sabbath?"

"I don't understand what you're getting at. None of the victims—"

"The man's still alive. Wolfgang Hartmann. The department store owner who's been protesting against mandatory closures on Sunday. His phone rang constantly on Sundays for a month this past summer. Get it?"

"You mean . . ."

Fritz was in full swing and slapped down a second piece of paper.

"The Seventh Commandment: 'You shall not steal.' Didn't your colleague Clarissa arrest one of the members several times for theft?"

"Beatrice Reichert, the former ballet dancer."

"There you go. And she herself was robbed. Oddly enough, only her favorite mementos were taken. That probably upset her far more than if expensive things were taken. Now the Fourth Commandment: 'Honor your father and your mother.' What stands out to you?"

Hannes stared blankly at him. "Mrs. Brinkmann. Her children want nothing to do with her. But then her children would be punished, not her."

"Mrs. Brinkmann also mentioned that she hardly goes to visit her parents at the nursing home. A little later, her own children receive a letter, after which they want nothing to do with her. Weird, right?"

"Yeah, but isn't that a little far-fetched?"

"Maybe. Let's wait and see. The Ninth Commandment is 'You shall not covet your neighbor's house.' The Grafs are trying to kick out their tenants so they can renovate their buildings and jack up the rent. Then their house burns down in early October."

Fritz rummaged through his small stack of papers and pulled out a fifth sheet. He was so excited that his ears were red.

"Now think about the murder victims. The First Commandment is 'I am the Lord your God. You shall have no other gods before me.'"

"Which includes Celtic gods, of course." Hannes eagerly leaned forward. "Antje Kramer was fascinated by Celtic mythology and even performed ceremonies. She was probably performing one when she ate the poisoned mushrooms. She also shared her fascination with others in the group."

"That's why the druidess had to die." Fritz nodded. "Just like her brother. He broke the Tenth Commandment: 'You shall not covet your neighbor's wife.' He was a ladies' man, both in his professional and personal life. And Sylvia Böhm was married."

"Isn't there also another commandment against cheating?"

"The Sixth: 'You shall not commit adultery.' She's also guilty of the Fifth: 'You shall not kill.'"

Confused, Hannes looked at him. "She didn't kill anyone."

"She had an abortion. That's probably why poison was injected into her abdomen."

"Right," said Hannes in fascination. "That would make sense. But what about Mr. Lück? As far as I know, there's nothing in the Ten Commandments about not being gay."

"Well, some hard-liners would say that it's implicit. But there's also the Second Commandment, which forbids taking the Lord's name in vain. Mr. Lück made no secret of the fact that he was gay. He also would always say—"

"That God didn't hate him, but loved him just the way he was." Hannes was amazed. All this made sense and was an unlikely coincidence. His head was spinning, and he stared at the list in front of him as he sorted through his thoughts and the Ten Commandments. "No commandment has been broken twice. If your theory's correct and it's been the same killer the whole time, then he's selected someone for each broken commandment. And that means there's still one missing."

"Or two," said Fritz. "So far as we know, we can only attribute one commandment to each victim, except for Mrs. Böhm. But if we say that she was killed for breaking the Fifth Commandment, then there are two more commandments left for which there are no victims."

"One I know: 'You shall not commit adultery.' But what's the other?"

Fritz pushed the last piece of paper toward him. "The eighth: 'You shall not bear false witness against your neighbor.' Either no one has broken that commandment yet or there's been an incident we don't know about. But I wouldn't count on the killer picking just one victim for each commandment. It could be pure coincidence that there's only been one for each so far. When he gets to the last commandment, he might start from the beginning again."

Hannes only half listened. He stared at the list and another thought popped into his head. He quickly shuffled through the papers to reorder them, then looked up at Fritz.

"If we arrange the incidents and murders chronologically, does anything stand out to you?"

Fritz rubbed the scar on his left cheek as he carefully examined the notes through his rectangular frames. Then he nodded and glanced at Hannes.

"They keep getting crueler. In July, harassing phone calls, relatively harmless. Then the mementos were stolen in August, which caused Mrs. Reichert emotional distress. And Mrs. Brinkmann likely experienced even more pain when her children stopped talking to her after the letter was sent in September."

"And in early October, the Grafs' property was damaged," Hannes said. "Maybe it was even attempted murder. It was sheer luck that the Grafs weren't in the burning house. Then by mid-October the first victim's killed: Alexander Kramer."

Fritz shook his head. "Who knows? Maybe he wasn't supposed to die. After all, the killer attached a footrest to the cross. The goal was either to make him suffer longer—"

"Or the perp assumed he'd be found in time."

"But then he realized how easy it was to kill and started to enjoy it. And thus the fate of Mrs. Böhm was sealed. Otherwise, maybe a few of her horses would have been poisoned."

"It's possible we don't know about every incident," Hannes said. "But we wouldn't have overlooked any deaths. The increasing cruelty over time supports our theory. But where do the attacks on Benjamin Lück and Thomas Beck fit into all this? They're not in your notes."

"That's true. However, it is conceivable that the attack on Mr. Lück was meant to be a warning. Maybe something similar happened to the victims, and we just don't know. If that's the case, then more people are in danger. Especially Mr. Beck, since he's already had several incidents."

"He's also sort of the group's unofficial leader," Hannes added. "With the death of Lück, the public outreach coordinator has been silenced. It's possible that the spiritual leader will soon follow. I wonder if . . ."

Hannes furrowed his brow as he weighed various possibilities. Fritz watched him intently.

"If I were the killer and considered New Way a personal affront to my deeply held religious beliefs and decided to wage war, where would I start? Sure, with the leaders. Mr. Beck and Mr. Lück make sense. Maybe Alexander Kramer, since his films gave him an audience. Maybe even Sylvia Böhm, because she organized a lot of the group's activities. But the others? The Grafs, for example, aren't in any sort of leadership role. On the other hand, the Schweigers are. Yet their somewhat conservative views don't seem all that in step with the group's stated principles."

"And so far, they haven't experienced any cause for concern. But maybe that's the reason why? Maybe in the eyes of the killer, they're not blasphemers?"

Hannes nodded as he took it all in. "True. But the killer would have to be intimately familiar with the lives of the members. He'd have to know that Mrs. Brinkmann 'banished' her parents to a nursing home. Or that Mrs. Reichert is a kleptomaniac. I doubt Mrs. Böhm told the whole world about her abortion. But at the same time, there's a lot of openness at New Way. Everyone's there because they're looking for a community that doesn't judge, where everyone shares their values. People know a lot about each other. Maybe the killer has an informant in the group. Or . . ."

"He was—or is—a member of New Way."

***

A number of journalists milled about outside the station. Lauer felt forced to hold a press conference to put an end to the wild speculation and counter the impression that the police were not on top of the situation. He had initially chosen Federsen to participate in the press conference, then changed his mind. Federsen was uncontrollable. It was feared that he wouldn't hold up under cross-examination from the press.

The last few minutes served only to validate his decision. Federsen had spent the entire morning lambasting every member of the team until Lauer had to intervene. Even Marcel didn't escape Federsen's wrath, and he was only a rank below the ornery detective. Lauer sighed. He had chosen Federsen over Marcel because of his age and experience, but the man seemed incapable of controlling his anger. He briefly took him aside and explained the seriousness of the situation.

"Henning, if you keep behaving like a rabid dog, I'll put Marcel in charge of the investigation. You can't treat your team like that. That's it."

"A bunch of amateurs," Federsen said. "How am I supposed to catch a serial killer with them?"

"You are not the only one who would prefer that this case be solved today rather than tomorrow, and I don't even want to think about what would happen if there's another victim. But I don't get the sense that your team's overwhelmed. Detective Niehaus just presented a brand-new theory. And in thanks you insult him in front of the entire team. How's your team supposed to explore every angle when they're only going to be met with ridicule?"

"Ridiculous," Federsen said. "A religious serial killer who's imitating a mass murderer from a horror movie? This isn't the US."

"The connection to the Ten Commandments sounds logical. It doesn't matter if the film was the inspiration for the killer, or if the killer came up with the pattern on his own. It may seem unlikely that there's an informant in New Way, but this is a lead that should have been investigated a long time ago. Be happy that someone's finally looking at the bigger picture. Let's head back inside. And pull yourself together. Marcel will join me at the press conference. I don't need you insulting anyone on camera."

He turned and opened the door to the conference room. Five officers stared at him as he returned to the room with Federsen in tow. The detectives had all been amazed when Hannes presented his theory regarding the Ten Commandments. Finally: a clear motive. Hannes was a little uncomfortable with the admiration it had earned. After all, Fritz did play an important part in this new break. But he of course had to keep that to himself and outwardly basked in the praise. Only Federsen had rained on his parade, calling it "a preposterous, harebrained idea."

The banter subsided as Lauer asked for attention and gave everyone their marching orders.

"Review everything you've got, and keep Detective Niehaus's theory in mind as you do. Then focus on the main suspects. We can't waste time with lukewarm leads. Marcel will join me at the press conference. I'll speak to the chief about what information we should reveal and how to proceed."

Federsen glowered until Lauer left the room. The other investigators kept glancing at him. There was no doubting the nature of the conversation outside the room.

"Let's start with Manuel Birkholz," Federsen said and nodded to Marcel.

"He's decided to cooperate, which is good for him. He couldn't have killed Mr. Lück because he has an airtight alibi for Monday night. He gave us the names of the two women he spent the night with. They weren't very pleased because . . . well, let's just say they're wives of two well-known individuals. We promised them discretion, and they confirmed that Birkholz didn't leave the house until two o'clock in the morning. One of the women said he was also with her on the night of the crucifixion. Her husband was on a business trip."

Hannes breathed a sigh of relief. It was in his interest that Birkholz be ruled out as a potential suspect on account of his careless remarks about Antje Kramer. The situation had brightened for Daniel Novak as well. The dealer was able to produce several credible witnesses to vouch for his whereabouts on the night Benjamin Lück choked on his own tongue. Novak had gone to his team's soccer practice, then got drunk at a bar with several teammates. A taxi driver confirmed that he had driven the plastered Novak home around two o'clock in the morning. Some of the investigators wanted to cross him off the list. Federsen said no because there was still no evidence to suggest that the recent killings hadn't been committed by several culprits.

For this same reason, Mr. Böhm also remained on the list. After all, he had a clear motive, at least for the murder of his wife and her lover. And as Marcel explained, there was a growing body of evidence against him in the tax-fraud case. But it had also been suggested that he could have lowered his tax debt in an entirely legal manner using a loophole. According to Mr. Böhm, he had been at home the night Benjamin Lück died. His employee Jonas Talmann had spent the night on the farm with the veterinarian helping to bring a foal into the world.

Both had confirmed that they had seen lights on in the house. Since Böhm wore a size twelve shoe, it was highly doubtful that he had left the footprint at the scene.

Then the investigators turned their focus to the Church of the Creator. The longer they discussed the Ten Commandments theory, the more convinced they were that the idea was the most promising lead they had. David Bach had fled; he didn't have an alibi for any of the murders; and he had a history of violence which suggested he was capable of committing such acts. However, doubts remained as to whether he'd acted alone.

"From what we know about him, he's easy to manipulate," said Isabelle. "He was probably glad to belong to a group that sees everything in black and white."

"Who is he closest to at the church?" Marcel asked.

"Frank Meister and possibly Ludwig Obermann," Clarissa said. "It's a little unclear what goes on inside that church. So far we've been unable to determine how it's structured or what its dynamics are like. They have a lot of members, but everyone's refusing to talk."

With his broken leg, Ludwig Obermann could only hobble around on crutches and was downgraded to a person of interest. It was possible he had constructed the wooden cross, which would make him an accomplice. Frank Meister was more difficult to write off.

"So far we can't pin anything on him, but he and Bach are close friends," said Per. "Evidently, he's the most intelligent of the three and indoctrinated in the Church of the Creator's ideology. He plays a very active role in the church and is as much a spiritual firebrand as the minister, Ahrendt. But he doesn't seem like the type who would get his hands dirty."

For that reason, Hannes voted that the minister shouldn't be written off either. While the older gentleman might have been physically incapable of committing the murders, he could still be the one pulling the strings.

Marcel looked at the list of potential suspects. "We can't ignore the incidents before the murders either. Bach could have used the printer in his apartment to print out that image of the Devil."

"We've also examined the letter sent to Mrs. Brinkmann's children," Hannes said. "Our experts are confident it was printed by the same model."

"How common is the model?"

"Pretty common, unfortunately. It's one of those all-in-one printers that lets you print, copy, scan, and fax. They're sold all over the place."

The investigation into the arson of the Grafs' house had yet to be closed. Isabelle had taken a closer look at the evidence and came across an important detail.

"Footprints were found in their yard. And—wait for it—the print is identical to the one at the scene of Benjamin Lück's murder. Of all the suspects we've mentioned so far, only one of them wears the right shoe size: David Bach. We went back to his apartment and checked all his soles again. Unfortunately, none of them matched."

"Well, that finally proves that the killer committed the arson," Hannes said. "Our theory's true."

"Still, the killer couldn't have acted alone," said Marcel. "From what we know about Bach, he's impulsive and not very intelligent. The killings were all meticulously planned. I'm convinced he's not acting alone."

"The bottles used to start the fire were beer bottles," Isabelle said. "Unfortunately no fingerprints were found. But the brand doesn't have a very wide distribution, and two of these bottles were found in Ludwig Obermann's refrigerator. He claimed not to drink beer and said Bach had brought them to a barbecue. His fingerprints were found on them."

However, there weren't any worthwhile leads with the break-in or the harassing phone calls. Mrs. Reichert had never reported the burglary to the police, and the phone calls Wolfgang Hartmann had received could no longer be traced. The telephone company had its own theory. If it wasn't a harmless prank, then the calls were probably made using a prepaid cell phone. The number could be traced, but usually not to a name. Although the law required the name and address of anyone who purchased a SIM card, the information was rarely compared against the buyer's ID.

It had also yet to be determined who was behind the anonymous complaint against Thomas Beck. The accusation that he was working as a psychiatrist without the appropriate credentials had been received in an envelope with no return address. The postmark showed only that the letter had been mailed from downtown.

Benjamin Lück hadn't reported the assault to the police either. His hairdresser confirmed that the actor had gotten hair extensions in February. However, he didn't remember Lück ever mentioning that he was attacked.

"What scares me the most," Isabelle said, "is that other members of New Way could be next."

The stunned silence suggested that Isabelle had just voiced what was on everyone else's minds. At that moment, Steffen Lauer walked into the room and was given a quick rundown.

"Someone should attend New Way's meeting tonight and talk to people," he said. "We need to stress that we're working very hard to solve the case and will do whatever's necessary to protect them. Any volunteers?"

As expected, the enthusiasm was muted. Since Hannes assumed Elke would be attending the meeting, he hesitantly raised his hand. Isabelle glanced over and reluctantly volunteered as well. Marcel, who had already thought he was off the hook, soon found himself roped in as well. That must have put a damper on the start of his weekend with his family. But Lauer thought it essential for a more senior detective to attend. And since it would be such a sensitive undertaking, Federsen was ruled out.

"I think Detective Niehaus's theory is the most compelling," Lauer said. "From now on, we'll pursue anyone who might be religiously motivated. The search for David Bach has the highest priority. We should also take a closer look at the Church of the Creator and its members. But let's not forget one thing: the killer's familiar with the members of New Way. Maybe he knows one of them. Although nothing suggests someone from New Way's actively involved in the murders, there might be someone who's helped gather information on the victims. Look for connections."

"Rebecca Köhler!" shouted Clarissa. "She dated David Bach long enough."

Lauer nodded, then looked at his watch and sighed. He only had twenty minutes to discuss the press conference with Marcel. It was days like today that made him wish he had followed his childhood dream of becoming a bus driver.

***

New Way's meeting that Friday night was packed. When the police arrived, everyone present knew that the evening would be different. Marcel was still sweating a little because the press conference had been chaotic. He excused himself to the bathroom and carefully dabbed his nose bleed. He was afraid that his face might appear in the evening news. The task that now lay before him was not any easier than talking to the press. Exhausted, he explained the evening's strategy to Isabelle and Hannes.

"I'll talk to everyone later. But first I'd like to talk to the board members in private. Hannes, mingle with the crowd and see what you can find out. Isabelle, talk with Bach's ex."

The three investigators split up and were bombarded with feverish questions. Hannes found Elke standing in a corner and casually made his way over.

"Still can't be persuaded not to join?" he asked quietly.

She smiled and shook her head. "Pretty exciting. I even filled out a membership form today. The choir group's really nice. I'd forgotten how much fun singing is. Besides, I get along with a few of the people. I think this is exactly what I was looking for."

Hannes sighed. He shared his theory with her, but even though he swore her to secrecy, he didn't disclose any more information than necessary. Still, it was enough for Elke to lose her cool.

"You think someone's punishing the members for breaking the Ten Commandments? Where would the killer get all this information?"

"Is there anyone here who doesn't have an antagonistic relationship with the Church of the Creator? Maybe the information's coming from inside the group."

"That's absurd. The Church of the Creator isn't held in particularly high regard here."

"Have you noticed any factions? Like stricter people versus free spirits?"

Elke thought for a moment. "Sure, the Schweigers. They sing in the choir and don't hide their disapproval of other members. They claim the moral high ground. They didn't like the guy killed on the cross, for example."

"Do they hang out with anyone in particular?"

"I don't get the impression that they have a better rapport with other people. Although, Mrs. Brinkmann seems to get along with them pretty well. But anyway, I find it hard to believe they'd pass on information to a killer."

"Might not be that way. It's possible Rebecca innocently told her ex-boyfriend a lot about the people here. Isabelle's questioning her now. We have to explore all possibilities."

"Now that I know what you're looking for, I can listen more closely to what people say. There's a choir getaway for two nights on the second weekend of Advent. Since Mr. Lück . . . well, a spot's opened up, so I'll be going. Maybe I'll hear something."

Hannes urged Elke to be cautious and reveal as little as possible.

"Does anyone know you're gay yet?"

"I mentioned it to Rebecca. She also sings in the choir, and we've become friends."

"Tell her to keep it strictly to herself."

Hannes hoped she would heed his warning. With Elke, he never knew.

***

Isabelle and Rebecca had walked up to the office on the second floor, where they could talk without being disturbed. She came across as being easily intimidated, and Isabelle was careful not to press her too hard. Apparently, she had located the leak through which all the internal information from the group flowed to the prime suspect.

"So you say Mr. Bach was interested in the members here. Did it strike you as odd? After all, you knew he didn't have a very high opinion of your group."

"Yeah, he always yelled at me, saying I had no business being here," a frightened Ms. Köhler whispered. "I tried to defend the people here, to prove that they're not so bad. And whenever David wasn't in a bad mood, I was glad he was taking an interest in my life."

"Did you tell him anything about the backgrounds of the members?"

"He already knew about some of them."

"For example?"

"That Alex starred in pornos and that Thomas Beck used to be a Catholic priest."

"What else?"

"He criticized Wolfgang for wanting to open his store on Sundays even though it's supposed to be a holy day. Said homosexuality was promoted here—by that he meant Benjamin Lück."

"What did you think?"

"I tried to defend them. But he would just yell at me, saying I'd been corrupted. I liked how Benjamin used to say that God loved him just the way he was, gay or not."

Isabelle stared at her in alarm. "Did you say that to your boyfriend?"

She nodded. Of course, she could put two and two together. It was bad enough her boyfriend was apparently behind the murders. What made her feel worse was that she had delivered him the necessary information. There were tears in her eyes, and even Isabelle had to take a few deep breaths.

Once more Isabelle went over all the information Ms. Köhler had given Bach. The woman grew more and more distraught, which made it increasingly harder for her to remember. Nevertheless, it was clear that she had provided her ex-boyfriend with enough information to give him a pretty good picture of the members. Isabelle even ventured to guess that this was the only reason he had become involved with Rebecca Köhler in the first place.

"What was I thinking?" she wailed and buried her face in her hands.

Isabelle sat down beside her and placed her arm around Ms. Köhler's shoulders. "Don't blame yourself. How could you have known that he—"

"But I knew that he was violent and was getting more and more fanatical!" she cried. "I hate myself for not breaking up with him the moment I realized that. Instead, I took advantage of my friends' trust. Alex, Sylvia, Benjamin, Thomas, Melissa . . ."

"Melissa?" asked Isabelle. She didn't recognize the name.

"Melissa Vogt. She's a trainer. She sometimes teaches fitness classes here and was especially close to Sylvia. She always comforted me whenever I had problems with David. She'd tell me he wasn't worth it, that it'd be easy for me to find someone else. But I'm . . . I'm pretty shy. She gave me tips on how to meet men."

"So your boyfriend must have been angry with Melissa."

"I didn't tell him about that. But David was always jealous, for no reason. I once told him that he shouldn't worry because I wasn't like Melissa."

"What did you mean by that?"

"Melissa's married, and her husband is the head of a construction project in Tunisia. She . . . well, she stretched the definition of fidelity and would occasionally tell stories about the men she slept with."

Isabelle breathed slowly. She was aware that the Ten Commandments prohibited adultery, and that no victim had been assigned to that commandment yet.

In the meantime, Marcel had gathered the group's board, which after the death of Mr. Lück had shrunk to four people, the Becks and Schweigers. But another man had joined the group: Bernd Graf, the owner of the burned house. Marcel guessed he was in his midforties. He wore a suit and rimless glasses, and his hair was meticulously parted. His pursed lips indicated that humor wasn't one of his strong suits. When Marcel asked whether any members were on good terms with the Church of the Creator, his question was met with collective headshaking.

"Absolutely not," Mr. Beck said. "The lines have been drawn. I've tried more than once to speak to the pastor over there in an attempt to reach some sort of civil compromise. After all, we do profess belief in the same fundamental values. The discussions went nowhere."

"Have any members left New Way? We've heard that some are toying with the idea."

"Fortunately, no," Mrs. Schweiger said. "We've even gained a new member. The young woman over there with the long blonde hair joined today. Her name's Elke Weber."

Marcel looked at Elke standing in her skintight jeans. He was surprised that someone would voluntarily join the group given the current situation.

"What was the group like before the murders? Are there any former members who've turned their back on the group? Anyone you've maybe had problems with?"

"We've only had six people leave since the group was established ten years ago," replied Mrs. Schweiger. As a founding member of the group, she was well versed in its institutional history. Of the former members, two had died several years ago. Marcel's ears perked when he heard this, but Mr. Schweiger reassured him that the deaths had been the result of a heart attack and old age. One woman and a couple had left New Way because they had moved for work reasons, and none of them had left on bad terms.

"What about the sixth person?" asked Marcel and glanced at Hannes, who had joined the conversation.

The detectives noticed an uneasy exchange of glances.

Mr. Beck said, "Carlos di Santo. He was a founding member. He has a very difficult personality. He suffered from depression and—"

"He's a real know-it-all," Mrs. Schweiger said. "He was treasurer and always wanted to enforce his opinion. If something didn't go his way, he'd immediately take offense. He left last March."

"What precipitated his departure?" asked Hannes.

Once again, the members exchanged sheepish glances.

"Frankly, we asked him to leave," Mr. Schweiger said. "He poisoned the atmosphere with constant fights. Then came—"

"There were some financial irregularities," Bernd Graf said. "I took over as treasurer, and I've never seen such messy bookkeeping in my life. Receipts were missing or incorrectly filed. He couldn't explain what had happened to 2,000 euros. Maybe it was just sloppiness, but . . ."

"You mean he embezzled the money?"

"We have no proof," Mr. Beck said. "Since Carlos was unable to give a satisfactory reply and on account of the general negative feeling toward him, we suggested he reconsider his membership."

"How did he react?" asked Marcel.

"Um, well . . ." Mr. Beck stared at the ground. "There was an ugly scene, and he said things he perhaps shouldn't have said. We haven't heard much more from him since. Maybe we should have been more sensitive . . . After all, he was depressed and—"

"We dealt with him for far too long," Mrs. Schweiger said. "If it had been up to me and my husband, we would have kicked him out long before that. Maybe then the 2,000 euros wouldn't have gone missing."

She glared at the chaplain, who obviously felt bad about it. Isabelle joined them too and nodded to her colleagues. Marcel and Hannes caught the signal, and the investigators excused themselves and moved off to the side to share what they had learned.

Marcel pointed to the group's new member. "I find it strange that this Elke Weber is just now joining the group, even though there's speculation in the press about a crusade against New Way."

Hannes cleared his throat. His colleagues' eyes bulged when he told them about Elke.

"That could play perfectly into our hands," Marcel said. "Nobody here knows she's friends with you, right?"

Hannes nodded.

"Do you think she could ask a few questions without raising suspicion? We need to know if there have been any other incidents. It's in these people's interest."

"She already sees herself as an undercover agent," Hannes said. "But I'm uncomfortable with the idea. Elke's gay, and I don't think we should play with fire. Not after Mr. Lück."

"Then tell her to be cautious about what she tells people," Isabelle said. "The best thing for her to do is come across as morally irreproachable."

"I'd advise the same," Marcel agreed. "Anyway, we confirmed that Rebecca Köhler was in fact the leak. I'm satisfied with our results."

Marcel addressed the gathered members. Although he confirmed the need for increased vigilance, his thoughtful and reassuring choice of words succeeded in dispelling the feeling that the police were in the dark. It was thanks to him that the evening ended so successfully.

After that, the board members stood up and announced that the group would be canceling all public activities. This also included the play. Even the traditional Christmas bazaar was axed. The members seemed glad that appropriate action was finally being taken in light of the murders. Only the group's regularly scheduled activities would continue, as well as the choir getaway.

Exhausted but satisfied, the detectives stood in front of New Way. There was an ugly cloud on the horizon.

"We can forget about our weekends," said Marcel. "We have a ton of work to do. I'll call Clarissa and Per . . . and Henning. We'll meet tomorrow at ten, then divvy up duties."

"We can at least still enjoy Friday night," Isabelle said to Hannes as Marcel called Federsen. She was surprisingly well dressed and even wore a touch of makeup.

But Hannes shook his head. For him, there was only one way to enjoy the evening, and Anna was waiting for him at her apartment. He quickly ran off to hail a taxi and didn't notice the disappointed look on Isabelle's face as she watched him leave.

CHAPTER 19

I've done so much already. All in your name. Exactly according to your will. All to set them back on the right path. To fight depravity. But they don't understand. Don't want to understand. Was I not clear enough? In the beginning, I was too kind. That's over now. Those who do not seek mercy deserve none. Those who deserve no mercy, receive none. I will judge on your behalf. If only they knew what I know. Lord, I will not let them drag your name through the mud. I will not let them challenge your glory. I am your instrument. May I do your will.

CHAPTER 20

Carlos di Santo, New Way's former treasurer, seemed to have been expecting the police that Saturday morning. He opened the door as soon as Hannes flashed his badge in the hallway of the four-story apartment building.

"Finally," Mr. di Santo said as he shuffled back into the apartment.

Isabelle and Hannes shot each other surprised looks and followed him through a dark hallway into a spacious living room. He must have been homesick, because evidence of his Argentinian origins were all over the room. Above the sofa hung the blue and white national flag, and since the World Cup wasn't taking place at the moment, it seemed to be a permanent installation. An oversize map of Argentina hung next to the flag. Most of the colonial-style furniture was made of dark teak, and the already somewhat faded color photographs on the walls showed the diverse landscapes of home. Only the large Persian rug seemed out of place.

The apartment was meticulously tidy. The unmistakable odor of cleaning agents hung in the air. Equally as immaculate was di Santo. His fingernails were precisely cut, and his pants had sharp creases down the legs. His patent leather shoes were polished to a brilliant shine.

He pointed to a black leather sofa, and the detectives sat down. Di Santo fiddled with a glass carafe in which floated several orange slices. His hands shook slightly as he filled three glasses. He wore a salmon-colored sweater and gray slacks. His face was framed by a dark mane which faded into a trimmed beard. Melancholic brown eyes stared from under thick, bushy eyebrows.

"Glad you take it seriously," he said and sat down.

"Of course we take this seriously," a confused Hannes replied. "I'm surprised you were expecting us."

Di Santo took a sip from his glass and pursed his lips. "What do you mean? I called the police yesterday. I was beginning to think no one was coming."

"Wait. Why did you call?"

"Because of my neighbors, of course. They keep making noise. I couldn't sleep. Not only do they trash the hallway, but—"

"Mr. di Santo, there's been a misunderstanding. We're not here because of a disturbance. We're investigating four deaths and have a few questions for you."

Di Santo stared in astonishment. The trembling in his hands grew worse. "Doesn't surprise me. No one will clamp down. I've tried."

"What have you tried?" asked Isabelle.

"To maintain order. There's no order here. The entrance is always blocked, kids are always screaming, people grill in the courtyard, there's always drilling and hammering, fighting, shouting, and the basement . . ."

"Mr. di Santo," Isabelle said, but he stared straight ahead and continued.

"Strollers in the stairwell, the trash is always overflowing, the laundry room . . ."

"Mr. di Santo," Hannes said.

The man jumped. He turned to look at Hannes, his eyes framed by a pair of silver-rimmed glasses. He ran his trembling hand through his hair and blinked.

"You've reported all that to the police?"

Mr. di Santo nodded. "Over and over. In the beginning, someone from the police would come. Now nobody comes. The neighbors call me names, and nobody does anything."

Isabelle rolled her eyes and glanced at Hannes.

"We're not here about your problems with the neighbors," Hannes said. "I'm sure you've read in the papers about the recent killings. It's been mentioned that the victims were all members of New Way. You were treasurer there until March, and we hope you can help us."

"Some new way," Mr. di Santo said. "It was my way. I was a part of it from the beginning. I've always tried to help, but everyone just thinks about themselves."

"Why did you leave?" asked Isabelle.

"I didn't leave!" he shouted in a booming voice. "They claimed I stole money and wreaked havoc. They were the ones who wreaked havoc."

"Who wreaked havoc?"

"The others. Sabine, Markus, Thomas, Sylvia, Antje . . . Benjamin."

"Benjamin? Benjamin Lück? What do you mean by 'havoc'?"

Mr. di Santo took a deep breath. "We wanted to do something different. No church, no religion. The Ten Commandments, fine, whatever, we kept those. But otherwise, we wanted to do things differently. But then they just did what they wanted. It became more and more like a church. They even got a priest. How's that different from church? Some even wanted to have him hear confessions. Dangerous. I know how the Church is. I had to go to Mass all the time as a kid in Buenos

Aires. I hated it. But the priest liked me. Really liked me. You understand? That shouldn't happen."

Hannes nodded in embarrassment and tried to make sense of what
happened. He could imagine that the group's books were a total mess
because of this man, who had evidently just indicated that he had been
abused as a child by a priest—which would explain his pronounced
aversion to ecclesiastical institutions.

"You mean that some members wanted to turn New Way into some
kind of church?" Hannes asked. "But it's supposed to be an alternative.
Live and let live."

"*Pfsh.*" He snorted. "It used to be like that. They were so clever
that no one noticed. It happened bit by bit, surreptitiously. The Ten
Commandments became increasingly important. They're all hypocrites.
No one's perfect."

"Who tried to make the group more religious?"

"A lot of people. I have to think about it."

"Who do you think killed the members?"

"I can't say. There are a lot of people who don't like New Way."

"But no one specifically comes to mind?"

He shook his head. "I have nothing more to do with the group. But
let me think about it. Maybe something will come to me."

"That would be good," said Hannes and handed him his card.
"Don't take this the wrong way, but I have to ask you where you were
last Monday evening."

"I am always here. I only go out to go grocery shopping. There are
a lot of bad people out there."

Mr. di Santo had no verifiable alibis for the times of the killings.

"Don't you work?" asked Isabelle.

He stared at the floor. "I used to be an engineer, but I've been
unable to work for two years."

Isabelle and Hannes asked about his relationships with the murder
victims, but it was impossible to tell whether he liked them or not on

account of his gibberish. In any case, Alexander Kramer had joined after Mr. di Santo's departure. The man appeared frustrated to have been forced out of New Way, and Hannes realized Mr. di Santo had lost the one thing he could hold on to. There was little help for a person incapacitated by depression. The twenty minutes of questions seemed to have exhausted him. As Isabelle slipped on her brown suede jacket on their way out, she suddenly stopped.

"Take a look at that photo," she whispered as they stood in front of a small dresser. Hannes gasped in surprise.

They headed back to the station, where they told their colleagues about their visit.

"There was a series of small photos on the dresser in his hallway," Hannes said. "Guess who was in them."

"Out with it already," said Federsen. "This isn't a quiz show."

"There were four portraits of Benjamin Lück," Hannes said.

"Did you ask him why he had the photos?" Per asked.

"Of course. But either he really does just talk gibberish or he's a master dissembler. He babbled on about some sort of gift and seemed flustered. He ripped the picture frame out of our hands."

"That's strange. Did he have any photos of the other victims?" Clarissa asked.

"No, but we did get a look at his shoes. He's a size nine, so the footprints at the scene didn't come from him. But it occurred to me: Benjamin Lück supposedly had a partner named Karl or Carlo. The breakup coincided roughly with di Santo's departure from New Way. I suspect the name of Lück's boyfriend wasn't Karl or Carlo, but Carlos."

For a moment, there was silence, then they all started talking over one another. Only Marcel remained silent, pensively rubbing his short beard. Finally, he hushed everyone.

"The other club patrons would have known."

"Not necessarily," Hannes said. "The witnesses stated that Lück never went anywhere with his boyfriend. It's possible di Santo isn't out. Lück would have had to keep his boyfriend's identity a secret."

"There's only one way to find out," Federsen said. "Ask around. See if the ex-boyfriend could have been Carlos di Santo. Maybe Lück mentioned that his boyfriend came from Argentina, or the people at New Way noticed something. You can tackle that this afternoon."

"But Isabelle and I are going to see that fitness trainer," said Hannes.

"Then Per can ask around," Marcel said.

"Someone has to visit that bouncer again tonight. Per?"

"No way. I'm not going there alone, besides—"

"I'll do it," Hannes said. "I'm meeting up with friends anyway. I can stop by."

***

The gym was ultramodern and located in a glass building next to a fast-food restaurant. From the treadmills, the exercisers could see what the restaurant customers were eating. Melissa Vogt was still wrapping up a Pilates class, so Hannes examined the state-of-the-art equipment.

At first glance, Melissa appeared to be a typical fitness trainer. She was slender and perfectly defined without overdoing it. Her form-fitting pants and pink top emphasized her figure. She had a thin face and dark-brown hair tied into a ponytail.

It turned out that Antje Kramer was the reason she had joined New Way. The sculptor had taken a class taught by Mrs. Vogt, who had a soft spot for meditation and spirituality. The connection she had with Antje Kramer was obvious. She hadn't attended New Way since her friend's death, because she wasn't particularly close with any of the other members. She seemed to strongly dislike Sabine Schweiger.

"She attended all my classes. She'd constantly complain whenever something didn't go the way she imagined it. She's overly opinionated and always gives unsolicited advice. She's a domineering figure at New Way, and people listen to her."

"Can you give an example?" asked Isabelle.

"When people share something about themselves, she explains how they should do it differently. She makes snap judgments and always knows best."

"Does she get along with anyone particularly well?"

"I always got the impression that people feared her more than liked her. She can have a very sharp tongue. Her husband's no different. I stayed out of their way. I think they're friends with the Grafs."

That made perfect sense to Hannes, who found both couples equally unpleasant. It wouldn't have surprised him if the Grafs had temporarily moved in with the Schweigers following the fire. But, as evidenced by their friends' extended stay at a hotel, the Schweigers probably weren't as charitable as they claimed.

"What do other members think of the Schweigers?" Hannes asked. "Is there any resistance to them?"

"Open resistance, no. Well, maybe the Becks, Mrs. Beck in particular. I don't think she can stand either of them. The Schweigers keep forcing her husband into the role of chaplain. The last time I went, some of the members were even asking him to hear their confessions. It was Sabine's idea. Everyone has something they want to get off their chest, she said. That's when it got a little too bizarre for me."

"You said Mrs. Schweiger likes to moralize. Did she target anyone in particular?"

"Practically everyone. She'd constantly be reminding us of the Ten Commandments. Yes, they're the principles of New Way, but most people saw them in a more general light. She, on the other hand, was very dogmatic. Mr. Beck would reiterate the spirit of the commandments in his speeches, but he mainly appealed to emotions. In her mind, some things were just unacceptable. Alexander Kramer, for example. She was displeased with his lifestyle."

"Because he starred in pornos?"

"Yes. She wasn't cool with that. Maybe she was jealous—he was a nice guy and had a knack for women. The female members adored him, but he steered clear of Sabine."

"Was there anyone he got along with particularly well?" Isabelle asked.

"You mean Sylvia Böhm, right? It was an open secret. Mrs. Schweiger caught them in the storage room and made sure the word got around. But he got along with everyone else—purely platonic, of course—despite Mrs. Schweiger's bad-mouthing him."

"For example?"

"Oh, it's completely ridiculous. This young girl, for example. I forget her name."

"Rebecca Köhler?" Isabelle prompted.

"Yes, Rebecca. She was being harassed by an ex-boyfriend, and Alex protected her. He probably felt like her big brother. She might have interpreted it as something more, but he was just being nice. He also got along well with Mrs. Beck, but it's completely absurd that Christine would cheat on her husband. Sabine caused some pretty bad blood with her accusations."

"Did she openly complain?" Isabelle asked.

"She's not one to mince words. Once a month, the group holds an open discussion. Members can say what bothers them and who they have a problem with. Matters are supposed to be resolved as a group. Sabine always seemed to have something to complain about. A lot of people would roll their eyes whenever she spoke up."

Isabelle and Hannes looked at each other. David Bach had squeezed much of his background knowledge out of Rebecca Köhler. The rest he had apparently researched himself, if what was found in his apartment was any indication. Rebecca would have never known that Mrs. Brinkmann had lied to her children about their father. And Bach could have hardly found out this story himself. But Elke had said that Mrs. Brinkmann was very close with the Schweigers.

"Did Mrs. Schweiger ever claim you were having an affair with Alexander?" asked Isabelle.

"No, I would have let her have it. Why?"

Hannes cleared his throat and related what Rebecca Köhler had shared. Melissa Vogt's eyes widened, but she didn't seem to harbor any resentment against her.

"That pig," she said about Bach. "He treated her like shit and was only using her for information. It's true, I sleep with other men. I've never made a secret of it. But not with Alex. My husband and I have an open relationship, so it's not like I'm sneaking around."

Isabelle hesitantly pointed out that not everyone agreed with open relationships, especially not the murderer. Although Isabelle was careful to conceal the fact that there had yet to be a victim for the Sixth Commandment, Mrs. Vogt recognized the scope of the situation.

"So you think I'm in danger?" Mrs. Vogt ran her hands through her hair. "I can't believe I'd become the target of a madman, but it's possible. I keep feeling like someone's following me."

"What makes you say that?" Hannes asked.

"At first, I thought I was just imagining things. But recently, I've been getting the impression that a man's been following me on a bicycle. It's always in the evening when I leave the studio. Yesterday, I thought he photographed me when I got home. But maybe he was just taking a picture of the building. I live in a beautiful old apartment building."

"Do you remember what the man looked like?"

"No, it was already dark. I'm not even sure if it was the same man."

"Have you had any problems with the Church of the Creator?" Hannes asked.

"Antje told me there had been incidents from time to time. I never experienced anything myself, but I only joined the group last spring. Supposedly there had been a confrontation at the summer festival, but I wasn't there. And I'm done going to New Way now. As much as I'm interested in the group, I wouldn't risk my life for it."

"That's understandable," Hannes said. It was clear Melissa Vogt had to be placed under police protection. The evidence was alarming.

"I can't imagine that someone from the Church of the Creator would be behind the killings," Mrs. Vogt said. "Antje told me they hold some pretty radical views, but the tensions seemed to have died down recently."

"What makes you say that?" Isabelle asked.

"Both sides were anxious to put the incidents of the summer behind them. I've seen Mr. Schweiger speaking with someone from the church several times, and it didn't look like they were about to rip each other's heads off."

***

Federsen was no longer at the station by the time Isabelle and Hannes had returned. Marcel was on his way out. It was his eldest son's seventh birthday the next day, and he still had some errands to run for the party. His Sunday was going to be particularly stressful, since he would be stuck entertaining eleven children all afternoon, and bad weather had been predicted. Against his wife's wishes, he had bought a children's movie just in case.

"The Little Ghost," Isabelle read with a grin.

"Do you think it's an appropriate film for seven-year-olds?" Per asked. "Your kids will joke about it for weeks if you put it on."

"You think?" Marcel asked. "Are they too old for this?"

"Your wife's probably right. You spend too little time at home," Isabelle teased.

"Whatever. It's not like I can put on a movie starring Alexander Kramer. Where are those DVDs anyway?"

"Why do you ask?" Clarissa smirked. "Do you need to entertain your wife at the party as well?"

Marcel gave her a withering look.

Per coughed in embarrassment. "Uh . . . well, they might be lying around my place. I couldn't bring myself to watch them here, so I took them home."

For a brief moment, there was dead silence, then the whole room shook with laughter. The confession had a cathartic effect. It had been too long since they had joked together.

"I know what you're thinking," Per muttered. His face was red, but he couldn't help but grin. "I just wanted to see if there were any . . . clues."

"And? Were there?" Isabelle wiped tears from her eyes. "Besides the fact that this Alex was a real stallion?"

"I paid more attention to his costar," Per said. "But seriously, the second film takes place in a church, and good luck finding a religious person who wouldn't be upset by it. Not only is Kramer tied to a cross while his colleague . . . Well, you get the point. I'm just surprised they found a church that let them film it on their premises."

"It definitely wasn't the Church of the Creator," Marcel joked, putting an end to the conversation. "Mrs. Vogt is now under police protection. She's the perfect victim for the perp. And it seems he's already had her in his sights."

Per was already thinking ahead. "What if he turns his attention to someone else? Suppose David Bach's following her. When he realizes she's under protection, he might look for someone new. His ex-girlfriend is also under protection, but who knows who else did something reprehensible in his eyes."

Marcel stared at him. "What do you want me to say? We're not able to provide police protection to everyone. We need reasonable suspicion."

There was a moment of frustrated silence until Isabelle spoke. "I think everyone's in danger. Hopefully anyone would contact us the moment they notice something suspicious. But as we saw today with Mrs. Vogt, sometimes you need to press the issue."

"Then we have to keep in close touch with all the members," Marcel said. "Per and Clarissa, that'll be your job."

"Agreed," Clarissa said. "I can also warn the three former members of New Way. A woman moved back to Regensburg last winter to take care of her parents, and a couple moved to San Francisco. He's been working for a consulting company there since May, and his wife takes care of their newborn."

"Thanks," Marcel said. "Carlos di Santo, on the other hand, is one odd duck according to you. It's no surprise he keeps calling us to complain about his neighbors. He has pictures of Benjamin Lück in his apartment and left New Way on bad terms. We can't rule out revenge. However, we haven't been able to find any connections between him and David Bach or the Church of the Creator."

"I spoke with members who've been around longer," Clarissa said. "It seems there are differing opinions about him. Some felt sorry for him because when he's not depressed, he seems to be a nice guy. Mr. Beck was concerned and asked what kind of impression we had of him. He blames himself for taking away the last thing Mr. di Santo had to hold on to. I tried to ease his conscience, but it sounds like di Santo didn't give you the impression of being too stable. Others had a more negative opinion of him. The Schweigers and Grafs had wanted to get rid of him for a long time, but couldn't get their way. It seems Benjamin Lück had always defended him."

"Were there any rumors that di Santo and Lück were a couple?"

"Well, I couldn't be that blunt. I hinted at it. Some thought maybe. Mrs. Schweiger immediately screamed, 'I figured!' Mr. Beck also guessed where I was going, but couldn't imagine it."

"He just doesn't have the excellent observation skills that Mrs. Schweiger has," Per joked. "I asked around at the theater and spoke with Lück's friends," he continued. "Carlos didn't ring any bells with them, but a colleague from the theater said it was possible."

"There's still a chance. Sometimes we're more likely to tell strangers certain things instead of our loved ones. Maybe Hannes will have more luck with the bouncer tonight," Marcel said optimistically.

***

Hannes was annoyed that he let Ben talk him into going bowling. The week had been exhausting enough, and he would have loved a quiet evening with Anna. Everything was still fresh, and they spent way too little time together to make the most of things. On the other hand, he didn't want to forget about his friends and looked forward to seeing Ines, Kalle, and Elke again.

Anna had been skeptical at first. She barely knew Hannes's friends, and she was certain that as Hannes's new girlfriend, all eyes would be on her. But as usual, Ben could be counted on to defuse awkward situations.

"So a hot brunette snatched our athlete!" he shouted with a grin as he turned the corner on his rusty bike and saw the pair waiting. They quickly let go of each other, and Anna wiped some lipstick off Hannes's neck.

"Rub all you want at the hickey, it's not going anywhere," Ben joked and tugged at the red wool cap covering his dreadlocks.

They had arranged to meet at a bowling alley on the outskirts of town and would head into the city for drinks afterward. That gave

Hannes the chance to make a quick detour and see the bouncer at La Bella Vita.

The others showed up shortly after Ben. Ines and Kalle had returned a week ago from their trip to the Seychelles—both very tanned. As always, Hannes had to suppress a smile as they walked over. Ines was stronger and a good deal taller than her spindly boyfriend. He looked a little bit like Harry Potter, despite his large nose. They formed a very odd couple, but a couple that was usually of one heart and one mind. Kalle was somewhat reserved, while Ines could strike up a conversation with anyone. She had turned thirty the previous summer, which made her the youngest in the group. That evening, however, the air seemed thick between them.

"Things aren't looking too rosy today, are they?" Ben whispered into Hannes's ear. "How was paradise?" he shouted to the newcomers.

"The Seychelles were amazing," said Ines. Her makeup was understated, but her pageboy haircut had been livened up with blonde highlights. "But we learned that all-inclusive vacations really aren't our thing."

Kalle concurred. "The first week was okay, but we started getting bored at the resort. Island hopping probably would have been better."

"Why didn't you take a few side trips then?" Elke asked.

"You get so used to the luxurious resort accommodations, you just become listless. We couldn't get ourselves to do anything," he said.

Ines excused herself from the group and pulled Anna inside the bowling alley.

"What have you been up to?" Ben asked Kalle, who stood with slumped shoulders.

"Christmas. She insists we go to her parents' and then to mine. You know how incredibly stressful her mother can be. I suggested we celebrate alone this year, and we've been arguing about it for days. I let it slip that she sounds just like her mother. She really let me have it."

"Well, that was stupid," Elke said and laughed. "You never tell a woman she's like her mother."

The group followed Anna and Ines into the building. Hannes hadn't considered Christmas—it'd be the last thing on anyone's mind when dealing with dead bodies. Anna's mother had died two years ago after a serious illness. She and her father had a somewhat ambivalent relationship, but she loved her younger brother dearly. Should he drag her to see his family for Christmas? It would be a three-hour train ride. And three days could be very long, especially since his mother had a habit of interrogating new girlfriends. He pushed the thought aside for the time being and was pleased to see that Ines and Anna were getting along. Ines was almost back to her old self. She sniffed her rental shoes.

"If we get into the habit of bowling, I'm buying my own shoes," she said. "Yuck."

"You could always play barefoot," Kalle joked.

They played three rounds, with Kalle placing dead last every time. But things seemed back on track with his girlfriend, so he didn't care. Hannes realized that Anna had regularly beat him.

After bowling, they headed to a bar downtown. Hannes figured it wouldn't be the last stop of the night, and excused himself for an hour around ten o'clock. Since Anna had just begun discussing job opportunities with Ines, he could leave her alone for a while. He wanted to get to La Bella Vita before it got too crowded.

***

The bouncer at the club recognized Hannes right away.

"Mr. Lück mentioned having a problematic relationship with his boyfriend," Hannes said. "Does that ring a bell?"

"Possibly. He had issues."

"Depression?" Hannes asked.

"Yeah. He took drugs, but wouldn't see a therapist. Benny said his depression was due to something else. His friend wasn't out and would always hide the relationship in public. That bothered him—he didn't want a secret relationship."

Hannes nodded. The description fit Carlos di Santo. He thanked the doorman and wished him a quiet evening. He had only taken a few steps when the bouncer called after him.

"You know, I think his boyfriend was from South America. Brazil or something."

CHAPTER 21

The party had raged all night. After stopping at various bars, the group had wound up at a club around two o'clock in the morning. Ben had met a petite exchange student from Vietnam and probably hadn't gone home alone.

Anna and Hannes spent Sunday afternoon by the sea. The strong wind from the north helped to clear their heads. Still, the walk didn't last long. They peeled off their thick jackets in a small café and made plans for Anna's future. Ines, who worked for the Red Cross as an aid worker, had inspired her the night before.

"It would be great if I could do something meaningful," said Anna as she rubbed her nose. She often did this whenever she was lost in thought.

"I'm sure there are companies that make meaningful products," Hannes said. "Maybe a solar panel manufacturer? Or wind power? That might be a better fit for the weather here."

"Yeah, I could see that. But I'd rather work with people."

They didn't get very far, but at least Anna seemed more motivated. That evening, she scoured the Internet for potential employers, and Hannes hoped she didn't discover her dream job in some far-off place.

Hannes gave Marcel a call. He sounded exhausted—a children's birthday party was no picnic.

"You should see what it looks like over here," Marcel moaned. "Think long and hard whether you really want to do this to yourself."

After venting his frustration, Marcel summed up recent progress. Isabelle and Per had paid another visit to Carlos di Santo, who had flat-out denied being gay and had flown into a rage at the very suggestion of his having had an intimate relationship with Benjamin Lück. It seemed like New Way's former treasurer was stonewalling. Hannes thought Clarissa might be better at breaching his defenses. He had portrayed himself as a victim of bullying and felt cut off from the rest of the world. The curtains in his apartment were drawn, and he only left to go grocery shopping.

After the chaos of the children's birthday party, Marcel had gone to see the Schweigers. He had wanted to form his own opinion of them, but following a memorable performance by Sabine Schweiger, he had to agree with his colleagues. But whether her judgmental ways made her a person of interest was a different matter. Asked about his relationship with the Church of the Creator, Mr. Schweiger said he had tried to mediate between the two groups. It was of mutual interest for the fighting to stop.

Hannes asked, "Who did Schweiger contact in his attempts at mediation?"

"Mr. Ahrendt and Frank Meister, who seems to be the pastor's right-hand man."

"So, ironically, two of the more hard-core members. That doesn't make sense."

"It does according to Mr. Schweiger. They're the opinion makers. If you want to change something, you have to go through them."

"Then let's hope that his efforts bear fruit. I don't want to have to visit another crime scene."

***

On Monday, Frank Meister's seized and encrypted laptop was evaluated. The results were devastating. They had already found a disturbing amount of information on the members of New Way at David Bach's apartment, but it dwarfed in comparison to what they found on Meister's hard drive. He had a separate folder with general information on the group, plus pictures and an Excel document listing nearly all the members and their addresses, license plates, phone numbers, and occupations. There was also a column in which an *X* was marked next to fifteen names, including the four victims.

The other eleven members were offered police protection, and only a few declined. Among them were the Becks and Grafs, who refused to be intimidated. Hartmann, the department store owner, and an elderly lady also refused. But even those who refused agreed to have an officer check in periodically.

E-mails between David Bach and Frank Meister confirmed the presumption that Bach wasn't acting alone. While Bach used an anonymous e-mail address, Meister used Outlook. The two of them had agreed to spy on New Way members, and Bach had passed on all the information he had obtained from Rebecca Köhler. It also emerged that the altercation during the summer festival and the destruction of the sculpture had been planned. And Meister had sent the picture of the Devil found in Mr. Beck's mailbox to Bach. The anonymous complaint filed against Mr. Beck accusing him of working as a psychiatrist was also found on the hard drive.

"Take a look at these pamphlets," Clarissa said and passed around the printouts. "We know he's very religious, but these suggest he's a fanatic. We already found religious literature at his place, but there were videos of some hair-raising sermons on his laptop. His web-browser history's also interesting."

Frank Meister was interested in militant antiabortionists and had scoured message boards that dealt with religious crimes. He had shown particular interest in the recent string of murders.

"But the same could be said for many people," said Per.

"True," Clarissa said and rolled her eyes. "But few people would have information on how to produce Rohypnol and what effect it has. Frank Meister did. But he only started looking two weeks ago, which doesn't quite fit our time frame. The drug was used about five weeks earlier in the death of Alexander Kramer."

"Maybe he wanted to alter the dosage? It might not have had the desired effect the first time."

Despite the new info, they couldn't bring him in. Meister had gone on vacation for two weeks and had disappeared without a trace—just like David Bach. Everyone had the unsettling fear that he would pop back up at a new crime scene.

***

Hannes found himself in the visiting room of the prison that Tuesday morning.

"Were you jumped?" he asked Fritz in disbelief.

Fritz's left arm was bandaged and in a sling. His face looked beat up, and he was limping more than usual.

"Oh, just a little prison fight," Fritz joked. "Some angry skinhead went after an African. The poor guy would have been ripped to shreds by the time the guards got there. So I stepped in."

"Stepped in? It looks like you were caught in the crossfire of a gang war."

"The warden's very grateful that I prevented a death. It's likely to help my situation here."

It seemed this was true; visiting restrictions had been eased. It was a good thing, since it took Hannes a while to update Fritz on the recent developments.

"Carlos di Santo's behavior's strange," Fritz said. "Of course, Bach and Meister got a lot of info from this Rebecca and sniffed out the rest. But there may have also been a second informant. Someone who hates New Way, but is familiar with the group. Since di Santo's unable to work, he probably invested all his energy and time into the group. Then they just kicked him out."

"But why would he ally himself with religious fanatics? He complained that New Way was getting too religious."

"That may be. But whether or not he's capable of an objective opinion is anyone's guess. Besides, there are always different factions in groups like these."

"Di Santo was forced out in March. He might hold a grudge against New Way, but definitely not Alexander Kramer, who only joined the group this past summer. It's highly unlikely they knew each other."

"Valid point."

"Unless . . . We found Kramer's pornos in Lück's apartment. If di Santo and Lück actually were a couple and kept in touch after the breakup, it might make sense."

"So di Santo saw the DVDs at Lück's, or perhaps Lück told di Santo that Kramer had joined. Di Santo realized Lück was attracted to the young man and assumed they were in a relationship. Maybe he even considered Kramer the reason for their breakup."

Fritz still doubted di Santo was involved. He noted that the detectives had lost sight of Matthias Böhm. After all, it was conceivable that Böhm wanted to take revenge against New Way. His marriage had deteriorated over the last few months, and he must have learned a lot from his wife about the members. However, there was no indication that he was in contact with the Church of the Creator. The focus of the investigation was obvious to Fritz: David Bach and Frank Meister had to be tracked down as soon as possible.

***

A few hours later, David Bach was back in the picture—quite literally. The detectives watched as the fugitive appeared in the slightly grainy footage of a surveillance camera. Although he had pulled his hood over his head when entering the gas station, it had slipped down as he brandished a knife in front of the cashier. Marcel paused the video at the moment Bach looked into the camera.

"That's him. He took 300 euros from the cashier, then tied him to a rack of shelves. On his way out, he stuffed food and drinks into his backpack. Wherever he's hiding doesn't seem to include board."

"Which would explain why we haven't been able to flush him out," Clarissa said.

"The gas station's located in a small town toward the coast," Marcel said.

"There have been reports of break-ins and shoplifting in the area over the past few days," Federsen said. "I wouldn't be surprised if Bach's to blame."

"The terrain's pretty open there," Isabelle said. "I go for rides around there in the summer. Mostly fields, sometimes you pass through small villages. If he's hiding in a forest, a nature preserve would be the only spot."

Per was skeptical. "In this weather? It was below forty last night. I don't think he's staying outside. Even in a tent he'd freeze his ass off."

"Bach's not a wimp like you," Hannes said. "There are things like thermal sleeping bags, and besides, there are a lot of cabins along the coast. It's only a few miles from the gas station. At this time of year, most of the houses would be empty. No one would notice if someone were squatting."

The others nodded. The area was touristy in summer and offered an array of accommodations.

"He wouldn't have gotten a hotel room," said Clarissa. "Too risky. But it would be a hassle to comb all the empty houses."

"But we can't rule out the possibility that he pitched a tent somewhere," said Isabelle. "The cashier said Bach took off on a bicycle. The guy must be running on empty. Robbing a gas station in broad daylight, then fleeing on a bike sounds like desperation."

"We'd need hundreds of people to scour the area," Marcel said. "Unless we can rule out the open countryside and the forest area quickly. Since the trees are bare, you could get a good overview from the air. On the ground, we could focus on the buildings."

He looked at Federsen, who was furiously scanning the map. "If we start now, we run into darkness. Bach would have an easier time escaping because we'd be unable to conduct the search without being noticed. Alternatively, we can hope he feels safe in his hiding place, especially now that he's got supplies. We prepare for the search now and start at first light. What do you say, Henning?"

"Damn it," said Federsen. "I hope you all realize what a clusterfuck this manhunt will be if the guy changes hiding spots. Someone's going to have to take the fall."

"Since he's riding a bicycle, I doubt it," Clarissa said. "He wouldn't spend hours riding through the countryside after robbing a gas station. He's not completely stupid."

"But he's got money now," Federsen said. "All he had to do was head to the train station, and he could be anywhere. The robbery was over three hours ago."

Hannes turned to the map. "The nearest train station's actually not too far. From there, the trains either head back to the city or farther east." He quickly pulled up the train schedule on his smartphone. "There's a regional express every hour."

"If he bolted, he's already gone," Clarissa guessed. "If not, he's likely to spend the night in his hiding place. So we're not risking much by waiting until the morning."

"He could have hopped on a bus too," said Federsen.

Marcel shook his head. "Bus drivers are more likely to remember a face than a train conductor. You need to make a decision now, Henning. We've never been this close to catching him. Maybe Frank Meister's with him. We should at least try."

Federsen grimaced. He fumbled through his pockets and lit a cigarette. No one dared remind him of the smoking ban. Short of breath, he shuffled to the window, opened it, and tossed out the butt.

"Steffen should decide. He's the chief," he said as he left the conference room.

Steffen Lauer's decision took ten seconds. He was desperate to move the investigation forward. It'd been made easier for him by the fact that the getaway bike had been discovered in a bush by the side of the road. Apparently Bach had been heading toward the Baltic Sea and had ditched the bike halfway to his destination. Steffen Lauer preferred risking an expensive bust over being accused later of hesitation.

The conference room now looked like a command center. Hannes had never experienced such an operation before. Lauer had drummed up several specialists who prepared for the manhunt with military precision. Two helicopters would scout the area, while four hundred officers would be deployed on the ground. A twelve-mile perimeter was drawn around the site where the bicycle was found.

The Baltic Sea formed a natural boundary to the north and west. Search teams would comb the terrain from east to west and south to north in a semicircle and draw the noose tighter. Boats would patrol the coastline. Hannes was impressed with the detailed planning: not a single aspect had been overlooked. A strategy for dealing with the press was also devised. Hannes felt a bit useless in the preparations and got the sense that he was in the way. Marcel apparently shared the sentiment and took him aside.

"There's not much we can do at the moment. We won't play much of an active role tomorrow either. We'll search the site in pairs. If we notice anything, the SWAT team will be on standby."

"What should we do in the meantime?"

"Everything's being taken care of. You've suggested that Clarissa should pay another visit to the Argentinian. It wouldn't hurt. Why don't you see if you can make him talk?"

Getting Carlos di Santo to talk wasn't particularly difficult, at least not for Clarissa. Hannes watched her pace around the living room. Di Santo squirmed on the leather sofa. The curtains were still drawn.

"Let's go over this again," Clarissa said. Her copper-colored earrings jingled. She never wore the same jewelry two days in a row. "Your relationship with Benjamin Lück was purely friendly, correct? Several people told us there was more between you."

"They're all lying."

"Plenty of witnesses have confirmed you were a couple."

"Impossible. We took special care not to . . ." Di Santo fell silent.

"You were never seen together," Hannes said. "But do you really think Mr. Lück didn't tell anyone?"

Di Santo gave up. His shoulders slumped. He looked forlorn.

"He promised he would never tell anyone . . . it was supposed to be a secret," he muttered.

Clarissa sat down. Her voice was a touch softer. "Why would it have been so bad if it got out?"

"I was ashamed. It's not natural. Two men together . . ." He shook his head.

"Where did you get that idea? Wasn't New Way open to everyone? Mr. Lück didn't experience any problems."

"If only you knew."

"What?"

"Some thought it was okay, but I heard others make fun of him behind his back. No one knew about me."

"But at least no one attacked him."

"Attacked? No, that's what the others did."

"Which others?"

"Guys from the Church of the Creator attacked him, cut off his ponytail, punched him. I was there. But they didn't know about me."

"Did you recognize who attacked him?" Hannes asked.

"Absolutely. Those two friends kept making trouble. Had fun doing it too."

"Who are they?"

"I don't know their names. One is thin, pale, wears round glasses. Has his hair combed to the side. He's always talking with their pastor. The other guy's younger. Tall, muscular, with ears that stick out even worse than yours."

He pointed at Hannes, who felt the blood rush to his ears. Clarissa snickered. The description matched David Bach and Frank Meister.

"Did you know Alexander Kramer?" Clarissa asked. "He joined New Way after you left and was nailed to a cross a few weeks ago."

"I read about that. He was the first sinner."

"What do you mean?"

"He made pornos. I met with Benny a few times. He thought he was cool."

"How was he the first sinner? Were there others?"

"There are many sinners. Everyone's a sinner, some more so than others. Sylvia killed a child, for example, and now she's dead. But the real sinners are the others."

Clarissa and Hannes tried to get more information from him, but the questions seemed to tire him. After ten minutes, they gave up. Di Santo's description of the attack on Lück had given them an important link in the chain of evidence against Bach and Meister.

***

Anna and Hannes cuddled on the sofa. He was amazed at how much he had been able to unwind that evening at Anna's apartment. She had a very positive effect on him.

Hannes leaned forward and took a sip of wine.

"Hey, take off your sweater and T-shirt."

Hannes didn't need to be told twice, and he excitedly began to undo his belt too.

"Hold on," Anna said and laughed. "You can take your pants off later. I just want to show you what I learned in my massage class yesterday."

While on her big trip, Anna had enjoyed many cheap Thai massages and was now taking a course. Hannes lay facedown on the floor and looked up at Anna over his shoulder.

"Why couldn't we have met ten years ago? It would have saved me a lot of time. You're a catch."

Flattered, Anna began working on his back muscles, and Hannes soon realized that a Thai massage had a painful side.

"Are you sure that's right?" he groaned as she pulled his arms back and stretched his spine.

"You'll feel like a new person afterward," she said. "Besides, you're extremely flexible. You won't believe what you'll be able to do later."

With that in mind, Hannes endured the pain, and Anna further distracted him with a recap of her day. She had applied to several jobs in the area, but one company in particular had caught her attention. LightFire specialized in selling stylish ecofashion produced according to strict ethical standards, and they were looking for a sales manager to start on February 1.

"I'm not a fashionista, but I think their business model's pretty cool. And I'd be working toward something. The company's only been around for a year. Ines knows a project manager there from school.

She's going to pass my résumé on to her friend. Maybe I'll have a better chance of getting a job that actually sounds interesting."

"Didn't Ines say there was an opening at the Red Cross?"

"It's just a temp job for a year. They need someone to cover for a woman going on maternity leave. By the way, she asked if we wanted to go to the Christmas market on Saturday."

"Is it that time again?"

"Sunday's the first day of Advent. We could go to the Christmas market at city hall. It's always the prettiest."

"And the most crowded," said Hannes. He suddenly realized they would soon have to discuss how they wanted to spend Christmas. "I have my boating test on Saturday."

"All day?"

"Yes, the written test is in the morning, and the portion on the water takes place in the afternoon. That reminds me, I need to study."

"You can do that tomorrow night," Anna said and moved her hands slowly to his waistband. "So what do you say? Should I tell Ines we're coming?"

She slid her hands seductively under his waistband. There was no winning against this tactic. Just then, his cell phone rang, and Anna stopped.

"Ignore it," Hannes said.

He rolled onto his back and pulled Anna down toward him. As their lips touched, the phone stopped, and she undid his belt. He gently caressed her stomach as he lifted her T-shirt. She reached to unbutton his jeans, but the phone rang again. Hannes slid a hand under her bra. Anna laughed, but before the mood was totally killed, the ringing stopped.

"I have something waiting in the bedroom," she whispered.

"Can't wait." Hannes grinned and ran his fingers down toward her pants.

The phone rang again.

"Damn it." Hannes sat up.

"Go answer it. It must be important. I'll be waiting in the other room."

Hannes watched as she walked into the bedroom. When the door had closed, he looked at his phone. He didn't recognize the number.

"Yes?"

"Um . . . hello?" The voice sounded vaguely familiar. "Is that you, Detective Niehaus?"

Hannes groaned to himself. Carlos di Santo. It was nine o'clock. What could he want?

"Yes, speaking. Mr. di Santo? What can I do for you?"

"You said to call if I could think of anything else."

"So what is it?"

"I'm not sure yet."

"Then why are you calling?" he asked in a barely restrained voice.

"I don't know, but I have an idea. Can we meet?"

"Now?"

"No, not now. I need to double-check first. But I'm probably right."

"Then tell me. What is it?"

"I'm meeting someone soon. I might know more then. The victims . . . it all makes sense. Can you come tomorrow at nine o'clock?"

Hannes thought about the forthcoming manhunt. "I'm sorry, but I'm busy tomorrow morning. Just tell me what you—"

"Then in the afternoon?"

"I don't know when I'll be free. It may take some time."

Apparently di Santo couldn't be persuaded to speak freely yet. However, the search for David Bach was expected to be over by nightfall. Either he would be found by then, or he wasn't in the area.

"I could come see you around seven." Hannes gave himself some extra time just in case.

"That works. I'll wait for you at home?"

"Yes, I'll come to your place. But Mr. di Santo, could you just tell me—"

Di Santo had already hung up. Hannes stared at the phone, wondering whether he should inform Marcel or Federsen about the strange call. He decided to call his boss, who wasn't pleased.

"The guy's been spouting nonsense the whole time. Go and see him tomorrow after the manhunt, but I'm sure it will be a waste of time."

Hannes shared this fear, even though he had a bad feeling about di Santo being left to his own devices until the next evening. But he couldn't do anything more than express his reservations to Federsen. He switched his phone to silent and placed it on the small coffee table. He took another sip of wine and cursed Carlos di Santo. Why didn't he tell him that afternoon what was burning him up?

Hannes was still curious what Anna had planned, so he crept to the bedroom door and opened it. One look, and he immediately forgot about Carlos di Santo and the investigation.

CHAPTER 22

The waves lapped against the hull of the small ferry which shuttled back and forth between the mainland and the peninsula. The crossing only took a few minutes, but the captain was still waiting for a container ship to pass through the fairway. Per joined Hannes by the railing, and they stared out onto the open sea. Since the sun had yet to rise, they did more imagining than viewing. A few gulls circled above them. It was drizzling, and Per pulled up the hood of his jacket. That early in the morning, there were few cars on the ferry and even fewer foot passengers.

Hannes rubbed his sleepy eyes, but the cold November air gradually banished his fatigue. The ferry had barely begun to move, when the opposite shore soon appeared. Hannes's heartbeat quickened. It was six in the morning, and the large-scale manhunt for David Bach was beginning. Uniformed officers reached the dock and checked every car waiting to head in the other direction. The twelve-mile perimeter had been established and roadblocks set up. Per steered the unmarked car off the ramp of the ferry and pulled over.

"What now? I have no idea what we're supposed to be doing."

"We're supposed to look around and not get in the way," Hannes said.

However, it would take a while for the search teams to sweep in from the other side. The officers at their current location were only responsible for preventing Bach's escape. A police boat patrolled the water, but it was unlikely Bach would plunge into the icy water and swim across the bay. But he could steal a boat and make a break for it.

"Let's go to the marina," Hannes suggested.

Per shrugged and started the engine. After a few yards, the street turned into a small road that led through some woods. A few sailboats languished in the water; the rest had already been hauled out for the winter. Uniformed officers were also stationed there, crawling under tarps and searching yachts. A retired majestic four-masted barque towered over the other end of the marina. It now served as a museum and wedding venue.

"There's a former campsite over there. Maybe we should check it out?" suggested Hannes.

"I didn't know it had shut down."

"They're supposedly building condos, shops, and hotels there. But as far as I know, they haven't finished demolishing everything. It'd make a perfect hideout."

Demolition had in fact already begun. A few abandoned RVs still stood around, and the detectives walked over to a decrepit trailer. The sky had turned from a deep black to a dark gray, and the sound of a distant helicopter could be heard.

"The door's cracked open," Per whispered and fumbled for his firearm.

"Keep cool," Hannes said. "You might end up shooting some homeless guy."

The door creaked as Per slowly pulled it open. So much for the element of surprise. Hannes climbed inside after him. The old upholstery smelled musty, but even in the dim light he immediately realized nobody was staying there. The four other abandoned RVs also showed no signs of occupation.

"That would have been too easy," Per said. "It's too bad. They probably would have given us a medal."

They returned to their car and asked their colleagues at the marina if there was any news.

"Both helicopters have been in the air for half an hour. The search teams have covered the first mile, but it was mainly open terrain. The press has already gotten wind of the action. The first news vans will be rolling in soon."

The rain was beginning to fall harder, so Per and Hannes decided to drive through the streets of the nearby village. The first few inhabitants were stepping outside their homes and excitedly sharing what little they knew about the day's surprising activities. As Per turned toward a sewage treatment plant, Marcel called Hannes.

"Where are you?"

"At the sewage treatment plant. What's up?"

"Not much. Our guys are making good progress, though. They've already searched the first couple of buildings and are showing residents photos. No one recognizes Frank Meister, but a lot of them think they've seen Bach. A man claimed to have seen him riding a bike two days ago."

"Where was that?"

"Near the maritime school. But that doesn't necessarily mean he's hiding around there. At least we now know he's been in the area awhile."

"I hope he still is. We've driven by everything already. Should we go somewhere else?"

"No, stay on the peninsula. We'll cover the remaining area. The closer the search party comes to you, the more likely the guy will get spooked. There's no way he can't hear the helicopters."

The search team was still far away, and their progress ground to a halt when they reached the villages. Per and Hannes spent the morning driving around the same streets. They had expected the day to be more exciting. Around noon, they stopped for fish and chips. Two plates of fried fish were soon placed in front of them. Per didn't touch his sides of boiled potatoes and spinach, while Hannes quickly cleaned his plate.

"You can always tell an athlete." Per grinned and pushed the remains of his lunch over.

"Your clothes would fit better if you'd clean your plate once in a while." Hannes speared a potato. "I think we've been looking in the wrong place. If you're looking to hide out for a long time, you'd choose something more secluded."

"But food's hard to come by in remote areas."

"That's why he had the bike. I suspect he broke into a cabin on the beach or a vacation home."

"Maybe. But I think he's gone by now."

"Seems you've changed your tune from yesterday. Let's pay and look around the beach."

Back in the car, Per asked, "Where do you want to start?"

"The beaches get really big over to the east. We should look there."

"You want to take a walk on the beach? The search team will sweep by at some point."

"Oh right. I forgot. In that case, let's just head home," Hannes said sarcastically. "I'd like to feel I'm doing something useful instead of aimlessly roaming around."

"But Marcel wanted us to stay here."

"We're not going that far." He pointed to the map on the GPS. "We're headed to this village. It's tiny, but there are lots of vacation homes and a huge beach. There might even be some secluded cabins. They'd be an ideal hiding spot this time of year."

They rolled past a small pond before Hannes turned left and headed back toward the sea. In the distance, they could already see a helicopter; the search team must have scoured half the area. Thatched cottages soon appeared, and Hannes drove through the village.

"Idyllic," Per said. "But you didn't want to look around town, did you?"

"The beach is over there," Hannes said. "I was here last summer, but I forget if there are any buildings. Let's just take a quick look around."

Hannes parked the car. They trudged along a narrow sandy path through the dunes and met with uninterrupted views of the Baltic Sea. One of the giant Scandinavian ferries motored in the distance, and Per scanned the horizon. The beach was deserted, which wasn't surprising. He pointed to the right.

"Isn't there one of those water-sports schools over there? I took a kite surfing class about five years ago. It was somewhere around here. But I only went once."

Hannes couldn't really picture him kite surfing. "Well, the school's got to be closed now. Let's take a look. If we don't see anything, we can turn around and drive back."

A relieved Per agreed. The stretch of coast ahead of them lay deserted and lifeless. There was almost no wind; tiny languid waves splashed against the sand. Suddenly, Hannes stopped and squinted through the rain.

"What's that?"

About two hundred yards away stood a red-and-white steel skeleton. On a platform supported by four girders was a tiny house with windows on each side. As they approached, they could see the white lettering on the wall: German Lifeguard Association.

"It's just a lifeguard tower," Per said. "*Baywatch* on the Baltic. I—"

"Quiet," Hannes said and pushed him toward the dunes.

"What's wrong?" Per asked.

"There's someone in the tower."

Hannes pulled out his binoculars and tried to make out the shadowy figure in the distance.

"Damn rain. I can't see anything. But there's definitely a man inside." He passed Per the binoculars.

"Short blond hair. Seems tall."

"Let's get closer."

"Wouldn't it be better to contact operation command?"

"And what if it's a false alarm? It could be someone out for a walk who wanted to enjoy the view," Hannes said.

"Then why would he break in?"

"Maybe it wasn't locked. We can use the dunes for cover. We'll get a better look over there. If it really is Bach, we can call for backup."

Crouching, Hannes made his way over to the tower, and Per followed. The winter vegetation offered little cover, but Hannes hoped it was enough. He ducked behind a bush about a hundred yards away and looked through the binoculars.

"I think it's Bach. He seems nervous and is constantly looking in the direction of the helicopter. Let's call for backup."

Per fiddled with his phone. "I don't believe this. I don't have any reception."

"Use the radio, but be quiet."

In a hushed voice, Per informed their colleagues of their suspicion. The SWAT team, which had been kept at the ready, was immediately dispatched.

"Can you keep watch by yourself for a minute? I've really got to puke. I hope the fish wasn't off."

Hannes grunted and lay down on his stomach behind the bush. Per darted in the direction of a tree, but he was oblivious to the root in his way. He stumbled and fell. Hannes chuckled, then turned his gaze back to the tower. The man hadn't seemed to notice them; his attention was focused on the helicopter which hovered in the air off to the east. Suddenly, he opened the door and stepped out onto the platform. Hesitantly, he looked around. Hannes caught a glimpse of the man's face through the binoculars. It was clearly David Bach, and he looked agitated. Hannes frantically looked for Per and cursed under his breath when he couldn't see him.

Bach began climbing down the ladder, and Hannes closed in on all fours. He quickly reached the edge of the vegetation; less than two hundred feet separated him from the tower. At that moment, Bach turned, faced one of the steel pilings, and unzipped his pants to pee.

Barking could be heard in the distance; the search team moved closer. Bach turned his head to listen. After zipping up his pants, he raced up the ladder. Hannes watched in surprise. Did he really think he'd be safe in that box up there? Then it dawned on him, and a quick look through the binoculars confirmed what he had suspected. Bach was frantically cramming things into a backpack. Hannes saw this as his last chance. With lightning speed, he jumped up and ran toward the tower. Adrenaline coursed through him as he reached for his gun. He hesitated at the foot of the ladder and struggled to control his breathing. Then the adrenaline took over again. He carefully grabbed a rung with his left hand while he tightly gripped his firearm with his right. He climbed the ladder as quietly as possible, but apparently not quiet enough.

Before heaving himself up, Hannes peered over the platform only to come face-to-face with a wide-eyed David Bach. They stared at each other in silence. Then their reflexes simultaneously kicked in. Hannes pushed himself up and pointed his gun in Bach's direction, but Bach had the advantage due to his elevated position. He leaped over to the edge of the platform and kicked Hannes in his chest, sending him backward. Hannes lost his footing on the ladder. As he fell, he heard what sounded like a shout coming from Per.

The fall seemed to take a surprisingly long time. Hannes saw David Bach slide down the ladder. Then Hannes turned, looked down, and hit the ground. A moment later, he saw nothing but the gray sky before it was swallowed by darkness.

***

The first thing Hannes saw when he came to was Henning Federsen's blurry face. There was an unpleasant throbbing in the back of his head, and he couldn't think straight. Federsen's lips moved like in a silent movie, and Hannes blinked. When he looked again, he saw two heads crowd over him. One was Per's and the other Marcel's. Then, suddenly, his hearing returned.

"He's coming to," Marcel said.

"He did a sweet backflip. Luckily he didn't land on his head," Per said.

"Good thing the sand cushioned his fall." This voice was unfamiliar.

Hannes carefully turned his head. A young female paramedic knelt beside him, and his memory suddenly came flooding back. He frantically tried to get up.

"Bach. He's . . . he's gone. Kicked me off the tower. Got to be around here."

"Easy, Hannes." Marcel eased him back to the ground. "Per arrived in the nick of time and arrested him. Bach's cuffed and sitting in the patrol car."

Relieved, Hannes closed his eyes and gave in to the exhaustion and dizziness. He tried to sit up again with help from the paramedic. Having tested his pupils, balance, reflexes, and ability to speak, she gave her diagnosis.

"Concussion. Mild to moderate. Again, you were lucky. But you need to be examined at the hospital as soon as possible."

"Oh, that's not necessary," Hannes said, but shouted in pain when the paramedic poked his torso. "What are you doing?"

"You have bruises, maybe even a broken rib. There's no way you're not going to the hospital."

Hannes let himself be led to the ambulance.

"Why did you climb up there? We had everything under control," Per said.

"We didn't. He realized we were coming."

Hannes felt another dizzy spell come over him and clung to Per, who helped him lie down on a stretcher carried by two other paramedics. They gently carried Hannes over the beach. Per stayed by his side.

"Has Bach admitted to anything?" asked Hannes.

"Federsen's interrogating him now. By the way, say what you will about our boss, but he seemed to be really worried about you."

Hannes shook his head. "Even if he was, it'll pass. Besides, you're the one who nabbed Bach, not me. How'd you do it?"

"Didn't take much. While you were practicing your high-dive routine, he was racing down the ladder. He was in such a panic that he wasn't looking where he was going. All I had to do was point my gun at him, and he knew he had no chance."

Hannes was glad Bach was now in Federsen's hands. Bach was probably sweating bullets. He closed his eyes and sank back into darkness. He had seen enough for one day.

***

No serious injuries were discovered at the hospital. Hannes had suffered a concussion and a few bumps and bruises. He was prescribed painkillers and bed rest, which wouldn't pose too much of a problem. They could wrap up the investigation now with the arrest of David Bach. But Per soon burst that bubble.

"I spoke with Clarissa, and Bach vehemently denies having anything to do with the murders. He has no idea where Frank Meister's hiding."

"Of course he denies it. We'll have to back him into a corner."

"Probably. So far, he couldn't give any credible alibis for the murders. But he did admit to the sculpture, the graffiti, the Devil in the mailbox, and the anonymous complaint, and incriminated his buddy Frank too. He denies slashing Beck's tires, though."

"Have you checked the soles of his shoes?"

"Yeah, of course. But they don't match the ones found at the scene of Benjamin Lück's murder or in the Grafs' yard."

"Maybe he bought new shoes and ditched the others?"

"He denies that."

"What about the other incidents? The phone calls, the robbery."

"He claims innocence."

"And Lück's assault?"

"He confessed to robbing the gas station. Nothing about assaulting Lück, though."

"Carlos di Santo was there during the assault and recognized him. We need to organize a lineup."

"Hopefully di Santo's a credible witness."

"If he's having a good day, it shouldn't be a problem. Which reminds me, he wanted to meet with me tonight. Supposedly he has evidence. We should hear what he has to say."

"Didn't the doctor tell you—"

"It's not like stopping by his place is a big deal. You can take me home afterward."

On the way to di Santo's, they picked up Hannes's prescription at the pharmacy, but the painkillers had yet to kick in as they sat in rush hour traffic.

"What reason did Bach give for hiding?" Hannes asked. "He denies murdering anyone. If he's telling the truth, why would he hide? He'd already been lying low when he attacked me with the crowbar. He only robbed the gas station after fleeing."

"He claims he was afraid because he already had a pretty long record. The minister from the church tipped him off that we were look-ing for him. He stayed with Meister for the first few days. That's when he figured out his ex-girlfriend had sicced us on him," Per explained.

"So he's not a total idiot."

"No, and evidently he has a short fuse. That's why he was waiting for Rebecca outside New Way with the crowbar. He was afraid you recognized him as Rebecca's ex and knew he needed to lie low. And when our colleagues called Frank Meister before visiting, he realized he needed to find another place to hide."

"So he remembered the factory where he worked."

"Exactly. He slept there at night and wandered the area during the day. He stole food because he was broke."

"Why didn't he just stay at the factory?"

"Fear of being caught. So he chose the lifeguard tower."

"And it was pure coincidence he'd chosen the night of Lück's murder to relocate?"

"He claims he saw us at the scene."

"So he was in the area?"

"Yes, because he was afraid to stay in the factory during the day. While he was wandering around, he saw the dead body being taken away. At first, he slept outdoors and in barns until he discovered the tower. Pretty far-fetched."

"So far-fetched it could almost be true," Hannes said.

"You've got to be kidding."

"Federsen and especially Clarissa know how to back a guy into a corner. His story's so complex it would be easy to trick him into contradicting himself. I'm sure they've tried. If you keep asking him to repeat the story, he'll inevitably slip up, especially since he's not that bright."

"Maybe we just need some time," Per said. "We can hit him with the lineup next. Di Santo will definitely be able to identify him, then his story will unravel."

Per parked the car. Most of the windows in di Santo's apartment were lit, and the lights on the fourth floor were also on. A woman just stepped out of the building as the detectives approached, and they slipped in after her.

"Can't wait to hear what he has to say," Hannes said.

They took the elevator to di Santo's floor.

"He lives here," Hannes said, nodding at a gray door.

Per pressed the doorbell, but nothing happened. He knocked on the door.

"Maybe he fell asleep," Hannes said and called di Santo. The phone rang, and a tango number started playing inside the apartment. After no answer, Hannes tried again but got the same result. Then he pounded on the door.

"What are you doing?" A neighbor had come out. It was a young man holding a baby.

Hannes flashed his badge. "We have an appointment with Mr. di Santo."

"Did he complain about something again?"

"No, we're here about another matter."

"Well, that's good. He's always complaining about something. But he was the one making noise last night. I thought about calling the cops on him for a change."

"What?"

"Our baby had just fallen asleep, and he started playing loud music. Seems he was moving furniture around. He even started drilling. He's one to complain."

"When was that?" Hannes asked.

"Around eleven. It was weird because you never hear anything from him. I went to the bathroom around one thirty and heard his apartment door close and someone walk down the stairs."

The investigators exchanged worried glances. Per knocked again. Nothing.

The neighbor retreated into his apartment. Per examined the door and pulled a credit card out of his wallet.

"The door's pretty old. The lock probably hasn't been updated either." He rattled the door. "There's a lot of give. If he didn't deadbolt it, I could open it with my credit card."

Hannes nodded. It was possible Carlos di Santo was simply asleep. Per stuck his credit card into the gap between the door and the jamb and slid it down.

"That's the latch. There's nothing else in the way. Doesn't seem like he turned the deadbolt."

He fiddled with the card until the door swung open.

"Your second heroic act of the day," Hannes joked.

They hesitated as they stepped inside. The only light came in from the hallway. Hannes called his name. No reply. He slowly walked past the small dresser where Isabelle had seen the pictures of Benjamin Lück. Something wasn't right. He opened the door to the living room and cringed in horror.

Hannes didn't notice Per's terrified gasp. He stared at the body, which seemed to float upside down in the room. Hannes saw only the back, but knew the man hanging there was Carlos di Santo. A rope had been tied around his ankles and attached to the ceiling with a hook, which explained the drilling noise. From the hook the rope led diagonally down to the floor, where it ended in another loop. It had been placed around the foot of a massive cabinet to prevent the body from dropping. He hung perfectly straight, his medium-length hair almost touching the ground.

Hannes shook himself from his stupor and raced into the room. There was plaster dust on the floor. He slowly circled the lifeless body. Di Santo's wrists had been tied behind his back; his arms stuck out to the side and pointed toward the ceiling. Hannes's gaze moved from the feet down to the body. When he saw the bearded face, he was overcome by dizziness. He pressed a hand to his mouth and took off, pushing Per out of his way, to vomit in the toilet. Panting, he clutched the ceramic bowl and laid his head on his arms. He struggled to get up, then flushed the toilet. He rinsed his mouth out several times and washed his hands.

Reluctantly, he approached the living room again. His stomach was rumbling, and he felt like his head might explode. Per was pale as a ghost. He had settled on the edge of the couch, unable to look away. Hannes forced the nausea down and knelt in front of the dangling body.

Di Santo's head was swollen. His dark eyes had lost their melancholic expression. Wide open, they seemed to be staring at the detectives. A thick black woolen thread zigzagged from one side of the mouth to the other. The killer had crudely sewn di Santo's lips together. Blood had pooled around the sutures and dried.

"I've already contacted our colleagues," said Per. "There's no pulse."

Hannes stood and sat down next to Per. They stared at the surreal scene. Hannes felt like his brain was shrouded in a heavy fog.

"Per," Hannes said, and his voice sounded fake to him. "Di Santo called me yesterday at about nine. Around eleven, the neighbor heard music and noise coming from this apartment, and at one thirty someone left the apartment. From here to the lifeguard tower . . ."

Per groaned and collapsed in exhaustion.

"David Bach couldn't have been the killer. He couldn't have gotten back to the search area in time. His getaway bike was discovered in a bush halfway between the gas station and the tower. There's no way he could have walked from here. The search began at six, but the area was cordoned off as early as five. He had at most three and a half hours. Not a chance."

"Unless he stole another bike. Or a scooter. Or a car. But it seems to me Frank Meister's now taken center stage."

CHAPTER 23

The coast had been blanketed by the winter's first frost, and the roofs were adorned by a layer of white crystals. Hannes ate his breakfast and took his painkillers. He had heeded the advice of his doctor and stayed home from work the previous day. His thoughts left him restless. The images of Carlos di Santo hanging from the ceiling played over and over in his head. That night, he had dreamed that Federsen had nailed him to a cross, while the other investigators sat at his feet stuffing their faces full of mushrooms. Hannes had jerked awake at five o'clock, his body soaked in sweat. He had spent the next few hours studying for his boating test the next day.

Fritz looked a bit better. His arm was still bandaged but no longer in a sling. He listened closely to Hannes's account of the successful manhunt for David Bach and the visit to Carlos di Santo's apartment. He would have loved to storm out of the prison and take a more active role.

"There were two glasses on his kitchen table, one full, the other empty. Traces of Rohypnol were found in the juice residue. It's the same pattern: the killer knocks the victim out, sets up the murder, and is careful to ensure that death only occurs when the effects of the drug have worn off."

"And that's what happened to Carlos di Santo," said Fritz.

"He called me at nine and said he was meeting someone. The person apparently came over to his place around eleven, because there was loud music and drilling. The guest must have slipped the drug into the juice and waited for di Santo to lose consciousness. The music was probably meant to cover up the noise. He moved the cabinet, screwed the hook in the ceiling, and grabbed the needle and thread. Soon di Santo was dangling upside down. His hands were tied, so he had no chance. Blood rushed to his head, his brain swelled, and organ failure did him in. The culprit sat and watched. The door to the apartment slammed shut around one thirty. Unfortunately, no one saw the perp. The time of death was sometime shortly before that."

"Not a pretty way to go," Fritz said and shuddered. "You wake up, realize you're hanging from your feet in your own living room, and your blood's all flowing to your head. And you can't scream for help because your lips are sewn shut."

"But that's not all. The inside of his mouth was torn to shreds by the thorns of a small hawthorn branch. He must have chewed on it in agonizing desperation."

"Incredible. The perp must have a real sadistic streak. It also supports the theory that the murders are meant as punishment. What could Carlos di Santo have done that was so reprehensible?"

"He was gay. But unlike Lück, he wasn't out. He was ashamed and kept it a secret."

"Anything besides that?"

"He fought with his neighbors and regularly complained to the police about noise, trash, and illegal parking. All the residents were questioned yesterday. He mostly kept to himself. His family lives in Argentina, and we haven't found any friends. He was a lonely man, especially after being kicked out of New Way."

"But it's worth noting that he hadn't been a member of New Way for six months, yet he was still killed. The circumstances of his death have the same pattern as the other murders. So why him?"

"He was a founding member of New Way. No one outside the group would have known he had been kicked out. Perhaps the perp didn't know either."

"Possible, but unlikely. So far everything seems to indicate that the culprit's very familiar with everything New Way. That's why we suspected someone within the group. Let's take another look at the commandments."

Fritz unfolded a piece of paper and pushed his chair next to Hannes. The prison administration must have been extremely grateful for his intervention in the fight, because the guard didn't seem to care.

"First Commandment: 'I am the Lord, your God. You shall have no other gods before me,'" Hannes read. "Antje Kramer thought otherwise and died as a result."

"Exactly. The Second Commandment: 'You shall not take the name of the Lord your God in vain.' Benjamin Lück told everyone God loved him despite his homosexuality."

"Third Commandment: 'Remember to keep holy the Sabbath.' Wolfgang Hartmann violated it and was harassed with phone calls on Sundays."

"Fourth: 'Honor your father and your mother.' Mrs. Brinkmann didn't do this actively enough and was punished with the estrangement of her own children."

"As for the fifth: 'You shall not kill,'" Hannes said, "the perp has already broken it five times. But he applied it to Sylvia Böhm, who had an abortion."

Fritz rubbed his large ears as he thought. "She also broke the sixth: 'You shall not commit adultery.' And Beatrice Reichert repeatedly ignored the seventh: 'You shall not steal.' Her favorite mementos were taken."

Hannes hesitated before tackling the Eighth Commandment. "'You shall not bear false witness against your neighbor.' So far, we haven't attributed a victim to this commandment."

"Because there hadn't been a victim until recently. Lück's tongue was cut out because he supposedly took God's name in vain. Carlos di Santo's mouth, on the other hand, was sewn shut so he couldn't bear false witness anymore. That's why he wanted to meet with you. He was onto something but was silenced just in time."

"But how did the killer know di Santo was dangerous?"

"Counter question: Who knew you contacted him?"

"Well, the people from New Way. They brought him to our attention."

"Aha. And I'm sure they also thought he wouldn't have anything positive to say about them. Who did di Santo complain about the most?"

Hannes thought hard. "He was so bitter, he lumped them all together. They had betrayed the original ideals of the group, he said, and wanted to transform it into a religious or at least a stricter association. He was outraged that a former priest had become involved. Oh, and he claimed that the Schweigers and the Grafs bad-mouthed Lück."

"The Schweigers keep popping up. But let's finish the list."

"The Ninth Commandment is 'You shall not covet your neighbor's house.' The Grafs' house was set on fire after they were planning to evict their tenants."

"That could have been a ploy, and they started the fire themselves. Has the investigation made any progress?"

"No. The Tenth Commandment also says, 'You shall not covet your neighbor's wife.' Alexander Kramer must have thought about that one for several hours on the cross. That's it for the commandments. Maybe the murders will stop now?"

"I wouldn't count on it. There's also the question of whether or not Mrs. Böhm counts for two commandments. If not, then 'You shall not commit adultery' is still free."

"Great," Hannes said. "So we need to find out who's been unfaithful and offer them protection?"

"Wouldn't hurt. I think the perp made a crucial mistake in killing Carlos di Santo."

"Why?"

"Di Santo was no longer a member. Presumably, he was killed because he knew too much. What other possibilities are there? Apart from New Way, he had almost no life. And it's highly doubtful his sympathies lay with the Church of the Creator. So he could only know something about members of New Way."

"Seems logical. Especially since we can rule out Bach as di Santo's killer. Frank Meister's still in the running, though. It's possible Bach committed some of the crimes, Meister the others."

"Like on Tuesday night, for example," said Fritz.

"I'm surprised by the killer's boldness. He must have felt safe. After all, he made all that noise. The neighbors could have easily called the police. And he stayed in the apartment for hours, instead of leaving as quickly as possible."

"Maybe he feels invincible. He's probably already planning his next target in his crusade."

***

Frank Meister finally showed signs of life. He had used his credit card to take out money at ATMs four times in the last few days and had maxed out the allowed limit every time. The first time had been four days ago at the main train station, then Tuesday night at the ferry terminal, and most recently in Finland. He had used two machines: one the day before in Helsinki and the other a few hours ago in Jyväskylä, 150 miles north of the Finnish capital. It was assumed that he had traveled by train, since the police had checked with all the car-rental companies.

The ferry line had confirmed that Meister had left the city early on Wednesday morning as a foot passenger and had disembarked almost thirty hours later in Helsinki. He must have headed straight to the main train station, because he withdrew cash half an hour later. He had probably also purchased a train ticket for the next morning, and had then spent the night in a three-star hotel near the station. He used his credit card to pay for the room. His cell phone had been off for days.

The ferry had departed at three in the morning on Wednesday, which would have given Meister exactly an hour and a half after leaving di Santo's apartment. He would have had no trouble reaching the ship in time.

The Finnish police had been sent a description of Meister. But if he switched trains in Jyväskylä, it would be very easy for him to disappear into the wilds of the great country. There wasn't much more besides trees and lakes farther north.

The investigative team was spellbound as they listened to Marcel's report. Hannes had joined them around noon, citing back pain and dizziness. Steffen Lauer had looked at him strangely, and Hannes had feared his visits with Fritz might be blown. He had felt his ears turn red.

"What does David Bach have to say about the fact that his buddy took off?" asked Lauer.

"Not much," said Federsen. "We'll take another stab at him soon, won't we, Niehaus?"

Hannes stared at him in surprise. Federsen had been really considerate lately. Apparently, he had earned his boss's respect, even though he hadn't been following orders when he'd climbed the lifeguard tower. Per had handled the situation with much more control.

"Bach's sitting in his cell. We're going to get the truth out of him," Federsen said. "Yesterday, he admitted a new detail. He'd gotten into an argument with Mrs. Böhm back in October when he distributed pamphlets to parents picking up their children from one of the playgroups. Alexander Kramer had also been there. Although Bach claims it was Meister's idea, he admits it had led to a heated confrontation. Once our Finnish colleagues nab Meister, we can finally consider the case closed."

Clarissa and Hannes looked at each other doubtfully.

"How can we be so sure no one else is involved? Frank Meister may be in Finland, but that doesn't mean other people aren't still in danger," Hannes said.

"What's that supposed to mean?" Federsen shouted. His opinion of Hannes had obviously returned to normal. "Since when did you start doubting that Bach and Meister are behind all this?"

"I agree with Hannes," Clarissa said. "We should at least consider the possibility that someone else is involved. So far, everything points to the two men, but we still lack hard evidence."

Federsen grew even more exasperated as the other colleagues began to voice their doubts. Lauer didn't want to take any chances.

"If we focus solely on Bach and Meister and there's another victim, we'll be publicly crucified. We don't have a confession, and we can't fully explain the motive, so we'll continue to investigate all possible leads," Lauer said.

At least Daniel Novak could be ruled out. The dealer had been able to account for his whereabouts on Tuesday night, which was more than Matthias Böhm could do. He said he had spent the evening preparing the documents to sell the horse farm and had gone to bed early without any witnesses.

"Mr. Böhm hates New Way," Hannes said. "Thanks to his wife, he was well informed about the lives of the members. But he had had no previous contact with Carlos di Santo."

"Di Santo was around long enough to have known Mrs. Böhm. Could something have happened that Böhm still resented?" Isabelle asked.

"We should check to see if there's any connection between them," Lauer said. "Is it possible there might be more accomplices within the Church of the Creator?"

"More than possible," Marcel said. "Ahrendt, for one, even if he's only the puppeteer. But unfortunately we don't have access to these people. We've tried to pressure them, but they either refuse to talk or say neutral things."

Ludwig Obermann, the carpenter with the broken leg, was eliminated as a suspect in the death of Lück. When di Santo had been killed, his mother had been visiting and confirmed that he had spent the entire evening at home. On the other hand, as Clarissa pointed out, Obermann's mother also belonged to the Church of the Creator. It was agreed that Obermann could only be considered an accessory. Clarissa and Marcel would question him again.

"Well, that's it for today." Federsen was ready to go.

"Wait," said Hannes. "We still need to discuss who we suspect from New Way."

"You and your damn ideas," Federsen snapped.

"Who do you have in mind?" Lauer asked.

"The Schweigers stand out. I find it hard to imagine them as murderers, but they do have surprisingly strong opinions."

"And that of course makes them immediately suspicious," Federsen said sarcastically.

"They didn't agree with the behavior of some of the members. They also had contact with Meister—Mr. Schweiger has already admitted that."

Lauer nodded and assigned Per and Federsen to interview them again. Isabelle and Hannes would see the Grafs, then take a second look at the rest of the members. First, however, Hannes accompanied

Federsen into the interrogation room to see the man who had nearly broken his neck.

The switchblade Bach had used to threaten the gas station attendant had been examined for possible traces of Benjamin Lück's DNA, but the analysis hadn't yielded anything. According to Maria's report, however, a knife like it could have been used to slice off the actor's tongue.

David Bach stared at his hands. It was the first time Hannes had seen him without being attacked. He was tall, muscular, and had an angular face. His eyes seemed cold, and his thin lips formed a straight line. His ears protruded from his head, and his short blond hair lacked any discernible style.

Federsen slammed a folder on the table and settled into a chair. He leafed through the folder for show.

"You already know my colleague," Federsen said. "You nearly sent him to an early grave."

"He doesn't look so bad," Bach said. Hannes was surprised by his high-pitched voice.

"I still have severe bruising and a concussion to thank you for," Hannes said as he sat down.

"Sorry," Bach said sarcastically.

"You should be," said Federsen. "Otherwise, we'd be questioning you about six instead of five murders. You're facing two additional counts for assaulting an officer. Maybe there's even enough for attempted homicide. Let's add it all up: five murders, one attempted homicide, robbery, several burglaries, assault, stalking, damage to property, and intimidation. Did I forget anything?"

"Bicycle theft," Hannes said and smirked.

It was a rusty old bike that Bach had taken. Despite an intensive search, no other bike thefts had come to light. Nor had any scooters or cars been stolen in the area, so it was looking increasingly unlikely that Bach was responsible for di Santo's death. There was no way he could have covered the distance on foot in such a short time.

"We're hot on your buddy's heels too," Federsen said. "He's in Finland."

The news surprised Bach. "What's he doing there?"

"Probably trying to evade us, but he won't have much luck. I'd advise you to put it all out on the table. Never know if there might be extenuating circumstances. If your friend comes clean first, he'll have the upper hand, and you'll be sitting in shit."

"I didn't kill anyone. I've already confessed to the other things, but I didn't kill anyone. I've got no idea why you keep assuming that."

"Because you've got a strong motive and no alibi," said Hannes. "You've threatened multiple people at New Way—"

"I did not. Sure, they annoyed us. They looked down on us, made fun of us. We're religious nuts to them. We wanted a little payback."

"Aha," Federsen said. "So you admit you wanted revenge."

"Nothing big—just create a stir. Distribute leaflets, then that picture of the Devil. We didn't hurt anyone."

"That's debatable. After all, Mr. Beck could have lost his livelihood because of your complaint. Property damage is no small matter either, not to mention the assaults."

"Yeah, it got a little out of hand. The complaint was Frank's idea. I wouldn't know how to engineer something like that. But honestly, I have nothing against this group. I'm not as religious as Frank. I feel welcome at the Church of the Creator, that's all. But I was annoyed by the way those people treated us. That's why I helped."

"Oh, so you just helped. Who else helped?"

"It was just Frank and me. He said we should teach them a lesson. It was harmless."

"What you intended to do with the crowbar was far from harmless," Hannes said. "You attacked me. And had I not been there, you probably would have attacked your ex-girlfriend."

"I just wanted to scare her. Frank thought she was the one behind it."

"Behind what?"

"That she was the one who tipped you off about me. I didn't want to get in any more trouble with the police. So we thought we could intimidate her."

"Let's move on to the murder victims," Federsen said. "Alexander Kramer once defended Rebecca Köhler from you, and his sister and Sylvia Böhm helped him. This past spring, you assaulted Benjamin Lück because he—"

"I already told you that's not true. I never assaulted him, and who's Sylvia Böhm?"

"Mrs. Böhm owned a horse farm," Hannes said. "But you put an early end to that."

"She was the one who was murdered?" Bach looked at Hannes and smiled mockingly. "She was always hanging around with that porn star. I get it now."

"Well? What do you have to say for yourself?" Federsen asked.

"I often saw her. Her husband is friends with Frank's sister—I've met him a couple times. He's even considering joining us."

There was a reassignment of duties shortly thereafter. Hannes and Federsen headed to the horse farm. Questioning Matthias Böhm became the highest priority, especially since Per had more news. He had called Thomas Beck to find out more about the relationship between Sylvia Böhm and Carlos di Santo. As far as the chaplain knew, the two hadn't been friends. He did, however, recall a conversation in which she told him she had joined because of di Santo. She had accidentally rear-ended him two years ago, and the Argentinian had suffered severe whiplash. She had felt guilty and had contacted him afterward. At some point the topic of New Way came up, and he had convinced her to attend a meeting.

Matthias Böhm denied any connection to the Church of the Creator at first. It was only when Hannes informed him that Frank Meister's sister was being interrogated that he conceded.

"It's a private matter, but yes, I know Ursula. We used to work at the same company."

"Why have you been keeping this a secret?"

"Because I didn't want to give the wrong impression. I am—I mean, I was—married. Ursula and I are friends. We've been getting together a little more often now because I've needed someone to talk to."

"You get along so well that you're toying with the idea of joining the Church of the Creator?"

"What's that supposed to mean?"

"Do you get along with Ms. Meister's brother as much as you do with her?" Hannes asked.

"Frank? We rarely see each other. I don't know him well, but he seems to be a decent guy."

"There's evidence to the contrary," Federsen said. "We're looking for him because of his possible involvement in several murders. He might be your wife's killer. Unfortunately, he's run off to Finland."

"That's ridiculous. Frank didn't kill my wife. Why would he?"

"You tell me. You know him."

"I know him well enough to realize your guess is nonsense."

When he learned that Meister had been a nuisance to New Way, he cleared his throat.

"It's understandable why he feels provoked by them. I used to listen to my wife make fun of the people at the church. She used to be a believer too, and I have no idea what this group did to her. She totally changed after joining."

"And why did she join?"

"Because we were going through a rough patch. She probably wanted to feel connected to a community."

"How did she hear about New Way?" Hannes asked.

"What does it matter?"

"Does the name Carlos di Santo mean anything to you?"

"No."

"He died two days ago. He was a founding member of New Way and used to handle their finances. Your wife accidentally rear-ended him about two years ago."

"I remember that. She was driving alone."

"He introduced your wife to New Way. Didn't you know that?"

"No. She felt unnecessarily guilty about that guy. She'd call him sometimes and meet with him." He looked at his watch. "I have some buyers coming soon, and I've almost reached an agreement with the tax office. Then this whole nightmare will be over."

Federsen nodded. "That's it for today. But your nightmare may be far from over. We're keeping an eye on you."

***

The team reconvened at the end of the day. There was no news from Finland, and Frank Meister hadn't used his credit card again. Hannes and Federsen gave a summary of their conversation with Matthias Böhm, which was then followed by an update from Isabelle and Per. They had paid a visit to the Grafs. Since restoration on their house continued to drag on, they were still living in a hotel. They had acknowledged that they were critical of some of the group members, just like the Schweigers, but they had also claimed that they would never drum someone out of the group. Carlos di Santo was a special case because he had apparently embezzled money. The Grafs also kept their distance from members of the Church of the Creator.

"We went over their alibis, murder for murder," Isabelle said. "They were somewhat taken aback, but we told them it was routine."

"What kind of alibis did they have?" Steffen Lauer asked.

"Nothing verifiable for the death of Alexander Kramer. But they had a meeting with their insurance agent at the time of Mrs. Böhm's death, which we've already confirmed. As for Antje Kramer, it's hard to pinpoint the time. We have no idea when the poisonous mushrooms were added to her stash. When Mr. Lück died, they were allegedly in their hotel room, and on the night of di Santo's death, they attended the symphony with friends, then went out to eat and headed back to the hotel around midnight. Their friends and a waiter confirmed this."

"So we can rule them out," Federsen said.

Hannes said, "As informants or accessories, yes. Besides, I had my eye more on the Schweigers. How did they react?"

"Outraged is probably the best way to put it," Clarissa said. "They supposedly contacted Meister in an attempt at mediation. They have alibis for every murder with one exception: Mr. Schweiger can't prove his whereabouts on the night di Santo died. He attended choir practice with his wife that evening, but then they split up. She went home to take over for the babysitter around ten. He says he had a headache and walked home alone. According to his wife, he arrived home around eleven. There are no other witnesses."

"Not very convincing," said Lauer.

Clarissa and Marcel had also conducted two interrogations. Although Ludwig Obermann wasn't a prime suspect, there was the question of his involvement as an accomplice. But he had clearly distanced himself from Bach and Meister once Clarissa started peppering him with questions.

"He claims he only wanted to defuse the situation in the summer and knows nothing about the other incidents. He didn't use the word 'fanatic,' but it was clear he considers Meister one. He described Bach as a hothead looking for recognition. He admitted that he could picture the two carrying out the attacks on New Way. And that was before we even told him about Bach's confession. He said he could have gotten involved, but had little desire."

"Was he credible?" asked Lauer.

"Yes," Marcel said. "He's very religious, but not fanatical. A little simple-minded, but good-natured. Just because he's a carpenter doesn't mean he made the cross."

"What did you learn from Meister's sister?"

"She corroborated Mr. Böhm's claim that they were just friends. Ursula Meister is as religious as her brother and would never get involved with a married man. Now that he's a widower, that could change. She's thirty-seven and—like her brother—was brought up very religious. She has a close relationship with him."

"But not so close she knows what he's been up to in Finland," Clarissa added. "His last vacation was in January, and she suggested he felt burned out. His trip might have been a snap decision."

Per shook his head. "If he's burned out, why would he visit Finland? It's dark nearly all day now and freezing cold. Wouldn't you head somewhere warm and sunny?"

"It's a pretty lame explanation. She wants to protect him and stated several times he wasn't capable of such acts. She said Bach is a liar and wants to pin the blame on her brother. She had always thought her brother shouldn't have gotten involved with him."

"Perhaps the perfect scapegoat," said Hannes. "Let's say Bach's telling the truth. He did a few stupid things, which Meister had put him up to. Maybe Meister's been the one behind the real crimes, but has been able to direct our suspicions onto Bach. He's fanatical and clever. He might have been using Bach from the start."

"Meister's sister would see it differently," said Clarissa. "In her opinion, Bach was a bad influence on her brother. But in attempting to portray her brother as innocent, she's maybe overshot her target."

"How so?"

"She talked about how well he got along with Mr. Böhm. When she told her brother about Mr. Böhm's problems, he offered to help. The two of them would often hang out and talk. Matthias Böhm seems to have downplayed his relationship with Frank Meister."

Chapter 24

With the last days of November came the first weekend of Advent. The sun shined warmly on Hannes. He yawned and turned over. Anna had tangled herself in the blanket. She faced him, her breathing deep.

Hannes had his boating-license test at ten o'clock. He stretched, remaining cautious as he arched his back. The pain had died down, and the pressure in his head had subsided so much that he decided against a painkiller.

After his shower, he walked out onto his little balcony. There wasn't a single cloud in the sky, and the temperature was almost in the fifties. The air felt unseasonably crisp. He took a deep breath and felt sorry his colleagues had to spend the weekend interviewing more witnesses.

He returned to the bedroom with a hot cup of coffee. Anna hadn't moved. He leaned over and fanned some of the coffee's steam toward her. He smiled as the aroma caused her nose to twitch. A moment later, her eyes opened. Anna stretched, then sat up and gratefully took the cup from Hannes.

"The sun's finally out again. What time is it?"

"A little after eight thirty. Breakfast is already on the table. I have to go in half an hour, so I can get to the port on time."

"It's a shame your test is today. Otherwise, we could take advantage of this great weather."

"I'm glad, because the sea will be calm today. Hopefully, the good weather will last through the afternoon for the second part of the test."

Anna looked at him longingly and stroked his arm. "I look forward to having a skipper for a boyfriend," she said and smiled. "Maybe we could walk on the beach in the afternoon? We said we'd meet everyone else at the Christmas market at seven tonight."

"That'd be great," Hannes said. "I'll call you after the written test. If I screw it up, I won't be going out on the water in the afternoon."

"You'll do fine. You can thank that guy for kicking you off the lifeguard tower. At least it meant you could cram on Thursday. Now give me a kiss."

On his way to the port, Hannes went over the test once more in his head. He could be given one of fifteen possible tests, each one consisting of thirty questions. On top of that, there was a nine-part navigation problem. That was the section he feared most, even if Ole had gone over everything there was to know about navigation.

Hannes fumbled in the glove compartment for his sunglasses, then his phone rang.

"Per and I are on our way to the horse farm," Clarissa said.

"I'm sure Mr. Böhm will be happy to see you," said Hannes.

"That's his problem. He owes us a few explanations. I'm sure there's a reason why he downplayed his connection to Meister."

"Do we know anything more about that?"

"No. And we haven't heard anything from Meister's credit card company either. He could be anywhere in Finland. He might have crossed into Norway or Sweden. We've alerted our colleagues there."

"At least he can't enter Russia. He'd be picked up at the border immediately."

"Right. And he can't take a ferry either—we've contacted all the ferry lines. But that really doesn't help, because Scandinavia's huge. Anyway, I'll call you later."

Twenty-four questions into the test, everything was going fine. Question twenty-five, however, threw him for a loop. Hannes chewed on his pen. "What does a sector light signify?" The answers all sounded right. He circled "Alter course when entering white sector." He quickly answered the remaining four questions and continued on to the navigation problem.

He nervously read the question and turned to the sea chart. He had twenty minutes. "A pleasure craft is traveling from Helgoland to Cuxhaven. The speed over ground is 10 knots. At 11:00 a.m., the craft passes the light buoy Helgoland-O, which is located 1.2 nautical miles south of Helgoland."

Hannes had to provide the coordinates of the vessel. In the second part, he had to explain that a marking on the chart signals the presence of a shipwreck at 56.3 meters below sea level. After calculating and charting a true course, describing a light buoy, and computing the travel time, he leaned back in his chair. The first six parts of the problem were done, and once he had answered the seventh part correctly, it was smooth sailing. Shortly before the hour was up, he laid down his compass and scribbled his answer to the ninth part, which had asked him to find out the so-called dead reckoning position.

Hannes walked outside and strolled down the quay toward *Lena*. She was one of the last boats still in the water, and he reverently ran his hand along her railing. He found it hard to believe he would soon be able to captain the boat.

"Can't hardly wait, huh?" Ole said as he strode over. "How'd it go?"

"Good, I think. Thanks for your help. Without you, that sea chart would have been tough."

Ole leaned against the railing and looked out at the sea. Hannes knew he wasn't one to waste his breath. A seagull landed on the edge of the boat. A moment of peace. Hannes could have stayed there forever. Just then, his phone rang. He looked at Ole, who furrowed his eyebrows, turned, and trudged across the footbridge.

"What's up, Clarissa?"

"Mr. Böhm claims Ursula Meister read too much into his relationship with her brother. She feels sorry for Frank and thinks everyone else does too."

"The guy doesn't exactly pull on your heartstrings."

"Don't fool yourself. He's well received at the Church of the Creator. Seems he's quite charismatic. I told Mr. Böhm that we were checking Meister's phone records. After that, Böhm admitted they had regularly spoken and met from time to time. He had needed someone to talk to, and Meister had helped him through a difficult time."

"A model of Christian charity," Hannes said.

"Which worked. After a heated debate, Böhm let slip that he had joined the Church of the Creator a few days ago, which I find strange."

"Why? He fits right in . . ."

"Because he knows we're investigating the church. That was his reason why he kept his relationship with Ursula and Frank Meister a secret. He even admitted he was aware of some of the nonfatal incidents. Frank had told him about them, but blamed Bach. So Böhm assumed we had something against Meister and Bach, that we'd think they might even be involved in his wife's murder. But he stays friends with Meister and joins the Church of the Creator?"

"And he said?"

"The two men are innocent. He sees the Church of the Creator as a place of refuge for true Christians and the people there as above suspicion."

"How credible do you think he is?"

"To the extent that his religious fervor matches that of the Church of the Creator. But he's also unreadable and could be hiding something. Especially since he admitted today for the first time that he knew about the sexual relationship between his wife and Alexander Kramer."

Hannes wandered back inside to find out the results of the written test. Despite three wrong answers, he had passed. The test on the water would take place in an hour. He went back outside and sat by himself. *Could Mr. Böhm be behind all this?* Hannes wondered. David Bach had admitted to meeting Matthias Böhm, but only a couple of times. Frank Meister was the link between them, and he was now hiding somewhere deep in the Scandinavian winter. At the same time, Hannes couldn't shake the feeling that the perp was involved in New Way. Or maybe that was just his dislike of the Schweigers talking. He was curious to hear what Elke would have to say.

He looked up at the sound of a car. Anna had borrowed her friend Tina's Mini and had pulled into the parking lot. She beamed as she walked over in her thin denim jacket.

"What a beautiful day. It's wonderful here." She waved a small backpack. "I brought some lunch."

They sat on two small rocks, and Anna pulled items from her backpack.

"Shrimp salad," Hannes said appreciatively and took a giant bite. "Where'd you get it?"

"From a deli near Tina's place. Congratulations on the first part of the test. When's the next part?"

"In a few minutes. But it'll take a while."

"Doesn't matter, I'll watch from here. There are worse places I could be. By the way, guess who e-mailed me?"

"You got an interview at LightFire?"

"Awesome, right?" she said and hugged him. "I have to thank Ines. She passed my application on to her friend there. I'm really excited."

Hannes was too, and he hoped she'd get the job. It couldn't get any better—the company was located in the city center, so she'd be close to him.

"All test takers to the boats!" the examiner shouted in a stern voice, and Hannes raced over to the dock. Contrary to expectations, Ute had decided to participate. The seasickness she had experienced in class hadn't deterred her. She was also the first one called. She had difficulty navigating by compass, but the examiner turned a blind eye when she took a few turns too hard.

Next was Hannes's turn. He performed the five mandatory maneuvers without complaint. Anna had left the spot where she had been sitting and stood beside Ole on the dock. Ole looked cheerful and was engaged in a lively discussion with her while they watched.

The examiner chose the two elective maneuvers that would take the shortest amount of time to complete.

"Good," he said to Hannes. "If you don't tangle up your knots, you're done."

Hannes leaned back and signaled with a thumbs-up to Anna and Ole that everything had gone well. While Karl grit his teeth and attempted cross bearing for a second time, Hannes's thoughts turned to David Bach. There was no questioning his inclination toward violence. His extensive criminal record proved that, and his actions on the beach only reinforced the opinion. But would he kill several people in such a sadistic manner? Especially strangers. Had he killed his ex-girlfriend, wounded pride or even heartbreak would have at least explained it. But she had been spared. Why? Was he driven by religious fanaticism? He didn't give the impression of being especially pious. And he wouldn't have become a crusader for nothing. This was where Frank Meister came into play. He was a brilliant proselytizer, able to sway others. But Hannes disliked the fact that the investigation hung on a single theory. Of course, it was an obvious one, and no other theory had suggested itself. But what if the Finnish authorities nabbed Meister and the theory turned out to be a flop?

'A flop' perfectly described Karl's performance. His seasick wife Ute had passed the test, while he had to take it again. The group had gathered on the quay. He stood there sulking as Ute demonstrated her knotting skills. Hannes ran into a little trouble with his bowline knot, but he managed to save face.

The successful graduates returned one more time to the small building where their licenses awaited them. Hannes stepped out into the sunlight and presented Anna and Ole with the turquoise-colored card.

"Congratulations!" she exclaimed. "I told you not to worry. Here—I got you a gift."

Surprised, he watched as she pulled from her backpack a white captain's hat with a navy visor.

***

That evening, the Christmas market in front of city hall was packed with visitors squeezing through the narrow corridors of stalls at the foot of the Gothic building. The old city center was adorned in festive lights and decorations, and everyone was thirsty for mulled wine.

Hannes sipped on his first cup while his friends were already on their second round. At least it wasn't cold, which was the first major strike against Christmas markets for Hannes. The second was the crowds. Ben's dog Socks apparently thought the same. He lay at Hannes's feet, his tail between his legs. He was, however, intrigued by the diverse smells. He constantly sniffed each passerby, and a little girl quickly pulled her cotton candy out of his reach. Hannes chuckled and patted Socks. The news of Hannes's passed test had been met with enthusiasm, and everyone was eager to know when he would take them out on the water.

"Doesn't make sense in the winter," he said. "There's not much space in the wheelhouse and cabin, and you'll just freeze your asses off outside."

Secretly, he wanted to embark on his maiden voyage with just Anna. That way, the others wouldn't see him make some clumsy mistake the first time he cast off.

"We could celebrate New Year's Eve on your boat," suggested Ben. "I don't know if Socks would come, though. We'd have to see."

"That'd certainly be a change from ringing in the new year in some crowded club," Kalle said.

"Or sitting in front of some boring raclette grill," Ines added with a grin.

Hannes stared at the five expectant faces. Judging by the look on Anna's face, she too welcomed the idea, so he bit the bullet. After all, it did sound like a good plan.

Hannes pulled Elke aside to ask about her recent impressions of New Way. Anna was talking with Ines about her job prospects, and Kalle had been roped into a discussion about women with Ben. Evidently, his romance with the Vietnamese girl from the club had its vagaries.

"How's the investigation?" Elke asked.

"We have a prime suspect."

"That's good. Maybe people will finally start relaxing at New Way."

"What do you mean?"

"Everyone's been on edge. There have been some heated exchanges."

"About what?"

"A few people think the group's being targeted for its excessive tolerance. That that's what triggered all of this."

"They're blaming the victims?" Hannes was stunned.

"Of course no one will say that out loud. But it seems that way."

"So who holds that opinion?"

"The group's split into two camps. The Schweigers head one group. Five or six people have rallied around them. The moderates seem to be leaving. Yesterday, only twelve people came to the meeting."

"Who's on the Schweigers' side?"

"The Grafs. They rarely used to attend, but now they've been showing up regularly. Then there's Beatrice Reichert. She's a little snooty—she's a former ballerina and thinks she's hot stuff. The Schweigers have also dragged two new couples with them who seem to be more or less cut from the same cloth."

"Who leads the other camp?"

"Those two clowns, Wolfgang Hartmann and his buddy, Bengt. But if this continues, I won't be going much longer. I thought it'd be different."

"Is the group on the verge of a schism?"

"Possibly. Mr. Beck is sitting on the fence, trying to keep the two sides together. His wife can't stand to be there anymore; she hasn't shown up in a long time, which is a shame, because she used to sing with the choir and has a beautiful voice."

"Have Beck's attempts at mediation been successful?"

"At least he's trying. But he's also part of the problem, because he doesn't stand up to the Schweigers and Grafs and gives in too fast. He lets himself be forced into the role of chaplain. On the one hand, he wants everyone to stick together, but on the other, he agrees that some things were a little too lax. He says he just wants to prevent someone else from getting hurt. That's why he's asked everyone to remember the Ten Commandments and not to make themselves a target."

"What's your opinion?"

"I don't know. I'm afraid some might consider me a black sheep for being a lesbian, especially Mrs. Schweiger."

"You told her?" Hannes asked, frightened.

"Of course not. Why would I? Only Rebecca knows."

"And she keeps it to herself?"

"She promised. She's been looking at me a little strangely, though. I suspect she's told someone. But I don't want to make any accusations. I asked her to keep it secret."

"Well, just be—"

"Careful, I know." She laughed. "You've already told me that a hundred times. But you're close to solving the case. What could happen to me now?"

"It's just that . . . Look, just be careful."

"I'll probably stop going. I'll attend the choir getaway next weekend because I've already paid. But if things don't change by then, I'll leave."

"Hey. What are you two chatting about?" Ben walked up from behind Hannes and put his arms around both of them. "Ines suggested we move to another stand. She's hungry."

The group wound its way through the avalanche of people, but their progress was slow because Ines, Anna, and Elke kept stopping to look at different stalls.

"What a small world."

Hannes felt a hand on his shoulder. He turned to find Mr. Beck and his wife. With his full beard, the chaplain could have easily been confused for Santa Claus.

"I thought I saw you," Hannes said. "So I wasn't wrong. Out trying to catch some Christmas spirit?"

"Yeah, but it's hard in crowds like this," Mrs. Beck said.

"Well, we're here, right?" said Mr. Beck with a grin. "Christmas always brings out the need for community and ceremony in people. Church pews aren't packed for nothing."

"Is it the same at New Way?" Hannes asked.

"Last year we had to set up extra chairs," Mrs. Beck said as she eyed Socks and took a step away. "This year . . . well, this year will certainly be different."

"We don't know that for sure," Mr. Beck said. "Our members are very upset right now, which isn't surprising. But we can be a wonderful community again. The perpetrator has been arrested, I hear?"

"The main suspect," Hannes said. "But the investigation's ongoing."

"At least everything's on the right track," Mr. Beck said. "But we don't want to keep you. Have a lovely evening."

"Who was that?" Ben asked as he watched the pair leave.

"That was New Way's sort-of chaplain."

"Oh, that cult Elke joined?" Kalle said.

"It's not a cult," Elke said as she, Anna, and Ines caught up with the men.

The group did run the risk of becoming a cultlike community. The five murders had not only cost human lives, but had also sparked further turmoil.

Chapter 25

Lord, I thank you. I thank you for your strength. I thank you for your counsel. They will not stop me. This I swear. No one will stop me. I am your servant and act according to your will. Eternal damnation awaits those who sin. For the kingdom, the power, and the glory are yours now and forever. Amen.

Chapter 26

On Sunday morning, Anna asked Hannes if he had to work.

"No, but I don't see how we're going to get anywhere with this investigation. One of the suspects disappeared abroad. Arresting him is our only—"

"Well, in that case, I have something for you. Or actually for both of us."

Anna handed him an envelope. Hannes pulled out an online coupon for a day pass to the Beach Spa.

"So you think I need to relax?" He laughed and pulled her close. "Thank you. That's the perfect gift to balance out this crazy week."

On their way to the spa, Hannes couldn't help staring at Anna. She hadn't once complained about his demanding job and the impact it had on his personal life. But was she only holding back because she had just fallen for him and found his job exciting?

"What are you thinking about?" she asked, noticing his change in mood.

"Honestly, I'm thinking about how long it will take before you start to find my job annoying. A lot of cops have trouble balancing their work and personal lives."

"Well, it hasn't bothered me yet. It's more exciting than having an accountant for a boyfriend. Besides, I know how to keep myself busy. And wait until I find a job—I tend to get caught up in my work as well."

"Well then, hopefully we'll still get to see each other," Hannes said.

"There's a simple solution: we reserve two nights a week for ourselves, so we're not liable to spend the entire weekend by ourselves and risk neglecting our friends."

"Sounds good. We should try it." But Hannes doubted the practicality of her idea.

The spa was crowded. The parking lot was so full that Hannes had to park on the side of the road. They were soon sitting in their towels, sweating and watching through a large window as the waves pounded the shore.

Hannes had left his cell phone in the locker and was enjoying the unexpected getaway. He couldn't help but admire Anna's body. Her residual tan shimmered in the warm glow of the sauna. He completely ignored the other women and only looked at her. She kissed him passionately, which surprised him.

The effects of the sauna had worn off by Monday afternoon. Hannes had spent that morning doing light exercise and found that his body had recovered from his fall. Federsen seemed to have forgotten about Hannes's injury and was as grumpy and surly as ever. He repeatedly complained about their Finnish counterparts, who had yet to find Frank Meister. Clarissa reminded him that their own hunt for David Bach took a while.

Fortunately, Federsen took his anger out on interrogating Bach.

"Fine, I admit it," Bach said, sweat dripping down his forehead.

"Be specific," said Federsen.

"We attacked that gay guy from New Way sometime in February. But we didn't really beat him up. We just went after his ponytail. It was disgusting how he just pranced around showing the whole world he was a homo. But it was Frank's idea."

"How did he know Mr. Lück was gay?" Hannes asked.

"Everyone knew that. You could tell. And besides, he was with some man that night."

"So? That doesn't mean anything."

"We saw them kissing in the street. It was disgusting."

"What did you do to the other man?"

"Nothing—he ran off. He was another one of the New Way people. We didn't see him after that, which was good for him because Frank wanted to jump him too. But that never happened. Probably shit his pants and never came back."

"Oh, but you hit your target, you dirty little—"

Hannes took over. He had to admit that his boss had conducted a pretty successful interrogation. "That man was Carlos di Santo. We found him dead in his home last Wednesday just after your buddy left the country. Evidently, he didn't just cut off a ponytail that night."

"Who's worth protecting more?" snorted Federsen. "You or Frank Meister? Maybe you should think about that until our next chat."

***

Isabelle and Hannes were sent back to the horse farm on Tuesday afternoon. As they climbed out of the car, Jonas Talmann was leaving one of the stables.

"You still work here?" Hannes said.

Grinning, Talmann walked over. "Mr. Böhm realized he needed someone familiar with horses. He's found a buyer and doesn't want the horses to look neglected. Yesterday would have actually been my last day, but I got an extension until the end of December."

"And then?"

"I don't know. Once the farm's sold, I'll talk to the new owners. I do know the animals. Every horse has its own quirks and personality, just like dogs."

"Your boss probably would have been completely helpless if left to deal with the animals on his own," Isabelle said.

"He doesn't know the first thing about them. They have to be dewormed again today, for example. At least he knows how to do that."

"Well, enjoy the rest of your day," Isabelle said.

"Wait, what do you mean?" Hannes asked Talmann. "How does Mr. Böhm know that?"

"He had no choice. Last summer, out of the blue, his wife decided to attend a horse auction, and I went with her. But I'd scheduled for the horses to be dewormed that weekend. Most horses are dewormed four times a year, in the spring, summer, fall, and late fall. We could have waited a couple of days, but Mrs. Böhm said her husband should finally learn how to do something."

"Is it difficult?"

"Child's play. We use a paste that's administered orally with a syringe. The important thing is the proper dosage. The syringe has marks for every hundred pounds. It's foolproof."

Isabelle was stunned. "When exactly was he taught how to administer the drug?"

Mr. Talmann furrowed his brow. "Must have been . . . hold on . . . probably mid-September. There had just been a huge storm. I remember Mr. Beck was here. He and Mrs. Böhm were discussing a field trip for disabled children. The visit was supposed to take place shortly thereafter, and they were worried the weather wouldn't cooperate."

"How did Mr. Böhm react?"

"He was surprisingly interested. He wanted to know exactly how much to give each horse. He didn't want to harm any of them. His wife laughed and told him a horse could handle a lot, but be careful not to swallow any because it's toxic to humans in high doses."

So Mr. Böhm knew the dosage. It would have been easy to determine how much was needed to kill a human. But the amount injected into his wife was so large that only someone who knew absolutely nothing about the process would have used that much to poison her. Also, the dewormer injected into Mrs. Böhm's abdomen was available online, so it didn't have to come from this farm. That much was obvious.

When Isabelle and Hannes began to walk toward the main house, Mr. Talmann stopped them.

"Mr. Böhm's gone for a few days."

"What?" Isabelle blurted. "Where'd he go?"

Talmann shrugged. "We're not on the best terms. He just told me he'd be gone for a few days and that I should take care of everything. He'll be back Sunday."

Hannes called Böhm's cell phone. It went straight to voice mail.

***

A few hours later, the investigators gathered in the conference room. Federsen had had the last straw.

"I just called Helsinki. They don't have any idea where our man is. I might as well just go up there and look myself."

An older colleague stormed in.

"Aren't you guys working on that New Way case?"

"Yeah, why?" Federsen asked.

"There's something going on in front of their meeting place."

"What do you mean?"

"We received an emergency call. Several patrol cars are already on their way. Apparently, there's been a fight."

"Unbelievable," Federsen said and stood up. "Niehaus, come with me. Maybe we'll put those muscles of yours to good use for once."

That wasn't the case. By the time they arrived, their colleagues had already defused the situation. Cops were taking down names and addresses. One was in the middle of interviewing Elke. Hannes shoved his way through and grabbed her by the arm.

"Hey," said the uniformed officer.

"I'll question her myself." Hannes flashed his badge. "What's going on?" he asked Elke after ushering her off to the side.

She was breathing rapidly. "Those fanatics ambushed us as we were heading to choir practice. They began insulting us and spitting. It escalated from there. Bengt grabbed a guy, and that's when all hell broke loose."

"Why did they ambush you?"

"They accused us of lying to the police. Said one of them had been arrested. Someone threw rocks at the windows." She pointed at the broken glass. It would probably be impossible to determine who had thrown the stones in the confusion. Hannes studied the scene in detail. Twenty members from the Church of the Creator stood opposite eight singers from New Way: Elke, Rebecca Köhler, Wolfgang Hartmann, his friend Bengt, the Schweigers, Mr. Beck, and an unfamiliar woman.

"Get out of here," Hannes said. "Then you won't have to give your name and address."

Elke grinned and hugged him. "Thanks."

She slipped away, and Hannes went over to his boss, who was already tearing into the minister from the Church of the Creator.

"If you're going to act like vigilantes, then you better be prepared to pay the price. Who do you think you are? You can't march over here and pick a fight."

"You think we started it?" Mr. Ahrendt said. "We're called murderers, and one of us is even in prison. God as my witness, that man's innocent."

"Careful lightning doesn't strike you," Hannes said.

"You again. I'm not surprised by your attitude."

"And I'm not surprised you attack people who you think have gone astray. No one from New Way pointed the finger at your pious flock. Your members did that on their own. Mr. Bach has already confessed to some of the allegations. So much for God as your witness."

"That's it," Ahrendt seethed.

Federsen turned around, grabbed Hannes's arm, and pulled him away. "A bunch of lunatics—both sides. I already spoke with Beck. The people from the Church of the Creator waited here until the choir members showed up. But the New Way members certainly didn't help the situation—they called the other side murderers. It went downhill from there. Let our colleagues take care of this mess. I've had it for the day."

"Why aren't any of our colleagues here? Isn't Ms. Köhler still under police protection?"

"She didn't want it anymore. A patrol car swings by her place every couple of hours. Same with most of the members."

Hannes followed Federsen to their vehicle.

"What a mess! They probably killed their own members!" Mr. Ahrendt shouted after them.

***

Fritz and Hannes sat across from each other in silence. The visit had been postponed to Wednesday morning since the prison staff had a mandatory meeting on Tuesday. Old Fritz's hoarse vocal cords finally sprung to life.

"What's your opinion?"

"What do you mean?"

"You just presented all the evidence to me. But I get the feeling you're not convinced."

"You're right," Hannes admitted. "But I don't know why. The evidence speaks for itself, even if it's not conclusive. I'm also troubled by Mr. Böhm's sudden trip. He seems to be involved. We don't know who played what role or why."

"It might be helpful to track down Böhm and Meister."

"What do you think we've been doing all this time? Still, I have a bad feeling."

"What's the problem?"

"Maybe it's because all the pieces fit a little too well. It makes me suspicious that we have no hard evidence. If only one of the men had shoes which matched the prints we found."

"The shoes could have been thrown out. At least Bach has the right size."

"It's not that I doubt the suspects' guilt. I just think we're missing the clue that ties them all together. Someone else is still involved. I just don't know who or why."

"Very good, Hannes," Fritz said with a smile.

"What?"

"Doubts are always good. They prevent you from making snap judgments. I have the same impression. Something or someone is missing—something or someone well hidden. But how do you shed light on something that wants to remain in the dark?"

"Any suggestions?"

"Rely on chance. The best clues often come up by chance."

"But that doesn't help. I can't just wait around until—"

"I didn't say to wait. Even chance can be controlled. So far you've stuck to the textbook procedures. Look for evidence, question suspects and witnesses, make the obvious or poorly hidden connections. Maybe it's time to loosen up, try something different."

Hannes knew Fritz had loved to ignore procedure. His unconventional methods hadn't won him any friends, but they had always proven successful.

"So you think I should follow in your footsteps and forget everything I learned at the academy? That'll certainly endear me to Federsen. Besides, look where that got you."

"You have to decide what's more important: popularity or success. I'm not saying to poke around haphazardly, but there's no harm in looking in other places. Don't just think of the obvious suspects. You'll overlook someone if you do that. In theory, everyone's a suspect. Don't forget that."

Hannes stared at Fritz and thought for a moment. "I don't care if Federsen likes me or not. I just want to solve this case. Maybe I should take a look at some of the people we haven't focused on."

"Exactly. Throw a couple of stun grenades and see who crawls out of the smoke. Maybe a good actor. Sometimes you've got to rip the mask off."

Hannes nodded. He had a vague hunch that he couldn't quite explain. But the wheels had been set in motion. Before he could try this new approach, he had to have another chat with David Bach.

***

"You wanted to talk? Then spit it out," Federsen said to Bach.

Hannes studied Bach, who seemed to have finally grasped the seriousness of his situation. But he looked so shifty that Hannes thought him capable of anything.

"I've been thinking," Bach said. "About Frank escaping to Finland."

"Do you know where he is?" Federsen asked.

"No. But the fact that he ran off got me thinking. He's always tried to convince me of his ideas. And usually they sounded good."

"How did you meet?" asked Hannes.

"I was a customer. I always bought my contacts at his store. After a while, we got to talking. He persuaded me to come to a church service. The atmosphere was cool. I'd never seen anything like it. Everyone stuck together. It was a real community, and I wanted to be a part of it."

"And now you don't?"

"I didn't say that. But I don't know if I still want to be friends with Frank."

"Why?"

"He told me we should pick on the New Way people. At first, I was against it because I'd already had enough problems with the police. Things were finally starting to fall into place. I had a job, friends, and no problems, really. But Frank kept pressuring me. Attacking the gay guy was a mistake. I was afraid he'd go to the police, and after that, I didn't want to screw anything else up. But Frank insisted, and we agreed that we'd scare them without attacking anyone else. That went on for a while."

"Then what?"

"Frank thought we should up the ante. That's where the crowbar came in. He insisted on targeting Rebecca."

"Why the anger against the other victims? The Kramers, Mrs. Böhm, Mr. Lück, and Carlos di Santo?"

"I had nothing against them. I also had nothing to do with their murders. But—"

"But what?" Federsen shouted as he leaned over the table.

"Frank was interested in the people from New Way. He got worked up. I found it exciting too. We gradually learned their names, read about them online, and secretly followed them. Frank was planning something. But when I asked him what, all he would do was grin. He's obsessed. It started to be too much for me. When the murders happened, he'd constantly talk about them and ask my opinion."

"What was your opinion?"

Bach shrugged. "I wasn't interested in them. But it was an exciting story, and it happened almost on our doorstep. We'd always argue over the motive for the murders."

"What was his theory?"

"That the sinners would now experience God's punishment."

The investigators were divided about Bach's statement. Half of them were inclined to believe him, while the others had their doubts.

"The little bastard wants to save his ass. Maybe there's some truth to his statement, but he failed to mention his own participation. We know he can be aggressive. I find it hard to believe he was the voice of reason in this friendship. Besides, he hasn't given us any proof," Hannes said.

"Because the proof would implicate him too," Clarissa agreed.

"I keep getting this feeling like we're missing something important," Hannes said. "Someone else is involved."

"Matthias Böhm," Per said. "He would have known all about New Way through his wife."

"No, not him. Bach mentioned something else. It wasn't random that Mr. Beck was one of their first victims. On the one hand, he's New Way's chaplain. On the other hand, Meister knew he used to be a priest in North Rhine-Westphalia and that he left his parish—or was kicked out. The Church of the Creator has several branches in Germany, including one in Cologne. Meister's a leader in his church here and regularly attends regional assemblies. He met a kindred spirit who knew about Beck's departure. Beck was the fallen priest. Before New Way, he proclaimed the Word of God, but now, in Frank Meister's view, he proclaims the word against God."

"Did Bach mention who this contact in Cologne was?"

"He claims he doesn't know. Meister told him that Beck was chased away because he broke his vow of celibacy. The guy in Cologne didn't know much more."

"And so now you think their brother in faith from Cologne is behind our series of murders?" Federsen asked. "How'd he manage that? Did he take the night train back every time?"

"It's just another possibility," Hannes said.

"And one we shouldn't rule out just yet," Steffen Lauer said. "Until we track down Meister and Böhm, we should investigate every possible lead. We need to find this guy in Cologne."

Per and Clarissa would question the local members of the Church of the Creator, while Marcel and Federsen would take care of the

Cologne branch. Isabelle and Hannes were given an entirely different assignment.

"Speak to Mr. Beck. Maybe there were conflicts with the Church of the Creator in his old community. The problems might have followed him here. If so, he might be able to help us with a name."

***

Mr. Beck was with a client when Isabelle and Hannes rang his doorbell. Since his office was in the attic, Mrs. Beck led them into the living room. The trials of the past few weeks had left their mark in the lines on the sensitive woman's face. She poured three cups of coffee and sat down.

"I'm sorry you've had to go through this," Hannes said, and her eyes filled with tears.

"I can barely sleep," she said. Her face was sunken, and she had clearly lost weight.

"I can imagine," Isabelle said. "But we're very close to solving the case. We have a suspect in jail, and more details come to light every day."

Mrs. Beck sighed. She had likely heard far too many comforting words from police officers in recent days. Hannes explained the nature of their visit.

"I don't remember meeting people from the Church of the Creator before. At least, there weren't any incidents like we've had here. Certainly no murders. It all started here, and I . . ."

Mr. Beck entered the room. He had just finished with his patient.

"I thought I heard the bell. Thank you for stopping by. How's the investigation going?" He grew tense as he sat down next to his wife. Isabelle summarized the status of the investigation and stated the reason for their visit. Mr. Beck cringed at the mention of his former life as a priest.

"There were a lot of problems back then," he said. "It wasn't a good time for me, and I don't like to dwell on it. That said, I never clashed with the Church of the Creator. The church didn't have a branch in the small town where we lived, so I have no idea who this contact in Cologne might be."

"How could he have learned about your resignation?" asked Hannes.

"Cologne's about twenty miles from where we were. Maybe he lived in our area. Besides, stories like mine tend to make the rounds."

"I can imagine. Is it possible someone from your former parish gossiped?"

"Sure. But it's been so many years."

"Some stories take a while to die down," Hannes said. "Is there someone from your former parish who might be able to tell us? Someone who can give a good overview of the people and the town?"

"Hmm." Mr. Beck rubbed his eyebrows. "I don't know who my replacement was. And I can't imagine anyone would remember what was said so many years ago. Have you tried the Church of the Creator? That might be easier."

"We're already on it," said Hannes. "Unfortunately, they don't exactly hold us in high regard. I'm hoping we can break the wall of silence."

Mr. Beck accompanied them to the front door. When Isabelle inquired about the current mood among the members, his face filled with sorrow.

"It's on the verge of splintering. Our group's divided into two camps, and I don't know how to stop it. One side accuses the other of wanting to convert New Way into a church. The other side claims dissolute morals led to the murders. Many have left, and the openness is gone. For instance, Rebecca told me in confidence that a female member asked her not to mention that she's a lesbian. I'm afraid the situation's only going to get worse."

***

By Thursday, the situation had indeed deteriorated even further. Per noticed it immediately after opening his laptop.

"Here, take a look at New Way's website."

"It looks different," Hannes said.

"They relaunched it with significant changes to the homepage. Do you remember the group's symbol, the outstretched hand? There's a new one now."

It was a uniquely Christian reference—a cross, though it had been slightly modified and was surrounded by ornate borders.

"Maybe the site was hacked?" Clarissa suggested.

"Or they've split into factions," Hannes said. "Per, what else has changed?"

"The presentation. The previous website went on and on about tolerance and only mentioned the Ten Commandments in passing. Now they're the focal point. Look, they're mentioned several times."

"Mr. Graf's IT firm built the old website," said Marcel. "Maybe he also handled the relaunch. I'm sure some of the members aren't very happy about this."

"And I'm sure others are," Clarissa said.

"We shouldn't interfere," Steffen Lauer said. "We have to remain neutral toward Christian and non-Christian groups alike. But that said, the group's about-face feels strange."

Lauer was also concerned that the members might soon get at each other's throats. They could only hope for a wave of resignations as a result of this change. But much more important to Lauer was the state of the investigation.

"Frank Meister has apparently run out of cash," said Marcel, who had kept in touch with the credit card company and their Finnish counterpart. Federsen had so insulted his Finnish contact, Jussi Mäkäräinen, that he had refused to talk to Federsen. Marcel spread out a map of Finland and placed his finger on a point between patches of green and blue.

"Kajaani. Probably not much more than an ATM there. Otherwise, trees and water, water and trees. And a train station too. Frank Meister's apparently still traveling by train."

"He's still got a ways to go until the North Cape," Federsen said. "Our colleagues haven't had much to contribute, and Meister's route is only going to get more remote from here. But I'm not surprised. That Finn is—"

"Doing everything he can," Marcel said. "If Meister's still in the area, there's a good chance we'll catch him. Unfortunately, he seems to pay for everything in cash. But Jussi promises they'll canvass all hotels, bed-and-breakfasts, and cabins in the area."

"What about down south?" asked Lauer. "Did we find Meister's friend in Cologne?"

The answers were discouraging. As expected, the Church of the Creator was not willing to cooperate. Ludwig Obermann had been the only one inclined to talk. According to him, Meister had once railed against Mr. Beck and his priestly past. Where Meister had gotten this information was unknown.

The church's contacts in Cologne must have been tipped off about the police. The investigators ran into a polite brick wall. All they could do was hope that their colleagues in Cologne would have a better chance tearing down that wall in person.

Hannes was exhausted and not up for any more challenges that day. Perhaps he should have given himself a little more time to recuperate from his fall. While his colleagues were left dealing with the Schweigers and Grafs, Steffen Lauer let Hannes go home early.

Hannes was glad he did. Anna's interview with LightFire was tomorrow, and she was extremely nervous. Anna spent the evening studying the company's website and memorizing details. She desperately wanted to get the job, and Hannes conducted several practice interviews with her. He realized that she wasn't great at showcasing her talents. It was only after several attempts and lots of coaxing that he was finally happy with her performance.

***

The next morning, Fritz and Hannes were in agreement. It was possible David Bach was grasping at any straw available. What could be easier than blaming a man who had disappeared into the Finnish wilderness? With regard to Matthias Böhm, Bach remained quiet. Meister was the only one he had ever discussed possible attacks on New Way with.

"It's probably true that Meister had New Way in his crosshairs first. But the footprint still contradicts Bach's statement. It was his shoe size, not Meister's."

Hannes felt reassured that Fritz shared his doubts. "Well, Meister's alive—he used an ATM, this time in Kajaani, so he's farther north."

"Why not block his credit card? He has to turn up when his money runs out."

"We considered that but thought it'd be counterproductive. This way we have some idea where he's staying. Besides, he could always rob someone when his money runs out. We don't want to risk that."

Fritz nodded. He was all ears when Hannes told him about Meister's contact in Cologne—a way to explore the case from a different angle.

"Unfortunately, we haven't had much success. I'll ask Mr. Beck again about people from his former parish. He didn't know anything about the Church of the Creator's activities at the time, but maybe someone else does. He also mentioned a group of militant atheists who made his life difficult there. They supposedly urinated in the baptismal font once. That of course doesn't sound like the Church of the Creator."

"Atheists," Fritz muttered. "I'd describe myself as one, but I'm no militant. If the killer was atheist, why would he reference the Ten Commandments?"

"I doubt he would. Plus, the Church of the Creator would be a much more likely target."

"There's another possibility," said Fritz. "It's good you're asking around Beck's former parish. After all, he did leave in disgrace. Maybe that wasn't enough for someone. Maybe he stepped on someone's toes and now, years later, that person's seeking revenge."

"I've already considered that. But then why wasn't he crucified? Why would others be forced to pay for his transgressions?"

"A sick mind doesn't always make sense. Maybe someone heard about Beck's current involvement and assumed New Way is a den of iniquity—and conveniently located just across the street is a bastion of true Christians who could be incited to join this holy crusade. Beck might be left for last so he realizes how others must suffer because he strayed."

"That sounds far-fetched, but I'll find out more."

Hannes called Elke in the car on the way to the station.

"Is this a bad time?" he asked when she picked up.

"No, hold on a sec." He heard her footsteps, then a door close. "Okay, I'm back. I'm still at work. The little ones are napping."

They chatted briefly about the confrontation on Tuesday, which had almost devolved into a fistfight. Elke was finished with New Way.

"The Schweigers and Grafs changed the website," she said. "No one knew anything about it. You should take a look. We could be confused for the Church of the Creator."

"I've seen it already. Why did they do that?"

"After the incident on Tuesday night, they claimed things couldn't continue like that anymore. Said we needed to be more upfront about what we actually stood for so the violence would finally stop. But not everyone shares their point of view."

"How have others reacted?"

"Same like me. Everyone's leaving. The choir getaway this weekend will be my last activity, since at least most of those people are normal. Wolfgang and Bengt want to start a new choir."

"Who would join?"

"Definitely not the Schweigers, nor the new chick they dragged into the group. Those three can sing as long as they want on their own."

"Are they still participating in the getaway?"

"I hope not. We'd have a nice time if they didn't. Unfortunately, Mrs. Beck canceled. She's just too upset. I wanted to back out at first too, but Rebecca convinced me to come. She's looking forward to it— she rarely gets out."

"Where is it being held?"

"We rented a house on a lake in the Holstein region."

"Are you going to attend the meeting tonight?"

"No way. We're leaving anyway. Wolfgang and Bengt are driving me and Rebecca."

Hannes had reached the station and said good-bye to Elke. Instead of wishing her a good time, he again urged her to be careful.

Everyone's nerves were shot. The fact that they were supposedly so close to solving the case was torture for them. Marcel called Jussi every hour, but inevitably returned empty-handed. The police had already visited all the hotels and bed-and-breakfasts around Kajaani without success and shifted their attention to vacation homes. They were afraid Meister had moved on. As for Matthias Böhm, there was no trace of him.

The Grafs and Schweigers justified their recent actions, claiming they had felt obliged to intervene. They wanted the group to return to its roots, which were, after all, Christian. Hannes's colleagues had pressed them hard, but they fiercely denied any involvement in the deaths and became indignant at the implication against any New Way member.

Hannes tried to reach Mr. Beck several times but only got his voice mail. He left a message, but Mr. Beck must not have listened to it yet. It was only after trying the landline around four that afternoon that he finally had some success.

"My husband already left for Holstein. He wanted to get a few things ready for the choir getaway. The others are supposed to get there around eight."

"You're not going?"

"No. It's just too much for me right now. I don't even feel like singing. I'd bring everyone down."

"Maybe you can help me then. We already told you about our Cologne lead. Unfortunately, we haven't gotten anywhere since then. I'd like to speak with someone in your former parish. Do you know anyone who might be able to help us?"

Mrs. Beck hesitated. "It's been so long, and we didn't leave on the best terms. I'd prefer to forget about that period in my life."

"We don't want to dredge up the past, but maybe someone noticed something. Your husband said he had problems with radical atheists there."

"Oh, that was just a bunch of ragtag teenagers. I don't think you'll get far investigating them."

"Probably, but it's worth a shot. Does any name come to mind?"

"Unfortunately, no. A few were from our town, a few from outlying villages. Eight or nine total."

"Maybe someone who still lives there might remember them? Someone from the parish council?"

"I don't even know if the same people are active."

Hannes rolled his eyes. Her fussiness was beginning to try his patience.

"Who was head of the parish council at the time?"

"Richard Jäger. There was someone else at first, but I can't remember his name."

"Do you have an address or telephone number for Mr. Jäger?"

"No. Like I said, it was complicated back then."

"I'll track him down," Hannes said. "Thank you for your time."

Richard Jäger's number was easy to find. A woman who introduced herself as Mrs. Jäger answered, and Hannes explained the reason for his call.

"I'm sorry," Mrs. Jäger said. "Unfortunately, I can't help you. I only moved here two years ago."

"But isn't your husband head of the parish council?" Hannes asked.

"Yes, for years. But we only got married two years ago. Before that, I lived in Dusseldorf. He once mentioned something about a scandal, but I don't know much more than that."

"When will your husband be home?"

"He has a business dinner in Münster tonight. He won't get back until late."

"Can I reach him on his cell phone?"

"Normally, yes. But he forgot to take his phone today." She laughed. "He always does that. Half the time he leaves it at home if I don't stick it in his pocket. He has too many things on his mind. But I'll gladly tell him to call you first thing in the morning."

Hannes reluctantly agreed and gave her his number. Although he didn't expect to get much out of this man, he at least wanted to know for sure. He had grown increasingly uneasy in the last hour, but didn't know why.

***

Anna twirled spaghetti around her fork and shoved the giant portion into her mouth. Hannes wiped a dab of tomato sauce from her chin.

He had taken her out to his favorite Italian restaurant to get their minds off things. It was a cozy place with a few small tables. Anna was unsure if her interview that afternoon had gone well.

"The guy really threw me for a loop. He was really hard to read. He could have thought I was great or a complete idiot."

"Who would think you're an idiot?"

"They have two more interviews on Monday," Anna continued. "He said he'd be in touch by the middle of next week."

"Would you want to work for him?"

"I don't know. He seemed really nice at the beginning and end of the interview. Maybe it was just a ploy to test me."

"What did he tell you about the company and what you would be doing?"

Hannes divided the pizza as he listened to her recount the rest of her interview. This was exactly the kind of evening he had wanted. And best of all, a free weekend lay ahead. After Anna had surprised him last Sunday with the day at the spa, he had tried hard to think of some way to repay her. Unfortunately, wind and rain had been predicted for that weekend, so his initial idea of a maiden voyage on the *Lena* wouldn't work. His pocket began to vibrate when Anna was in the middle of describing her potential new job, and he knew it would be a bad idea to answer the phone. Then it vibrated a second time as she rested her leg across his knee under the table.

"Something's vibrating," she said.

"It's my phone."

"Don't you want to see who it is?"

"It's Friday night."

"Maybe your suspect finally confessed."

The mere suggestion made Hannes fumble for his phone. It was Marcel.

"We've got him!" he shouted.

"Who?"

"Frank Meister! Well, actually, the Finns have him. He was renting a cabin from a family. They thought it strange that a German would want to go on vacation there in the middle of winter. That's how he lay low for so long. He obviously couldn't pay them with a credit card."

"That's amazing! When can we question him?"

"Tomorrow. He's being brought to Helsinki, and he'll be put on the first flight out in the morning."

Chapter 27

Tensions ran high Saturday morning. Frank Meister had been extradited back to Germany and would be whisked from the airport to the station. By ten o'clock, he would be sitting opposite the detectives, refusing to talk. Clarissa sat cracking her knuckles. The interrogation would be led by Federsen and Marcel, while their colleagues would follow the proceedings from behind the two-way mirror.

Hannes sat off to the side, piecing together news footage of the crucifixion on his laptop. A shiver ran down his spine as the eerie scenes took him back six weeks. With his outstretched arms and flawless body, Alexander Kramer seemed to embody a saint. The gray sky and heavy rain clouds reinforced the almost magical effect, creating a dark atmosphere. Hannes saw himself duck under the tape behind Federsen and run toward the large wooden cross. The cameraman had then zoomed out again and captured the assembled pack of reporters, yellow journalists who sought to quench the public's thirst for sensational news.

Hannes suddenly jumped. He stopped the video and rewound. Standing next to a camerawoman was a tall figure holding a digital SLR camera. The head was mostly covered by the hood of a green parka, but it was clearly a man. There was no close-up of him. Hannes rewatched the sequence and pressed pause when the man appeared in the background. He leaned forward and squinted. He would have to ask a technician to enhance the video.

His cell phone rang.

"Richard Jäger. My wife said you wanted to speak to me?"

Hannes had almost forgotten about him. He went out into the quiet hallway and explained to the chairman of the parish council the reason for contacting him. There was dead silence; he thought Jäger had hung up. But then he heard him clear his throat.

"Your call surprised me. Of course I read about the murders, but I didn't know Thomas was involved in the group. It's just that . . . Well, let's just say it doesn't seem like a group he'd join. At least not the Thomas I knew."

"What do you mean?"

"You asked me if there had been any conflicts when he was a priest at our parish. I've never heard of the Church of the Creator before. However, we were targeted by a group of young people back then."

"Mr. Beck mentioned that. Atheists, right?"

"Correct. But it was no accident this group chose our parish. The town has about ten thousand residents, half of whom belong to our parish. So it's not as if no one had heard of us. There were always public debates about us. Thomas Beck was the one who started it all."

"Because he was a priest living with a woman who he married after leaving the priesthood?"

Mr. Jäger cleared his throat again. "I take it he didn't tell you he'd been the subject of earlier criticism?"

"He indicated there had been some sort of scandal. He didn't go into details."

"I can imagine. He was a very dogmatic man. His homilies certainly took some getting used to in the beginning. But after the first six months, his inhibitions seemed to fade. He promoted an unusually hard-line interpretation of morality. Mass attendance dropped significantly because people began to feel excluded. Some even called him the hate priest. Then the newspapers started to write about how our town's pulpit was being used to spread backward, almost fundamentalist messages. So it was no coincidence this atheist group knew about us."

Hannes had to steady himself. He hadn't expected this. That didn't sound like the Thomas Beck he had gotten to know over the past few weeks.

"He must have done a complete one-eighty," Mr. Jäger continued. "He would have condemned a group like New Way as the work of the Devil. That said, he became a little more relaxed just before leaving. After he met Christine, his behavior changed. She sang in the choir. They quickly became friends, and he started to distance himself from his more radical views because of her. Then there was a new problem. There were rumors they were more than friends, which was too liberal for some people. So we asked him to stay away from her. He had fallen for her, though, and she had an admittedly positive influence on him. It seems from your description of Thomas that his wife continues to exert a strong influence."

"Conceivably," Hannes said. "Mrs. Beck is warm and friendly. Still, I'm surprised. Did he anger anyone in the community?"

"He stepped on the toes of anyone who didn't get out of his way fast enough. The atmosphere was very tense, until Christine entered the picture and he changed his behavior. But he'd already burned a lot of bridges."

"Did the atheists stop protesting then?"

"The incidents did taper off. We haven't had any problems since."

Hannes thanked him for his insightful information and paced up and down the hallway. Mr. Beck had upset both moderate believers and atheists with his strict interpretations of the Bible's teachings. Then he seemed to displease some members of the community with his surprisingly liberal interpretation of celibacy. He ran hot and cold, a mix of emotions. He seemed completely transformed today, advocating tolerance of different lifestyles. Was it possible for someone to change that much in only a few years? Was his wife's influence that far-reaching? The doubts gnawed at Hannes until he entertained a completely new possibility. Was Mr. Beck's change of heart only for show? Was he actually pursuing a different path—a truly fiendish one?

He swung open the door to the conference room and summed up his recent phone call to his colleagues.

"So you think Beck has only been pretending to be tolerant but is in reality a fanatic? That he's the one who killed these people?" asked Federsen. "We're about to interrogate our second main suspect, and you want to dish up this nonsense?"

"I'm not saying Bach and Meister are innocent, but we did consider the possibility that the two of them might have had an accomplice in New Way."

"I think it's bullshit. Beck doesn't have fanatical tendencies. And if he used to, he's changed. He's pitted himself against the Schweigers, who've been gunning for a much more religious group. How does that fit into your theory?"

Steffen Lauer spoke up. "That would certainly be odd, but it's worth a closer look."

"I'll go see Mrs. Beck now," said Hannes. "She's home alone. She's not participating in the choir getaway. Maybe I can get her to open up. She seemed reluctant to speak yesterday on the phone when I asked about their former parish."

Lauer agreed. "All right, who wants to go with Niehaus?"

Hannes looked around. Everyone wanted to watch Meister's interrogation. Isabelle finally raised her hand.

"Thanks," Hannes said. "By the way, something else occurred to me. I've been looking at news footage from the crucifixion." He waved his colleagues over to his laptop and pointed to the still. "There, next to the redhead with the camera. You can't make out his face because he's standing in the background, but there's something about that guy. We should get the image enhanced."

"I'll take care of it," Per said.

"It's just a waste of time," Federsen said as Hannes and Isabelle left the room.

***

Mrs. Beck was apparently not at home. Nobody came to the door.

"If we head back now, we'll only miss the beginning of the interrogation," Isabelle said.

"Absolutely not. I'd like to look around."

"Do you really think Beck's implicated in the murders? So far there's been no sign that he had any connection to Bach or Meister."

Hannes walked alongside the house toward the backyard. He had no idea what to think. The garden looked even more cared for than before. The plants had died back for the winter—the apple trees were pruned, and the few flower beds were cleared of weeds. Both the lawn and the flagstones which led to the small garden shed had been cleared of moss. Its sides had been painted red, while the window frames and roof edges were white. The door was ajar.

Hannes suddenly stopped, and Isabelle bumped into him. He stepped off to the side and examined a large bush.

"What's wrong?" she asked.

"Only thorny plants," Hannes said and pointed to the shrub. "Remember what was in Carlos di Santo's mouth?"

"Yeah, a hawthorn branch. But there's a lot of hawthorn in this city."

"I'm not very good with plants, but I wouldn't be surprised if this one's a hawthorn bush. Marcel likes to garden—he should take a look."

Hannes turned back toward the door and entered the large shed. Although the Becks had only moved in that summer, the shed was full of junk. He scanned the contents. Garden furniture lay next to the mower; flower pots had been brought in to protect the plants from the impending frost; and paint cans and various tools sat piled on a shelf. In one corner, wooden beams and planks leaned against the wall. Hannes examined the dark wood closer.

"The Becks seem to be very handy and do a lot of the work on their house themselves. I'm not an expert, but couldn't this be oak?"

"You mean like the cross? Hannes. Oak is one of the most common types of wood out there. You can probably find it in every other garden shed."

"I'm just saying."

"I'm going to take a look around outside. But I think we should head back now."

Hannes wasn't ready to give up. He watched through the window as Isabelle walked across the lawn, then turned his attention back to the shed. At the far end was a heavy workbench covered in bits of potting soil. Hannes wiped a pile of sawdust off the bench. There were screws and nails of various sizes in a large toolbox with several compartments. A heavy iron hammer in front of the toolbox immediately stood out. But did it really mean something? Isabelle was right. These things could be found in any toolshed.

His eye fell on a square object pushed up against the wall under the workbench and covered with a gray blanket. He knelt down and lifted the cloth. The heavy wooden box was apparently meant to be hidden from prying eyes. He grabbed the metal handle and pulled the chest forward. The lid didn't have a lock, so he flipped it open. A shiver came over him when he saw what was inside. Ballet slippers, old and worn, just like the other contents. Hannes pulled out a leather-bound photo album and opened it. Although he had spoken with Beatrice Reichert only over the phone, he knew that he was looking at the face of her youth.

Isabelle shouted. Hannes dropped the album on the workbench and rushed to the door. He didn't see anything menacing in the garden. Isabelle was standing in front of the bay window and frantically waving her arms. He bounded over to her.

"What's wrong? I thought someone was attacking you."

"Look through the window," Isabelle said. "Mrs. Beck is just lying there."

Hannes cupped his hands and peered through the window. Mrs. Beck lay half on the sofa, half on the floor. Her curly hair was spread out over the armrest. But he saw something else. There were pill bottles on the small coffee table, and she had slashed her wrists.

"Call an ambulance!" Hannes shouted and sprinted to the terrace.

He grabbed a flower pot and threw it as hard as he could at the glass doors. They both shattered. Hannes quickly stuck his hand inside and unlocked one of the doors. It creaked open and he raced to the couch. Mrs. Beck's face was pale. Her left arm hung motionless by her side. As he searched for a pulse, he knew they had arrived too late. Her arms were rigid. Hannes sank to the floor and leaned against the couch.

"Forget the ambulance. Call the coroner," he said to Isabelle, who stared down at him, her eyes wide. "Rigor mortis has already set in. Mrs. Beck must have been dead for several hours. She probably mixed herself one final cocktail last night before cutting herself." He pointed to the coffee table in front of him: two bottles of vodka and two empty pill bottles.

Isabelle picked one up and read the label. "It doesn't tell me much, but it's prescription only. Mrs. Beck mentioned on Wednesday that she could hardly sleep anymore. She probably got her doctor to prescribe her sleeping pills and saved them. She wanted to play it safe. But why would she go through all that trouble to kill herself?"

"I don't know. And we don't even know yet if it's real or staged to look like suicide."

He told her what he had found in the shed.

"So Mr. Beck was behind the break-in at Mrs. Reichert's. That makes sense. As the chaplain, he's familiar with the lives of the members," Isabelle said.

"Exactly. And what do you confess to a chaplain? You talk to him about things that have been eating you up inside. He also probably wrote the letter to Mrs. Brinkmann's children about their father."

Both fell silent. Hannes stood and walked over to the terrace door. He needed some fresh air. Once outside, he took a deep breath. He didn't feel like he had to vomit. He was slowly making progress. Given the number of bodies over the past few weeks, this didn't come as a big surprise. Even the weakest stomachs harden at some point.

Isabelle followed him outside. A thought dawned on him.

"Elke. She's with Beck at this choir getaway. His wife mentioned yesterday that he went early to prepare a few things. We have to call the others."

"I've already called them," said Isabelle. "They're on their way here. Federsen and Clarissa will handle Meister's interrogation. But why would Elke be Beck's—"

"He knows she's a lesbian!" shouted Hannes. "Rebecca told him. And he probably knows she's friends with me. He saw us together last Saturday at the Christmas market."

He nervously paced back and forth. It was a fucking stupid idea for Elke to join this group. It was an even dumber idea to have her play private investigator. If anything happened to her, he could never forgive himself. He grabbed Isabelle by the shoulders and looked into her eyes.

"I'm heading there now. Wait here for the others. I'll contact you as soon as I find out where they are."

Hannes sped down the highway and kept trying to reach Elke on her phone. But either she didn't have any signal or her phone was off. Hannes's concern grew. Who else might know where the choir was staying? The singers, of course, but they were already there. Or maybe not. Given the recent conflicts, it was unlikely that Mr. and Mrs. Schweiger were participating. Hannes called Per, who was shocked by the new developments and offered to track down the address. Five minutes later, he called Hannes back.

"I reached Mrs. Schweiger. They're not attending. She was surprised I wanted to know, but I didn't tell her my reason for asking."

Hannes's fingers flew across the screen as he entered the address into the GPS. He would arrive in thirty minutes. He slammed on the accelerator and told Per to send backup. As he exited the highway, his thoughts turned to the relaxing day he had spent with Anna at the nearby spa. Though it was only six days ago, it seemed like a lifetime. Instead of heading toward the beach, he made his way inland and was glad he had decided against an unmarked car that morning. Even though there wasn't much traffic on the streets, he turned his police lights on. As Hannes barreled down the road, his phone rang. It was Marcel.

"Hannes, you have to hurry. The choir members are in big danger."

"I'm going as fast as I can."

"We searched Beck's house and have already noticed a couple of things. Beck wears a size ten and a half. We're collecting all his shoes to compare prints. There's also a case of beer here—same brand as the bottles used to set the Grafs' house on fire. And we found a book about mushrooms in his desk drawer with several toxic varieties highlighted. It seems we bet on the wrong horse. The culprit was right under our noses the whole time."

Hannes cursed. Whether Bach and Meister were still somehow involved was irrelevant right now. They had clearly identified the mastermind.

He rolled down the gravel driveway of a single-story house on the edge of a small village a few minutes earlier than predicted. The house had a lakefront view. It was pouring rain and a cold wind blew from the north. Hannes got out and ran toward the house. He flung open the door. Rebecca Köhler, Wolfgang Hartmann and his friend Bengt, and another woman sat at a wooden table, playing cards and drinking coffee. They all looked up at him in shock.

"Where are Elke and Mr. Beck?" asked Hannes.

"They've gone out for a walk," Ms. Köhler said.

"In this weather? I thought you'd be singing here."

"We thought it was strange too," Mr. Hartmann said. "We were up late last night and slept in this morning. Elke and Thomas got up earlier and left a note saying they were taking a walk down to the lake."

Hannes looked at his watch. It was already noon. "Where's the note?"

Rebecca pointed to the kitchen counter. Hannes recognized Elke's handwriting.

Good morning, sleepyheads. Had too much to drink last night? ;-) Thomas and I went for a walk around the lake. Already made some coffee. See you later.

Hannes walked back to the table, stunned. "How long have they been gone?"

"We don't know. We've been wondering why they haven't come back yet. Did something happen?" Mr. Hartmann asked nervously.

"When did you find the note?"

"I woke up first, around ten," Mr. Hartmann said. "I was still groggy, and it took me a while to get going. And I didn't even drink that much last night."

It was the same for the rest of them. The group had gone to bed around one o'clock after a few bottles of wine—but not enough bottles to explain the slow start to the day. Everyone had seemed to get suddenly tired the night before. It was clear what had happened. Beck had served a final round and had slipped a strong sleeping pill into four of the glasses. He hadn't put anything in Elke's glass, so she had woken up long before the rest of them. It must have been easy to persuade Elke to go for a walk while the others slept. Hannes rushed to the window. There were three vehicles in the driveway, not counting his police car.

"How many cars did you drive here?" he asked.

"Three," Mr. Hartmann said, walking over. "What's going on?"

Hannes pulled him outside while the others watched them with skeptical looks on their faces. He told him about that morning's discovery. Mr. Hartmann shook his head in disbelief.

"I don't want to start a panic," Hannes said. "Please keep this to yourself, but make sure everyone stays together. My colleagues will be arriving in a few minutes. I don't think you're in danger, but Elke might be. Do you have any idea where they might have gone?"

"Yesterday Thomas kept raving about some beautiful path which leads to the Immenhof estate. You know, the country estate where they filmed a bunch of movies back in the fifties. The path starts at the end of the road."

"As soon as my colleagues get here, please send two of them after me."

Hannes jumped into the car and bounced down the gravel driveway toward the road. He was forced to leave the vehicle when he got to the end of the road, because the path was more of a narrow dirt trail. Hannes began to jog. To the right, he could see the lake whenever the rain didn't pelt his eyes. The icy wind stung his face, and steam escaped his mouth. There wasn't a single other person out. He crossed a small wooded area before reaching open meadows and fields again. Panting, he updated Marcel over the phone. Several colleagues had arrived at the cottage. Per and Isabelle were already chasing after him.

Hannes squinted. In the distance, he thought he saw smoke. He picked up his pace. The slippery ground made it difficult for him to move quickly. After he passed a small stand of trees, he could clearly see the smoke. Panic gripped him. What could Beck have devised this time? He briefly stopped to orientate himself, then left the path to run across the fields in the direction of the rising smoke. He thought he could make out a human figure standing a little more than five hundred yards ahead of him. He blinked and rubbed his eyes. He was frantic.

The person seemed to stagger. They fell to their knees and struggled to get back up. Hannes sank ankle deep into the mud. Didn't Elke have a blue windbreaker like that? He then recognized her long blonde hair and was relieved. But when she fell to the ground again, his relief faded.

He finally reached her a few minutes later. Elke was lying on the ground. She looked up at him with tears in her eyes. Her hair lay like a golden fan unfurled across the mud. Hannes knelt down beside her and patted her on the cheek.

"I'm so glad I found you."

"Hannes?" She murmured his name in disbelief. Her eyelids fluttered.

He patted her again on the cheek, this time a little harder. "Elke. You have to pull yourself together. Stay with me. What did Beck do to you?"

"Do to . . . ? Nothing. Wanted to warm up. Barn. Then . . . fire. Were . . ."

Hannes didn't understand the rest of what she said. He shook her shoulders.

"Where is he, Elke? Where's Mr. Beck?"

"Wanted to save me. Fell. I . . . tried . . . to help him. Was too . . . hard."

"Where, Elke?"

"Fire. Barn . . . on fire. He . . . still inside."

Her eyes closed again, and Hannes was unsuccessful in getting her to say anything else. But he could feel a pulse, and her breathing seemed regular. Smoke inhalation? He stood up. Where were Isabelle and Per? He pulled out his cell phone. Per answered immediately. Hannes shouted his location into the phone. In the background, he could hear Isabelle requesting an ambulance. A little later, he saw his colleagues emerge from behind the clump of trees. He waved his arms above his head.

"Elke's here!" he shouted. "A barn's on fire over there. Beck's inside. Take care of Elke. I'm going to see what I can do."

Hannes ran off. He decided on the most direct route, which meant wading across a small creek and crawling through thickets.

Flames leaped from the top of the roof, and he wondered how this building could burn so fiercely in the wet weather. The air was filled with acrid smoke, and he began gasping. He covered his nose with his arm and looked around, breathing through the wet fabric.

In the rear of the hay barn raged a flaming inferno, and the fire crackled as it jumped onto another bale of hay. Hannes shouted for Mr. Beck. He scanned the various farm equipment located to the left of the entrance; hay was stored on the right.

He understood why the roof had caught fire. The loft was crammed with hay that was going up in flames. A burning beam detached from the ceiling and hurtled to the floor in a shower of sparks. Frightened, Hannes took a step back. Then he thought he heard a faint moan. The fire had not yet reached the entrance, so Hannes was able to take a few steps inside. He cautiously pushed a trailer plow over and looked in the direction of the noise.

Hannes looked near the foot of the ladder leading to the hayloft. A body lay twisted on the ground, not yet engulfed in the nearby flames. The heat had to be deadly. The man moved a little and turned his grimacing face. Hannes recoiled. Thomas Beck's beard was completely singed, and his skin was covered in blisters. A heavy wooden beam lay across his chest, flames licking at one end. Hannes understood why Elke couldn't have dragged him out with her in her condition.

He glanced at the roof. Should he risk his own life for a killer? The flames might have been a fitting punishment for Beck, but Hannes couldn't let him be reduced to ashes. He coughed, and his eyes began to tear up as he felt his way forward. Another beam dropped from the ceiling and crashed next to Beck. He stretched out his arms, imploring Hannes, who lifted the intact end of the beam from his chest and tossed it aside. It was unbearably hot. Hannes tried not to look at Beck's skin. He grabbed Beck by the shoulders and pulled him away from the relentless flames. The unpleasant smell of singed hair and skin stung Hannes's nose.

He backed against a harrow, which blocked the way to the entrance. Hannes took a moment to gather his strength and looked down at Beck's motionless body. His leg was bent at an unnatural angle and must have been broken clean through. The fallen wooden beam had probably also shattered several of his ribs. There was a risk that the shards of bone might pierce a vital organ, but burning to death was an even greater risk. Without any further hesitation, Hannes grabbed him and slung him over his shoulder with a groan. No cry of pain rang out—unconsciousness could be so gracious. He carefully climbed over the piece of equipment, trying not to ram his leg into the tines. Overcome by coughing, he was forced to stop.

Hannes could taste the fresh air only a few feet away. His body was shaking, and his leg buckled under him. He managed to shift Beck's weight just in time to avoid falling. The hayloft collapsed behind him in a thunderous roar, kicking up a whirlwind of sparks. Hannes squinted and protected his face with his free arm.

Beck hung motionless over Hannes's shoulder and bore the brunt of the sparks. Hannes staggered forward, his eyes fixed on the entrance. He gritted his teeth and counted the steps. He needed oxygen. It was now a matter of sheer will, and at that moment, he wanted nothing more than to carry Beck to safety.

As Hannes staggered out of the barn, gasping for breath, he felt like a dragon exhaling smoke. But it was just his breath condensed in the cold air. He tried to put as many steps as possible between them and the barn, but the weight of the heavy man pushed him closer and closer to the ground. From his hunched position, he could just make out the blurry figures of Marcel, Isabelle, and Per running across the soggy meadow before his legs finally gave out. He crumpled to the ground, his cheek soothed by the cold, wet grass.

CHAPTER 28

Four days later, Hannes read the headline on the front page of the newspaper Isabelle had brought to the hospital. "Police End Religious Crusade" ran in bold letters, a half-burned barn pictured below. Absolved of any blame, the Church of the Creator could devote itself once more to its search for the one true way to God.

Isabelle brought Hannes up to speed. David Bach and Frank Meister remained in custody, although there were doubts as to whether they had collaborated with Thomas Beck. Meister claimed that he'd fled to Finland because he realized the investigators would find things on his laptop that would put him in a bad light. He had suspected his friend David Bach and had repeatedly confronted him about New Way. He was afraid of being dragged into the investigation. It had been a knee-jerk reaction, and he had chosen Finland because customers had raved to him about the solitude.

Matthias Böhm had returned to his farm on Sunday evening. He had wanted to get away for a few days and put some distance between him and the turbulence of recent weeks. On a whim, he had decided to visit Denmark and rent a cottage for five days.

News footage of the first crime scene had been examined. After enhancing the images, Thomas Beck could be clearly seen standing among the reporters and cameramen. The police had found photos of the crime scene on Beck's digital camera, some of which had been taken a few days before the cross had been discovered. He had also photographed Sylvia Böhm. She had still been alive and had stared absently into the camera as if already under the influence of the Rohypnol. There was no mistaking the pain in her face.

Beck hadn't photographed any of the other victims, but in his desk, the police had found a small shoebox containing Rohypnol pills. His browser history had eliminated any remaining doubts. Although Frank Meister had also researched the drug, he had simply been curious about the murders and had read in the papers that the drug was used in the crimes.

A pair of worn-out shoes had been found in Beck's shed. The prints matched those discovered at the scene of Benjamin Lück's murder and in the Grafs' yard following the fire. The hawthorn bush next to Beck's shed had been painstakingly examined. There was evidence that a branch consistent with the one found in Carlos di Santo's mouth had been recently clipped.

"Beck was probably also responsible for the calls Wolfgang Hartmann used to receive on Sundays. We found a receipt for a prepaid SIM card he bought at a discount store. He must have then gotten rid of the prepaid card," Isabelle said.

"What about the other incidents?" asked Hannes.

"Well, you found Mrs. Reichert's stolen items in his shed. She said she had confessed to him that she was a kleptomaniac and had once showed him her memorabilia when he had been at her home."

"He was a perfect actor. We noticed that when we saw him at the play rehearsal. Have you questioned Mrs. Brinkmann?"

"Of course. She had trusted Beck, just like everyone else. She often cried about her problems to him. She had told him about her parents in the nursing home and the father of her children. We found the letter addressed to her children on Beck's computer. He didn't even try to cover his tracks."

"He probably felt untouchable. His first real mistake was leaving the shoe prints in the Grafs' yard."

"And filling bottles of his favorite beer with the accelerant."

"What about the wooden cross?"

"He probably cut the beams in his shed and assembled them onsite. We also found a pack of the nails he used."

"And Mrs. Böhm?"

"She discussed the pros and cons of abortion with him. He had visited the horse farm once while she was in the middle of explaining to her husband how to use the dewormer. She had mentioned to him that it was dangerous to humans in high doses. Beck must have grabbed a few bottles of it when no one was looking. Antje Kramer's death is the only one we can't pin on him. All we have is the book in which he highlighted several poisonous mushrooms."

"That was slick," said Hannes. "He's the one who called us. He hadn't seen her in a few days and was supposedly worried about her. He'd visited her at her workshop to discuss the arrangements for her brother's funeral. He could have slipped her the poisonous mushrooms then."

"At the very least, he knew she ate hallucinogenic mushrooms."

Rebecca Köhler blamed herself for carelessly jeopardizing Elke's life by mentioning her homosexuality in front of Beck. Traces of Rohypnol had been detected in her blood—Beck had used his tried-and-true method on her while slipping the others sleeping pills. Elke hadn't suspected anything when he had persuaded her to go for a walk. Mr. Beck must have prepared the barn the day before. When he and Elke passed by, he suggested they take refuge from the icy wind and rain. A shivering Elke agreed, and they ducked inside to have a cup of hot tea from Beck's thermos.

"We'd chatted the whole way there, and he was so nice. He scrambled around the barn and called down from the hayloft that he wanted to show me something. I climbed up and saw him kneeling in front of a small fire pit. He said some hobo had probably passed through and made a pit to warm himself. There were still ashes on a piece of sheet metal surrounded by stones. I hesitated when he proposed that we start a fire with some of the wood left, but I didn't think it was going to be that dangerous—there had obviously been a fire there before. It was only a small fire, and we huddled close to the flames. He gave me tea, and after a few minutes I became incredibly tired. He said it was okay if I took a quick nap."

When Elke had opened her eyes again a little while later, Beck was pulling her toward the ladder. He seemed surprised she wasn't asleep. "Fire!" he had shouted, but she was too dazed to respond. As he continued to drag her, Elke became a little more cognizant of her surroundings and struggled to her feet. She thought he wanted to carry her to safety. He started to go down the ladder, and she turned around to follow him, kicking him by accident. He fell and broke his leg. The fire had grown in strength, and the adrenaline set in, shaking Elke from her daze as she climbed down the ladder. She began to pull Beck from the barn, but he only cried out in pain. How she managed to make it all the way to Hannes remained a mystery. Either Beck hadn't used enough Rohypnol or Elke had a high tolerance.

"I've never been a lightweight," she explained. "At the dentist's, the Novocaine hardly ever works, so they always need to give me more injections. It was probably the same for the stuff he slipped me."

After Elke had regained consciousness in the hospital, she had anxiously asked about Beck and even blamed herself for leaving him in the barn to get help. She was stunned to have been so fundamentally wrong about him. But Elke had emerged relatively unscathed and had fared even better than Hannes.

The detectives assumed Beck had wanted to stage an accident. Had he thrown her from the hayloft, his claim that she had fallen in a panic and seriously injured herself wouldn't have been credible. He probably meant for it to go some other way. But he would have had to answer why he lived while Elke burned to death.

"How is he?" asked Hannes.

"He's still alive," Isabelle said. "But he's in no state to be interrogated. Should he wake up, he'll remain disfigured for the rest of his life. He was severely burned and has already had multiple skin grafts. You could say God punished him by sending you to his rescue."

"Enough with God," said Hannes. "His name has been abused a little too often lately. I wonder how Mrs. Beck could be so oblivious to all this."

"Maybe she did know. She looked like a living corpse toward the end. The news affected everyone, especially her. Maybe for good reason? If she knew what her husband was doing or suspected it, she could have told us and put an end to her husband's rampage. Instead, she withdrew and suffered in silence."

"And when she learned that we'd be contacting her former church in North Rhine-Westphalia, she realized everything would probably come to light. Has her cause of death been determined?"

"At the time of her death, Mr. Beck was picking up the key to the cottage, so it's likely suicide. Federsen's compassion for her has its limits, though. He suspects she must have had some idea and accuses her of cowardice. On the other hand, your dedication seems to have impressed him."

Hannes shook his head. "Wait a few days, and it'll fade. But he did actually visit me briefly and even left me something." He pointed to a bouquet on his bedside table.

Isabelle was skeptical and impressed. "Would've never guessed he'd go that far. Kudos to him."

"I've been wondering if his wife isn't behind it," Hannes said and grinned.

Anna meanwhile had bagged the job at LightFire and would begin in February, but she didn't seem too excited yet because she had spent the last few days at his bedside and slept on a guest bed. Hannes had suffered moderately severe smoke inhalation, but the doctors did not expect there to be any permanent damage. Only time would tell how his burns would heal. In addition to numerous smaller burns on his body, he had also suffered a large blister on his hand. His face, though bright red, wasn't hurt. His spirits were high, since he would be leaving the hospital the following day. He looked forward to his own bed and what he would do there with Anna.

***

Christmas Eve promised to be a cold, clear night. It was nearly a full moon, and the white disc with its characteristic craters already hung high as Anna undid *Lena*'s dockline. Hannes took her hand and pulled her aboard. They were bundled in thick winter clothes.

Hannes hurried back to the wheelhouse and began to maneuver the boat away from the dock, just as he had learned a few weeks ago. He waved to Ole, who watched them from the jetty.

"Struck gold, I see," Ole had whispered with a wink to Hannes and pointed to Anna.

"Sure did. We're headed to Denmark," Hannes had replied with a grin. "Won't have to prospect for blondes there."

As he passed the small lighthouse at the end of the pier and headed for the open sea, his thoughts turned to the events of the last few weeks. Thomas Beck had awakened from his coma a week after Hannes had been discharged from the hospital. Given the overwhelming amount of evidence, he had quickly confessed to the crimes. The death of his wife, which he found out about shortly after awakening, had sapped him of any resistance. He insisted she hadn't known, but it was obvious she couldn't have been completely clueless.

Another detail emerged that at least in part explained the secret radicalization of the former priest. As Mr. Jäger had noted, his wife had had a mitigating effect on Beck. He increasingly relied on her judgment and grew to idolize her. But a rift occurred when he noticed how well she got along with Alexander Kramer. Jealousy had always been a flaw of his, and several members of New Way stated in hindsight that he had always kept close tabs on his wife. Some even said he was very controlling. When Mrs. Schweiger began spreading the rumor that the porn star had been flirting with not only Sylvia Böhm but also the chaplain's wife, his jealousy exploded.

Beck had been convinced that Kramer and his wife were in a relationship. The suspected infidelity had pulled the rug out from under him, and he fell hard. Their relationship foundered once he began accusing her of betrayal. He had then taken a critical view of New Way and what he considered the inappropriate behavior of its members. In the end, he chose to take corrective action. When his punishments proved ineffective, he simply increased the ferocity of his efforts. Beck had finally returned to God, and God himself had shown him the way. He had merely been his instrument. The culmination had been the crucifixion, which he had intended as a clear signal to the others. He had assumed that the young man would be discovered in time and had been careful to ensure that no one would be able to identify him as the killer. Alexander Kramer had attended Melissa Vogt's fitness class, and Beck had been able to slip the Rohypnol into Alexander's water bottle without being caught. Afterward, he had followed the young man, and when he had collapsed at the bus stop, Beck pulled him into his car. He had gotten the idea for how to fake his alibi in Mrs. Böhm's death from an old whodunit on TV, and had bought the ticket to Sea Life in the morning before seeing his counseling clients. As he'd recounted all of this to the investigators, he'd left them with the impression that he was downright insane.

Hannes shook his head as he thought about all the dead ends their investigation had encountered. But at least his hunch that the answer could be found in New Way had been correct—even if he had initially suspected the Schweigers. But Mrs. Schweiger wasn't completely innocent; after all, she had been the one to spread the rumors of Beck's dramatic reconversion. Nor could Frank Meister and David Bach be considered entirely innocent, since they were responsible for the other incidents, like the attack on Benjamin Lück and the property damage. Meister had worked himself up into a state of religious zealotry and had infected his friend. Ironically, they would also be held accountable for the threats and slander against Thomas Beck. Only Mr. Böhm had managed to escape prosecution—the investigation into his suspected tax fraud had been suspended.

Fritz had been very proud of his former colleague when Hannes had visited him a few days ago. He downplayed his own contribution to the investigation's success. Instead, they agreed that they had complemented each other. Fritz had been touched by the box of Christmas cookies Anna and Hannes had baked for him. For a moment, his eyes had appeared suspiciously moist before he loudly blew his nose. Hannes wondered what Christmas would be like for Fritz in prison.

Anna opened the door to the wheelhouse. She walked up from behind and put her arms around him.

"Well, captain, is everything under control? No shoals ahead?"

"Nope. So far, so good."

"When do we drop anchor?"

"Have you had enough?" said Hannes. "Or are you getting seasick?"

"Of course not. The water's almost as smooth as glass. I was only thinking about your presents under the tree."

So that was what Anna had been up to. Hannes smiled and placed her hands on the wheel.

"Keep her going straight. I'll be right back."

Hannes strode across the planks of his ship, then climbed down the stairs to the cozy cabin. *Lena* hardly pitched in the faint swell of the placid sea. In the afternoon, he had bought a tiny Christmas tree that was perfect for the space. Given his recent experience with burning barns, he had decided against decorating it with real candles and used a string of electric lights instead. He had also heeded Ole's advice: "No open flames on board."

Anna had piled a mountain of small packages under the tree. Hannes pulled his small, clumsily wrapped presents for Anna out of his bag and placed them next to the others. He was glad Anna had been gung ho about spending Christmas on the water. He didn't want to think about what it would have been like if they were sitting in his parents' living room instead. They were headed to Copenhagen and would return shortly before New Year's. There would be an entirely different atmosphere at that celebration. Hannes chuckled, remembering the discussion with his friends about what to drink on New Year's Eve. He gave the decorations on the tree a little fine-tuning, fluffed a few pillows, then ran back up to replace Anna at the wheel.

They anchored for the first time shortly before reaching the Danish island of Lolland. Anna had already uncorked the bottle of red wine and was waiting for him in the small cabin. As Hannes stood on the stairs and saw her sitting in the soft light in front of the tiny Christmas tree, the stress of the past couple of months drifted away in the mild sea breeze. Anna shook one of her gifts, and a warm feeling flowed through him. He cleared his throat, and with a smile of feigned guilt, she put the package back. Hannes climbed down the steps and pulled the hatch down. The moon cast a glittering ribbon across the water, and the lights of the tiny Christmas tree twinkled in the reflection of the Baltic Sea. High above the small boat, in the vastness of the night sky, shined the constellation Cygnus, also known as the Northern Cross.

About the Author

Photo © 2015 Ruediger Schapmann

German author Hendrik Falkenberg studied sports management and works in sports broadcasting. The magical allure that the sea holds for him comes alive in his stories, which are set on the north German coast. His first book, *Time Heals No Wounds*, was a #1 Kindle bestseller in Germany.

About the Translator

Patrick F. Brown studied French and German at Georgetown University in Washington, DC. He currently lives in Philadelphia, PA, where he does freelance translation.